PRAISE FO

"There are few who can write of the early Far West and the era of the fur trade with as much authority and insight as does Win Blevins. When you open one of his novels, you'd best be prepared to jump bareback on a half-broke Indian cayuse that will tear off beneath you, the wind whipping across your face as you are carried hither among the high and distant places without let-up, without stop until you reach the last page."

—Terry C. Johnston, author of *Cry of the Hawk*

"Win Blevins is the modern master of early frontier fiction. In *The Snake River* Blevins artfully deals with yet another legacy of white expansion—a boy disinherited from two worlds. Tragic, humorous, and vivid, this is the literature of the New West."

—W. Michael Gear and Kathleen O'Neal Gear, authors of *People of the River*

"*The Snake River* is an unconventional yarn of free-spirited mountain men, Indians and missionaries, told with bawdy humor, action, and a good measure of the unexpected."

—Elmer Kelton, author of *Slaughter*

"Over the years since I read his *Give Your Heart to the Hawks* I have come to think of Win Blevins as an exceptional chronicler-in-fiction of the great fur trade and mountain man era of our Old West, a writer of the school of A. B. Guthrie, Jr., Vardis Fisher and Will Henry—very fine company for any writer.

"In *The Snake River,* as in his previous books in the 'Rivers West' series—*The Yellowstone* and *The Powder*— I see the wonderful conjoining of story, character, history, and lore that I admired in his work from the beginning."
— Dale L. Walker, *Rocky Mountain News*

"Win Blevins in *The Snake River* has written an exciting tale of action and high emotions with a real love for the northwest country, its people, and its history. It's a story about a transitional time in American history, involving intrigue, duplicity, and courage."
— Robert J. Conley, author of *The Way of the Priests*

"*The Snake River* transcends ordinary frontier novels as *A River Runs Through It* transcends fishing yarns. It is filled with people we care about immediately, engaged in living lives which are the stuff of fable. Deeply satisfying!"
— Norman Zollinger, author of *Rage in Chupadera*

"Win Blevins knows the mountain man years so well, he gives all his heart to doing what he loves to do best—tell a whale of a tale."
— John Byrne Cooke, author of *South of the Border*

RIVERS WEST
Book 8

THE
SNAKE RIVER

Win Blevins

BANTAM BOOKS
NEW YORK • TORONTO • LONDON • SYDNEY • AUCKLAND

Because it tells of father and child,
this story is dedicated to my three children,
Pamela Jo, Adam, and Ethan.

THE SNAKE RIVER

A Bantam Domain Book / November 1992

ISBN 0-553-29770-8

Published simultaneously in the United States and Canada

Bantam Books are published by Bantam Books, a division of Bantam
Doubleday Dell Publishing Group, Inc. Its trademark, consisting of the
words "Bantam Books" and the portrayal of a rooster, is Registered in U.S.
Patent and Trademark Office and in other countries. Marca Registrada.
Bantam Books, 666 Fifth Avenue, New York, New York 10103.

PRINTED IN THE UNITED STATES OF AMERICA

0 9 8 7 6 5 4 3

Rivers West
Ask your bookseller for the books you have missed.

Acknowledgments

The Honorable Clyde M. Hall of the Shoshone-Bannock Reservation at Fort Hall, Idaho, has helped me greatly with the matters of Shoshone language, culture, and worldview in this book (for the Shoshone words he used Wick R. Miller's *Newe Natekwinappeh: Shoshoni Stories and Dictionary,* and his own knowledge of the Shoshone language). Murphy Fox of Helena, Montana, helped me cope with other realities of the historical West, especially mountain men. Both have been my guides in such matters for several books now—my deepest gratitude to them both.

Michael and Kathleen Gear, archaeologists and anthropologists, provided wonderful suggestions. Ian Fallows and Alan Smith, of Kendall, Cumbria, England, helped me with matters of Irish, Scottish, and English speech.

Bob and Inger Koedt came up with something crucial at an urgent time. Bill Gulick walked ahead of me in Snake River country. Dick Wheeler and Lenore Carroll lent their wisdom.

Profound thanks to you all.

The world is full of stories, and from time to time they permit themselves to be told.

—OLD CHEROKEE SAYING

Prologue
The River

It is a strange river, the Snake. It has been strange for aeons, back to the time when volcanoes gave birth to this land in unimaginable violence. The Snake is one of the children of that violence.

The river still flows from a country that will thrill you one moment and terrify you the next. And into a country that, besides thrilling you and terrifying you, will boil you, freeze you, and scour your skin off with sun and wind. It is no country for the timid.

Officially, the Snake begins in the high mountains just southeast of the border of Yellowstone National Park, some of this nation's most remote wilderness. Unlike the Yellowstone River, which gets its start nearby and crosses the continent to the east, the Snake goes fiercely west. The river's fountainhead—wonderful word, *fountainhead*—is a big spring. From there the river rampages toward the Pacific.

The beginning of the journey is idyllically alpine, along the southern edge of the park, then south through the grandeur of Jackson Hole. In these first hundred miles or so it parades through mountain meadows and forests of fir, spruce, and aspen, with the Tetons as a spectacular backdrop. If you hike and fish and float this part of the river with alert eyes or a good guide, you'll see moose, elk, buffalo, and the bald eagle commonly enough, and on occasion the river otter or the grizzly bear. One kind of paradise.

Originally this stream was known as Lewis's Fork (and today it's sometimes called South Fork). Out of the mountains on the west side of Yellowstone Park flows its brother, Henry's Fork. Another alpine stream, swift, cold, and dazzlingly clear. Another sojourn through mountain meadows and grasses and forests. A parallel paradise.

At the wedding of these two forks the Snake crashes into hell. The river roars over a great falls and charges forward through a high, dry, broken, lava-flow country, a country that gives unforgettable meaning to the term *malpais,* bad country to travel through. The lava is deeply fissured—sometimes you have to go forty miles out of your way, they say, to get around a crack. There's little water. The lava rock soaks up the heat on summer days and radiates it back at you, helping the sun simmer your brain.

The animal life runs to grasshoppers and lizards. There's so little game the Indians here used to eat the grasshoppers, broiled on sticks or mashed into cakes. Mountain man Joe Meek, run onto starvin' times in this country, reported licking ants off his bare arms, and glad for the opportunity.

The river travels mostly in chasms, out of reach of man. It goes down stepping-stones, through the big waterfalls. It surges through whitewater canyons. The first white men to try to navigate it were astonished by the river. "Its terrific appearance beggars all description," wrote Wilson Price Hunt in 1811. "Hecate's cauldron was never half so agitated when vomiting even the most diabiolical spells."

What Hunt didn't know was that the Snake River drains country that was and still is even wilder and crazier. The mountains of Yellowstone start the river. From the south the deserts of Idaho, Utah, and Nevada add their bitter comments. From the north come the turbulent waters of some of the continent's great mountain fastnesses.

Names tell part of the story: the Bitterroot Mountains, Hell's Half Acre, the River of No Return, Craters of the Moon National Monument, Hell's Canyon. Nine million acres of tumbled, wild-hair-up-your-ass desert and mountain feed the Snake. They turn it so wild, men curse it.

The name Hunt and the other first white navigators

gave the Snake was a curse—Maudite Rivière Enragée, Accursed, Enraged River. It's so wild that modern men have trapped and tamed it with dams, partly for irrigation and partly for peace of mind. Nowadays you have to do your floating mostly on the far ends of the river, upper and lower. Dams clog the main artery.

After about a thousand miles of adolescent hell-raising, far downriver in the state of Washington, the Snake gives up its identity to the Columbia River, and turns west for a majestic processional to the sea. Just as well. Maturity and tranquillity would not become the Snake.

Before Wilson Price Hunt and his fellow fur traders came, human beings had lived along the Snake for centuries. They were, to modern sensibilities, a strange people.

Now we call them the Shoshones. They called themselves by names such as the Root-Eating People, Squirrel-Eating People, Salmon-Eating People, Pine Nut–Eating People, Seed-Eating People, Dust-Eating People, and Sheep-Eating People. The early trappers called them the Snakes. This name is said to be an error based on the sinuous movement for the name of the people in sign language. Some of their traditional enemies among the Plains Indians to the East also called them Snakes.

They lived in the huge vastnesses from the Rocky Mountains to the Sierra Nevada, from the heights of the mountains of Yellowstone to the depths of Death Valley. They lived in the mountains to the north and east of the Snake, where salmon ran the rivers and sheep grazed the high country. They lived in the Great Basin south and west of the Snake, where they foraged for roots, nuts, and seeds, and sometimes hunted small game.

They were different from the Indians white Americans are most familiar with, and in prehistoric times sharply different. They dwelled not in tipis but in brush huts, and sometimes in holes in the ground. They did not hunt the buffalo. They wore little (though it was taboo for women to wear nothing). Instead of riding horses and shooting arrows, they walked and prodded at the earth with sticks—two of the white-man names for them were Walkers and Diggers.

During this era before they had the horse, they had little
in a material way. All their richnesses were spiritual, for
they did know Duma Apa, Father Sun, and Duma Sogobia,
Mother Earth, and Wolf and Coyote and Spider, Blackbird and
Crying Cloud, and many other powers. They had not theology
but mythology, ritual, and dream. Their awareness of Spirit
came from old, old stories. They did not debate the nature of
God. They did not know much *about* God. But without such
analysis, they knew Spirit. They knew Mystery.

They came to know by mythology, ritual, and dream.
The old stories showed them Power afoot in the world. Ritual
put them in harmony with that Power. And in waking dream
or sleeping dream they were granted blessings of *puha,*
guardian spirits, and were told ways to live as channels of
puha, the power those spirits can give. This religion was not
what they figured out but what they knew from experience.

Some of these people lived near the eastern edge of their
vast territory, in the Rocky Mountains, and therefore near the
Indians of the Plains. As time went on, these Shoshones
integrated the ways of the Plains Indians into their own—they
became horsemen, tipi dwellers, buffalo hunters—they mixed
their original Great Basin culture with a Plains culture. These
Shoshones are known to us as the Wind River Shoshones,
Green River Shoshones, Fort Hall Shoshones, and by other
white-man names.

This cultural adaptation was a great change for them, so
great they even integrated the central religious ceremony of the
Plains Indians, the sun dance, which they called the dry-
standing dance, into their own sense of Spirit.

Before long, as we are speaking of time, these eastern
Shoshones encountered yet another culture, very alien to
their own, and underwent changes far greater still.

The first whites the Shoshones encountered were fur
traders, led to Henry's Fork of the Snake River by Andrew
Henry in 1810. The next year brought more fur traders, led by
Wilson Price Hunt, and the next year still more. In 1818 the
British sent a Hudson's Bay Company fur brigade to the
upper Snake River. In 1824 the Americans followed suit, and
soon there were white men in the country every year.

The Shoshones welcomed them. They made friends with the whites. They traded them horses. They lent and traded them women. For a long time they could boast that no Shoshone had ever killed a white man. They absorbed what the whites had to offer—guns, metal knives, powder, lead, blankets, beads—and used these things to enhance their own way of life.

The white men liked the Shoshones. They were good Indians in a grand country rich with beaver. The whites trapped beaver in Shoshone country in spring and autumn, rendezvoused there in midsummer, and often spent winter with the tribes. They married Shoshone women. They learned the language and adopted the ways. They had Shoshone children.

Simply because of what they had in their heads, the whites made everything different. Quite by accident, the mountain men brought new ways of seeing the world to the Shoshones. Implicit in their guns and compasses lay applied science. In their knives and blankets, manufacturing. In their exploring, a kind of imperialism. In their minds in every way, a new worldview.

Great changes came on the outside as well. In the 1840s the white people turned the old trail along the Snake River into a great highway to Oregon, and then a highway to California. Whereas the mountain men admired the eastern Shoshones, the immigrants mostly despised them, as they despised all Indians. Small trading posts in Shoshone country grew into big enterprises serving the wagon trains, Fort Hall and Fort Boise on the Snake itself, Fort Bridger on Black's Fork. Eventually there were troubles. Eventually soldiers came, and there were greater troubles, including massacres of Shoshone people. Eventually the Shoshones were confined to reservations, the largest being Fort Hall in Idaho and the Wind River Reservation in Wyoming, both still with us.

Then the railroad came, and brought with it surveyors and farmers and bartenders and sheriffs and preachers and real-estate agents and district attorneys and the whole kit and caboodle of the vitality that passed for civilization in the mid- and late-nineteenth century. The Shoshones had to find a way

to live in the midst of all this alien progress. They managed.
They still manage, with difficulty. Their old ways are making
a comeback, and give them peace of spirit in the whirlwind of
change.

Now the old road along the Snake River, part of the
Oregon Trail, has become Interstate 84. You can drive from
the headwaters of the Snake to its mouth at the Columbia in
two easy days. You will not see the great falls. Most of the turbulent water has been turned into reservoirs. You won't need
to eat lizards, grasshoppers, or ants. You may pay no attention
to the lava flows everywhere. Even on the hottest August day,
thanks to air conditioning you may not even notice Duma Apa,
Father Sun, as you cruise along. All that is both a gain and a
loss.

The story that follows is of the kind that is invented but
true. Invented in its particulars, true to the spirit of the times,
the 1830s, and of the peoples, both red and white. They
were strange people, from the modern perspective, and we
must reach across a distance of mind to embrace them.

The story began with a fur trader who came among the
eastern Shoshones with that Hudson's Bay Company brigade
in 1818, and planted his seed in a Shoshone woman's belly.

Part One

A BAND OF PILGRIMS

Chapter One

 Michael Devin O'Flaherty stirred. In dream his mind roamed through green, sun-spangled fields of Erin. A voice barked his name gratingly.

He stirred. He sat up and quickly lay back down. He tried to clear his head. He'd sworn off drinking, so why did his head feel like it was about to bust? Neck hurt, too. When he twisted his neck, it felt like dry grasses cracking.

The voice came again. "Mr. O'Flaherty?"

Boots walked into his prone view, black boots. Flare hated boots. Whenever an Irishman saw boots, he thought of the British and the Year of the French at home and fancied the boots were about to crunch his neck. He'd been born the Year of the French, 1798, so naturally hatred of the Brits ran in his blood.

What kind of man would walk around to the front of a canvas lean-to, where he could peer in? Plenty of room at the back. More polite. A Brit would be impolite, to get the upper hand.

It was a big man, strapping, gussied up in a black frock coat. Which was strange enough, here at Fort Laramie, a thousand miles from the settlements. A man with a big, fine, leonine head of black hair in a pompadour. A man bristling with male vigor and authority. The sort of man Flare despised.

Michael Devin O'Flaherty divided malekind into two groups. The first was essentially Irish, men delighted by the world and its poesy and song and wanting nothing on earth but to enjoy nature and art and life. The second was essentially British, men whose only pleasure was in ruling, dominating, controlling other men, and as an afterthought women. They didn't know what pleasure was. This bastard was a Brit in spirit.

"Mr. O'Flaherty?" the man said a third time.

"Right enough," murmured Flare, sitting up.

"I'm Dr. Full, Samuel Full." He made three very distinct syllables of "Samuel."

"I'm sorry to wake you, but I was told you might be pulling out for rendezvous anytime. Are you up to a guiding job?" He looked around Flare's low home and few blankets disapprovingly. "Mr. Robert Campbell recommended you." He let his doubt show in his voice.

Flare knew the doubt and disapproval weren't necessarily real. This sort of man would act that way just to throw you off balance. This Dr. Full missed his calling by being American instead of Brit.

"I'm leading a group of Christians to the Methodist Episcopal mission on the Willamette. Do you know where it is?"

"Aye." Flare rose out of his blankets, nude except for the Celtic cross on a chain around his neck. It was a cross of an ancient style, the symbol of the crucifixion with a circle around it, like a halo.

Flare slipped on his moccasins first, letting his bare arse shine whitely at the interloper, then draped his breechcloth from a belt. The man stared at him. Rude bugger. Would he want to watch Flare squat, too?

"We need to travel fast, and will pay top dollar for a good man. You're highly recommended. Are you interested?"

"I'll talk about it if ye'll give me coffee."

"Coffee. Is that all you drink, Mr. O'Flaherty?"

Flare looked at him hard. "I swore off the whiskey. For good."

"When?"

"Yesterday."

It had been a six-day binge. For years he'd said an Irishman was not drunk as long as he could hold on to the spinning earth and not fall off. Then he got the letter. He was through with boozing, he swore, and he meant it.

The coffee was strong and bitter. Flare liked it with sugar boiled in, and plenty of it, but these Christians had no more sugar. Which only meant they wouldn't pay Laramie prices for it.

They were a strange lot, as he knew they would be. He'd met Dr. Whitman at rendezvous a couple of summers ago, and the two missionaries and their wives last summer. He thought Americans were peculiar people. They had a grand country, wide open to all the adventuring a man might have in his heart. Yet a lot of them bid fair to be as priest-ridden as the Irish. Protestant priests, of course, which meant they didn't have a thousand years' experience crushing people's spirit.

He drank his coffee and chatted amiably.

He made them out as two families and some strays: Dr. Full, his wife, a quiet woman who seemed older than he, near on forty, and her children. A blacksmith, Alan Wineson, who appeared overendowed with shoulders and biceps and underendowed with wit, and his wife and three unruly children.

The strays were an older man, perhaps sixty, with a round body and a beaver face, and a cheerful spirit. Name Parker Jones. They called him Parky, and it was impossible not to like him. Sheppers Smith, a younger Dr. Full, in training for bastardy but not yet fully accomplished. And three maiden ladies, of all things, two schoolteachers and one bound to join her intended.

To tell the truth, a slight outfit to be traveling from here to the Pacific Coast. They'd come this far with one of Sublette and Campbell's trains supplying Laramie, which was well enough. But they had only four grown men, two of them preachers, and the others likely more practiced at praying than shooting. The Indians didn't care a farthing if the Christians passed through, but might prefer that they left their horses. As a toll, or tribute.

Also, the party was late. They'd gotten off late from Missouri, and the Laramie outfit had been in no great hurry, having plenty of time to get out and back. Long way yet to the Willamette, and the middle of July already here.

His main thought was that it was another party of missionaries, like Marcus Whitman brought before. Bloody nuisances. Flare thought he'd tell Full to stuff his bleeding job, even though the Irishman needed it.

"More coffee, Mr. O'Flaherty?"

It was the first time he'd really noticed her. He rose. From natural courtesy, though others would attribute his manners to Gaelic blarney. "Thank you, Miss . . . "

"Jewel. Maggie Jewel," she said with a fine smile.

"Sure and you are a jewel," he said as she poured. She gave him a merry come-off-it look and passed on to the next empty cup.

A tall lass, with hair the rust color of pipestone, full in the bosom and bottom, as Flare liked them. Tall as himself, Flare would wager, and would go near Flare's eight stone, he'd wager again. Flare was always hard and lean, and right now, hung over and broke and starved for a few days, he was gaunt. She was graceful with her fullness— tread lightly upon the earth. Beautiful, as Narcissa Whitman had been beautiful. He liked the look of her. But no schoolmarms for Michael Devin O'Flaherty, you can bet on that.

"What about it, Mr. O'Flaherty, are you our man?" It was Dr. Full interrupting Flare's fantasy of Miss Jewel.

"Might be. Don't know. What'll ye pay?" Flare noticed that all eyes were on the two of them. But from the look of it, everyone took a back seat to Dr. Full, especially his mouse of a wife.

"Five hundred dollars."

It was no fortune, truly. Three or four years ago a good trapper got three times that in wages from American

Fur Company for a year's work, and Flare, a brigade leader, made near double that again. But this wasn't three or four years ago. Beaver had bottomed out, and a child could hardly make enough for lead, powder, and tobacco.

"Don't know," said Flare softly.

"Will we be able to get to Vancouver before the snows?"

"Should do. You'll be wanting to leave the wagons here."

"No, Mr. O'Flaherty. Those wagons are essential. We were told we could get them right through to the Willamette."

"Might do. Terrible risk. Slow you down. I wouldn't chance it." Flare had to smile at himself for saying that. There wasn't a chance he wouldn't take, the more fool he.

"Do we not need the food?"

"Consider the lilies of the field, how they grow. They toil not, neither do they spin." Flare spread his arms to the horizons. "Buffalo country." Flare noticed Miss Jewel watching him with a saucy smile.

"But man, those wagons bear our clothes, our silver and china, our furniture, our books—"

"Everything that makes you civilized."

"Yes."

"To survive out here, you need to be *un*civilized."

Miss Jewel was much amused.

"Far from it," said Dr. Full huffily.

"Oh, Samuel," she burst out, then corrected herself: "Dr. Full, Mr. O'Flaherty is just having some fun with you."

"Is that true?" Full demanded.

"A bit of fun, perhaps. It's true you want to leave the wagons here. The clerk will trade you some mules, and you'll need them." Flare didn't add that the wagons would go cheap and mules would come high.

"What else?"

"We'd travel every day, rest when I say so." Flare had heard about other missionaries demanding that every sabbath be spent resting . . . and praying and reading

Scripture . . . and preaching. Flare wouldn't be able to bear the preaching.

"What else?"

"I'd be in command and you'd take orders. All of you." A fine test for Dr. Full. Bad enough to herd pork-eaters across the mountains, impossible if you weren't in charge.

"No, thanks, Mr. O'Flaherty." He spoke decisively. Flare didn't think he would pass the test. "We'll apply elsewhere."

"Oh, Samuel . . . Dr. Full," Miss Jewel put in, "you don't hire an expert and then tell him how to do his job."

He ignored her.

He said curtly, "Thanks for your time, O'Flaherty."

Keep your leprechaun spirits up after that set-to, laddie, he teased himself. He was chewing on pemmican at his lean-to. Out of fresh meat, he was, and out of nearly everything else. Hadn't eaten for drinking in several days, didn't have a day's worth of pemmican left.

He envied Wolf Tone, picketed nearby, munching on grass. Wolf Tone was a handsome black stallion—black Irish, Flare liked to say. Not an Indian pony but an American horse, sixteen hands. While Flare was hungry, Wolf Tone had plenty to eat. Flare often wondered if he shouldn't learn to eat grass and leaves and twigs, like the critters.

Truly, he hadn't had such a bad spring. He'd trapped with Barnaby Skye in North Park, and they'd come in to Laramie with a dozen packs of skins. When it came time to go on to rendezvous, Mr. Skye went. But Flare had got that letter, and went on another binge. Drank for six days and gambled at the hand game for the last three days while stuporous. Now he had nothing.

The letter was from his oldest brother, Padraig, in County Galway. His old mother, God rest her soul, had passed on in her sleep. Seventy-five, she was. Mind not right in her last couple of years, she was, but talked often of Michael Devin, and hoped for a letter from him.

Padraig listed all of Flare's nephews and nieces, and two grandnieces, and said they all prayed for him. And truly hoped this letter reached him—it was being sent to American Fur Company, Michael Devin's last known address.

Padraig always called him Michael Devin, as his mother had. It was the American beaver men who gave him his odd nickname. They shortened his name successively to Flaherty and then Flare. Once a brigade clerk asked him how to spell it. When Flare gave the full version, the clerk asked for the short one. "F-l-a-i-r?" He suggested. "You do cut a fancy figure."

"No," said Flare, "F-l-a-r-e. An Irishman's life is brief enough, but bright and fiery."

All in all it was a nice letter Padraig wrote, such as made Flare feel shamed enough to get drunk. His eldest brother was almost as good as their mother, God rest her soul, at making Flare feel ashamed. Flare had loved his father, God rest his soul, dead twenty-five years, and despised his mother. Which he showed by a binge in her memory, and gambling away everything.

Yes, Ma, I'm a drunk and a wastrel. And ashamed. Shame was very Irish. The Jews have guilt, a Jewish fur trader had told him in Montreal, and the Irish have shame.

Truth is, lad, you need that job.

Nursemaid bloody preachers.

You're flat broke, laddie. You've not supplies to get to rendezvous. If you get there, you've no plews to trade.

This child has always survived.

Oh, leave off with that. You're a thirty-nine-year-old, worn-out, washed-up drunk and gambler. Maybe you cut a figure once, maybe you could have made something of yourself, but that's behind you, laddie.

Beaver's bound to rise.

The devil. It's silk hats now, my friend. And black boots.

I can guide someone other than a self-important ass. We'd be at each other's throats.

True enough, laddie. Going to try your credit again at the post?

He listened to the footfalls on the other side of his lean-to. "Mr. O'Flaherty?" It *was* her. Usually he could tell, but it had been hard to hear her steps for sure around the campfire with others moving about.

He stood so she could see him. "Aye, Miss Jewel. Will ye come and sit a bit with a wastrel? So my honored mother would warn you, God rest her soul."

She cocked her head and studied him. "You don't have the face of a wastrel, Mr. O'Flaherty. An idealist, perhaps, and a little worn."

He chuckled. "Aye, lass, you bet, all the Irish are worn, and this one more than a little. Would ye share a bite with me?" He held out the last of his pemmican. "I've no coffee."

"No, thanks. Dr. Full has gone over to the fort to try to hire another guide. But the only man on Mr. Campbell's list who's at the fort now is you."

Flare let it sit.

"Dr. Full says he heard over there yesterday that you need the money. Why don't you take the job?"

"It wasn't offered, lass."

"Shaw," she said. "I can get Samuel to offer it."

"I liked the way you put your oar boldly in. Got the impression he didn't like it."

She grinned like a mischievous kid, which made her look marvelous. "Samuel thinks I'm too forward. He says I don't honor the respective spheres God gave men and women in this world."

"Words of a man who would like any place, just so it's on top."

"Oh, Samuel, Dr. Full, is a good man. I just know him too well."

"Well enough to fight like brother and sister," Flare said with a smile.

"We are, sort of. But he doesn't like to admit that. His mother and father raised me from the time I was thirteen. He wasn't there much—he was apprenticed to a physician. He's a medical doctor. And an ordained minister."

"Why is it that you switch between his Christian name and his family name?"

"He's asked even his family to call him Dr. Full except when we're entirely alone. He says us treating him with respect will show others they must. And he addresses us formally."

"Out here, lass, a man who doesn't know poor bull from fat cow won't get much respect."

"I think a man of God is always due respect," she said with a hint of heat.

"I left civilization behind, not God, *musha colleen og*" (dear little girl), Flare said quietly. "An Irishman can run, but he can't leave God behind."

She eyed him, hesitated, then blurted, "I think you're a good man."

"I think you're a winsome lass," he answered.

"I want you to guide us."

"Dr. Full doesn't want me."

She pursed her lips, wagged her head. "He can be persuaded. Come at noon." She got up, grinned back at him, and walked off.

Sure and you're heading for trouble, Flare said to himself. You like her too much, which will never shine in her crowd.

Well, he'd taken jobs for worse reasons.

Dr. Samuel Full rode away from the Laramie stockade irked. The clerk, one Vernon Scharp, would recommend no guide handy at the post now. He said he needed his employees, and the free trappers were gone to rendezvous on Green River. The man didn't even speak heartily for Mr. O'Flaherty. A good man, said Scharp, but into his cups, far into his cups. But who said Scharp was an honest man?

Dr. Full needed to think, and he needed horseflesh under him while he thought. Being high, having a sense of

sovereignty and domain always made him think better. He
would walk his horse slowly back to camp.

It all started when he cornered Jameson LaLane after
the fool's sermon at the church in Philadelphia. LaLane
was squirming, and Dr. Full had no idea why. Lalane was
the head of the Oregon mission, the man given the job Dr.
Samuel Full and other every enthusiastic minister of God
of the Methodist Episcopal Church coveted. He was the
object of everyone's envy. And the fool was unsure of
himself.

Dr. Full said nothing. He watched LaLane feint,
duck, and dodge—when there was nothing to dodge. He
was the guest of honor. The church women were treating
him with respect, even awe. The man had the world in his
hand. Why all the fancy footwork?

Dr. Full waited until the women were gone. He was
taking LaLane home for Sunday dinner, but that could
wait. LaLane looked at Dr. Full sheepishly. Dr. Full
looked back. And looked and looked.

When the question came, it came whole, polished, a
gleaming gift from God. True, it was an insane question—
rude, confrontational, wildly out of order. But gloriously
on target.

"How many Indians have you converted?"

Jameson LaLane did not hesitate, feint, or dodge. He
blurted it out, a man flinging his burden to the ground:
"None."

None! In four long years in the wilderness? None?

The sacrifice of Christ had balmed not a single savage soul in Oregon? Dr. Full couldn't believe it. Yet
LaLane's eyes told the truth. They were direct—shamed,
but direct and open, confessional. The man had gone to
Oregon to convert the heathen, spent three years at his
labor, and accomplished nothing.

Now he was touring the United States to tell of his
effort, of his desperate need for more money, more Christians, more help. He was come to sing the necessity of
bringing the Gospel to the heathen. And on all his tour, no

one had dared ask the man of God a simple question: How many savages have you brought to Christ?

None.

Yes, the man had accomplished something physically—buildings built, crops in, a working wilderness post. But nothing toward the goal he was sent for.

Dr. Full saw his great fortune.

Then the excuses began. At first they were general. LaLane knew Indians were children of darkness—the Scripture tells us that—but he had not realized how benighted they were. The most terrible curse of all was not to dwell in darkness but to be blind, unable to see the light when it shone forth all about you. Jameson LaLane had held high his beacon, and no one had seen it.

Then, with prompting, the facts emerged. The Indians had moved away from the missionaries—they'd abandoned the traditional sites of their villages to get away from the whites. The first two years they lived nearby, and a few even let their children come to the mission school. When LaLane and others went among them to teach, they listened politely and sometimes asked questions, but the questions showed they understood nothing. "Nothing," said LaLane bitterly, his mouth twisting at the memory. "They thought if they prayed, guns and whiskey would rain down upon them as manna from heaven."

He switched plans and tried to get them interested in farming. If they learned industry, diligence, and perhaps a little cleanliness, he thought, they might begin to get a glimmer of the light. At least farming would keep them from gallivanting about all the time, Lord knows where, sometimes in search of food, but often to perpetuate their abominable devil worship.

They responded a little. Some could see the benefit of crops, though none was inclined actually to plow, plant, and hoe. But the country was forgiving—it would grow anything, and with the merest hint of effort.

Then they began to get sick. Fevers, dysentery, agues—every plague known to man. The children, especially, sickened and often died.

It was an old story. The mountain men had told LaLane of how white men brought diseases the Indians were not accustomed to, and how they seemed to die of any fever. LaLane heard, but he didn't realize.

By the end of the second summer the mission had no Indian neighbors. A few children stayed at the school, after elaborate, barbaric ceremonies to ward off evil spirits. The ceremonies disgusted LaLane utterly, but he saw no chance of talking the pagans out of them. He accepted the children. Otherwise they not only couldn't convert the Indians, they couldn't find them.

If they left their children at the school, though, the savages would come back for them.

"But not a single convert?" Dr. Full knew where his leverage was.

LaLane gave an involuntary cry, half laugh, half wail. His face was the face of a man who had ventured forth into the darkness, gazed into its heart, and found despair. "The truth is," he rasped hoarsely, "they are Indians."

It took Dr. Full no time at all. It was easy to persuade LaLane that the mission's first need was now a doctor like himself: How could you save the Indians' souls if you couldn't keep them alive? The mission board, though it ignored most of LaLane's urgings, quickly approved this proposal. Its other decisions fit nicely with Dr. Full's plans. LaLane would stay in the States another year, traveling and lecturing with the two Indian boys he'd brought East as an appeal to sympathy, visiting churches with hat in hand. The mission board itself had no way to give LaLane the funds he said he needed.

Some of the board members saw that by sending the manly and energetic Dr. Full a year ahead of LaLane, they might be changing leadership. They didn't care. LaLane saw it, too. He was too worn down to care.

So Dr. Samuel Full got his due. Four years earlier, when Jameson LaLane was chosen head of the Oregon mission, the board passed over Samuel Full because he had less experience with congregations than LaLane. He had less experience because he'd apprenticed himself to a physician, learning to heal the body as well as the soul. Nearly two years he'd spent in that apprenticeship, and he had a touch for pulling teeth. The two years once seemed to cost him his ambition, the greatest opportunity for bringing lost souls to the Gospel since the early centuries of the Christian church. He wanted to sing out the Gospel in the darkness of the great American wilderness.

And now he was justified. Now his knowledge of doctoring got him what he wanted.

Last winter, in the East, he put together a small group of the faithful with the skills he wanted in Oregon. The mission had veered from its purpose. It had become too mindful of worldly matters, had sent back word to the States for carpenters, farmers, mechanics, blacksmiths.

Samuel Full would continue to build the settlement, the outpost of civilization on the Pacific Coast. He would also return it to its high purpose. He would save Indian souls.

To that end the assembled people who would be tools in his hand. Another minister, Parker Jones, an older man whose wife was dead and children grown, congenial, without personal ambition. A young Christian with under-standing of account books and numbers, Sheppers Smith, and a particular admirer of Dr. Full. Another blacksmith, Wineson. A schoolteacher for the white children, Elvira Upping. And most crucially, a teacher for the Indian girls, Maggie Jewel.

Aside from their skills, they all had a quality that would serve Dr. Full well: They were malleable, they could be forged into the shapes that his great purpose re-quired. Sometimes he wasn't sure of Miss Jewel, but she was especially well trained, his sister in Christ, and a woman. She would learn. His band of the called needed people with the self-discipline, the sense of station, to make good followers.

That was the problem with Mr. O'Flaherty. The man

was a wild hair. Dr. Full had a subtle eye for people, and he was seldom wrong about them. The man O'Flaherty would not bend.

The question was: Did it matter?

O'Flaherty would take them to the Willamette and be gone, gone to his Indian sluts or into his cups or taken by his juvenile yearning for adventure. Who cared where he went?

If he wanted to struggle with Dr. Full for supremacy within the traveling band of the chosen, why not? It would be amusing. Maybe even an Irish sot could learn something.

"No wagons." Flare had to make sure of it.

"Agreed," said Dr. Full. "Will you help me trade them?"

Flare nodded. "And I will be in charge."

"Yes."

"That means I choose the route, say when we set out and when we stop, choose the watches, choose the fords—the lot."

"Yes." The fellow didn't like having it put to him strong. Flare didn't blame him.

"Listen, man, when we deal with Indians, you and all your outfit must follow orders. If any man reaches for a weapon, a lot of hair might be lost."

"I understand."

"It'll be a thousand dollars," Flare said.

"I'm prepared for that."

"I'll need some in advance. Truth to tell, I'm flat broke."

"So we heard," Dr. Full said.

"Two hundred here, three hundred at Fort Hall, five hundred at the Willamette."

"At the mission," Dr. Full corrected

"Aye." Flare held out a hand. "You bet." They shook.

That phrase, "you bet" was a fine American affirmative. Flare liked it.

Dr. Full disappeared into a wagon and came back with a handful of gold coins. He handed them over.

"I've business at the fort," Flare said.

"You won't get drunk on us?" Dr. Full asked.

"No more in this lifetime," Flare said simply.

Full just turned away.

The trouble with one like that, Flare reflected, is that you can't win. He'll just come back meaner.

Chapter
Two

"Would you like to hear the story of the putrefied forest?" asked Flare. The kids clamored for it.

Miss Jewel rolled her eyes comically. " 'Putrefied' is mountain-man funny for 'petrified,' children," she said.

"Mr. O'Flaherty," said Dan doubtfully, "is this true?"

"You bet," said Flare.

This was the time Flare liked. They'd made their miles. In fact, he had this greenhorn outfit whipped into pretty good shape, into the routine without complaint, and even with pride. So at night, before he took the first watch (he also took the last), they could enjoy the campfires and his yarns.

What kind of mountain man would he be if he couldn't stretch the kids' ears with twenty years' worth of tall tales? Even if they seemed a spiritless bunch of kids?

"Us beavers was riding up on the Snake River, across that malpais. Lava-flow country, terrible stuff. Hit was summer, and we wuz froze for meat." Flare liked to mimic American backwoods talk. He could mimic anybody's words, or their walk. "Over there ain't buffler country. You'll see when we get thar. Old Gabe and me, there was, and Black Harris, and Mr. Skye, and three or four other hosses as know what way the stick floats."

He looked merrily at Miss Jewel. She got a kick out of good yarns.

"Well, we rode up Henry's Fork and into some mountains. If you went a long way on that ways, you came to whar was the boiling springs, as I told you about, and whar the water shoots into the sky and you can smell the sulfurs of hell down below.

"As we come into these mountains, it turned peculiar, like you never see in that country. For half a day we rode in a fog, so's we could scarce see whar we was headed. Finally we got to feeling lost and made camp.

"When we woke in the mornin', it was a puzzlement such as you never did see. We was in a hole, open meadows surrounded by forested hills, and this child noticed right off everthing was quiet-like, no sound at all. That's onnatural in the woods. And it was onnatural still— seemed like the grasses didn't wave nor the leaves flutter in the wind. But I thought nothing of it. Just ain't no wind, I told myself.

"This child walked down to the little crick to fetch water, and the water was froze. Not just ice on the surface but froze solid to the bottom. In the middle o' August.

"I goes back to tell Old Gabe, and I sees that hoss holding offhand on somethin'. There's the elk, right close, only a couple of hundred steps away and in the open, an easy mark for Old Gabe. He let fly with Old Bullthrower, and right back comes the loudest THOCK! you ever did hear, like an ax hitting a tree. Echoed everwhere. The elk just stood there like nothing happened.

"'Old Bullthrower don't miss,' said Gabe suspiciously. He throwed down and nailed that elk agin. THOCK! Echoes. Elk standing up handsome. Gabe began to look around like the place was full o' haunts.

"Right then Mr. Skye hollered out from the edge of the woods. He'd walked up there and took his wiping stick in case he saw a fool hen, and he did see one, and whacked it, and it broke the stick. Oh, was he a-hollerin'.

"Gabe and this child and another'n or two run over there, and you wouldn't believe it if'n you didn't see it. Mr. Skye, with the biggest chest and arms I ever saw, was whomping and whomping away, till his wiping stick was splinters. That fool hen was stone, solid stone."

Miss Jewel put in, "That's what petrified means, children, turned to stone."

"And hit really do happen, don't it, Miss Jewel?"

"Certainly," she said.

"Wall, then all us hosses begun to look around good. Everthing was putrefied. The trees was stone, their leaves was stone. That elk was putrefied solid, you could've broke your head on it. The birds was putrefied. Finally I figured out that even their songs were putrefied, and that's why it was so onnatural silent.

"Now Old Gabe, he's some, he's seen everthing and remembered it all, but he's superstitious-like. So that hoss says, 'Boys, let's get out'n this queer place.'

"We was packed and saddled and ridin' before Gabe could cuss at us. But we couldn't see how we come in through the fog, on account of the putrefied ground showed no trail. So we headed for the divide on the north. When we got to the crest, there was a chasm half a mile wide, with a river far down in the bottom. We rode east and west and all around, and everwhere was that chasm. Seemed that river run in a circle, penning us in that putrefied forest.

"This nigger was about to say there was some way out, we damn well got in, when Old Gave said he had an idea.

"He backed his horse up a little and galloped straight toward the chasm. We thought he was gone loco. Comin' to the edge, he spurred good, and horse and rider just flew over the chasm like a kite in a fine wind. Clear on across. And then waved to us to come on over.

"Well, we did. Never had such a feelin', afore or since. Mountain men soarin' like eagles.

"As we rode off, this child says to Gabe, 'How'd you know?'

"'Figgered it out,' he says. 'The law of gravity was putrefied, too.'

"You bet."

*   *   *

At first Miss Jewel thought fleetingly it was the glow of the sun setting. She looked up at the real sun, still two hours high. She turned every which way. And saw.

The fiery glow on the crest of the hill ahead wasn't the sun. It was flickering, crawling down the wind like a red worm, bright and malignant.

"Prairie fire," Mr. O'Flaherty said softly.

Cold went through her like lightening.

She looked sideways at him. Mr. O'Flaherty stared hard at the flames, in good view now on the crest of the hill and sweeping this way. He looked to the right into other hills, to the left toward the Platte, back toward the flames. He was erect, motionless, seemingly calm. She could see calculations running through his eyes.

"The river!" he shouted, and started loping downhill. Following his example, the rest of them kept their horses to a canter, in no great hurry.

At the river he rode forward toward a bend, but also toward the flames. In faith, Miss Jewel followed.

Below the bend stretched a gravel bar. Mr. O'Flaherty went onto it, into the shallow water downstream of it, and splashed his horse all the way across the river, knee deep to the rider. As the others crossed, he rode back and yelled at the packhorses to make them move along.

On the far bank Miss Jewel suddenly discovered she'd been holding her breath. She exploded it out, and a tear or two almost came with it. She'd been badly frightened.

Riding up, Mr. O'Flaherty gave her one of his mad Irish grins.

"Are prairie fires common?" she huffed.

"Sure and they are when Indians set 'em, you bet."

"Indians?" sputtered Dr. Full.

"Indians," Flare repeated quietly. "Let's camp on that bench!" he hollered to everyone, pointing just above.

"We don't want to camp with Indians close by," said Dr. Full.

"That's just what we want to do," said Flare. They needed to get set, and he had no time for fools.

"But—"

"Dr. Full," Flare said menacingly, "get your mules unloaded, your horses picketed, and your tent up. Now!"

The man's face flushed ripe red, but to his credit he went and did it.

Flare started getting the gear arranged in a line to lie down behind. A poor defense, but better than none.

"Will we be able to hold 'em off, Mr. O'Flaherty?" It was Sheppers Smith, the fellow Flare thought of as Dr. Full the younger, sounding melodramatic. Flare nodded toward the gear to be stacked.

"Won't have to, lad. They're playin', not fightin'."

"That fire wasn't any play!" He grabbed an armload and set to work.

"Aye, lad, it was but play. They knew what we'd do when they set it. Big trouble, if they'd meant to make it, would have come quieter. Naturally, if we'd been foolish enough to let the mules run off, they'd have accepted the gift."

"So what now?" It was Alan Wineson, the addled blacksmith, pitching in, too. Dr. Full came up behind. Maybe the big man wasn't ashamed to soil his fine clothes.

"They'll be along tonight or tomorrow morning. Expecting some presents."

"Swine," said Dr. Full. "Thieves."

"Don't know as I'd call 'em thieves," said Mr. O'Flaherty. He lifted. Stacked. Lifted.

"Maybe you wouldn't."

Flare ignored the slight. "Dr. Full, you say your object is to create a colony at first, and then a real settlement, and finally to settle the Willamette valley thoroughly."

"It is. We will not merely preach the Gospel but teach the white way."

"Takes a lot of bodies and souls to do that." Lift and stack. "The whole lot traipsing across this trail. Killing the game, drinking the water, burning the firewood."

He stopped and looked at Dr. Full. "This is *their* land, Dr. Full."

"They have no title," he said.

Flare suppressed a chuckle and surveyed the work. It would do. He didn't expect to need it, and if he did, it would do. "No, Indians don't deal in titles, Dr. Full. But it's theirs. When we take a little, we'll pay a little. And feel grateful for the bargain."

"Can we stand them off with this?" Full gestured at the barricade.

"No. We'll be outmanned." Maybe not in raw numbers, but in numbers who could fight. "But they won't attack a defended position. Unless they're drunk."

Drunk was what they were. Drunk descending to hung over.

They were Arapahos, eight of them, young men, surely out to steal horses from the Crows. That had more cachet than stealing horses from Americans, who were easy targets. But Americans would do, especially if the youths had gone against the Crows and were headed home empty-handed.

They came a half hour before dark. Flare didn't like it. Clearly they meant to camp with the whites, damned dangerous in their state of inebriation.

"Disgusting," Dr. Full said bitterly, like that was the worst of it.

"Sit on my left," said Flare. "Smoke the pipe when it's passed to you. And no matter what happens, keep your mouth shut."

Flare got out his pipe, sat and invited his guests to sit, and took his time filling the bowl while he thought.

Flare had a lifelong thirst himself, and fellow feeling for another man with thirst. But he didn't believe the Indians and firewater mixed. He'd given Indians whiskey when he traded for the Northwest Company those first two years, but not when he traded for Hudson's Bay Company. The Bay didn't believe in it. Which was the only thing that bunch of Scottish and British bastards got right.

Whiskey ruined Indians. Flare had seen brother kill brother, and father rape daughter, all because of drunkenness. A Flathead friend had even broken Flare's nose in a drunken stupor.

Ten years ago, drunk, he'd quit the Bay and come over to the Americans. Trouble was, the Americans gave Indians whiskey. Good way to compete with the Bay, they said. It was, if you didn't give a damn for consequences. Some outfit had given these Arapahos whiskey yesterday, and today Flare and his lot were facing the consequences.

Maybe after a generation the Americans would learn. It took the Bay longer than that. If the God-cursed fur trade lasted another generation.

So he decided. He would give these Arapahos a little whiskey—there wasn't any way out of it. But he had a little trick to make it safer.

He lit the pipe. He watched the smoke rise. In English, translating into sign language, he offered the pipe to Mother Earth and Father Sky to the West, where the thunder lives, the North, from where the cleansing winds come, the East, home of the dawn, and the South, where we are always looking.

This was always a solemn moment for Flare. He didn't *believe* anything about it—those cursed with a Catholic education believe little they're told ever again—but you didn't have to believe in the earth and sky. They were terms of your life. And it was a ritual he used to say something. With smoke he honored the earth he walked on, the sky he lived under, the four directions in which he wandered. By sharing the pipe with fellow human beings he promised truthfulness and goodwill.

Then he passed the pipe in the ritual manner, and each man smoked in silence. Flare hoped no one noticed the look of distaste on Dr. Full's face when he put his mouth to the stem.

When the smoke was done, Flare gave them a little tobacco, a few strands of beads, and some cloth. He spoke his friendship, of his appreciation for being able to cross the country of the Arapaho on his way to where the white people lived by the big water, of his pleasure in smoking with these men.

The leader simply said, "Awerdenty." It was the trapper and Indian mangling of the Taos word for whiskey.

Flare was offended at the man's bad manners, and distressed at his abasement. But it would not do to give any sign of unhappiness. Instead he told the man that this was a group of Christians who believed whiskey was bad for all men. He himself had given whiskey to many Indians, and his heart was low because it hurt his friends. He asked his new friends, these Arapahos, to drink no whiskey. He himself would drink no more whiskey as long as he walked the earth.

"Awerdenty," the man said, crudely, and perhaps dangerously.

Flare would make one last try. He started out sincere and turned into a terrible hypocrite. As he spoke, Flare developed an epic thirst, the thirst of a sailor surrounded by water, water everywhere, and not a drop to drink. Flare had tasted a dram or two before he left Ireland, 1814 it was, but he'd come to love drink in Montreal. Brandy in particular. And after he learned truly to love it, to take it to his bosom like the wife he never had, he was plenty fond of even Indian whiskey. He hated to think, even now, what ingredients he put into the trade whiskey. Tobacco was the most pleasant, snakes' heads the least.

Now he could feel the glow in his veins, like letting a heavy glass with a candle inside warm your hands on a cold night. He imagined the brandy glass once more warm in his hand and lifted to his eyes, and the yellow light in its center like a will-o'-the-wisp. When you chased that will-o'-the-wisp, when you let the whiskey roar through your veins, you were witty, you were wise, you were strong and long-lived as gods, and damn all.

Thirsting, he made himself finish his little preachment on temperance to these Indians, but couldn't remember what he'd said. His palms were sweaty with want.

"Awerdenty," the leader said, and Flare knew that was the last time.

"All right," Flare said, "whiskey."

* * *

He had to give Dr. Full credit, the man didn't open
his mouth in front of the Indians, not even when Flare
promised them whiskey. Sure and he took that as a privi-
lege to go on and on about it now.

"O'Flaherty, you'll get us all killed!"

That was merely the most moderate of Full's state-
ments. He mentioned that he didn't know Flare had
brought whiskey, as though it would be possible to get on
without it. He insisted he would have forbidden it—he
thought those kegs were water. He made dire predictions,
caroming from rape to torture to postmortem mutilation in
delicate areas.

Wonderful how these pork-eaters believed their own
scary stories. Wonderful how they kept their nerve except
when they needed it. Their manners likewise.

Flare had told the Arapahos naught but that they
would get the whiskey in the morning, when the white
people could get gone. They growled, but they understood. Indians regarded drunkenness as a license to do
anything, anything at all, because they weren't responsible. Nor would you get more than a sympathetic look
when they sobered up and found out they'd maimed you
or your son. They knew why Flare wanted to get clear
first.

They watched when Flare and Sheppers Smith began
to dig. Flare told the others they'd have to trade off with
the two—it would take hours into the night, and they had
only the two shovels. He even made Dr. Full do his fair
share. Parky Jones worked cheerfully, but tired fast. Sheppers pitched in, and Alan Wineson used the blacksmith
muscles with a will. The three teenage lads did well, as
much as they could, especially Dr. Full's eldest stepson,
Dan. Flare excused only the little boys.

By turn-in time, the hole was the size of a big closet.
All the Arapahos but one were passed out—hangovers did
that to you. Flare set the jug in the middle of the bottom,
showed the last fellow where it was, and motioned that he
intended to put the dirt back into the hole. The Arapaho

nodded sullenly. While Dan distracted the fellow, Flare moved the jug to a corner of the hole and got all the men to push dirt back in fast.

"They'll just dig it up and come after us," said Dr. Full, puffing. Flare supposed his idea of high station didn't let him get much exercise.

"Aye, they were talking about that, you bet. In discouraged terms, I must say."

"Talking about it? Why did you use signs to them if you speak their language?"

"Don't speak it much. Understand it middling well." Flare added with a grin, "Never pays to tip your hand at cards."

The dirt was back in the hole. At last everyone could go to sleep. Flare took all the watches himself. Too much danger too close. With the luck of the Irish, they'd get away with it.

At dawn they bade good-bye to their Arapaho friends and kindly left them one of the two shovels.

Chapter

Three

The insubordination broke out that evening. Dr. Full could feel it coming. Dan and Miss Jewel started it with their hero-worshiping talk about Mr. O'Flaherty.

Actually, Dr. Full found himself more amused by than offended by the guide. Mr. O'Flaherty used his charm instead of his authority, which showed him to be subtle. His regimen was hard—up before dawn and the men taking turns on watch all night, a big meal and a nap at midday to make up for it. Ten miles or so before nooning, another ten or so after. But Mr. O'Flaherty persuaded people to follow his regimen willingly, and take pride in their toughness. Even today, when they'd gone hard all day without a nooning, trying to leave the savages far behind, no one had complained.

While Mr. O'Flaherty slept, dead under his blankets, Dan got started and wouldn't quit. The boy went on and on: Mr. O'Flaherty saved them from the fire, Mr. O'Flaherty powwowed with the Injuns, Mr. O'Flaherty fooled them good, Mr. O'Flaherty saved our skins—all the while, Dr. Full noticed, giving his stepfather sidelong looks. Finally the boy said in awe that Mr. O'Flaherty was a real man, and Miss Jewel agreed with him. That was too much, too damned much.

"Mr. O'Flaherty can truck with savages and a godforsaken land, of course," snapped Dr. Full. "He is a savage, worse than a savage. He has forsaken God."

Thus started, Dr. Full didn't want to stop. Mr. O'Flaherty's insubordination before God and God's authority—these were sure signs of his lack of grace. Dr. Full would use Mr. O'Flaherty gladly and get rid of him at the earliest possible convenience. Such a man had no place around a mission.

The man had roamed this wilderness for twenty years. In that time he probably had not darkened the door of even one of his papist churches, though he wore one of their crucifixes around his neck. He surely had lain with Indian women. He was a drunk and a mad gambler. He indulged his appetites wantonly, and lived for no more than the pleasure of the day. If you thought man was an animal, he might be a real man, but not if you thought man had a soul.

"Oh, Samuel, you're intolerable," said Miss Jewel calmly.

"Dr. Full," he corrected her sharply.

She rolled her eyes.

The silence around the campfire was embarrassed. Dr. Full noticed more sidelong looks toward the sagebrush, lots of them, to make sure Mr. O'Flaherty hadn't woken and heard.

Actually, Mr. O'Flaherty thought the whole thing was rather a hoot.

Sweeter far to have Miss Jewel on your side than Dr. Full. You bet.

He was careful not to stir and alert them.

In fact, the better he knew Miss Jewel, the more he admired her. She stood up to men. Stood up to everyone, for that matter, firmly but with grace. She loved music, and sang prettily. She had wit, in both senses—humor and intelligence. She had sand in her craw, and did what was needed without complaint or hesitation. She even rode astride, not sidesaddle.

The way she rode astride was a tickle. Before this

trip she'd never sat a horse. Now she rode with fierce enthusiasm, even recklessness, but as yet little balance. And
she had an oosick quirt she used with a will.

The fine part was, she didn't know what an oosick
was. A beau had given it to her as a souvenir, she said. He
was a whaling fellow out of Nantucket and brought it
back from Esquimaux country.

Clearly, he'd never told her an oosick is the penis
bone of a walrus. So she stitched some rawhide to it and
in lovely ignorance used it to flail her mount.

Ah, if only the missionary men knew, wouldn't they
take that as fraught with meaning?

He shifted in his blankets and looked up at the stars.
That scientist Nutting had said they were seven thousand
feet high here. Sure and you saw more stars from up high,
far more. More all of nature. Why did the white people
see God's nature as something to be controlled and reduced? Why not simply enjoyed?

He'd never seen a lady ride astride before. Indian
women did it, with high horns and full skirts to protect
their modesty, but white women never. Miss Jewel had
split her skirts up the middle and stitched them into legs.
When she stood, they looked like skirts. When she
wanted, they divided like pants.

The other women, especially Dr. Full's wife, Annie
Lee, thought Miss Jewel had her nerve. Which made Flare
like her the more.

And made him uneasy. He didn't feel attracted to
women he admired—he simply didn't. He wasn't interested in white women. Among his scores of lovers was
nary a one. He wasn't interested in more than feeling hot
as a poker and getting a nice douse. He knew himself.

So, why, laddie, are ye turnin' soft over a lass that
don't know where it is or what's it for? Nigh thirty years
old and never been touched. Her Puritan religion has dried
it up forever. Nothing there for the likes of you, laddie.

Besides, she wouldn't have ye. When all is said and
done, she don't want a man with spirit but one with a
soul. Like Shep Smith, working to become a martinet for

the Lord. Or Alan Wineson, with the wit of a tree stump. Aye, a man with a soul, you bet. Funny how spirit is fine and high, but soul is hangdog.

She'd scream and run from you like you were something nasty that lives in dirty hair. You bet.

And who'd want her, what wouldn't give a man comfort between the blankets until she checked with the Almighty? Who would make her say no anyway.

Besides, it ain't so much that you have that lovely wantin' for her, is it? Different kind of a feeling, isn't it?

If you mean to turn sentimental like this, better you should go back to drink.

Flare was right. She wouldn't have him. She was telling Dr. Full something like that at the moment.

"Yes," she said hotly, "I find him attractive. And no, I'm not going to come-hither him. And what business is it of yours?"

"I'm your spiritual counselor, Maggie."

"Well, Samuel . . . " She wished he'd said he was her brother. But he'd never do that.

"Samuel, I know body from soul and earth from heaven. I know what comes from God's grace and from man's unaided struggles."

She let it sit.

"Then perhaps you won't act so enamored of him."

"I'll think on that."

"Maggie," said Dr. Full, "Oregon will be a great growth for you. Keep faith with God and he'll keep faith with you." Which was just his way of telling her a man would be waiting for her in Oregon, the sort of man he thought she ought to have, one who would use a strong hand.

He didn't know she'd decided never to marry. Her engagement had ended in bitterness, and she would now devote her life to Indian children.

He touched her shoulder. She shrugged it off. He walked off into the darkness.

Funny, she felt uncomfortable now calling him Samuel.

Dr. Full felt more natural. Wasn't that queer? For your brother?

They were taking their noon meal together, as they usually did. She didn't give a care whether Samuel liked it or not.

"What's a fine lass like you doing in . . . a wilderness like this?"

She thought with amusement that he'd been about to say "in company like this."

"I've been called," she said.

"Called, is it?"

"When I was a child, near Pittsburgh, people were full of Indian-fighting stories and horrific tales about Indians. You know the kind. Save your last bullet for your wife, and keep her from a fate worse than death."

"Aye. The people who tell those stories might want to save you from the likes o' me."

She smiled at him. He was intuitive. "I didn't believe those stories. It seemed to me that Indians are God's creatures, just like the rest of us. And the ones I saw around me were not bloodthirsty or rapacious. Just ordinary and beaten down. And we were killing them every chance we got."

"This is heresy, lass." She wondered what he would really say in their defense. Poor, defeated creatures.

"They live in darkness," she hurried to add. "They were dirty and diseased. They couldn't read or write. They had no art or beauty in their lives. They didn't know God."

She saw that Mr. O'Flaherty was fidgeting, but she wanted him to know her mind on this. And if the boot fit, let him wear it.

"Then it came to me, simply and beautifully. Indians are what man is without God's grace. Without His light in one's life. What we Methodists called Unredeemèd Man." She looked him full in the face. "With that understanding came the call. God wants me to teach them." She brightened. "I went to the Wilbraham Academy in Massachusetts and learned to teach them. It's difficult, but very worthwhile. And when they've learned from me, they can learn from Dr. Full."

Holy mother of God, ye've found the answer, Michael Devin. Talk to her about her religion. That conversation will wither the most rambunctious pecker, you bet.

Change of subject: "How is it Dr. Full is your sort of brother, as you put it?"

"I never knew my father. I'm an only child. My mother died of smallpox when I was ten. I got passed around from house to house, and then Reverend Full, Dr. Full's father, took me in. I moved in when I was thirteen, and Dr. Full was funny about it."

She mused on it a moment. "I've never quite understood. He didn't accept me as part of the family. He was the oldest, sixteen, and very much the leader."

Flare could well imagine that.

"I was unruly, I guess, and hoydenish, and . . . he thought I needed to learn a female's place." She grinned. "He still does."

She seemed lost in thought for a moment. "Anyway, he insisted the family introduce me as Maggie Jewel, not Maggie Full, and he treated me differently. I asked him once to call me his sister, and he said, 'Maggie, you are my sister in Christ, but not in the flesh.'

"That time in my life taught me something great, and even Samuel's contrariness helped. I went to camp meeting and was saved. My mother taught me to pray but never took me to church. She thought church wasn't for the poor, the likes of us. When I was saved, I felt God's presence in my heart for the first time. And when I joined the church, I learned what it means to belong to something larger than yourself, to be part of a community."

She brightened. "So it didn't matter if Samuel treated me like a lost waif. Besides, in less than a year he was gone off, apprenticed to Dr. Chambers. Dr. Chambers was a very fine physician. After that, we saw Dr. Full only on holidays. Then he studied the Gospel. He's an accomplished man."

She smiled in a brittle way at Flare.

"Miss JOO-wuhl." It was Annie Lee Full, calling her pot-scrubbing assistant. Mrs. Full never failed to call Miss Jewel to her duty. Seemed to Flare Mrs. Full didn't see much in life but duty.

Miss Jewel shrugged helplessly and went off.

Holy mother of God, but didn't people spoil it? Bloody people.

Flare had turned them out in the dark as always and set them on the way before first light and sunrise. The way was unmistakable along the narrow Sweetwater River, and he could leave them to it an hour or so. He told Dr. Full the savages would surely not come after them, but he needed to ride out and check for sign. Which was true enough. He also needed to get clear of human beings for a while.

How they scratched and clawed at one another! A lad wouldn't call an adopted child "sister." Fifteen years gone and her still wanting.

He remembered as he rode, eyes in the present, mind in the past. His eyes took in all, from long habit, restlessly checking out hilltops, the shadows in coulees, the edges of tree lines, the myriad signs of life of the high plains.

Flare had never been more right than in running off from home. Nothing for him there. His father owned a printing shop, and there was a living in it. Not enough for five sons, however, and certainly not for the last of them, Michael Devin. So he traded his birthright to his eldest brother for the traditional mess of pottage, in this case a berth to the New World.

Wasn't his financial prospects that drove him off, though—rather his prospects in spirit. He'd seen that in his father, God rest his soul.

Liam O'Flaherty had been a good enough sort of man. Good to his five sons and two daughters, taught them to love above all things song and poetry and Ireland.

Taught them to love drink without wanting to, and to love his weakness.

At the time Flare only knew he had to get out to save his spirit. Not the soul the priests talked about, the spirit. Later he figured it out.

Liam O'Flaherty was a trapped man. In his spirit was adventure, as in every man's spirit. To roam the fine world God gave us, to brave its difficulties, conquer its obstacles, love its maidens. But the only maiden he ever got to love was Flare's mother, God rest her gaol of a soul.

They married early. And it was probably early on she learned to keep him bloody well obedient. He went to the shop he would one day inherit from his father. He went to Mass. He confessed. He brought his wages home. Sure and he had the occasional aberration, especially at the nearest pub, where he sang the songs of his heart with his mates and staggered home at an indecent hour. When he did that, he slept on the floor.

Aye, she punished him by holding out. So Liam O'Flaherty became a well-behaved man. Except for spending more and more time in the pubs. And slinking home. Still she held out. And he tried to be more obedient yet.

He died of the cold one winter night, lying drunk in a gutter. Why did God permit the Irish to invent whiskey? he'd asked his sons ritually. And they answered, ritually, to keep them from ruling the world.

Flare's brothers took over the business.

Flare left for America.

Occasionally, through the Northwest Company or Hudson's Bay or America Fur, he got a letter from his eldest brother, Padraig. News—mostly the names of new nephews and nieces. Hints that he should write more often and come home soon—your indifference is killing our mother. The Irish dollop of shame in every dram. Flare wrote every two or three years, but never spoke of coming home.

He had learned the lesson well from his mother.

Never give a woman the chance to have that kind of sway
over you. *Country* matters, as the Bard called it.

Flare had been . . . as he could not help but be. From
the start he loved the fair earth, and especially the sky, the
region of dreams.

> this most excellent canopy, the air, look you,
> this brave o'erhanging firmament, this majesti-
> cal roof fretted with golden fire.

Skies gave him itchy feet. Horizons looked grand to
him. Sunsets stirred his heart. He'd wanted to see where
the sun went down, and now had gone as far as a man
could go without becoming a sailor.

He'd dipped his wick. Aye, plenty, and with hot lust,
you bet. He loved women, and liked 'em, too. Liked their
company, their laughter, even their tears. Didn't just like
to frig 'em. Liked to hold them, talk to them, sing a song
and hear one back, ride fast against the wind with them.

True, he'd kept to red women.

And he'd kept in mind the lesson of his father.
There's always a fair land over the horizon. And a fair
face as well, and a willing body.

He urged his horse up to nearly the top of a butte, got
off, dropped the reins, walked near the summit, crawled
the rest of the way. He took his time and looked good.
Must have spent a quarter of an hour watching for motion,
or the unnatural lack of it. Nothing. The Arapahos probably thought their chances for more awerdenty were better
back toward Laramie.

He'd paid for his freedom. He'd given up his home.
He thought about that during the cold nights in the north
country when he couldn't sleep. He had no home. No father, no mother, no brothers and sisters. No wife and no
children. When none could claim ye, you had a claim on
none. He simply moved along, restless, you bet. Like a bit
of water that melted on the three Tetons and dribbled into
a rivulet and ran into a creek and then flowed into the
Snake River, then the Columbia, then the mighty Pacific.

And was raised into a cloud and headed back for the Tetons. Repeated the journey again and again. Sometimes it felt pointless, bloody pointless.

It had its compensations. The grand one was that he loved the West—forests, mountains, plains, deserts. And he relished it. Riding across the cold river in high water. Climbing the mountains. Outwitting the Indians. Crossing the deserts thirsty. Eating hump ribs. Riding among the herds of buffalo on a rampage. This is what men did before rules and religion and self-doubt spoiled it.

Eventually, people would spoil it.

The missionaries would spoil it.

Their ways would spoil it, even if they didn't mean them to.

Even Miss Jewel would spoil it.

And then where would Flare go?

Chapter

Four

It was an uneventful trip: up the Platte to the Sweetwater with the one episode of Indian trouble, up the Sweetwater to South Pass with good water, good grass all the way, no troubles. At Pacific Spring they celebrated their crossing of the continental divide. Miss Jewel and Miss Upping made lemonade from crystallized lemon they'd brought all the way from St. Louis. Flare had a yen to celebrate the crossing the way he usually did, whiskied up, but he drank the lemonade, without sugar, sour, like Miss Upping's personality. He told himself it made him a new man.

It was Flare's pride that it was an uneventful trip. The better he did his job, the less eventful it would be.

He rode out looking for Indian sign morning, noon, and night. Dan Full went along for a while, and learned something. Then Dr. Full decided he didn't like his stepson aping a barbarian, and made the lad stay in camp.

At the Big Sandy Flare himself caused an event: He decided to try the short way to Fort Hall. It would save days—straight west to the Green, up LaBarge Creek and down John Grey's River and through the mountains onto the Snake River. They might get to the fort by the time the Bay outfit took the furs down the Snake to Walla Walla.

If that happened, they could travel in safety. Maybe they would even be willing to travel without Michael

Devin O'Flaherty, who was getting weary of pork-eaters, and felt his summer's case of itchy feet coming on. And another itch, too, fleshly.

The only trouble was the forty miles between the Big Sandy and the Siskadee—no water. He told them how they would do it. Stay all day at the Big Sandy, get the people, horses, and mules well watered and fresh. Fill every keg, can, and bottle with liquid. Set out in the cool of the evening, ride through the night, get to the river before the heat of the day.

He watched them as they rode. The danger was the mind, not the body. You thought about the two or three hours until you could rest and sip out of a keg. Not long—the body could wait two or three hours easily. Did wait, when you knew water was plenty. Didn't want to wait when you knew it wasn't.

If you got to fretting, you made a problem. Went stiff in the saddle. Made your mount work harder. Made yourself work harder. Used up more energy. Sweated. Needed more water.

It could get worse. You looked out across the sagebrush flats and saw no end. Desert, you told yourself. Your mind tried not to remember the scare stories you'd heard about desert, desperate men, horrible deaths. You got panicky. Sang that to the horse right through your body, made him edgy. Burned horse and rider up.

Not that it was fantasy, entirely. Deserts were dangerous, you bet. Once, Flare had killed a horse to drink its blood. He'd heard stories of men who did that to their *compañeros,* but he didn't believe them.

He needed to help the fantasies of the fearful. So Flare stopped and let people behind catch up, then rode ahead, stopped again, checking, chatting with each person, helping all relax.

He flirted with the women, all but Annie Lee Full, who was too sober-sided to enjoy it. He told the men jokes. He told one about ye olde sod several times.

An Irish rebel sneaked up on an English camp one dawn, looking for a shot. He saw the British general come out of his tent. The rebel drew a bead. But the general was admiring God's dawn, and the rebel couldn't shoot even a Brit at such a moment. The general walked toward the creek. The rebel drew a bead. But then the general dropped his drawers, and the rebel couldn't shoot even a Brit at such a vulnerable moment. The general relieved himself. He stood, pulled his pants up. The rebel shot him dead. Bugger insulted ye olde sod.

They rested, drank, watered the animals. Went on.

Flare sang Irish songs to keep them easy:

> 'Tis the last rose of summer
> Left blooming alone;
> All her lovely companions
> Are faded and gone;
> No flow'r of her kindred,
> No rosebud is nigh,
> To reflect back her blushes
> Or give sigh for sigh.
>
> I'll not leave thee, thou lone one,
> To pine on the stem;
> Since the lovely are sleeping,
> Go, sleep thou with them.
> Thus kindly I scatter
> Thy leaves o'er that bed,
> Where thy mates of the garden
> Lie scentless and dead.
>
> So soon may I follow
> When friendship decay,
> And from love's shining circle
> The gems drop away!
> When true hearts lie wither'd
> And fond ones are flown,
> Oh, how would I inhabit
> This bleak world alone.

Middle of the night now. They rested, drank, and watered the animals. Went on. They would do well enough as long as Flare kept them fighting real troubles and not imaginary ones.

When his fuzzy brain wouldn't bring back any more fine Irish songs, he switched to a voyageur song or three, sprightly affairs, with a rhythm of paddles dripping, or hoofs clopping.

Joy to thee, my brave canoe,
There's no wing so swift as you;
Right and left the bubbles rise—
Right and left the pine wood flies;
Birds and clouds and tide and wind,
We shall leave ye all behind.

(chorus)
Joy to thee, my brave canoe,
There's no wing so swift as you,
Joy to thee, my brave canoe.
There's no wing so swift as you.

Gently, now, my brave canoe,
Keep your footing sure and true,
For the rapid close beneath,
Leaps and shouts his song of death;
Now one plunge and all is done,
Now one plunge, the goal is won.

(chorus)
Joy to thee, my brave canoe,
There's no wing so swift as you,
Joy to thee, my brave canoe,
There's no wing so swift as you.

Finally, a little before dawn, they used the last of their water on themselves and the horses. They slept an hour or so, and ate a little. As they packed up, he spoke to them about not losing control of the animals. The horses and mules would smell the water well before they saw the river. And want to take off for blessed liquid. Horses suffering from lack of water were weak and didn't look where they were going. Too often they fell—sometimes they broke their legs, or the bones of their riders. Don't let them have their heads, truly.

Before they got within smelling distance, Flare tied the pack animals nose to tail and took the lead line himself.

Soon the mounts began to act up. In a couple of minutes, one by one, every rider but Flare lost control of his horse. Pell-mell they went for the river.

Flare let his animals come up to a trot but kept tight rein. Until he heard the screams from the river.

He dropped the lead line and put the spurs to his horse. Mad you are, lad, he thought, eyes on rough, stony desert ground and mind trying to shut off the screams.

They were by the near bank and . . . and it was over. The screams stopped.

Thanks to Dr. Full.

Annie Lee Full stood there in the water waist deep, her skirts floating around her like flower petals. Her horse was standing, drinking, at the far bank. Dr. Full had hold of his wife's hand. She was gasping and wheezing like she'd never get air again. But her hair wasn't even wet.

Flare counted mounts and riders and got the right number.

Not hard to figure out what happened. The horse, out of control, jumped in where it happened to hit the bank, which was where the river happened to be deep. Mrs. Full, her leg wrapped around that silly sidesaddle horn, lost her seat. The horse blithely swam itself to shallower water and started drinking.

Mrs. Full, for the moment, was held up by her skirts. When they got soaked, they would drag her under, whether she could swim or not. So she screamed and screamed. Funny how quiet, controlled ones shattered when trouble hit them.

Dr. Full went off the bank some way below Mrs. Full, no telling how far. Took him a minute or so to swim the horse upstream to near where she was. At that point his horse got its footing and stood. Mrs. Full did the same.

"All safe, then," he said.

Dr. Full continued to murmur gently to his wife. But he was looking triumphantly at Flare.

"Well done, Dr. Full," Flare said pleasantly.

The power-hungry of the world don't lack for nerve, he thought.

*   *   *

The last night before Fort Hall, Flare had to make his try. He wasn't a lad afraid of the slings and arrows of outrageous fortune. And to have one white woman, well, it seemed a temptation.

If he couldn't put it off on drink, he could blame it on restless balls. He was naught but an animal anyway, the way they saw it.

He and Miss Jewel had developed a custom of walking a little after dinner. He suspected both of them took pleasure not only in the other's company, but also in tweaking Dr. Full.

This evening he took her arm, lest she step into a crack in the lava rock. "Nasty stuff," he said, "a bloody nuisance."

"I've been thinking you might like to hear some songs in Gaelic," he said. "'Tis a lovely language, and a language of love."

"Wonderful," she said. He'd recited Thomas Moore poems to her, and sung the grand songs Moore had made from Gaelic tunes and English words. Now something new. He held her hand while she sat on a boulder. He always stood while he sang.

He sang softly of a lass calling her lover back to her, in a world that one day, inevitably, takes the lover away forever. Michael Devin O'Flaherty let his light, graceful tenor spin the words ethereally into the last light in the plum-colored sky.

> Is go dee tu mavourneen slaun
> Shule, shule, shule, aroon
> Shule go suckir agus shule go une
> Shule go deen aurrus aguseilig lume
> Is go de tu mavourneen slaun.

Then he sang it once more in English:

> I wish I were on yonder hill,
> 'Tis there I'd set and cry my fill,
> Till every tear would turn a mill.

(chorus)
And safe for aye, my darling be.
Come, come, come, oh, love.
Come quickly and softly,
Come to the door and away we'll go,
And safe for aye, my darling be.

I'll sell my rock, I'll sell my reel,
I'll sell my only spinning wheel,
To buy for my love a sword of steel.

(chorus)
And safe for aye, my darling be.
Come, come, come, oh, love,
Come quickly and softly,
Come to the door and away we'll go,
And safe for aye, my darling be.

I'll dye my petticoats, I'll dye them red,
And round the world, I'll beg my bread,
Until my parents shall wish me dead.

(chorus)
And safe for aye, my darling be,
Come, come, come, oh, love,
Come quickly and softly,
Come to the door and away we'll go,
And safe for aye, my darling be.

When he finished, he could see her eyes gleaming wet.

He lifted her chin gently and kissed her.

She turned away, pushed him away.

"No, Mr. O'Flaherty." It was a gentle rebuke, not stern. But a rebuke.

"I'm drawn to you, Miss Jewel," he said. He'd never felt so witless.

"Yes. I'm attracted to you," she answered softly, gently, yet forthrightly. "I'm not going to pursue it."

She reached and took his hand.

"May I tell you why?"

"Add to my torment, lass?"

"You're a man of the world, Mr. O'Flaherty," she said throatily, and smiling. "You're a fine man. I've known you wanted us to be lovers. I can't, and it's not just a matter of wedlock. I'd like you really to understand me."

She gripped his hand in both of hers. "You're as fine a man as . . . as a man can become on his own, without God's grace."

"Unredeemèd Man," Flare murmured.

"Yes, exactly. That's not enough," she asserted. "Only God can lift us up to be . . . more than human, can remake us like Him. That's the kind of man I want.

"But I treasure you," she went on. "I treasure your company. I like flirting with you, and I mean to flaunt it in front of them all the way to the mission . . . and then say a fond good-bye."

Flare withdrew his hand. "It may be there's a brigade going from Fort Hall down the Snake soon. In that case, the good-bye might be sooner."

In the moonlight he saw the hurt on her face. "So . . . you see what I mean by unredeemèd?" She tried to recover her sense of humor, tried to chuckle. "This was love 'em and leave 'em."

But they were too late at Fort Hall. The outfit had gone to Walla, and the clerk had no plans to send another one soon. It was strictly buy beans and flour, trade worn-out horseflesh for fresh, and hit the trail.

Miss Jewel told Flare how glad she was. Now they'd get to flirt all the way to the Willamette.

Part Two

A PILGRIMAGE

Chapter
Five

They called him Web, and he hated it.

The name came from his mother's brother, Rock-chuck, when Web was born. Rockchuck immediately saw the skin between the baby's two big toes and the next ones, like duck's feet, and mockingly called him Web. A sure sign that he was the son of his father, Rockchuck cracked. And his father was a no-good *divo*, a white man.

Besides, Web knew he should have outgrown his childhood name by now. He deserved a name he had earned, or one given him from his first coup. But he had no vision. He had purified and prepared himself, twice, and gone onto the mountain and deprived himself of food and water, twice, but he had seen nothing.

He also had no coup. He had only once been invited on even a pony raid, and then permitted only to hold the ponies while other men stole Crow horses.

Also, his hair was rust-colored, not black, like a true Shoshone's. Another bitter gift of his white-man father, as everyone knew.

It was all a disgrace. He was eighteen years old, and a disgrace.

These people mocked him, and would always mock him. *Numah-divo,* they called him. It was the people's word for half-breed, their word for *Shoshone* spliced onto the word for *white man*. They could make similar words that meant Shoshone-black white man and Shoshone-

Mexican. All were words of scorn. Web was the first *Numah-divo* of his people.

But tonight he would earn another name. This very night.

In his own mind he kept another name for himself anyway: Sima Untuasie. When he found out why he was named Web, he asked his grandmother, Black Shawl (his *un kakau,* his mother's mother), whether his mother had spoken before she died, shortly after bearing him.

Yes, his grandmother had said. She murmured, "*Sima untuasie.*" My first son.

His grandmother added, "She loved you."

He liked the Sima part: first. He was something new, a *Numah-divo,* yes, the first, the only. *Sima Numah-divo.*

Tonight he would show them.

He was waiting now, frustrated. Waiting for his *hi-antseh* (friend) Yu-huup, which meant Fatty. He knew a lot of being a young man was waiting—waiting to go on your first pony raid, waiting to get to help steal ponies instead of just holding the horses, waiting to get into a real fight, waiting to get a coup, waiting to marry, waiting to be recognized for what you are, a man.

He had been tortured with waiting. He would make it end tonight. If Yu-huup ever came.

He bent his attention back to the rock. He'd come to this outcropping because the warm lava rock drew the lizards, and he could hear the shoosh of the creek churning by. He found flowing water soothing. And he liked to catch lizards with his quick hands. While his friends clowned around and missed and acted like they didn't care, he could catch ten, two hands' worth, sometimes more, without having one dart away. Like the sound of the water, catching them eased him mind. When he was watching a lizard, he thought of nothing, not his intolerable situation, not his future, nothing at all. It took his mind off the festering within him.

Tonight.

He festered all the time. He raged half the time. He hated his life.

Web hated the trapper who fathered him. Back when

the Frenchies first came to hunt beaver on the Snake
River, this man had spent a winter with his people, with
his mother, Pinyon. When spring came, the trapper simply
left, abandoning a people who had adopted him, and abandoning a child in his mother's belly.

The Frenchie didn't give a goddamn. That was what
Web always called the man out loud. Goddamn Hairy. He
chuckled whenever he said it. The whites said each white
man had two names—not a secret name and a public
name, like a Shoshone, but two public names, which they
called first and last. No one knew his father's name, so
Web gave him one: Goddamn. The second one the people
gave him because he had *Inqa-moe-zho,* red hair all over
his face. Rockchuck said the fool accepted the name without a complaint, didn't even know it was an insult.

Goddamn was one of the few *divo* (white-man)
words Web had learned, and he knew it well. The other
trappers who had come Americans, they called themselves—had told Web all about it. It was a word of bad
medicine, a curse. It meant plagued by the spirits. The
Americans seemed amused at his interest, but they joined
in. Hairy was a member of another white-man tribe, they
said, a Frenchie, so they goddamned him heartily. They
explained that not all Frenchies were Frenchmen, some
were Englishmen, but Web didn't understand that.

Another bad-medicine word Web learned was son of
a bitch—son of a dog. But that didn't seem so bad to Web.
It might be a man's medicine to be given power by a dog
in a dream, so to be the spirit child of a dog. So Web pre-
ferred goddamn—cursed by the spirits.

In his mind he called his father Goddamn instead of
Hairy always. Then maybe his father's *woah* would burn
when he pissed, or the Crows would steal all his horses, or
his children would all grow up to hate him.

Web hated him. One day the goddamn son of a bitch
would come back and Web would show him.

Like tonight. Tonight he would show everybody.

It started the summer after the big fight against the
Blackfeet in Pierre's Hole, the year the white men called

1833. That summer Web went with his band to the big trading fair on the Siskadee, what the Americans called rendezvous. There Web talked with white men a lot for the first time. And when the people left that rendezvous, he found out how deep was his humiliation.

Rockchuck took him hunting in the high country of the Tu-nam pai-okai-pin. It was a bad time for the family. Web's grandfather, Beak, died a week before. No one knew why. He complained a lot going over the last divide from rendezvous, said he had a terrible gut ache, and sometimes rode on a travois, like an infant. Then suddenly rolled onto his knees, shook and jerked violently, and pitched into the dirt, dead.

Since Web's mother died in childbirth, he had been raised by his mother's parents. That was usual enough. Many first children were raised by their maternal grandparents. But Web was being raised with half the family anyone was entitled to, among a people to whom family was everything.

So Beak was the only father Web had ever known, and he was gone. They boy would not miss him much. For several years Beak had been withdrawn, remote from the family. But Web felt for his grandmother, Black Shawl, and he knew he now had no male protector.

After the mourning, Black Shawl asked Rockchuck to take Web deer-hunting. The boy was fourteen winters old, she pointed out. It was the Shoshone way.

Actually, Web's father's brother, his *hai*, should have become his teacher, to show him the ways of the earth, the ways of the rooted, the winged, the water-dwellers, and the four-legged. This man should have taught him how the four-leggeds leave their signs on dirt and sand and mud and snow, and how to follow them, how to know what they will do, how to catch them and take some of their power, or their lives and their power. This man should have prepared him to find a dream that would show him his power, his personal, special way to walk the earth.

So Rockchuck complained—that's not my job, he said, I'm the kid's *mother's* brother, his *tami*. Old Black

Shawl spat in the dust. She wasted no time pointing out the obvious—she just ordered Rockchuck to take Web hunting.

So they set out resenting each other. Rockchuck left Web on stands alone for several days, entirely alone, with nothing to eat or drink, and the necessity of absolute stillness. Rockchuck said it was to teach him patience. Web suspected it was to inflict punishment. He thought Rockchuck was not out trying to jump deer, but in camp, napping. And there was nothing Web could do. He refused to be caught off his stand. At night, in camp, Rockchuck acted sullen, and occasionally arrogant. If Web had good medicine, he hinted, they would not be taking so long to find so common a thing as a deer, and kill it.

When they did find one, it was only a buck so young the antlers hadn't branched. Still, Web kept the dewclaws as a sign of his first hunt, and gave them to his grandmother. He knew he had learned something, alone there in the beating sun. He could master not only his hunger and his thirst but his anger.

In front of the people, Rockchuck seemed to shrug the kill off. A small deer, a nothing, his manner said. Web could almost hear them whispering, "*Numah-divo.*" Halfway of the people, not exactly one of us.

That night Web learned something else: He learned not to cry when his feelings were hurt. He learned not to care about these people who scorned him.

He did care about his grandmother. Only she felt truly like family. But a woman could not teach a boy the ways of men. She always held out the hope that Goddamn Hairy, Inqa-moe-zho, would come back and be a father. But Web didn't want him back. Web would learn carefully the lessons Rockchuck had for him, and despise him every moment. And Goddamn could go to the Ninabee, the devils with tails who eat children. No, to Joahwayo, the big fool with a hairy face and scaly body who ate grown-ups.

Now, four years later, Web had passed eighteen winters. And he had learned.

He saw a lizard by his right foot, a tiny one. The innocent creature came out between Web's feet, stood still, peered about, its head frozen still. Then it scurried up between Web's calves, stopped, peered.

The fool. Web would wait until it came within reach and catch it. Even catch it with his awkward hand, the right hand. And fling it away. This lizard would be easy.

He had learned the patience his uncle forced on him. He had learned quickness with his hands—Web could do anything that required nimble fingers, especially whittling with a knife or drawing or painting. He had learned cunning. And he had learned not to care.

The little lizard was up between Web's thighs. This was an affront. For this the lizard must become like a winged one, and fly. Web eased his hand off his upper leg, felt the warm rock with his fingertips. He moved with the gentleness, the stealth, the calculation, and the cruelty of the hunter. The lizard was confused—even Web's right hand would be plenty quick for this prey.

Snatch!

He held the creature up to his eyes and studied it. It jerked its head back and forth, looking about stupidly, understanding nothing. It flailed its legs in the air, then held them utterly still, then flailed them again.

Web pinched hard with his thumb and forefinger. The lizard squashed all over his hand.

Guilt and shame lifted him like a great wave. You are angry, he accused himself, so you take it out on a lizard.

Miserably, he wiped the goo off on his breechcloth.

Yes, I am angry and upset, goddamn you all.

Tonight I will show you.

Wh-r-r-r!

Rattlesnake!

Web jumped up. He couldn't see it. Which way should he run?

Goddamn!

He jumped off the rock, fell to the ground, scrambled away.

Whomp. Someone landed on him from behind. Held his head down. Grabbed his scalp lock.

Web felt the hot prick of the knife. He shook himself, but the man was too heavy, too strong.

Hah, hah, hah. Hah, hah, hah. A laugh, slow, elaborate, mocking.

His captor stood up. Web rolled over and looked up at his big friend Yu-huup. His grin was big, his eyes wild as moons. One open palm held the rattlesnake rattle, a big one. Web remembered when he and Yu-huup killed the snake together.

"Cousin," said Web weakly. He reached up for a hand and heaved to his feet. "You could have hit me with the poison." He was still getting his breath. Web was a slight, wiry youth, Yu-huup a big one, and fat.

"A Crow would have lifted your curly hair," said Yu-huup, putting his knife away. Web was always sensitive about his hair, which not only was brown but also curly. His hair and his light skin gave away that he was *Numah-divo.*

"So what do you want, cousin? What's such a secret?"

Now Web looked at him in the eyes. Here was a real test for Yu-huup. The deed would be daring, and exciting, but tomorrow some people would shun Fatty. He might have to take the full blast of One Bull's anger, and One Bull was a plenty mean old man.

Web felt cold in his gut, hurting. Maybe Yu-huup would say no. Maybe Yu-huup would say yes and, just when he was needed, run like a coward. Maybe Yu-huup would tell his mother and father and spoil the plan.

Web sat down on the lava rock and motioned Yu-huup to join him. He looked at his cousin and best friend nakedly. "Tonight I'm going to steal Paintbrush." He let it sit. The cousins looked at each other hard. Fear appeared there—and boldness and daring and excitement . . . and the uncertainty of teenagers.

Finally Yu-huup said, "One Bull will kill you. Horn's kinsmen will kill you."

Web shook his head and smiled a wicked smile. "I have a plan," he said.

*   *   *

Web first saw Paintbrush the summer when they were both twelve, the year before the great rendezvous on the Siskadee. She and her brother came to live with One Bull. Their parents had been killed by the Crows, a terrible thing, and One Bull and his wife were their uncle and aunt. Since Paintbrush and Web had not come to the changes—to young womanhood and manhood—the two played together as children.

Paintbrush was lonely. Occasionally she cried for her parents and her band, but more often Web would find her sitting alone by the river, her eyes far away and infinitely sad. He felt for her—she, too, was a stranger among these people. He befriended her.

And Paintbrush brought Web a great gift. With childish pleasure she showed him the implement she was named for. She showed him how to make tools for painting from bones, or from willow sticks, and how to chew the end of the stick to make a wide implement for some strokes.

Web loved painting. Though women did quillwork and beadwork and decorative, geometric painting, men did paintings showing real objects, men and horses at war, and the like.

The two kids gathered colored rocks and crunched them into powder, dug out black and yellow minerals, scraped up yellow earth, and mixed it all with clay to make paints. They mixed the colors with grease, fat, or water, or for painting on hide with a glue made from hoofs. And they painted gaily and merrily, all day long, as long as their parents would permit it.

Paintbrush stuck to the women's style, geometric, decoration of small things she was learning to sew, and with a nice eye for design and color. Web was different. He painted what he saw by night, in his dreams, and the grand story figures of the Shoshone people whose lives were told during the winter moons, Coyote howling at the full moon or acting foolish or wise, his brother Wolf, Rabbit, Bear, the tiny Chickadee, the Thunderbird, and the like. When he was painting, he felt right with the world.

Somehow it was all beautiful—gorgeous—and the people marveled at Web's art.

Web thought how lucky he was that Paintbrush had showed him her namesake tools. How lucky he was to have a flair for painting. How lucky he was to be able to play at painting with her all day, every day.

Now, five years later, he knew he had fallen in love with her that summer.

Black Shawl knew it then, Web saw now. She mentioned to Web, pretending to be casual, that Paintbrush was not betrothed to anyone. She was new to the band, and her betrothed one had died as an infant. Black Shawl did not need to say that no girl child had been offered to the child Web for betrothal, because Web was *Numah-divo*. Or that here might be a woman for an outcast, a man with no betrothed.

Felicity. Web saw the working of spirit here, *Tsaa nevmu-da-hi*. He loved Paintbrush.

The next summer, at the great rendezvous, Web came by chance on a white man drawing. The boy was taken aback. The white men painted nothing, as far as Web knew. They hardly decorated anything except maybe the handles of their knives and guns. It was as though they didn't see, didn't dream.

What this man was drawing was still more amazing. He made small sketches of plants, exactly as they looked. The man invited the Shoshone boy to watch. It was strange to Web. Yes, rooted things did have power, but few men dreamed of rooted things, or got their life's medicine from them. Why would anyone draw them? This man sketched one plant after another, and not as in vision, but exactly as they looked to the undreaming eye. Yet they were *Tsaa-na,* beautiful—he had the gift of *pohan-apusa,* dreamed power. Scientist, he called himself several times. Other times he said his name was Nutting.

Later came more events sent by Spirit. Web brought his hide paintings for Scientist to see. Scientist got a Shoshone-speaking trapper to explain to Web what Scientist was doing. Somehow Scientist would see the plant with great exactness from the drawing, study it, understand it, and extract its power that way. Web didn't really understand. But he started following Scientist into the fields and learning to draw as Scientist did, from life rather than dream. Scientist even made him a gift of a pad of what the whites called paper, and colored pencils. A treasure to Web.

That brought trouble. When the people saw these new-style drawings, they shrugged their shoulders. No one saw any point in drawing from observation rather than vision. There goes Web again, they whispered, thinking and acting like a *divo*.

Web kept drawing from life—everything he could find to draw, every chance he got—but he kept the sketches hidden.

Near the end of the rendezvous came the crash. Paintbrush became a woman, bleeding with the moon, and was initiated into the ways of a woman, *waippe*. She and Web could no longer play together as children.

Then One Bull let it be known quietly that his daughter Paintbrush, a most beloved daughter, was betrothed. Betrothed to a young man of great promise, from a great family. Horn, the son of the war leader Raven.

Web was desolate. He could not believe it. Could they not see the hand of spirit drawing the best future for him and Paintbrush?

So came four years of agony: His grandfather died. His uncle Rockchuck humiliated him. Except for his family, people seemed to shun Web. Until Yu-huup insisted, no one invited him to hold horses on a pony raid. No betrothed appeared for him. Web was only halfway one of the people.

Aside from his grandmother, he had one great good in his life: Paintbrush loved him. Or so he thought. She told people that his good medicine showed in his painting. She favored him with glances, looks, even furtive touches. It was risky, but she did it. She let him know.

So Web decided he must take a risk. Among these people the great crimes were to kill a kinsman, to steal a kinsman's horses, or to steal his wife. Any could mean blood or banishment.

But there was one way out.

* * *

"In two moons you will join us among Nakok's people," Web told Yu-huup. Nakok was a rebellious Shoshone leader, and his band lived on U Ah Die, the Wind River.

Yu-huup's eyes locked on him. Excitement? thought Web. Fear? Both?

"Then in the moon when water begins to freeze at the edge of the streams, you and I will go against the Crows. Alone." His eyes gleamed. Just two young men against the Crows, a daring stroke. "We will bring Horn so many horses he will forget a mere woman." His lips tossed off the words mockingly.

Yu-huup knew Web was right. It was a bold plan, but workable. Horn might feel humiliated, rejected by his woman for another man. But neither Horn nor his family could refuse the payment of the horses. That was the custom. Then Web and Paintbrush would come back to the tribe, in their own lodge, a full-fledged family of the people. Their children would be true Shoshones, *duvish-shaw-numah.*

And Web and Yu-huup would be looked on with new eyes. To go alone against the Crows and run off their pony herds! Deeds of valor! Coups!

"*Ha-uh!*" Yu-huup exclaimed in excitement.

Web shook his fist in the air. He wanted to fill the sky with shouting, but that might give something away.

"Here's the plan," he began.

Chapter
Six

Web was ready.

He'd been lying here in the shadow of the lodge for almost enough time to see the Seven Sisters move against the black sky. He had walked quietly through the village, not exciting the dogs, which knew his smell, then letting One Bull's war horse, staked by the lodge, snuffle him without getting alarmed.

Web was entirely naked, scales painted all over his body, hair painted on his face, like Joahwayho. Since he had no *poha* (medicine) of his own, this was as good a choice as any—Joahwayho, he who came in the middle of the night and ate grown-ups.

He streaked hair all over his face, not just on the upper lip and jaw but also on the nose and forehead. He made crazy patterns of the hairs, angling wildly, many of the streaks bolts of lightning. His eyelids were white, and they made a weird effect when he blinked. Yu-huup greased his rust-colored hair, twisted it into horns, and tied it high and spiky.

Web was worse than a *zo-ahp,* a ghost. It anyone saw his face, not only would they not recognize him, he would scare them half to death.

Since the night was cool, the lodge skirts were down. Now even the last of the fire was out, and everyone asleep, One Bull and his wives at the center rear, their last daughter on the buffalo robes at their feet. Paintbrush.

He took a deep breath to ease his tension, then another, and another. He wondered how Yu-huup was doing in the ravine with the three horses. Yu-huup was his only friend, his *haintseh*, but Yu-huup acted dumb sometimes. What if he got scared of the real ghosts and ran off?

No time for doubts now, time for action. He crawled several steps and sat still in the shadow. He waited. No man or beast had heard. No one raised the alarm.

Web lifted his knife and began, ever so slowly and ever so softly, to cut the thongs that held the hide cover of the lodge to the stakes in the ground.

Black. Black like he had a white-man kettle on his head. Black like the stomach of a grizzly bear. Black like the heart of One Bull. Web couldn't see anything.

So he would go by feel. He knew very well where everyone's buffalo robes were, that Paintbrush was just to his left, her feet near him, her head at the far end. He would ease around and get next to her ear and whisper to her ever so softly.

He couldn't be sure she would come with him. A man simply did not ask such a thing. It would get you rejected, then and forever. But once, within her hearing, he'd told the story of Red Forehead, who stole Lance's wife. He had watched Paintbrush's face. Everyone knew Red Forehead and the woman had been happy, had stayed together for years and had lots of children. The flicker of eyelashes seemed an answer.

A flicker of eyelashes. But unmanly to ask more.

Web lifted himself slightly on his palms and moved to his left. Again. Once more.

M-m-m-m?

Goddamn!

His foot touched flesh. Goddamn you, you stupid . . . !

He lay still as the earth itself.

M-m-m-m.

Stirrings over there. Were they looking around the lodge, trying to see what moved? He thanked *Itsa-ppe,* Coyote, the trickster, for the blackness.

Rustling of robes and blankets. Scrapings. Maybe Old Bull was sitting up, looking around. The first moan had been female, the second male.

Web wanted to sink into the dirt like spilled water.

M-m-m-m.

M-m-m-m.

More rustlings.

A couple of more moans.

Then other sounds, touchings, stirrings, little sounds of pleasure.

Goddamn.

And then the ancient, rhythmic slurp of human beings obeying the force of life within them. The sound Web had heard hundreds of times in his life, though he never had touched a woman in that way. The sound Paintbrush had heard hundreds of times and never made herself.

Tsaa-yogo-sic, he thought amiably—there's a little humping going on here.

Web lay next to Paintbrush, close enough to hear her breathe. He thought maybe he could feel her breath on his face. He lay stiller than still. He felt his *woah* fiercely erect. He squeezed the handle of his knife so hard he thought the bone might crack.

He wondered which of his wives One Bull was on top of. One was old and fat, the other not so old and comely. The old fool was so lecherous, so *nia-shup,* he probably liked both of them, and any other woman he could get. Pictures arose in Web's mind, the heavyset old man bouncing around on top of one, then the other, playing lewdly, throwing her legs around, laughing, mocking Web, who had never had a woman.

A fantasy touched him. Paintbrush's body lay the length of him, warm, soft, luscious. She was still, gentle, not yet beginning to move against him, her long hair on his cheek and chest. He felt the lips caress his neck. That caress was more real than any human touch he'd ever felt.

He shook himself and broke the illusion.

Fortunately, he bumped no one when he shook himself.

Paintbrush was so close. She exhaled deeply, and he felt her warm spirit on his eyes.

The two lovers were quiet, except for an occasional stirring, a sigh of satisfaction, a wordless murmur.

Web would have to be quiet for a long time before he whispered to Paintbrush. The lovers would lie awake for a little while, and half awake for a long time. He needed them deep in their dreams.

He could be patient. Thanks to Rockchuck. He could put his mind into a kind of stillness, a peaceableness, and wait for hours. He had plenty of time. He was where he wanted to be. He would think of Paintbrush as he often thought of the animal he was stalking, think of her and bring her those final inches, from enticingly close all the way into his arms. He pictured the parts of her, her slender limbs, her lissome body, her small girl's breasts, her undulating hips . . .

He never knew he was falling asleep.

Paintbrush heard breathing, rhythmic, relaxed breathing, one of the sounds of the earth. She enjoyed it dreamily. It made her imagine running water, the lulling sound of water flowing lightly over rocks.

Then two awarenesses began to seep into part of her mind. One was the predawn light. The other was breath on her face.

The wind, it must be the wind. She lolled pleasantly in her mind, shushed by the sound of water, warmed by a soft breeze.

But it was warm. It was moist. It was animal.

Paintbrush, the adopted daughter of One Bull, born to the Tukku Tekkah, opened her eyes and saw the monster Joahwayho.

She flinched. She froze.

The monster opened its eyes, its mad, white eyelids wagging at her.

Paintbrush screamed like a woman-child about to die, a shrill, ululating, horrific, mind-shattering cry.

From behind, One Bull saw not a monster but a boy in his virgin daughter's robes. The man was on his feet instantly, he leapt, he slammed one shoulder into the boy. Hard against the lodge skins they went. One Bull rolled on top of the enemy and pinned him with his heft. Then he grabbed the greasy hair, jerked the head back, and turned his face sideways.

He looked hard. Then he snapped in disgust, "*Numah-divo.*"

Paintbrush screamed and screamed.

One Bull started slapping Web's face hard, deliberately, over and over. He held the hair with one hand and made Web's face jerk with the other.

"*Na-nik-kumpah,*" he said with a growl. "I'll kill you later."

Chapter
Seven

But One Bull did not kill Web. The two clans, One Bull's and Horn's, sat in a lodge and smoked and talked. There was a good deal of cackling over a boy who came to steal a girl and fell asleep. They had no debate because the punishment was a foregone conclusion: Web would be banished.

The accused demanded that he be allowed to speak to the clans in his own defense. Rockchuck brought the message. Why? they asked. Anyone can see he tried to steal Horn's woman. Yu-huup, found holding the horses, even confessed.

Rockchuck didn't know why. He simply repeated Web's request.

Web sat in the place of least honor in the lodge. He sat with his eyes on nothing, seeing nothing, but refusing to cast his eyes down, to act obsequious in front of the circle of men who mocked and condemned him.

He drew on the pipe defiantly, and offered the smoke as a prayer. Without knowing what he was going to say, he began.

"I do not care what you say." He spoke in a controlled voice, so they wouldn't hear his anger, his fear, his outrage.

"I do not care what you think of me."

He nearly shook. He had no idea what to say next.

"You have treated me as a *divo*," (white man). "From today I will be a *divo*."

He was shocked at himself.

Yes, this was it.

"I will go to my father's people. I will get my father's *poha*" (medicine). "I will never even think of the Shoshone people again. Good-bye." When Shoshones said good-bye, instead of *un-puih-ha-he,* meaning "See you later," they meant they hoped never to see you again.

He stood, ready to leave. Then he thought. He walked between his host and the fire, a deliberate insult, and strode out of the tipi.

The men in the circle muttered angrily. When they were calmed down, they decided to ignore the manners of a boy, and a *Numah-divo* at that. They talked a little more. Then they banished Web for life.

The old woman found him beside the little creek. The blanket was pulled over his head, and it was shaking. The boy was sobbing.

Black Shawl was sorry. She loved him. But he was different—he had always been different. Even his painting was different. It was painful, for both of them, but finding his own way would be best for Web.

She sat down beside him, close, letting him feel her shoulder and her knee as she sat. She waited, and waited, and after a while he stopped crying and looked at her.

"People told me what you said," she murmured to him. "Sometimes even anger is wise. I think maybe your *poha* (medicine) is with the *Hookin-divos.*" It was their word for the French trappers, the ones who came from Vancouver.

That was all she said. There was no need for more words. She would give him a pony, unfortunately a poor one, a blanket, some moccasins, and a little pemmican. He would take his weapons, his colored pencils, his few sheets of paper, and the one object his father had left behind, a compass. After sunset today, anyone of the people who spoke to him or gave him anything would be punished. Even his grandmother.

After a long while, she added, "I'll get your things ready." She looked at the boy's wet cheeks. "They've sent Yu-huup out hunting with his father so you can't say farewell."

The tall, skinny teenager and the short, skinny old woman walked side by side away from the pony herd, in the bottom land along the creek. They said nothing. The old woman held the boy's elbow, perhaps for steadiness, perhaps from affection. She turned her face up to his. Her skin was creviced almost as deep as the bark of the cottonwood. Her eyes were rheumy, and she no longer saw well. She couldn't see her grandson's face clearly unless she held it close.

She had him a few years, and now she would lose him to his father. She had always felt the oddness in him anyway, surely from his father's people. Maybe it was something good for him. Even Frenchmen, though they acted the fool, had some sort of power. Every living creature had its power. With Frenchmen it was the clever things they made—like traps and guns, and pencils and paper.

Lucky. The boy had spoken in anger and bitterness, and wisdom had come out of his mouth. Luck was not chance—it came from Duma Apa.

She held him back and eased herself onto a log. She could not walk far these days. This was all the distance she would go with him. He must make the journey alone.

"Well?" she asked.

"It's all right, Grandmother," he said.

She held his face close and looked at it clearly for the last time.

"Tell me about the journey," she instructed.

"I go down the Snake River for about twenty sleeps. There the river goes east of north into a deep canyon, impossible to travel through. The Frenchmen call it the canyon of hell. I leave the river there and follow the old lodge trail north. After perhaps twelve more sleeps the trail will come back to the river, and it will turn west. Then the river will flow into a huge river coming from the north. There I will find the Frenchman fort Walla Walla. Maybe from there I can find someone to travel with to Fort Vancouver, which is almost to the sea."

"*Tsaa-yu*," said the old woman. It is good. "We call the big river the Snake. What do the Frenchmen call it?"

Web laughed sardonically. "Mad, Accursed River."

The old woman made a severe face. "It is mad. Keep your distance."

"And what will I find among the Frenchmen, Grandmother?" Web said bitterly.

"Your *poha*," the old woman said. Your medicine.

"And maybe my father," said Web. "Goddamn Hairy, my mad, accursed father."

She stood and embraced him.

"I will come back, Grandmother. With many horses and many presents."

She hugged him. She didn't think he'd come back.

"*Tsaa-paitt-sig,*" she said. "*Oosie-oie-yound.*" Go well. This is all I ask of you.

He mounted, looked back once, tried to smile, and set the overloaded pony to walking.

He had a hard way to go, and dangerous, through the country of a lot of bloodthirsty people. He'd have to travel at night. The pony probably wouldn't last—it was old and broken-down—but he could always eat it. It was more than fifty sleeps to Vancouver, by the western sea. No man of her people, in the memories of the grandfathers of the oldest men, had traveled that far. She hoped he made it to the Frenchmen. The ways of the powers were unpredictable.

It was hard to see a grandchild leave, almost unheard of among the people, a loss grievous as death. She had raised him as her own. But he had to go where he belonged.

And it was time for her not to be responsible for a

child. Since her bleeding stopped, she had worked to learn medicine. She knew how to use snowberry tea to help a woman after childbirth, and self-heal to improve eyesight. Her friend had promised to teach her how to prepare the wild geranium to heal ulcers in the stomach, skullcap to ease heart pain, and other remedies. It was time for her to become a healer.

She was sad. It was hard to imagine him living among strangers, in some foreign place. Those people ate a lot of fish, or so she heard—barbarous. And some flattened their heads. The Frenchmen stank like fetid feet, left their women at home, and took everybody else's.

There were no people like the Newe-i, the people.

She couldn't see him clearly now, not with these eyes. Surely that dark shape against the horizon was him. She waved. If you come back, grandson, she murmured, I may no longer be walking the earth.

The worst part of getting old was losing the people you loved.

Chapter
Eight

The exile wandered. He drifted. He walked and rode like he was drunk, or opiumed, or like the air of the whole world had turned foul and fogged and soured his spirit.

Web rode slowly through the heat of the moon when the berries are ripe, which the white man called August. He went along a nameless creek toward the Snake River, and then over the lava plain to the white-man trail. One sleep away for a strong, lone man with no women, no children, no travois. It took him two days to get there.

The exile was half-hoping Yu-huup would track him and catch up. Maybe his cousin would bring him some gifts, some extra pemmican, extra moccasins, another blanket—maybe even another horse. It would be some company. Yu-huup could at least wish him a good journey, though never say good-bye.

So he drifted along toward the big river, where he would turn west toward Fort Walla Walla, toward Fort Vancouver. Toward his father's people, and his father.

It would be a hard trip. The Snake River here ran through lava flows, sagebrush plains, and desert flats. The river made its own canyon and ran crazily over big falls, through terrible rapids, a mad, accursed river for sure. But he would follow the trail the white men used. They came every summer to Fort Hall, to collect the beaver pelts and

pack them downriver—to Fort Walla Walla, Fort Vancouver. A moon ago he might have been able to ride downstream with some of them. But they had gone back to Fort
Vancouver by now. The names of the forts made a kind of
thumping music in his mind, like drums, lulling and irri-
tating at once. He almost fell out of his saddle, drowsy in
the heat, his spirit murky.

Web knew he would have to be lucky to make it all
that way. Anybody might take his scalp. He snickered to
himself. Maybe one of the Frenchmen who were now his
only people would lift his hair and give it to his father,
lordly there in Fort Vancouver. And his father, knowing it
for what it was, would roar and roar with laughter, and
hold up the red scalp of Web, his red son, for all to see.

Yu-huup didn't come.

Web spent the third day lying by a seep, a half mile
below the trail. He told himself he was resting his pony,
but the creature didn't need rest yet. Web lay in the shade
of a rock all day, occasionally drinking, eating too much
of his pemmican. Far too much. He was torporous. He had
eaten the first night greedily, like a man consuming his
last meal. He needed to remember to make it last more
than a moon, until he got to Fort Walla Walla. Now he
would have to hunt. Which would take more days, make
him later getting to Walla Walla, make him need more
food.

If his spirit weren't so heavy, the exile might see
something. Might get *poha* (medicine) from Spirit. Might
be brought help by a lizard, or a spider. But he knew his
spirit was fouled.

Yu-huup didn't come.

The next day Web lay around again. He daydreamed.
He fantasized.

His imaginings were ugly. He began to think he
would lie here forever, until he died. When he thought of
the people finding his bones here next summer, he smiled
with wry satisfaction. Or maybe the pony would go back
to camp, and the people would know. He chuckled bitterly. He liked to imagine how they would be sorry and

know they'd been wrong, and how Paintbrush, especially, would weep over the body of the exile.

Sometimes white people gave their horses names. Now that he was a white man he would name his pony. Maybe Mom-pittseh. Owl. Among his people the owl was the messenger of death.

Yu-huup didn't come. Rockchuck didn't come.

On the evening of the fourth day he decided to change. Simple as that: He decided. His decision went like this: True, he had abandoned his first people, or been abandoned by them. But he would never abandon Spirit. He would now ask Spirit to enlist its *poha* on his side. He would pray. He would renew his promise to avoid the behaviors Spirit forbade. He would ask for the strength to make a sacrifice as his bond for that promise.

It was a simple thing to decide, and necessary. At first it made no difference. He lay there, torpid, his strength lulled, his will limp, his spirit listless. When he made the decision to go through these gestures, he felt no better, no stronger, no more hopeful. His pledge was simply to make the gestures, to do his part, to see if he could act better.

He gathered sticks and built a small fire. Then he gathered the needles of the cedar and burned them. He rubbed the smoke on his body, purifying himself.

He took two valued possessions out of his old, ragged parfleche bag, sweetgrass, and the compass his father had left with his mother. Web had always felt odd about this compass. According to Black Shawl, his father left it with some words and a promise. He explained that the stick always called toward the north, where the white buffalo lives. While Pinyon had the compass, all Hairy's travels would lead him to Pinyon. The words said the compass had power. Yet his father had not come back.

Nevertheless, the compass still showed the direction from where the white buffalo sends the cleansing winds. Web would honor its power, however small. With a bow drill he made a small fire and lit the braided sweetgrass.

He passed the compass four times through the thick, curling smoke.

Then he stood. Without even a *toih,* pipe, he faced each of the four winds, the west of the Thunderbird, the north, home of Magpie, the east, where Meadowlark comes from, and the south, where Owl lives. Without even tobacco to offer, he lifted his arms to Father Sky, made obeisance to Mother Earth.

Then he prayed. *"Ne Nahgai Ook,"* he said—Hear me, Spirit. *"Ne shone deah"*—Have mercy on me. *"Ne tsaanani-sunte-ha"*—I pray well.

He promised to bring an offering of tobacco in the future. To behave as Spirit had taught Shoshones to behave. To make a sacrifice of flesh to Spirit.

He asked for strength to start on his great task, finding his father. Strength of spirit to do what he must do. Strength of body to set out firmly on the long journey. Strength of will to persevere for many sleeps. Strength of mind to make wise decisions.

He finished his prayer with thanks to Duma Apa for the earth, for living things, and for his own life.

When he was finished, he felt scarcely different from the way he felt when he decided to change. He was a little more hopeful. At least he could do what he had decided to do, whether it was futile or not.

Now was the time for his sacrifice. He took his knife from the belt of his breechcloth. He kept it very sharp. As he looked at the blade, his hand jumped.

Taking control, he sat cross-legged by the fire, once more threw cedar needles on the coals of the fire, once more purified himself. He took the knife in his right hand. With his left he lifted the skin a finger joint's length above his left nipple.

He forbade his imagination to go ahead of him. He had seen this done but never tried it. The pain of imagination, he knew, would be greater than the pain of the flesh.

Deftly, he made a downward cut with the knife point. Blood popped like beads of red sweat from the thin line.

Quickly, not quite frantically, he made three more cuts, outlining a square of flesh the size of his thumbnail.

It worked. He felt a mad glee. It worked. He'd done it. Now he knew that he'd doubted he could do it.

The next would be the hardest part. He put a stick in his mouth and clamped down hard. With his fingernails and his knife point he loosened a corner of the square.

Then he got a good grip on the corner, opened his eyes wide and staring into the night, and pulled. Steadily, his mind screaming, he peeled the patch of flesh off his breast.

It was in his hand. He had done it.

His chest welled blood, and it spilled down his belly.

He realized he was half-lying in the dust. Instead of yelling, he said a quiet thanks to Spirit for giving him the strength to do what he must. Then he cast the patch of skin to the earth.

Then he cupped his right hand over his bleeding left breast, pulled his blanket over his body and slept.

At dawn he saw something simple and practical. He realized it was past time to get Mom-pittseh, Owl the Messenger of Death, some real water. The poor old horse had been forced to lick at the seep for two days. With the river right there within sight, though through a hell of a broken gully. Web needed to get Messenger down to the river. Probably he could lead Messenger carefully through the gully. A quick trip down and back.

But leading the horse down there turned out to be tricky. It was all lava rock, jumbled and crazy. Messenger went gingerly. It was a skittish, unpredictable horse and probably wouldn't have gone at all if it couldn't smell the water. They squeezed between boulders, watched their feet around cracks in the lava rock, clambered over boulders. It was goddamn awkward.

The exile talked to this pony, stroked its muzzle, kept it calm, kept a good hold on its bridle. Web could feel the trembling urgency of the horse to get to the river, within sight, within smell. Web began to feel a little better about himself—he was doing the right thing for Mom-pittseh, and doing it well. And now they were through the worst, to where the floor of the gully was mostly clear.

The light changed. That was what he thought afterward. The quality of the day's light shifted somehow—darkened maybe and came back tinged with red.

Mom-pittseh, Owl, appeared in the sky.

Transfixed, Web watched owl flap down the gully toward them, from the south.

It was the middle of the day, when owls don't fly. It was a region where owls didn't live. Owl was huge, twice the size even of the great horned owl, which was as big as the war eagle. This was Magic Owl.

Web could not move. He was rigid with fear. And if Magic Owl was flying toward him, he didn't want to move. He mustn't show fear. He stood at attention. He held the horse Mom-pittseh, named Owl the Messenger of Death, tightly. He watched the spirit-bird come.

Magic Owl flew directly at them, fast as an arrow and straight, unvarying, not at all like an animal. He seemed to be headed for Web's face. The exile stood fast. He gritted his teeth, but he refused to let Owl see him flinch.

At the last instant Owl veered off slightly. His wing slapped Messenger the pony impostor in the face.

Messenger tossed its head and bolted.

The jerk threw Web off balance. He stuck out one foot to catch himself. And stuck it straight into a lava crack—in above the ankle.

He let go of the bridle with one hand to keep from falling . . .

Messenger's hindquarters bumped Web. The exile went over hard.

Falling, he thought Owl had truly brought death.

The rim of the crack snapped his leg.

"*Ataa!*" he roared, a cry of pain. And lost consciousness.

His mind rose through waves of pain. All was shimmering, unclear, like the air next to the ground on a hot day. He was swimming in pain.

Web came up from the little death. The little death
had taken him for a while, he knew. Owl brought it.

He blinked, and cleared his mind a little. Lifted his
head.

Pain knocked him back down.

But the little death didn't get him this time.

He wanted to lift his head enough to see his leg.
Maybe that would tell him the big sleep was going to take
him.

He was sure he would get far enough past the pain of
moving to get his head up. After two more tries he did.
His leg lay crooked on the rock, bloody and bent at an un-
likely angle.

Web thanked Duma Apa. The leg was broken, but it
was not caught forever in the crack. Maybe no big sleep
yet.

He rested, then lifted his head again.

Pain. His head fell.

Gingerly, he lifted his head again and looked. The
horse named Messenger of Death was in the river, drinking. He wondered if the horse would drink too much and
kill himself. He supposed it didn't matter.

His tongue hurt already, dry, yearning for water.
Later today or tomorrow it would swell and crack. Until
he got to the seep.

He intended to survive. Or at least do everything
needed to survive, and leave his life in the hands of the
powers.

He would get back to the seep, whatever it took.
There he had water and food. There he could survive for
weeks.

He would do that much. Then he could give himself
up to the powers. And submit to the big death with honor.

He would rest first. And hope that Messenger came
back, and he could at least hold on to the saddle and drag
himself up the gully.

He lay still. His mind wandered, drifted, half-
dreamed.

Messenger didn't come.

Yu-huup didn't come. Rockchuck didn't come. Black Shawl didn't come. Goddamn Hairy didn't come.

Owl didn't come.

He heard a snuffle. Messenger. Out of reach. Looking at Web.

Impossible. How could he have heard the snuffle and not the clops of hooves?

Didn't matter. He would catch the reins. Get Messenger close. Use the stirrup to try to pull himself up.

He talked softly to the horse, gently, winningly.

Messenger stood off a few feet, sideways to Web, still, looking at the rider.

Wariness was in the horse's stance. It didn't eat, didn't look around at the world. It eyed the exile warily.

Web cooed at Messenger. He spoke to the horse seductively.

Web's grandfather said the four jobs of a horse are grazing, drinking, mating, and running. If a horse wasn't doing one of these, he said, it was looking or listening or smelling for something to run from. And you better figure out what.

Web tried to think about what the horse was wary of. His mind didn't think of anything well. Its answer to all questions, right now, was pain, pain, pain. Maybe Messenger was scared of the pain.

Web almost managed a smile.

Well, maybe it was the blood. Maybe Messenger smelled Web's blood and was afraid of it.

"Mom-pittseh, *ne punku haintseh,*" Web addressed the animal softly. Messenger, my horse friend. "You are my life. Come here. Let me touch you, let me stroke your muzzle. Don't trot away with my life."

The horse put its head down and began to nibble at grass. The reins lay on the ground now, puddled. It jerked at grass with its teeth, chewed grossly, and swallowed. The jerking seemed rough, unnecessarily rough. The pony did not even look at Web, but tore at the grass, indifferent.

It swung its head a little away from Web. Shifted its hindquarters toward him. Tore at other grass.

Web come-hithered the horse again. Messenger ignored him.

Web felt desperate, and his desperation felt crazy-funny.

Maybe he would have to move to get the reins. Shift, slide, roll, move somehow.

He would try to move and see if he could do it.

He waited. He held his breath.

He rolled his shoulders.

Pain raged.

He lay still and tremulous. He did not pass into the little death. He could not permit that now. He had to catch Messenger.

He watched the old horse.

His tongue parched in his mouth.

He watched and occasionally cooed.

He woke suddenly. Messenger was near. The reins lay an arm's length out of reach.

He waited. He breathed deep and steeled himself against the pain.

He rolled and lunged.

He felt the leather of the reins.

Messenger jerked its head up.

Web clutched hard.

Messenger threw its head.

Web lurched into the dust.

The reins were gone.

He held himself and shook with dry tears. He noticed he had broken the scab on his left breast, and blood dripped. It was bright red and silky on his chest, dark red and glutinous in the dust.

When he woke from the little death, Messenger was standing near the river. Looking up the gully in Web's direction. The horse stamped its hooves lightly, hesitated, and began to trot. Trotted out of sight.

* * *

Web dragged himself.

It couldn't be called crawling.

He couldn't use the right knee to crawl because of the pain. He threw himself onto the right hip while he brought the left knee up.

At first he dragged himself up the gully once or twice or at most three times, a foot or so each drag. Then he decided to count the drags and force himself, regardless of the pain, to make five drags before he rested.

Between rests, he advanced about the length of his own body. Once or twice, resting, he went into the little death.

He knew a man could go four days without food, water, or sleep. Men who sacrificed themselves in the dry-standing dance did that. He thought he would die of thirst before he could get back to the seep.

When he rested, he asked for help from Duma Pia and Duma Apa, Mother Earth and Father Sky, from the directions of the four winds. He asked also mercy from the sun, *tapai*, that it not dry him out fast.

A simple thought rose in him: Rest during the day. Drag yourself at night. He thanked Duma Apa for the thought.

He dragged himself sideways into the shade of a big boulder. He lay back and let his body feel the cool of the shade. He turned his head and touched his lips to the cool rock, and imagined the cool was wet.

Now he would sleep until twilight. Then drag himself through the night. He knew he didn't have the will, within himself alone, to drag himself to the seep. So he would ask Duma Apa for the will. He would ask aloud sometimes. At other times, when he rested or slept, he would make every breath a prayer. Tonight when he dragged himself, he would make two rhythmical efforts, alternating. He would exert his body to gain a few inches upward. Then he would ask the powers for the will to exert again, and again.

The thought of asking, the thought of giving his life into the hands of the powers, gave him sweet solace.

Sweetness. Thought of drink. Of putting his lips to the seep. A sweet fantasy.

After he drank, he would sink into the little death, or the big one—it did not seem to matter, they were the gifts of Owl—and he would dream.

Time came apart, loose fragments in his hands, like strands of a willow basket falling apart.

Night, day, dawn, sunset, noon, midnight, Web couldn't tell one from another. Sometimes he dragged himself. Sometimes he slept. From time to time he would remember to ask for power. Then he would lie still and speak his prayer aloud, and then breathe it with every draft of air.

He dragged himself perhaps half of the first night, half the second day. After that he could not guess. Periods of light and dark passed at random, not in the magisterial half-day intervals dictated by Duma Apa, Our Father, but arbitrarily, nonsensically, in great shards and in tiny splinters.

He dragged himself. He prayed. He breathed.

His existence was nothing but this, his consciousness nothing but this. Glancingly, once in a while, he thought it odd that he suffered no thirst, no hunger. He hardly noticed.

He would have guessed it was on the sixth or seventh day, but it was in fact on the fourth, that Owl came to him.

Owl did not appear mysteriously, obliquely, glimmeringly. He flew up in a matter-of-fact way, perched on a rock close to Web's ear, and spoke like a friend. "I will help you," he said.

Web broke into sweet tears.

"You must heal. You must begin to walk again. Prepare yourself in the proper way. Then build a trap and bait it. Wait beneath the trap four nights without eating or drinking, or especially falling asleep. An owl will come to eat. Catch it by the feet with your bare hands. While you hold it, here is the song you must sing."

Now Web was frightened. No Shoshone would touch

an owl, a taboo bird that tells of death. If he must touch an owl, maybe he must never again be a Shoshone.

But an Owl went on. "First you will call in the animals of the four winds.

Hiyo koma wey, Hiyo koma wey
Hiyo koma wey sheni yo
Hiyotsoavitch, Hiyo tsaovitch
Hiyo tsoavitch sheni yo.

Then sing to the owl:

Mom-pittseh, Mom-pittseh,
Mom-pittseh, Mom-pittseh,
Coming to me through pieces of light and dark.

Mom-pittseh, Mom-pittseh,
Mom-pittseh, Mom-pittseh,
Coming to me through pieces of light and dark.

As Owl sang the song, he did a little dance on the ground, darting back and forth, fluttering his wings, hopping, weaving forward, circling, repeating the series of motions.

Web's eyes were opened, his ears alert. Owl's notes clanged like gongs, and his movements burst on the eyes like sun rays.

Web understood the challenge being given. He saw the danger if he lost the owl, even in pain from the pecking and jerking and beating. He saw the *poha*, animal-spirit power, being offered. He wept with gratitude.

"When you have sung and danced," Owl went on, "you will wring its neck with your bare hands. You will cut its heart open and hold it high overhead and let the heart's blood run down your arms. After that, when you fight, you will paint yourself with owl's blood where it runs on your arms.

"You will cut off the owl's feet," he went on, "and tie

one on each upper arm, between the chest and arm, claws into the arm."

Web understood that he was being given the power to grip strongly.

"You will take the heart and the skin and keep them in a bundle."

Web knew that if he lost the bundle, he would not only lose the power but also would become crippled or otherwise handicapped.

Owl began once more to sing the song:

Mom-pittseh, Mom-pittseh,
Mom-pittseh, Mom-pittseh,
Coming to me through pieces of light and dark.

He did the dance, weaving, hopping, fluttering his wings, going up the gully, back to the south, the home of the Owl. The moment he flapped his wings and lifted off the earth, Web saw him no more.

Seemingly, without lying down, sitting down, or even falling down, Web passed into a restful sleep, free of dreams.

Chapter
Nine

Flare eyeballed it. He wondered why the others didn't see it. He always wondered. The wondering stirred him to high-flown thoughts. The mission folk kept their heads so high in the sky, hunting for Truth, that they couldn't see what was around them. Which was a bleedin' horse with a bleedin' saddle and no rider standing a couple of hundred yards out.

To Flare the missionaries were a source of infinite variety and amusement.

The saddle was Indian. Flare couldn't see what tribe it was this far away. But it meant trouble for some poor critter.

He looked around. They were all jawing away, as usual. Their eyes must be on heaven, 'cause they surely weren't on earth. Mother of God, you run from the Holy Church in Ireland and get caught by Protestants in the deserts of the New World.

Funnier yet: There was no God in this forsaken country, that was clear enough. And Michael Devin O'Flaherty, who'd spent his life getting away from God-ridden people, who'd left civilization to live among the pagans, was bringing Jehovah to the country, in the form of superstition-bound missionaries. Mother of God, but it was rich.

He looked at Miss Jewel, who had some sense to go

with her fine, plump bottom and fine, rounded bosom.
Which made him want to get her into his blankets and
jolly her good. He smiled ironically. Faint hope of that,
me lad. She was discussing the doctrine of transubstantia-
tion with Dr. Full.

He nodded slightly at her. "Miss Jewel, I'm going to
get that horse." Don't explain, just inform.

She looked, saw. "Yes, Mr. O'Flaherty. Of course."

She probably didn't see the saddle. Well, it wouldn't
do its owner any good anymore. But it would tell a story.
And someone would want to know.

Miss Jewel stopped her horse. Flare would never
quite get over her forked there on the saddle—he'd seen
no other white woman do that. The whole party stopped,
wondering what was on the mind of the guide who pushed
and pushed and never let them stop. He reined away and
walked his horse. No sense spooking the lost critter.

Funny, though. The lost critter didn't act spooked.
Waggled its head back and forth, making the reins flip
about. Trotted a few yards. Stopped and looked back at
Flare. Trotted again, looked back, trotted. Finally headed
for that gully.

"What *do* we have here?" asked Dr. Fool.

Flare just let it sit.

"A fallen child of nature, to be sure," said Dr. Fool.
"But aren't they all fallen?"

He knelt over the boy and started mumbling. Over
the weeks of the trip Dr. Full had become pure fool to
Flare. Or sometimes Flare called him Dr. Full-of-Himself.
Like the Brits, fundamentally not worth thinking about.

But Flare was not amused by Dr. Fool's officiousness
now. Time to do some doctoring.

The boy had a broke leg. Maybe Dr. Fool could set it
and save the lad's life. If they could get enough water in
him in time, and fever didn't get him. If Dr. Full would
stop praying and start setting. If Dr. Full could get his
mind out of his notions long enough to see not a child of
God, a creature of Darkness, a fallen angel, or a sinner in

need of grace, but a lad with a broke leg—Shoshone lad,
surely a breed lad.

The lad moaned.

Flare squatted next to the lad and squeezed his wet
handkerchief. Water dripped into the boy's mouth. He didn't
react, didn't move lips, tongue, anything. After a while Flare
saw his Adam's apple bobble. Flare squeezed a few drops
onto his forehead, thinking ironically, I baptize thee, in the
name of the Holy Mother-bleedin' Church. . . . He wiped the
face and forehead and laid the handkerchief on the lad's hair
line to cool him a little.

Lad was in rough shape. Flare took the float stick
he'd brought back, hacked it in half with a few swings of
his tomahawk, and handed the two pieces to Dr. Full for
splints. Tore up the flour sack for ties—now the flour
these pork-eaters brought along was paying its way, anyhow.

Flare walked back to read the tracks. The boyo had
dragged himself up the gully—plucky boyo, almost got up
to his gear. Half mile uphill to here, tough going. Could
have stayed alive for weeks up there, what with food and
water. Didn't make it, though, did he?

Flare read the spot where it happened. Horse was
walking, being led, broke into a run. Flare couldn't see
just what went wrong for the lad—it happened on a rock
with a big crack. Maybe the boy stuck his foot in the
crack and went over. Would fit his break, it would. Yes,
blood on the uphill side of the crack.

The lad's crawl, and all his resting spots, were clear
to those as had their eyes on earth. Flare followed the
marks back up. In one place the feathery marks of owl
wings brushing the sand—damned peculiar, must have
been made before or after. Nothing else here but a tale of
struggle and pain. A plucky boyo in truth.

The boy was unchanged. Breathing easier, maybe.
Dr. Full had the leg set. Looked reasonable enough. Nothing Flare couldn't have done himself. The doctor was
going on with his tongue, in his elaborate, Dr. Fullish

way. He talked as a creek ran over a waterfall, because he
had to.

Flare looked at the sides of the gully. Not too bad,
but . . . he looked up the boulder-strewn gully. Not a job
for a horse.

"Mr. O'Flaherty," Dr. Full said, "I'd be obliged if
you'd fetch the smith." Muscles to heft the boy out of
here.

Flare squatted again. One of the reasons the missionaries thought he was a barbarian was that he squatted
comfortable as an Injun. Well, he was a barbarian. Flare
wet his handkerchief from his flask again and dribbled
water into the lad's mouth and onto his forehead. An
Irishman didn't hop to another man's order too quick.

Mind rose, and fell. *Mu-qua-yizikanzi*—soul fog flew
up.

Mind rose toward consciousness, and fell.

Swayed, rose, drifted, drifted, swooned. Bumped.

So. I have passed through a little death. Maybe the
big death. But I have passed through the death Owl
brought me. I am here.

Where is here?

Lie still, feeling. Mouth. Mouth hurts, tongue hurts.
Head—move neck slightly. Okay. Trunk, okay. Arms—
wiggle one finger—okay. Legs. Yes, the leg hurts. Won't
move that. The pain is there, waiting.

Maybe I've passed through a little death. If it is the
big death, leg would be perfect. It's broken. I hope I am
below the sky. I want to do as Owl told me.

Let the eyes flick open, closed. Glare. See nothing
but Apa the sun spirit, glaring.

So, where am I? Beyond a little death.

Bump!

Ataa! Ouch! Where am I?

Open yes. A horse's behind. A woman. Unbeliev-
ably, a white woman. With red hair, the color of the sacred
pipestone. Looking at me. Smiling at me.

I am with white people.

Mind-swoon.

Miracle. Owl sends me through a death and brings me out with white people, my new people. Not after a moon of travel. Now. Owl my guardian makes miracles. Soul fog lifts.

Lots of words. Booming. A man's voice. *Divo-taik-wag.* White-man talk.

Yes, know some English, a little, but mind won't work those words now.

A man rides into view, in front of the woman. The man has a big smile, too big. He is, he is . . . acting like my friend so he can talk me into something. Yes. Funny. He's booming the words. He has on some sort of fancy black coat.

A few of the words are understandable. The man is telling his name, Doctor Full. Too many words.

Where am I? Who am I?

Tired. Want to see more of the miracle, but very tired, very sleepy, and the words are very many. . . .

"Pehano."

The voice is male, gentle, soothing. "Hello, how are you?"

Still in the Shoshone language: "You're a brave boyo. You're going to be all right."

I am Sima Numah-divo.

I'm not as hot now. A man is speaking my language to me in a funny accent. Yes, one of those Americans, or Frenchmen. I passed through the little death and came out among the white people. Miracle from Owl.

Water dribbled into his mouth. Sweet, cooling water, wonderful water.

I will open my eyes in a moment and see where I am, beyond the little death, what country, and whether fair or foul to the eye.

Now am I truly Sima Numah-divo, the first Shoshone white man.

"I've brought him some broth."

I am a new person, beyond the little death.

A woman's voice. Speaking English. I will have to learn this language, really learn it.

"Sikkih, tain-apa tekkah." Here, boyo, eat.

Let eyes open. Flutter. Close. Sweet darkness. Open again.

Twilight. Faces close. Beyond, a camp with a few trees. Pleasant shade. Long shadows. A lovely scene. I want to draw it. With my colored pencils. Bright. New world.

Faces of a man and a woman.

"Sikkih, tain-apa tekkah."

The man is smiling a little. His face looks like . . . He wears a circled cross. Miracle. Circled cross. Red road, black road, wholeness. . .

Bowl against my hands. Grasp. Smell of meat soup.

The woman is a vision. She has bright, bright pipe-stone hair. More strange, it's piled on top of her head. Strange new world, where women do such things. She's beaming. My new people like me. Love me.

Soup. Spoon. Take it and eat. Am lying down.

Look at the faces. Oh. The tastes in this new world are wonderful.

"You've had a bad time," says the woman. "You're going to be all right."

Am lying on a travois.

"Hi-na en-nan-i-hai, tua." What's your name, lad?

First, My name is First.

Throat doesn't work.

Swallow some more soup. Swallow a couple of times.

Look into the faces.

"Sima." My voice rasps. Say it clearly to these creatures. "My name is Sima Numah-divo."

Chapter

Ten

Sima's English improved faster than his leg.

"Urinate," he said.

Miss Jewel heard and came to help him.

He was leaning against the travois, as he had been for the last week. He rode there, tied to the lodgepoles so he couldn't fall out and mess his leg up.

He wouldn't be able to ride anyway. He wasn't up to Messenger for a while. Owl, the messenger of death, had scared the horse named Messenger of Death. Had broken Sima's leg. Had sent Sima through death, the little death. Had used Messenger to bring Sima back to life, to bring the white people to Sima in a miracle. Though he could not ride for a while, he was glad Owl had used Messenger.

For now his life was the travois. He ate there and slept there. He rested on it in camp, the poles propped against a tree, as they were now. His only relief from the travois was when someone helped him away to urinate or defecate. His tasks: Heal, walk, prepare, trap an owl.

Miss Jewel pulled him up on his good leg, got her arm around his waist, and walked him toward a cedar to stand behind. She was tall, almost too tall for him to get a good grip on her shoulder, and strong for a woman.

Urinate and *defecate*. These were new English words he learned from Miss Jewel, who helped him with his English. Flare thought this was funny, and offered different words for the same things, but Dr. Full forbade Sima to use Flare's words. Which made Sima think English was a weird language. Why have good words and bad words for the same thing? Did people on the red road speak good words, and people on the black road speak bad ones?

The whites shortened his name to Sima. Like Flare shortened his real name, O'Flaherty, to Flare. They liked to shorten names. That was okay. He liked Sima. The First.

Everyone but Flare and Miss Jewel found Sima's need to go to the bushes embarrassing. They pretended not to hear, or were too busy to help. Dr. Full clearly thought it was beneath his dignity. Sima knew grown-up Shoshones who were too good for things, and was amused by them, too. Now he waited until Flare or Miss Jewel was nearby to say his new English words, and they helped him gladly.

Now Miss Jewel let him go, he got balanced, and she turned her back while he splashed. After growing up in one family after another, and more brothers than she could remember, she said, she had no delicate sensibilities. Sima like to have her help him. She always seemed tickled at the others' embarrassment.

He liked Flare to be around him because they spoke Shoshone. But when Dr. Full caught them, he would correct them. Only English, he said sternly. The way from barbarism to civilization is to learn to speak English.

Sima didn't know what barbarism was, but he wanted to learn English, and he wanted to be civilized. Flare called this a dubious proposition, but Sima didn't understand.

Flare didn't know about Owl. No one would know about Owl.

Miss Jewel helped Sima back toward the travois.

She and Flare were the damnedest pair. He was short, wiry, and a wit. Also a skeptic about everything. You had to watch his lively eyes, which spoke—roared—passions he'd never own up to.

Miss Jewel was tall and had that attention-getting hair. She wore it high, and artfully arranged, like a head-dress she'd grown herself. It shone beautifully in the sun, like the wire of a copper bracelet, and made her look even taller than she was. (She spent a lot of time fixing it in the morning—he'd seen that.) With her hair up, she looked taller than Flare.

The odd thing was the way the two of them acted around each other. Not only did he think she was some punkins—that was his own phrase—she also noticed it, liked it, watched him back like she had the same thing on her mind, and teased him about it. No Shoshone woman would have been so brazen. From the look of the other women, they wouldn't, either. Just Miss Jewel.

But Miss Jewel wasn't Flare's woman. No, he said, she was a schoolteacher. Lots of times it was hard to ask anything—the white-man way seemed to be to figure things out without asking.

That schoolteacher business bothered Sima. He'd noticed the three women teachers slept together in one tent, without men, like women separated in a taboo. They couldn't all be bleeding with the moon all the time. He wondered if *teacher* meant a woman who had never started bleeding, or at least a woman who had no man. If they'd started bleeding, why would they have no men?

At least Miss Jewel wasn't scrawny and dried-up-looking, and sour, like Miss Upping.

Miss Jewel helped him lower himself onto the travois. "Talk?" he asked.

She leaned against the tree next to him. They often practiced his English after she helped him. Today he was going to take advantage, just a little, of his right to ask anything.

"Why you say the devil is in Flare?"

She took a minute to speak.

Sima had lots of things about it figured out. The devil was a bad spirit. He'd heard a lot about the devil in the past week. But what did the devil have to do with Flare, who was a good man?

"Flare isn't wicked," Miss Jewel said, "he's good. When we say the devil's in someone, sometimes we really mean he's bad, and sometimes we mean he's full of fun. It's really hard to tell what we mean, Sima, I know."

She hesitated, and for a moment Sima thought she wouldn't go on. But this was a woman to say what should stay unsaid. "If I were to speak seriously about Flare, I'd say he doesn't know God. I'd say he's as fine a man as *nature* can make."

She chewed a lip. "What I want to do with my life is rise above my nature. I ask God to bring out my higher nature."

Sima didn't understand that at all.

"But," Miss Jewel went on, "that doesn't mean we can't enjoy the juices of life. With discretion. Even if this bunch of sticks in the mud *disapproves*." She drew the word out mockingly.

Sima smiled at her and touched her arm in thanks. Listening to English wore him out. She put a hand on his shoulder, and they enjoyed the evening in silence.

"Why don't they think you act right?"

"I'm not demure," she said, "or shy, or deferential." She spoke with a hint of resentment. "I'm not what the ladies' magazines call a True Woman. The four virtues of a True Woman are purity, piety, domesticity, and submissiveness. I fail on the last." She searched for better words. "Among the Shoshones, do women keep their eyes down, not look men in the face, not speak up about what they think in public, not speak in council, and not let on which man they're interested in?"

Sima nodded.

"Well, white people do, too. And I don't care—I won't live that way. God made woman the equal of man. Which this bunch of lamebrains hasn't figured out. They're too busy *disapproving*." She emphasized the word with her voice, and her merry eyes.

"Miss Jewel," called Dr. Full. She snatched her hand away from Sima's shoulder and went to Full. Sima thought one of the things Dr. Full disapproved of was their touching.

Sima wondered why Miss Jewel said Flare knew nothing of God. He wore the circle cross around his neck. That was an ancient symbol among many Indian people. The two bars of the cross meant the good red road against the turbulent black road, light against dark, good against evil, east-west against north-south. The circle resolved all the conflicts in the wholeness of life. It was the symbol of a man of spirit power.

Flare seemed like he was walking the good red road. Maybe Miss Jewel said that because Flare was what Dr. Full called a papist, which was another kind of Christian. But wasn't Christian all the same white-man spirit power? If you had one kind of power *(poha),* guidance from the eagle, perhaps, or the kit fox, why did that make wrong someone else's power, maybe the *poha* of the owl? Why should two kinds of Christians be mad at each other?

Whether it made sense or not, Sima was determined to learn it.

Miss Jewel had asked him about his religion, too. Sima said honestly he didn't have any. Asked what he believed, he said at first, "Nothing." When he understood better, he said he didn't believe—he *saw.* Saw the power *(poha)* of the sun, of the thunder and the water, the four-leggeds, wingeds, and rooteds. And, of course, he honored these things, as was plain good sense. Many of his people could do more—ask for such powers to be theirs, ask for *poha.* And have the request granted. He didn't mention Owl.

Sima did say he'd sought a vision with no success. Though he prepared himself, and made the sacrifice, no vision power came.

Miss Jewel kept her lip buttoned, but Sima could see she didn't like hearing about the powers he saw. Well, he might add some white-man powers for himself. But they would be added. He had Owl. He had Apa. And others anyone could see plainly.

Dr. Full wanted to teach Sima the white-man powers. If these powers could be understood only in English, that made sense. He would learn excellent English. He would say his Scriptures in excellent English. He would tell his father, Goddamn Hairy, in excellent English what an ass he was. Or he would say something else to his father—he hadn't thought that out.

But he would definitely learn about the white-man powers. With Shoshone powers you could make the thick rawhide of a war shield hard like metal. You could make your arrows fly straight. You could bring food to the people. You could see at night, evade the enemy's blows, and chase away ghosts. And you could have your eyes cleared, to see the good, red road for yourself and for the people.

But with white-man powers you could make metal, which was a great medicine. And from the metal you could make guns, knives, kettles. You could make blankets, find lots of tobacco—so much you traveled with it in big ropes—whiskey. His father's compass. You held it in your hand, and a stick inside pointed to the direction where the white buffalo lives, which the white men called north. Even in the dark. Sima didn't know why you would want such a machine, but it was a wonder.

They were odd, white people. Most of them didn't see the red road. They lived quarrelsomely, with no attention to the common good. They even killed each other sometimes, and acted like it was no great matter, or actually congratulated one another on murder. Sima had seen it.

But that didn't matter. Sima wanted to get the power to make wonders. He wanted his father's power. And then? He didn't know. Could you live among the white people and still walk the red road?

"Miraclee?" Sima repeated, testing the word. He looked at the writing paper he held and pronounced the last syllable, *klee,* as it looked to him.

They were passing the miles on horseback. The good Lord knew, Dr. Full thought, there had been many miles to pass in this mad country. They'd been spending it teaching Sima to spell.

"Mira*kuhl*," emphasized Dr. Full. "Like the virgin birth," he said again. Dr. Full had told the story of Christ Jesus's coming to earth by a virgin several times. If he weren't feeling so good, he would have been frustrated with his first savage pupil. The boy didn't get the Christian meaning of *miracle*—something divine, something done by God, not by nature. Something not in the ordinary scheme of things. But the boy couldn't make the separation. He had some funny heathen notion of what a miracle was, and kept saying the hand of Spirit was in everything, and nature was Spirit.

Sima's face lit up. "Like you find me dead," he exclaimed.

"No," said Flare, chuckling, "that was not a miracle."

"I think maybe it was," said Miss Jewel. "I see the hand of God bringing Sima to us."

Dr. Full motioned with his hands for them to keep it up. The boy was intelligent, and would profit from a discussion like this.

"It wasn't even that much of an accident," Flare protested. "You were lying within less than a mile of the Oregon road. I saw your horse and followed him to you. Because I was looking, not by accident." He cast a mirthful eye at Dr. Full and Miss Jewel. "If one of you priests had seen it, *that* would have been an accident." He loved to call them priests, because it tweaked their blue noses. "You don't look."

"Miracle," said Sima firmly. "You not understand." He considered his English carefully. "I dream white man be." He had not admitted to them that he was kicked out of the tribe. "I long way to white man go. All to Fort Vancouver. Dangerous. Many days. Want with white man be."

"I fall down." He patted the splint on his leg. "Break. To little death go." He mimed passing out.

Sima gave thought to his words. "Flare me wakes up. Different. Different world all way. Splinted leg. Thirsty not. Main thing, *among white people*. Went long, long way while little death. Among white people. Safe, not dangerous. Fall down to little death, rise up to new world."

"Now wait a minute," said Flare with a little heat. "You woke up right where . . .

Beholding this conversation, Dr. Samuel Full beheld his luck. He could hardly keep from grinning night and day. It was delicious.

The boy Sima was riding astride. For the first day. The boy had been impatient, extremely impatient, to get on horseback again. Dr. Full had prevented that, on medical grounds, for the boy's own good—spiritual good, not physical good.

Oh, perhaps the boy could have ridden a few days earlier, perhaps even a week, now that Dr. Full saw that he rode without his feet in the stirrups, and was beautifully balanced, graceful even with the splint on his broken leg. It must feel a lot better than scraping along on that travois, thumped by every stone this miserable country put in the way. But Dr. Full couldn't afford to have the boy ride too well. Not until today, when they left Fort Boise, a new and miserable pretense at civilization in this vast wilderness. Not until they were so far from the boy's homeland that he'd never think of going back. Back to savagery. Oh, no. This little savage was going to be saved.

He was the one Dr. Full had dreamed about, the one Dr. Full thought of as the Alchemized Savage. The alchemists were false scientists who studied endlessly to find ways to turn dross into something precious, to convert lead into gold. Dr. Full knew how to use God's grace to convert the barbaric to the redeemèd. Thus the Alchemized Savage.

And being converted, Sima would become Dr. Full's luck.

For who would be the instrument of this alchemy?

Dr. Samuel Full, at your service.

Of course, it was the hand of God, any soul could see that. The boy said he was going to the white man to find his father, a man known only as Harry. The fool. A father who sired him in a casual act, bestial, mere rutting. A father who showed how much he cared by disappearing the next day, or next week, or next month, his appetites sated. A father who didn't know of the boy's existence.

Dr. Samuel Full would bring the boy to know the father who mattered. His heavenly father.

It was immensely important. Jameson LaLane had labored for three years in the mission field without a single convert. Dr. Samuel Full would make his first convert before he even got to the mission.

That would bring other savages into the fold. It would make Dr. Full's leadership manifest. The missionaries, discouraged at sowing but never reaping, would flock to Dr. Full's strength. To the glory of God, and Dr. Samuel Full.

Dr. Full smiled in ecstasy. Samuel Full was born—this was the theme of his life—to show what God meant men to be. It was grand how all things came together for the good of those who love the Lord.

Dr. Full looked at Sima and grinned. To arrive with an Alchemized Savage. The boy was a gift of God. Maybe even a miracle.

Chapter
Eleven

The boy drew exquisitely. Miss Jewel felt awed.

He was modeling Flare's head. The mountain man was grumbling but holding still. Sima had put his head just so. The boy knew exactly what he wanted. The evening sun struck Flare's profile so that shadow created a line down the middle of his forehead, nose, and mouth, light and dark on either side. If Flare moved his head even slightly to the left, light bled onto the dark side of his face, and Sima sternly put it back.

Miss Jewel had taken drawing lessons. Though she drew poorly, she had learned to see well. Well enough to know this boy saw naturally, beautifully. He drew from life accurately, but with a gift of sight that made everything lovely.

Miss Jewel's teacher had said, repeatedly, that you did not draw or paint objects, really. You drew the light that was on them. And that was what Sima did—drew sunlight enhancing the things of the world. He also had a fluid, graceful line.

The boy was not without thought, either. He put Flare's head that way and made a little joke. Flare was a mountain man, he said—half white and half Indian. So Sima would draw him half and half. The Indian half light, he jokingly suggested to Miss Jewel, and the white half dark. But he made the white half light, and then altered the eye and cheekbone subtly on the dark side to look Indian.

She wondered what that meant to Sima, who was himself half white and half Indian. He was going to his white father, which was a beginning. But he was divided about his father. Sima was going from his home to an utterly alien world to find the man, but the boy spoke of him sadly. Or bitterly. She felt an inchoate passion in him about his father, and wondered what went into it of love, and what of hate.

Well, he had a right. He was abandoned.

The past was past, though. Whatever Sima's feelings, God had given him genius, and God's gift of genius was not to be wasted.

That was why he was going to be Miss Jewel's prize pupil. She would civilize this heathen child, and he would make a contribution to the world. He would show God's beauty to men. And women. Miss Jewel didn't like saying "men" for the human race. Men did enough putting themselves first.

Sima held the drawing up. Miss Jewel could see in it how good-looking Flare really was. Sima showed how finely shaped his face and head were, under the long hair and ragged whiskers, and Sima had replaced the dust and the hints of gray with the original sandy color.

"Sima," she said, "it's not enough to be half white, half Indian. You must be all civilized."

"Why?" said the boy. He was concentrating on a small touch of modeling on Flare's nose.

Miss Jewel smiled devilishly at Flare. "Take Flare here. He's a man of intelligence and ability, a man who could contribute. Instead he's roaming around to no point."

Flare gave her a mock evil eye, and Sima pushed his head back where it was.

"Back and forth, back and forth," she said. "Missouri, Oregon. Taos, Oregon. No point."

Sima shrugged. "Prolly right," he said. "My father half white, half Indian. He ever done no good."

"What's civilized?" objected Flare.

Sima moved Flare's head back. The lad was a nuisance.

"If you want to help the boy, don't talk about civilized," Flare pushed on. "Tell him good men, and what they did."

"Like Martin Luther, for instance, Mr. O'Flaherty?" It was Dr. Full, come to spoil the fun.

When Flare turned his head to look at Dr. Full, Sima pushed it back and put a bulldog look in Flare's face. Meaning, Keep still, damn you. Flare saw the doctor was bearing his black medical bag.

"Martin Luther had a splendid righteous anger," said Flare, "I'll grant him that. But you give the boyo Martin Luther as a model. I'll give him Wolf Tone."

"We thought Wolf Tone was your horse, Mr. O'Flaherty."

"Only an American could be so ignorant."

Dr. Full smiled, appreciating the banter.

"Wolf Tone was an Irish hero of the Year of the French, first of a thousand heroes."

Flare saw Sima was going to quit pushing his face around and let him talk. "See, the Brits captured him, they did, Wolf Tone. And hanged him. But he didn't die, did he? That's starters for heroic, nay? Bounced at the end of their bloody rope and lived.

"Then comes the good part. He's lying in hospital, and a doctor warns him he mustn't move his head.

" 'Why not?' says Wolf Tone.

"Bloody doctor tells him, 'Your neck's broke, if you move your head, you'll die.'

" 'Thank you for your kindness, Doctor,' says Wolf Tone graciously. Then he jerks his head to one side, and is gone."

Dr. Full paused to comprehend, then challenged, "Heroic?"

"Bloody magnificent," said Flare, "to those with eyes to see."

"Tincture of laudanum," said Dr. Full.

Sima lay between Dr. Full and Mr. O'Flaherty, asleep, or whatever you called passed out from laudanum. The doctor held up the vial. He grinned at Mr. O'Flaherty and said mockingly, "A miracle that sends the boy to his little death. And we will raise him up—Lazarus."

Mr. O'Flaherty, in his usual half-insolent way, started cutting with his John Wilson knife. Down the brittle, cracking splint from Sima's knee.

The new splint was ready. Mr. O'Flaherty had shot the elk during the two days they stayed over at Fort Boise. Now the piece of hide was half stiff—still flexible enough to wrap around Sima's leg and tie, but hardening fast enough to give him support. In a couple of days it would be rigid as a board.

The camp was quiet. Miss Jewel wasn't helping. Though she said she wasn't a bit squeamish, Dr. Full knew all ladies were. She should learn her rightful sphere.

The only thing was to get it done fast, before Sima woke up to the pain.

Mr. O'Flaherty flung the old hide splint away and reached for the new one.

"Wait," said Dr. Full. "We need to check this leg carefully." He began to wash the area around the wound.

Impatiently, Mr. O'Flaherty fingered Sima's toes.

And then the man acted crazy, even for him. Went down to one knee, spread the big toes away from their companions, felt of them.

Threw Dr. Full a mad look.

Dr. Full took Mr. O'Flaherty's hands away and spread the toes himself.

Between the big toe and the second toe was a web, as on a duck's foot.

Unusual. But why did the man look like he swallowed a frog alive and kicking?

Mr. O'Flaherty ran. He stumbled, heading anywhere. Away.

Dr. Samuel Full watched him with the greatest interest, suspecting an opportunity for advantage.

Flare was sitting on a boulder, chin propped up on his knees, staring somewhere toward the goddamn sun, which was setting somewhere over the goddamn Pacific Ocean. Seeing nothing. Dr. Full had said he would make Sima comfortable for the night. The boy would just pass from the laudanum sleep to natural sleep, Full said.

Flare had both moccasins off, and was holding his toes between palms and flattened fingers. He felt like he was cradling them. And practically rocking yourself, lad, like a wee child.

Flare heard Full's footsteps. "Let me see," said the doctor. When Flare hesitated, the doctor reached out and pulled his hands away.

Dr. Full spread the toes with professional matter-of-factness and looked at the webs between the big toe and the one next to it, one web on each foot. He felt them, looked again. "Even the same big wrinkle," he said. "I've never seen one of these, much less two. There's no doubt about it."

He looked Flare hard in the eye and spoke hard. "So are you going to tell him?"

"Not yet," murmured Flare. "Not yet."

"You're right," said Dr. Full briskly. He looked at Flare hard, then nodded, as though to himself. "It's not you he wants." He studied Flare. The mountain man hung his head. "Or maybe he does. So he can rise up and strike you down." Dr. Full was amused. Suddenly his voice changed. It was almost intimate, a parody of understanding. "No, you can't tell him, can you?"

What have I done, Flare's soul wailed, with my wretched life?

* * *

"What was your mother's name?" asked Flare.

He looked at Sima's face. The boy looked young in the dawn light, and vulnerable. He had just wakened from the little death. Flare had brought him coffee, thick with sugar Flare bought at Fort Hall, the way Flare and Sima liked it. Sima lay on his travois, and Flare stood beside him.

The outfit would not move today. They had changed Sima's splint on Saturday night to give him a full day of rest before he rode again.

Flare had no rest. He'd sat by the fire all night, and remembered his life phantasmagorically, a nightmare. He'd remembered his women. He'd pondered the progeny he might have, all over the West. My get, as the Americans called them. None of them white.

Flare had come out with the Northwest Company from Montreal twenty-three years ago, a sixteen-year-old lad. Instead of going back to the city with the pork-eaters, he'd spent the first winter at Fort William, and headed to Slave Lake in the spring. Before he was twenty, he was an old hand, not only a *hivernant,* a man who'd spent a winter in the wilderness, but also a clever and respected one. When the Hudson's Bay Company offered him a smart bit of money and the chance to go to the Pacific Coast, to Fort Vancouver, he grabbed it. And then he led brigades into the lands the Americans claimed, reaping fortunes in furs. He cared nothing for the fortunes other men made on his efforts. He loved the life, and scorned them for caring more for the money than the adventure.

When the time came to make contact with new tribes, it was often Flare who was chosen. He had the knack. He was superb with the sign language, he picked up spoken languages quickly, and he understood the Injun mind. He'd lived among tribes the boiled shirts on the HBC board of directors in London had not imagined in their most fevered nightmares of barbarism.

He'd had women in every one. It was the way you

became one of them. Country wives, the HBC called them, privately approving. A woman for a summer here, a winter there. An adopted family, adopted people, adopted loyalties. It was politic, it was good business, and it satisfied Flare's nature.

He liked the women, by God he did. He liked their company, truly. Though he liked adventuring with his comrades, he liked long camps with a big family and a companionable female. He liked sharing his thoughts, which was easier with women than with men. And he liked the feel of them in the buffalo robes, the ancient, rhythmic rub of them, for sure. He'd been a young man, uninhibited, and heedless of consequence.

Besides, it was the way of the country. His principle for living with the Indians was, When among wolves, howl.

Twice he'd nearly settled down for good. The first time he'd got sent away from her, far to the Pacific shore, to Fort Vancouver. It was a great opportunity, he told himself, and he couldn't stay behind. The second time he'd even had a child, a girl, by a Cayuse woman he lived with for two years. But his infant daughter died during the second winter, driving Flare half mad. Right then old Skye suggested that he and Flare join the American trappers— to hell with HBC, anyway—it didn't have the old Northwest Company spirit, and the Americans did. Flare rode with Yanks ever since, and stayed away from the Cayuses.

Did he have progeny all over the West? Wondering, he looked into Sima's face.

In the Shoshone language, he said, "What was your mother's name?" He repeated in the Shoshone language, *"Hi-na enin pia nani hii-ukkan?"*

"Epa Waapin," the lad said. "Of the *Pia Kuittsun Tekkah,* her father Beak, her mother Black Shawl."

Yes, as Flare thought. He remembered Pinyon of the Buffalo-Eating Band well. Comely, she was, with a devil of a sense of humor, on the wild side, that girl. He'd

lodged with her the very first winter he came up the Snake
River. Stayed all winter, an open winter, and the brigades
came upriver early that summer. He'd had three or four
months with her, all told. Liked her a lot. She was the
cheerfulest woman he'd ever been around, and a little
wild.

It was a long time ago. He'd been twenty. Now he'd
take her to his lodge and his robes and spend an eternity
there with her—hell, an eternity every night. Then he'd
told her he'd be back in the autumn, meaning every word,
even leaving his compass with her, and headed downstream. When it came time to go back to Pinyon, he got
the bloody fever. Sick for a month. When he healed, the
Snake River brigade was gone, McLoughlin ordered Flare
south, down to the Umpqua, instead. And there another
fine bottom had caught his eye. His eye wandered, those
days.

"What happened to her?"

The boy kept his eyes cast down. He didn't like talking about it. Flare thought tears were close. Speaking his
own tongue made the lad more emotional, too.

"She died a few days after she bore me. I never knew
her."

Flare thought how it would have been. Pinyon would
have held the boy, nursed him. Held him, at least, before
the fever came on her. Murmured to him, surely. Then the
fever would have taken over her body and mind, until she
didn't know her child, and lost her hold on life itself.

Black Shawl and Beak would have blamed the white
man who abandoned their daughter, partly. Among them
the father was forbidden in the birthing hut. If he so much
as looked on a woman while she was menstruating or giving birth, he would bleed from the nose or mouth until he
died. He had certain duties while she was in labor and in
childbirth. He was to eat only light food—no meat—and
drink lots of water. While the newborn was being washed
in warm water, the father went into the cold creek and
washed his genitals. For the next several days—the

mother would not be restored to him for a full moon—he was to rise early and move about, to inspire like behavior in the child.

Pinyon's parents would have thought Flare's failure to act in the right way contributed to disharmony of the physical and spirit world, and so to Pinyon's death.

Bloody rotten world. That's how he knew there was no God, or God had wound up the world like a clock and gone off to play billiards with his mates and pay human beings no mind. Surely He wouldn't kill teen-age mothers as they brought their children into the world.

Most likely He's off in a far corner of the universe rutting, Flare thought self-mockingly. He flings his get about creation, filling the skies with new solar systems.

"And your father?"

Sima shrugged, feigning indifference or scorn. "He went fur-trading with some Frenchmen. He said he'd come back, but he never did." His eyes out across the long distance, unfocused.

"Did he know you were on the way?" Flare hadn't known. He wondered why Pinyon didn't speak up. Had she not known herself, before he left? Or had she understood, all along, that he was footloose and fancy free?

"I don't know. Grandmother said she never knew whether Mother told him or not." Silence.

"So maybe he didn't know."

"But he didn't care enough to find out, did he? He didn't care what happened to me. Or my mother. He abandoned us. Her."

Aye, lad. I didn't see, those days.

One tear came now, drifting crookedly down Sima's cheek. The lad brushed it away. Weak, with his broken leg, or he wouldn't have let it flow. Flare was glad for the weakness.

"Man are stupid animals, sometimes," Flare said bitterly.

Sima said nothing.

"When you find your father, what will you say to him?"

Sima's voiced crawled with feeling. "I'll spit in his face."

Why ought I tell the lad anyway? Flare asked himself. It was a moment of pleasure for me, and the gift of a lifetime for him. Enough, a man would think.

He thought on the lad behind him. The lad who'd said he wanted to be alone for a while and nap. To be alone, at least, thought Flare. And why do you care that he doesn't want you there? Hasn't the lad a right to forty winks?

Flare crossed his legs, sitting Indian fashion by the squaw fire. He got out his white clay pipe and stuffed it with kinnikinnick. A pipe would make him think clearer.

Aren't you ashamed, man? Better sleep with your moccasins on, and never wash your feet, lest your son find you out.

The lad touches my heart. He's making a passage, a difficult and dangerous passage. He needs me.

Then help him out and keep your bloody mouth shut. No reason to make him feel obligated.

He tweezered up a hot coal with a pair of sticks and lit the pipe.

Aye, you bet, tell him you're his father, you fool, and he'll spit in your bloody face and be gone.

Why should it matter, a moment of pleasure for me, a life for him? The bull mounts the cow only for the sake of his urge.

I have no right. I gave up my right.

"Well, Mr. O'Flaherty, did you tell him?"

Flare was surprised. Dr. Full studied and prayed all day when they rested, and sometimes preached to the brethren and sistren, as he called them. Maybe Flare should feel flattered that he'd drawn the doctor from his holy silence.

"No, I didn't."

"No, you can't, can you? You gave up your paternal rights at the start."

"Watch yourself, Dr. Full."

Full gave a big, self-conscious smile and spread his arms, indicating he meant no offense. The two of them had jousted verbally before, and enjoyed it in a prickly sort of way.

"You said you're a sporting man, did you not, Mr. O'Flaherty?"

Flare looked at the bugger hard. "Aye. You bet."

"Will you play at chance with me then?"

Flare just stared at him.

"You dare not tell Sima his paternity. Yet in your confused way, you want to act a father to him. To set his feet on the right path.

"I want to set him on the path that's truly right. So I propose a contest, one to be strictly fair."

Full waited, evidently much amused. "Go on," said Flare. He felt a hint of an urge to go for his knife and cut the man's throat. But there was no cause for that.

"My path is the word of God. Faith. Thus obedience. Thus certainty of salvation."

"Mystic mumblings, and a lack of common sense, more like."

Full ignored this amiably. "Your path is the arrogance of relying on your own fallible observation and judgment above all else."

"Using me brain, more like."

"The results of our paths show in our lives. I am a minister of the Gospel and a doctor. You are a vagrant in the wilderness. I build self, family, church, community. You wander, the slave of your impulses, building nothing, abandoning all, even your own children."

"You're pissing into the wind," Flare said with a growl.

"I prepare the way for the next world, and you merely shuttle back and forth on the face of the earth, aimlessly."

"You offer delusion, I choose reality, I'd say," Flare put in caustically. Mad exchanges were entertaining, but this was nigh too bleedin' much.

"I offer God and heaven. You offer bleached bones on the desert."

Flare snorted.

"So let us put it to the test, which way is better. Your son will be the judge. You and he will come with us to Mission Bottom. Each of you may stay as long as you like, and may leave together or separately. We will let Sima see what God's civilization has to offer. He will attend the mission school under Miss Jewel, and I will instruct him in the Gospel. You may teach him whatever you like—hunting, trapping, your cunning ways with brute nature, whatever you like—even your libertine pleasures.

"I am willing to wager that Sima, in a fair contest, will respond more to the enlightenment of mind and soul than to the appetites of the body.

"At any rate, I so propose. Sing your song to him—your base melodies of this vile earth. And Miss Jewel and I will sing celestial melodies. Then you may ask him freely: What does he choose? Your way or mine? Man's way or God's?"

"It's a bet," declared Flare. That was all he said.

A thrill ran through Dr. Full. I've won—Mr. O'Flaherty is playing my game.

"I make you a promise," said Dr. Full with a look meant to seem cunning. "I will not cheat by telling him of his paternity, and setting off his fury at you."

"Each man will hold his tongue," Flare agreed shortly.

Dr. Full smiled hugely and offered his hand. Flare shook it. "I'm supremely confident," said the doctor. He felt exhilarated. He'd already won.

"I'll hold me own," said Mr. O'Flaherty. A confession of weakness.

Dr. Full considered, then spoke. "You rutted like a beast, Mr. O'Flaherty, and then ran off."

"I'm a man, for all that," said Flare.

"Beasts have no higher feelings. You abandoned your son, Mr. O'Flaherty."

Flare said nothing.

"Do all the men in your family have the web?"

Flare nodded. "On my father's side," he mumbled. "And the women on my father's side."

"Always so high, almost to the nails?"

"Some more, some less."

Dr. Full snorted. Smiled. They are such simpletons, people, he thought. Shook his head. "I will enjoy our competition, Mr. O'Flaherty, and look forward to the prize."

Full spun and walked away, swinging high the hand with the Bible in it.

The man is a son of a bitch, thought Flare. But he's right.

And the question is, laddie, if you didn't care twenty years ago, why do you care now? All of a sudden like?

Explain that, Mr. O'Flaherty. Explain it to your son.

Well, Sima is right about one thing. The boyo went looking for his father a thousand miles away. He went through a little death. And he woke up in his father's arms. It's a bloody miracle.

Flare tapped his pipe out on a moccasin.

My son despises me, he thought.

Part Three

A MAD NEW WORLD

Chapter
Twelve

Dr. Full set his foot onshore, looked back at his small band of Christians, lifted a hand toward the fort, and said ceremoniously, "Through His grace, safe in Oregon."

Flare ignored the slight to the real guide, himself, who'd kept the Pawnee from running the horses off, found water when they needed it desperately, figured out the safe places to cross the rivers, judged when to trade the horses and take canoes, stood guard through the dangerous nights, and, of course, spotted Sima before the lad died. Full better not be thinking of giving the good Lord Flare's thousand-dollar fee.

Flare turned his back to Dr. Full and strode briskly up toward the stockade. Flare was feeling grand.

What Flare liked about Fort Vancouver was the mad new world. He stopped to look.

For a couple of thousand miles crossing the continent you saw almost no one. A few Indians here and there, though they mostly stayed away, and seeing them usually meant trouble. A few traders and mountain men at the posts, Laramie, Hall, Boise, Walla Walla. Otherwise no one. A vast continent of solitude.

And now, before his eyes, a whole world. The stockade, with eight substantial buildings inside. Outside, clumps of huts here and there. Everywhere people strut-

ting about, comings and goings, things happening. Perhaps a hundred white men lived here permanently,
French-Canadians, Métis, English and Scottish artisans,
Scotsmen in charge for the Honorable Company. Plus visiting sailors, British and American and sometimes Russian. The fort had in addition probably three hundred
Indians, Delawares, Iroquois, Chinooks with high-caste,
misshapen skulls and their slaves. Plus visiting chiefs.
Plus Kanakas, natives from the Sandwich Islands. Fort
Vancouver all in all was a fine little piece of the world,
and in Flare's view, it was very cosmopolitan.

Flare whirled and looked back. His son was standing
beside the canoes uncertainly, about to start helping the
men unload. "Sima!" cried Flare. He grinned and jerked
his head and waved up the hill. Sima smiled and came
running. Dr. Full got into gear behind him.

Flare stood and looked at it all. Men of every color.
Men who spoke many tongues, had many ways, wor-
shiped many gods. They bore studying, these men, and
Flare liked that. They were as various as mankind itself.

The women were of only one color. Saving those
they'd brought with them, and they were aberrations, no
offense to Miss Jewel. White women didn't shine in the
wilderness, they wouldn't last, they didn't belong. It was a
big wildness, from Taos to Hudson's Bay to Russian
America. Flare had traveled it for a quarter century and
seen the whole kit and caboodle, as the Americans said,
from Esqimaux to Spaniards. There wasn't a place for
white women in the whole vast lostness. Praise be. The
way he saw it, without the oppression of white women,
maybe civilization would have a chance.

Flare would take a woman tonight—he'd not touched
one save in imagination for months. An Indian woman,
naturally. Strange land, where a white man takes only heathen women, and gets a heathen son.

Sima limped up alongside, and Flare put a comradely arm around his shoulders. At least he hoped Sima
would think it was comradely. Dr. Full gave them an odd

eye. "We'd best be seeing the doctor right off," Flare told Dr. Full. "Around here *the* doctor is Dr. John McLoughlin, chief thumb-up-the-ass factor. He'll want us for dinner tonight."

Flare jerked his head, gave them his best Irishman-at-your-throat grin, and they set off uphill toward the stockade.

Dinner. Flare thought on it greedily. He loved to eat Dr. John-be-damned McLoughlin's food and drink his fine brandy. For the emp got a sour stomach from every rich quaff Flare got in life. Tonight he would spoil Dr. John's digestion for a week. If only he could prick Dr. John's pomposity as well. Flare and Skye called him the emp, very short for emperor, because he was the most pompous man they'd ever known.

Flare looked at Sima. "It'll be fine doings tonight, lad."

"Surely you wouldn't corrupt the boy, Mr. O'Flaherty?" asked Dr. Full with light mockery.

Flare eyed him hard. Does the prude read my mind?

"Either with spirits or with the flesh?" Dr. Full went on.

Oh, bugger off, thought Flare.

"Aye, and see the devil!" came a bellow.

Sima felt himself jump. It was a voice fit for a wicked giant, the roar of a cavern-mouthed monster accompanied by the cracks of bullwhips. Where did it come from?

"Up here, dunderheads!"

Sima looked up as ordered and saw a man the size of a grizzly on the rampart above the stockade.

"You've changed, Skye," said Flare. "For once I heard you before I smelled you."

The man named Skye laughed, a sound like a boulder crashing downhill. "I smell of Satan, as always," he roared. "Like you."

Silhouetted against the sky, he looked like the biggest

man Sima had ever seen, tall and wide and not a bit fat. Sima felt his chest tighten and his breath run hard through his throat.

Skye put a hand on the top of the stockade and vaulted down. The distance must have been ten feet, and he looked like he weighed as much as a buffalo bull, but he landed lightly on his feet, rumbled forward, and shook both of Flare's hands with both of his own. Maybe he wasn't as tall as he seemed at first, but he was bulk enough for two of Flare. His eyes were small, obscure, and blue.

"Skye," said Flare, "this is my friend Sima, a Shoshone. Sima, Mr. Barnaby Skye."

Skye stuck out a huge paw and Sima shook it. "Come to eye the white-man doings, have ye?"

"Yes, Mr. Skye," said Sima. "It seems a fine place."

"It's a grand place," the giant roared. "Here ye can broaden your horizons. So broad ye'll get the clap in six languages, and it pains equally in all."

"He comes seeking his father," put in Dr. Full severely. Skye turned his attention slowly, searchingly on the preacher. "It is my hope to persuade him the one he needs is his heavenly father. I'm pleased to meet you, Skye."

The giant touched Dr. Full's hand like he was brushing it off. "*Mr.* Skye," he said. He eyed Full's black ministerial clothing balefully. "Especially to those who corrupt the young."

"Dr. Full is headed to the mission on the Willamette," said Flare.

"And good riddance," he said to Flare. "It's *Mr.* Skye," the giant reminded Full, and turned his back on the parson magisterially.

"What brings ye Vancouver way, Skye?" Flare was damned curious. Skye stayed away from this fort like the smallpox. As a lad he'd been press-ganged into the British Navy—press-ganged was a fancy word for kidnapped— and after several years jumped ship in Vancouver. He always spoke with hatred of the Navy, and feared being

abducted back onto one of the ships that visited the fort—
if the giant was afraid of anything now.

He carried a pair of special weapons in memory of
his years of sea slavery—belaying pins, which he used
with wonderful savagery to break heads by throwing or
clubbing. He'd carved them with death's heads.

"Mr. Skye goes where he pleases," said Skye. "The
report at rendezvous was that the Honorable Company
would pay more for plews. Which was a damnable lie."
The giant shrugged.

"And how about you, my friend?" Flare steered clear
of Vancouver, too. He was a trusted man, a brigade leader,
and then got himself into trouble with the emp. Flare and
Skye skipped Vancouver one summer together, went over
to the Americans. What put the spice into their defection
was that they took nine thousand dollars of prime beaver
plews with them. The squared it with the emp later, giving
up their salaries and performing some services.

"I escorted the missionaries. They paid me handsomely to do it. What with the price of beaver . . . " For
two decades the trappers of the Far West had lived as
cocks of the walk. Flare and Skye despised fashion anyway, but to lose your livelihood to a silk hat . . . at thirty-
five or forty to find yourself useless.

Skye regarded Dr. Full with imperious disdain,
looked at Flare, shook his head ruefully. Then he laughed,
a warm, rumbling laugh.

"Let's have a private word, mate. I've got a bit of a
deal afoot, and you're just the man for it."

"Sima's in, too," Flare said firmly.

"All right, mate," Skye said, patting Sima on the
back and almost knocking him down. "The three of us."

"The problem," said Flare, "will be Full."

"Any why would Full-of-Himself give a bloody
damn?" asked Skye. "McLoughlin will see he gets where
he's going with the legbone connected to the hipbone."

Flare nodded toward Sima.

"Aye, the young chap. Why?" Skye put a huge arm around the boy's shoulders.

Skye had put the proposition to the two of them, and it was a good one.

A Russian ship had broken up at the southern shore of Puget Sound, a week's ride to the north. Some of the sailors and fur hunters had drowned, others had been killed by Chickeele Indians, and the cargo of otter and seal furs was gone.

It was a delicate matter. The Honorable Company did not tolerate depredations by Indians, even against the company's competitors. Its policy was strict fairness. The company would be here for centuries, and nothing short-sighted would do. The Indians must be punished and the furs returned to their rightful owners. So McLoughlin had explained to Skye.

On the other hand, McLoughlin at present had no men to execute his policy. Rather, he had men but no leader reliable against Indians who might still be bloody-minded. And the matter must be taken care of immediately. The Chickeeles, McLoughlin said knowingly, must be made to feel the wrath of the Honorable Company as soon as possible after their unacceptable acts.

So McLoughlin was prepared to hire Sky and Flare to get the job done. The three negotiated. The ultimate price was what Flare and Skye wanted. They got the fur themselves, which they would *sell* to HBC at fine prices. The market for beaver might have gone to hell, but not the market for otter. Skye boasted afterwards that they'd make a couple of thousand dollars each, two years' wages per man. A boon, even after Flare shared with Sima.

It always surprised Flare that Skye was invariably eager to make money. All he ever did with it was go on sprees of epic proportions. But then Flare had nary a dime to show for a quarter century's labor either.

Skye repeated himself. "Why would Full-of-Himself be concerned about this young chap?"

Flare shrugged. He couldn't tell his friend the truth in

front of Sima. "He wants to make Sima an example. What a fine Christian an Indian can become. He won't think our influence will help the boy."

"Sima, let me handle this."

"Yes, Skye," said the boy.

"*Mr.* Skye," the big man corrected him.

John McLoughlin set the best table west of St. Louis. And presided in a manner that softened his formality and austerity. Flare had to admit, in fact, that McLoughlin had become gracious. He was much taller than even Skye, and of a huge voice like Skye's, but he knew how to comport himself to guests.

The food was splendid. For meat, great slabs of beef, mutton, goat meat, and pork, all from stock raised by the fort, and geese brought down by fowlers. Potatoes, peas, and other vegetables grown in fort gardens. Fresh fruit—apples, grapes, peaches, strawberries, praise Godawmighty even figs and oranges, a tribute to the emp's enterprise and ingenuity, as he never tired of telling them. Pies. All sorts of breads, since the fort had a flour mill. Flare noticed that Sima's favorite was the hot buns with raisins and a sugar paste on top.

The missionaries, he saw, had no favorites. They treated all the foods circumspectly, as though McLoughlin's papism were dietary. And they answered Mac's polite conviviality with coolness. Well, they were God-ridden, even Miss Jewel.

Flare whispered to Sima to ignore the wines as they were served. It was tempting to irk Dr. Full by encouraging the lad to imbibe, but Sima wouldn't be able to keep pace with old sots like the emp and Skye. Dr. Full, his wife, Annie Lee, and Miss Jewel made rather a point of refusing the liquors.

Skye, of course, was drunk. The man never drank without getting drunk, and always relished the prospect. Huge in body, in his cups the man seemed to grow enormous in spirit; his appetites, enthusiasms, and energies became incredible. Flare felt that his friend became the full-scale Mr. Skye only when inebriated. He had seen the drunken Skye wrestle a buffalo bull, grab hold of its horns, and throw the critter. Then the bull got mad, and Skye jumped and rode it. Flare had never seen the like.

Unfortunately, Skye drunk soon became Skye helpless. It was Skye's habit to drink and drink and drink until even he couldn't stand up, then to drink lying down for a couple of days, until he was physically incapable of lifting cup to lip, and finally to sleep it off for half a week. In these states Skye needed nursing.

Occasionally, Skye asked Flare if he should marry. It would help during his drunks, he said. Flare answered that men of spirit should never marry. Marriage penned a hoss in a tiny pasture. What Skye needed was not a wife but a slave. When Skye started railing about freedom—he knew what it meant to be enslaved—Flare replied firmly that the alternative was to learn to drink like a civilized fellow instead of a beast.

Nevertheless, the men cared for each other. They'd helped each other escape from being subjects of the crown, and become subjects of nothing but their own wills. Which was bad enough, Flare often reflected.

Maybe, with Skye in his cups, and Dr. Full-of-Himself, there would be some amusement tonight yet.

After the dessert and tea and coffee—dessert and coffee were wonderful—Dr. McLoughlin's huge frame led the men to another room for brandy and cigars.

Sima thought the hardest thing about white people was their many little ceremonies, like this one. And their rigid distinctions of higher and lower among each other. The two men called "doctor," for instance, demanded and got deferential treatment. If they didn't demand it, as Dr. McLoughlin didn't, it was because they were sure of getting it anyway. Mr. Skye was demanding it by insisting on *Mr.* in front of his name. Which was odd, because like Flare he seemed not to need it. Among whites, some people were treated respectfully simply because of their personal qualities, like Flare.

Among the Shoshones, everyone got more respect than these whites offered each other. Everyone was thought to be on a journey of spirit, following his medicine, and so deserving of respect. Except, of course, halfbreeds, who were despised.

Among whites, on the other hand, women were always treated as unimportant, even very smart women, like Miss Jewel. It was like both sexes were needed, but one came first and the other second, like parent and child. But Miss Jewel was always getting even with little words and gestures. Sima liked that. Now the women were sent to another room while the men talked about what was important. Which was typical.

Since Sima's English had gotten good, he could keep track of most of these things. It you were a white man, you wouldn't talk to someone else, in effect, unless he bent his knees to you a little first. Even the expression "bending the knee" was white-man talk. It was very peculiar.

Now Dr. McLoughlin made a small ceremony of lighting his cigar. (Was the cigar a little like the medicine pipe? Did you speak only truth when you held it? Dr. McLoughlin didn't pass the cigar, but offered each man his own. Sima declined because he didn't know how to treat the cigar ceremonially. Dr. Full also refused. Did that mean Dr. Full wasn't going to tell the truth?) "Dr. Full, may the Honorable Company be of service to you in any way?"

Sima had to be careful. Sometimes offers of generosity were genuine, sometimes merely ritual. This one seemed genuine.

"I think not," replied Dr. Full stiffly.

Sima's translation: I not only refuse your kindness, I am offended by it.

"I beg you to speak freely to me," said Dr. McLough-

lin. "You at the mission are our friends, and in times past
we've been glad to lend a helping hand."

Sima had heard Flare tell Dr. Full what had happened. Flare had been at pains to point out that McLoughlin had given Full's predecessors seed when otherwise
they would have had no crops, and would have faced star-
vation. He had outfitted some families for the winter and
never called for repayment. He had provided guides and
equipment at no charge. He even answered insults with
kindness. He had gone far beyond what his own masters
required of him. It seemed that all this was generosity.

"Instead of a request for you," said Full, "I have
questions." His eyes gleamed with a white-man madness.

Sima's translation: I intend to challenge you.

McLoughlin spread his huge arms wide and smiled.
Apparently he had nothing to hide.

"You are a Scot and a Catholic, Dr. McLoughlin.
Why do you not oppose those who come to claim the
country for the United States and for the true Christ
Jesus?" Glint of superiority.

This was getting hard for Sima. There were nations
of white people, just as there were nations of Indians, but
these were of one nation—they spoke the same language.
And Flare had explained that there were two kinds of
Christians. Catholics and Protestants, and they spoke the
same language and read the same Bible, but they fought
with each other. Sima didn't get it. Didn't they all see the
same Spirit? Were they enemies because they had ceremonies that were a little different?

"We are a few white men in a sea of red men, Dr.
Full. It seems to me that we ought to help each other. No
more than that."

That made sense, Sima thought. He must remember
that the white men stuck together against the red men,
which might mean against him. Or might not.

"Unless you oppose us secretly, sir."

Sir—one of those little words whites constantly used

to show rank. But Dr. Full seemed to use it mockingly. After all, he was a sir, too.

Sima saw the anger rise in Dr. McLoughlin's voice. The doctor sat still, evidently gaining control of himself. Sima admired him for that. "I am kindly disposed to you," he said simply. The anger was really gone—this McLoughlin was a man. "And we have business to discuss."

Flare put in, "I wish to leave your employ here, Dr. Full. Dr. McLoughlin has consented to provide you an escort upriver to the mission. The escort knows the way well, and will provide more security than I can."

"We hired *you,* Mr. O'Flaherty." Sima saw Dr. Full was uncertain what to make of this, but inclined to see enemies everywhere.

"So you did. Dr. McLoughlin requires my services urgently."

"To reimburse you for the loss of Mr. O'Flaherty," Dr. McLoughlin put in, "the Honorable Company is prepared not only to provide you with an escort, but also to pay you one quarter of Mr. O'Flaherty's fee."

"I don't understand."

White people again. Dr. Full understood. He was looking for trouble.

"It's a right bargain, Dr. Full," boomed Mr. Skye. "You're paying Flare a thousand dollars for four months of his time. For passing by one week of that, you get two hundred and fifty dollars back. Ought to please a skinflint like yourself."

Mr. Skye didn't like Dr. Full. What did "skinflint" mean?

"Two hundred and fifty dollars is a lot of money to your mission, Dr. Full. For giving up nothing, in truth."

Dr. McLoughlin disliked Dr. Full, but he concealed it well.

"How about it, sir?" roared Skye.

"I would like to be free," said Flare.

Dr. Full shrugged. "What do you want O'Flaherty to

do?" His eyes went from man to man, ravenous, wanting to know. But the money meant a great deal to him—he was a white man. What would he want more? "What exactly?"

"Mr. O'Flaherty and Mr. Skye will go to the Puget Sound," Dr. McLoughlin said, "to recover furs from a wrecked Russian ship. Indians have taken the furs. They may also have killed some sailors. It may be necessary to punish them. The company requires experienced men for such work."

"Is it dangerous?"

And why did Dr. Full ask? He would not go far to protect Flare. His eyes hopped rapidly from McLoughlin to Flare to Skye, probing.

Dr. McLoughlin shook his head no. "We will send an overwhelming force." the man told simple truth—he was a good man.

"What's missing here?" Even the question was a difficult admission for Dr. Full. The man was sure he was being taken advantage of. Such a man would always be sure of that.

Flare said quietly, "Sima goes with us."

Flare and Dr. Full looked at each other hard, warring. What was going on? Sima saw for the first time something new, a fresh opposition between them. And it centered on him.

"The devil he will," said Dr. Full. Flat, like that.

"We talked to him," said Flare. "He wants to see the big water. And what else is to be seen."

Skye put a huge arm around Sima's shoulders. Sima would always feel safe around this big man.

Dr. Full spoke to Sima directly, intimately, as though no one else existed. "You would pass up the chance to come to know your heavenly father."

What was it Dr. Full really wanted? Sima wondered. Why did the man want Sima to *arrive* at the mission with him?

Sima decided he couldn't figure that out now. "I will

come to the mission at the beginning of winter," Sima said softly. He meant it. Like a white man repeating a promise foolishly, he said, "I give my word."

"My son . . . " began Dr. Full.

"I will come to the mission in the winter," Sima said again. Even he could hear in his voice a new quality, a new authority, a refusal to be denied.

Flare and Dr. Full glared at each other, neither giving in. What are they fighting over? Sima wondered. Dr. Full couldn't win—Sima would do what he wanted.

"It's settled then," Dr. McLoughlin said. "I propose a toast to a safe journey and return." He raised his brandy glass high. So did Skye. Sima raised his—his brandy was untouched. At last Dr. Full raised his glass in agreement, but set it back on the table without drinking. Dr. Full did not approve of spirits.

Sima took the tiniest taste of his brandy. Harsh. With a hint of sweetness, but harsh. White men were strange to drink such stuff.

"Our escort will be ready at your earliest convenience," Dr. McLoughlin said to Dr. Full. "I've taken the liberty of drawing up this note of credit on the Hudson's Bay Company for two hundred and fifty dollars American."

Sima studied Flare. His face was triumph, Full's defeat. White men were strange.

He sipped his brandy again. He didn't know everything yet. But he was getting skilled in reading white people. You had to read them, for they seldom said what they meant. There were rules that interpreted from what was said to what was meant. He didn't know why they had this slant way of doing things. But he was getting so he understood them. Soon he would understand them better than they understood themselves.

Peculiar people.

Chapter

Thirteen

The moment Flare came into the room, he could see the old tricks still were being worked. McLoughlin was not only big but imposing, a figure of weight and authority. The room—large desk, shelves of books, flag of the Hudson's Bay Company, weapons on the wall—conspired to make the chief factor intimidating. As a younger man, Flare had resented this posturing, this assumption of greatness by the emperor of Oregon. Come to the New World as a free man, Flare despised such arrogance. Though Skye said the man was a mere piker beside any sea captain you could name.

It caused their troubles. McLoughlin always said Flare was looking for ways to undermine his authority, and thousands of miles from the seat of power, such authority must be absolute. So the emp looked for ways to make Mr. O'Flaherty bend the knee. Flare scoffed. Their strife chafed. And when Mr. Skye suggested he and Flare go over to the Americans, Flare said sure—at least Americans didn't have emperors.

Flare studied McLoughlin while the big man went through the little ceremony of pouring brandy. The Frenchies said he'd changed, become almost generous, was even capable of gentleness. Flare didn't know. He'd been genial last night at dinner, but he was showing off for the missionaries. He was perfectly capable of taking revenge on Flare now. Revenge for years of back talk and insubordination, if not for taking the furs to the Americans.

They toasted each other's health, exchanged pleasantries.

Flare had come on a strategy. You always needed a strategy to deal with McLoughlin.

He had decided to throw himself on McLoughlin's mercy. Which was damned scary.

But Sima had just now brought it up, and Flare was out of cards to play. He smiled grimly at himself. And *why* are you trembling like a quaking asp, my mate?

He made himself begin. "Dr. McLoughlin, the Shoshone lad Sima will be here in a few minutes. He wants to speak to you. I invented an errand for him first."

Flare swore he could see a look of sneaky glee flit across McLoughlin's countenance. Maybe the bastard would turn out to need killing yet.

Now Flare spoke one word at a time. "I ask you not to tell him the truth."

McLoughlin gave a theatrical shrug. "The company believes in truth. What does the lad want to know?"

Flare put it carefully. "It's personal. He will ask the full name of a company trader who spent the winter with his tribe. When you work it out, the winter will have been 1818. The records will show he was from McKenzie's brigade. Sima believes the man's first name to have been Harry."

The doctor nodded, bring the year and the events to mind. Flare was sure McLoughlin had grasped all by now. "And why should the company withhold that name? Did the man commit a crime?"

Flare said simply, "He fathered a son." Time passed. "Sima."

McLoughlin studied Flare. At length. "And who was this man?"

"Me, sir."

McLoughlin simply waited. It was one of his tactics,

to ask nothing, but use his eyes to demand more, and see what came forth. Flare decided to give in. "I spent that winter among them, Dr. McLoughlin, in a lodge with Sima's mother. And left in the spring. My name among them was Hairy, sir. H-a-i-r-y, not H-a-r-r-y."

Dr. McLoughlin just kept waiting. Irksome, how well it worked. Flare gave his own elaborate shrug. He could not meet McLoughlin's eyes. "Later, the mother died in childbirth. The lad has been an orphan. And a half-breed. Which among Shoshones is a terrible thing."

Flare stopped himself. There was no need to run on. McLoughlin had heard this sort of story often enough.

"Are you sure?"

"Yes, sir. You know my duck-webbed feet."

Flare had the pleasure of taking the chief factor by surprise. McLoughlin barked a laugh. "Pass on your best qualities, eh?"

Flare ignored it.

The doctor rose, paced, turned the force of his personality on Flare. "The lad needs a father. Why should he not find you?"

"He must find me, Dr. McLoughlin. But not yet." Flare didn't know how to explain this. "He hates me. Hates his father," he corrected. "He thinks his father didn't give a damn about him."

"That appears true enough."

This was lawyer stuff. McLoughlin knew very well how this happened, and why. But Flare restrained himself. "I didn't know she was with child, sir."

"And you assumed she'd marry within the tribe and any child would be well enough taken care of," McLoughlin said bluntly.

"Yes, sir." No sense pretending.

"Do you care, Mr. O'Flaherty? Do you really?"

Time for nakedness. "Yes, sir."

"Why? You've done this a hundred times. You've avoided responsibilities. You've been vocal about your pleasures and your freedom. Something about the nature of a bull and its urges, as I recall."

Flare eyed the doctor with wry amusement. Aye. The bull must be a bull, he always said, when it is time. Implied was, The devil take all else.

"I can't explain it, sir. Sima came to me eighteen years late . . . somehow. He calls it a miracle. He is in midstride, sir, becoming . . . something else. A white man? A man. I want to be there, sir."

"To set him on the right path?" McLoughlin queried.

"Yes. He needs that." Flare hesitated. "And just to see." He didn't know if the words were enough for McLoughlin. Or for himself.

McLoughlin spoke intimately. "And six months from now?"

Flare squirmed, closed his eyes, finally looked McLoughlin full in the face. "He'll have naught to do with me if he finds out now. In a few months I'll tell him, come what may."

"What could come, Mr. O'Flaherty?" Flare thought the words were sharp.

"He'll go over to the missionaries."

"Aye?"

"He's smart, so Dr. Full wants to make him a model convert. Tells him to seek his heavenly father instead of his earthly father." ·

Dr. McLoughlin took a pace, turned back, pulled at his beard. "What are you not telling me?"

"Dr. Full and I have a sort of contest, sir. We compete for Sima's soul. We show what we are and let Sima choose."

"Anarchist or Methodist?" McLoughlin was much amused by this. "What a choice! Then Dr. Full is in on your secret."

"He knows, sir, and is sworn not to tell."

"Mark my words, the man is a schemer. He will trade knowledge for power."

Flare said nothing. He could not afford to smile at the emp saying this of someone else.

"How does the lad find life among the missionaries?"

"Sima is tempted. He likes Miss Jewel. She's his teacher. He'll spend the winter with them."

"Any red-blooded man would like Miss Jewel," said McLoughlin. "Including yourself, my innocent O'Flaherty, I'd say, from the way you look at her."

Flare gave in to desperation. "I beg you, sir—"

A soft tap at the door.

"That's him, sir. First let's—"

"Nay," McLoughlin said with a fierce look at Flare.

"Sir, I must—"

McLoughlin whirled at Flare and said evenly, "May God help you, Mr. O'Flaherty." He crossed the room, flung the door open, welcomed Sima politely.

May god help *you,* you bastard, thought Flare, glaring at the emp.

Flare was intrigued to see that Sima was not awed by the man or the room. The lad looked around curiously, declined brandy, replied politely to McLoughlin's pleasantries, and went straight to his request. He showed self-possession in front of the emp. Flare was proud.

"Do you have every way, Dr. McLoughlin," Sima concluded, "of tell who lived with my people that winter?"

McLoughlin rose from his chair behind the desk. He looked at length at Sima, evidently considering. Finally he said, "Yes, Sima, I do. I am sympathetic to your plight. I deplore the use of native women for our men's convenience without responsibility. I always have." He indulged himself in a hard look at Flare. It was true, McLoughlin had cleaved to his Indian woman faithfully, and been a true father to his children. "I can find out who your father was, and I shall. The company keeps records of what man went where."

McLoughlin turned his back, waited, perhaps pondering. He turned again to his visitors. "Those records, however, have been shipped to Montreal. I will send word back, and have it looked up. In a few months we will know. By spring, perhaps."

He said these last words directly to Flare. Flare understood. No way on earth would word come and go to Montreal over the winter. But Flare had no longer than spring. Then McLoughlin would tell.

Flare heard his own breath rasp.

"I understand you're spending the winter at the mission. In the spring, we will not only tell you who your father is, and where, but send you to him at the company's expense. Wherever he may be. If he's retired, probably Montreal. Will that be satisfactory?"

Sima nodded slowly. "Yes. Good. Very. Thanks you." The lad seemed truly satisfied.

"Until spring, then," said McLoughlin. And offered his huge hand to Sima, then to Flare.

Flare shook it hard.

Chapter
Fourteen

 At the end of each story, Sima and Palea had to sum up the tale, to show Miss Jewel that their English was coming along well enough for them to understand.

The fisherman found a brass bottle in the sea and opened it, they agreed. Smoke poured out of the bottle, and an Efrit, a monster as big as a hill, formed himself from the smoke. The Efrit announced that he had been in the sea one thousand eight hundred years, and now he would kill the fisherman.

Afraid, the fisherman pretended not to believe such a huge Efrit could have ever fit into such a small jar. When the Efrit proved he could get into the jar, the fisherman popped the stopper back on and held it fast.

The Efrit begged to be let out once more, but the fisherman was too clever now. He was going to throw the jar back into the sea for another one thousand eight hundred years. Citing the commandments of God, though, the Efrit begged the fisherman to let him out. Finally the fisherman agreed. Then the Efrit gave the fisherman a new kind of fish. It was so wonderful the king paid handsomely in gold for it.

They loved this story from *The Thousand and One Nights,* and agreed that the fisherman had done right to take a chance and repay malice with kindness.

"Palea understands these stories better than we inland people," Miss Jewel said, breaking the spell. "His people are people of the sea, and fishermen."

Sima breathed out. It was a wonderful story, and a wonderful book, full of monsters and mysteries. Miss Jewel had a whole volume of it, and a fund of other stories she could tell from memory. Sima and Palea had spent the whole afternoon sitting in front of the tent in the autumn sun, hypnotized.

Palea was Sima's new friend, a youth his own age from the Hawaiian Islands, slender, brown, shy, with a beautifully shaped head and speaking a soft, hesitant, melodious English. His people were truly seafarers, he said. He had taught Sima and Miss Jewel from the first moment to say not Sandwich Islanders, as the whites called them, but Hawaiians. The white men took your home from you, he said, and they even took away its name. Sima had decided never to use the name Sandwich Islands, and Miss Jewel agreed.

Sima thought Palea was like Mr. Skye. Mr. Skye had been forced into the British Navy, and Palea had been forced into the service of the Hudson's Bay Company. Both of them were torn away from their families, and ended up far, far from home with no way to get back. Mr. Skye jumped ship and made a place for himself in a new land. Palea wanted nothing but to go back to his home country. He spoke of the flowers there, the rich smells, the soft rains, and the gentle sweetness of life, though oddly, he didn't mention his family. Palea hated the chill of this country, which did not seem cold to Sima. But in Hawaii, said Palea, it was never cold, or for that matter hot, but always gently warm. Hawaii was the perfect place. The gods gave it to the Hawaiians, and the whites took it away. Worse yet, they took it away in the name of saving it.

Here Mr. Skye showed that he had white man's disease. For Skye, being forced into the Navy was enslavement. For Palea, Skye said, being forced to serve the

Hudson's Bay Company was a chance to improve himself. Skye put this view with simple conviction. It angered Palea and amazed Sima.

Of course, Dr. Full had the same disease. Disappointingly, Miss Jewel did, too. Sima wasn't sure about Flare.

Sima was coming to understand white men better and better. Their main affliction was thinking that their way of looking at things was the only way. The way of progress, they called it. Other attitudes they regarded simply as childish, and gave them no further thought. White man's disease.

Sima had made up his mind he would not get this affliction. He would merely add white-man knowledge, or medicine, to his Shoshone understanding. He would become something greater than either. He would turn his father's curse into a blessing.

His gullet tightened. He ignored it. He must not think of his father. Spring would be time enough for that.

Meanwhile, he was going to make a book of drawings of the wonderful creatures in *The Thousand and One Arabian Nights*. Miss Jewel's copy had one illustration, and Sima was going to make a book full of them, starting with this Efrit, whose head was a dome, his legs masts, his mouth a cavern, his teeth stones, his nostrils trumpets, and his eyes lamps. Hearing of his skill with colored pencils, Dr. McLoughlin had given Sima a drawing tablet. He started with one eye like a lamp.

Crack!

"Ow!"

Crack again!

Sima grabbed his head, laughed and howled at the same time, and ran. Palea just ran. It was Mr. Skye again. Sima ran like hell.

"Enough!" bellowed Skye. "Excuse, Missy," said Skye to Miss Jewel softly. He always called her Missy. "Come here!" he hollered "I warned you!" He tossed a belaying pin in each hand, like a juggler. "Got to have a different kind of lesson now," he told Miss Jewel.

"If you say so, Mr. Skye," she answered, and took her book into the tent. She said she enjoyed Flare's spirit, but Mr. Skye's wildness was beyond her tolerance. The boys crept back.

Yes, he'd told them. Any time he could sneak up on them, he would crack their heads with belaying pins. If an Injun got close to them, they'd get scalped, not whacked. He was teaching them the habit of constant alertness, he claimed. Sima thought he was also having a good time cracking heads.

Mr. Skye said he kept his belaying pins for sentimental reasons. When he got pressed, he was a young chap of just fourteen, and of only middling size. The older men had bothered him—he didn't give details—until he learned to use the belaying pins. He practiced and practiced, and learned with an expertise that turned heads. He not only could lay about him with the pins with an astonishing clatter and devastating accuracy—like a bloody savage beating a jungle full of drums, he boasted—he also twice knocked men cold with thrown pins. Later he got his growth, and became truly terrible with them.

When he told Sima and Palea about it, he showed them the carving on the pins. He'd wanted to learn scrimshawing at the time, he'd had nothing but time at sea, but lacked ivory. The bosun's mate suggested he put his mark on a couple of pins. He carved the face of Thor on one pin, and his hammer and thunder on the other. Skye's insignia.

When he jumped ship, the pins and a dirk were the only weapons he could lay hands on, and he was more deadly with the pins. When he earned a tomahawk, and later pistol and rifle, he kept the pins. For sentimental reasons, he said. And, besides, truly, a man never knew.

"Chappies," he said, "tonight Mr. Skye teaches ye something of import. Aye," he said, grinning broadly, "something of import."

"Where's Flare?" asked Sima suspiciously.

"Belay that," ordered Mr. Skye. "He's acting serious

about leaving at dawn. But you chaps and Mr. Skye are in for a sailor's last night in port." He raised high a jug and chuckled.

Somehow Sima became aware just before it happened. He felt light seeping into Mr. Skye's tipi for a while, down the smoke hole and through the hide covers. Then a faint scratching sound. And a shadow across the floor of the lodge.

Sima didn't care. He didn't give a damn about anything in the world but the warmth that was against his stomach and thighs. In a moment he would get back inside that warmth, maybe not even moving this time, just back inside the warmth. From behind, here as he lay, from behind, without effort.

In a moment. His mind was so—

Came a roar: "Asses!"

Flare's voice. Sima knew it, but he didn't care.

Whack!

"O-o-w-w!"

Whack!

"O-o-w-w!" This time the screamer was Sima. He covered his bottom with his hands, and the cords bit into his hands. "O-o-w-w!"

Whack! Whack! The girls were crying out and Mr. Skye bellowing and Sima himself wailing. The warm bottom rubbed against him and was gone and he wondered fleetingly if it was gone forever.

The cords got him again.

Bedlam!

Girls running. Out into the day with no clothes. Flare gave them parting slashes. Girlish shrieks.

Mr. Skye dived for Flare, but Flare dodged easily, and brought the quirt down on Mr. Skye's naked back.

Then on Sima's ass again.

The little Irishman was laying about him violently, in grim silence, and beating the hell out of both of them.

Sima decided he'd get into the spirit of things. He

lunged for Flare. The earth rocked back and forth fast.
Sima fell flat. When he got up. Flare put a moccasin into
his back and shoved him into lodgepole. He went down in
a heap.

"Bloody hypocrite!" yelled Mr. Skye.

Flare said nothing, just faced Mr. Skye, ready for his
charge. Mr. Skye lurched forward on all fours. Flare
dodged easily. Skye hit a lodgepole with his head, and the
pole split. Skye lay dazed. Flare larruped his naked ass.

"Drunk as skunks, the two of you," he said.

Mr. Skye struggled to get up but couldn't.

"*Bloody* hypocrite!" said Skye with a snarl.

Flare stepped back, lowered his quirt. Suddenly Sima
saw Palea standing in the door of the lodge. Why wasn't
he here with the two of them? How long had he been
gone? Why had he brought Flare here? Or had Flare just
come to Skye's tipi first thing anyway?

"*Bloody* hypocrite," Skye tried once more, at half
volume.

"The brigade is leaving now," Flare said. "Catch up.
If you can ride hung over."

Sima thought on poontang.

That was a word for it he'd learned from the Frenchies.

It was wonderful.

He rocked to the rhythm of his walking horse, half
asleep, half drunk. The rhythm kept him half asleep. It reminded him of one of the rhythms of ye olde rub, as Mr.
Skye called it. Sima had never imagined it would be so
grand.

Ribbon, she said her name was. He had always fantasized about a Shoshone girl named Paintbrush, not a
French-Canadian girl named Ribbon. All right, Ribbon
would be his woman. While he looked for his father, he
would hump Ribbon, body length by body length, from
here to Montreal. No matter how far it was, he would get
there hump by hump.

Palea rode beside him, all fresh and alert. Palea had
hardly touched the firewater, and Sima thought less might
be a good idea next time. He didn't know how much
Palea had frigged Ribbon. Or Berry, the older woman. It
had been dark in the tipi. The women had come and gone
from robe to robe. Sima had topped Berry a couple of
times, but he'd been attracted mostly to Ribbon. She was
his age, and had a perfect shape, and a humor impish and
sardonic at once.

All night long there'd been the sounds of ye olde rub
in the lodge, and rasping cries of pleasure, and no man
cared what the others were doing, or weren't.

But Palea had left the lodge early. Sima supposed it
was his first time, too, so he was embarrassed or the like.
Sima couldn't imagine that. Godawmighty, as Flare liked
to say, once you discovered poontang, your mind was between your balls.

Two women. Sima wanted Ribbon plus one, at least,
on his journeys. And whatever women caught his eye
along the way.

"So lads, are your minds where your cocks were all
night?"

Sima's eyes scratched as he looked at Flare.

"Aye."

"I guess so," said Palea.

"Well, they should be. Natural," said Flare.

They rode in silence for a moment.

"I want you to know something," said Flare. "They're
whores."

"What's 'whore'?" asked Sima. Not that he gave a
damn.

"Skye gave them a cup of booze and a few beads for
their tails. Some other man will do the same tonight. And
tomorrow night. And every night. The whores don't care."

Sima thought about it. He shrugged. He didn't know
if he cared what Ribbon did, as long as she . . .

"They'll give you a disease," Flare said. "It'll hurt when you piss. It'll hurt when you fuck."

Still . . .

"For a little more trouble, you can have women as won't give you a disease."

Sima looked sideways at Palea. For some reason Palea seemed standoffish about the whole thing. Sima was ready to whoop and holler and reminisce, when he felt awake enough, but Palea acted indifferent.

"It makes sense not to get sick from sex," Sima ventured slowly.

"Aye," Palea spat out bitterly. "Aye. Remember the Hawaiians, and you'll see that."

Sima noticed Flare looked as puzzled as he felt.

"You don't know, do you?" Palea went on, almost accusingly. He looked at them hard. Then, not so harshly, he told his story.

Captain Cook, said Palea, came to Hawaii when Kelolo, Palea's father's uncle, was a boy. Now Kelolo was an old man, perhaps seventy years. When Cook came—in the arrogance of the white men he said he discovered Hawaii, though the Hawaiians already had done that—the Hawaiians thought the white men were gods. There was an honored story, known for many generations, that one day gods would come to the island, and they would be white-skinned. So naturally the Hawaiian women took every opportunity to have sex with these seafaring gods and so become mothers of gods.

They became mothers of disease, diseases gathered by the white men in every foul port of the world, but unknown to the Hawaiians. Soon the Hawaiians discovered that the white men were no gods, and the women lost interest in the sex. But they spread the diseases to their men. And in the span of two generations, three fourths of the Hawaiian people were dead. Killed by white-man diseases. Palea snapped out these last words.

Sima looked at Flare questioningly.

"They say it's so, lad. Course, no one did it on purpose."

"They did it," said Palea.

"I'll not be telling you otherwise," Flare said.

They rode in silence for a bit. "I came to give you boys a bit of friendly advice about poontang," Flare went on. "Here it is. Stay away from the whores. God's truth, there's one under every skirt, and you don't need whores."

"Stick to one woman, like Dr. Full say?" asked Sima.

"Truly, I wouldn't get my mind fixed on just one piece of poontang, either," said Flare in a kindly way. "There's one under every skirt. God's truth."

Sima looked from Flare to Palea and back. He didn't know what to think.

"There's something more," Flare said. His face wasn't so stern now. "Palea is getting paid for this little trip of ours, but perhaps not enough. Sima isn't getting paid at all. So . . ."

Flare handed Palea a fine new John Wilson knife, gleaming and sharp. "A bit of a present for you, lad." Palea lit up, and mumbled words.

"For you, Sima, more than a bit to help you get started in this mad new world." Out of a cover made of blanket, Flare slid a rifle. He handed it to Sima.

Sima held it gingerly. A real rifle, not a fusil. It was new and beautiful. He could hardly believe it was his.

"Percussion cap," said Flare. He handed Sima some caps wedged into a piece of deerhide. "When we stop this evening, perhaps you'd like to learn to shoot."

"You bet!" said Sima, using Flare's pet expression.

Chapter
Fifteen

"A month," said Palea, pointing, entire arm extended. The arm seemed to languish with sadness. "It took us a month to sail here." Sima knew his friend was homesick a lot, but he had never seen him as forlorn as he was today. Palea didn't mention it until Sima asked, but he looked constantly toward the western horizon, his eyes far away.

Flare and Skye had gone across to the wreckage in canoes with the local Chinooks, to make sure there was nothing salvageable. Was it the sight of a wrecked ship and thought of death that saddened Palea, or just the look of the long reach of ocean that separated him from the Hawaiian Islands?

The two teenage boys sat on a big rock and looked at the gray sky and said nothing more. They were at a great point reaching into the sound, their view toward Hawaii blocked by islands. At Vancouver Mr. Skye and Miss Jewel had shown Sima a big drawing of the earth, as they called it. North America, this piece of land, was huge. Sima saw where the Shoshones lived, and where this coast was, and where the Hudson's Bay Company's main houses were in Montreal, and more on a big bay to the north, and where Miss Jewel came from, inland from the ocean to the east. Skye showed them how one captain had sailed all the way around the earth, and how the disease-carrying Cook had found many islands, including Hawaii.

The earth was so huge, and the drawing so full of knowing. Sima felt awestruck in the presence of such medicine.

Now he had seen this big water for himself. He had always known about it, always had the sense of it, for the salmon trout (as the white men called them) came from this Pacific Ocean up the Snake River a thousand miles to the streams of his homeland. The Shoshone name for one of the bands of his people was Salmon-Eaters.

He had not known it was so huge, this ocean, the biggest on the earth—an ocean big enough to throw two or three of the North and South Americas in, and lose them. Yet an ocean the white men sailed easily in their enormous ships. The furs Flare and Mr. Skye intended to recover would cross the ocean to a country named China. The white people had strong medicine to sail such seas.

In fact, the big ships never stopped circling the earth with goods to trade. They started in England, an island, and took knives, guns, blankets, and other goods to Fort Vancouver for trade to the Indians (a white-man name) for furs. The furs they took to China, and traded them for tea, spices, and a fine cloth called silk. These items they took to London and exchanged them for knives, guns, and blankets again. And so on, a ceaseless circling.

Sima understood circling. Men lived in a circular tipi to acknowledge the never-ending circle of a day, a year, a life, the life of the tribe. The circle honored life, but the white men had no sense of this honoring. He didn't understand the point of this circling until they mentioned money again. Money explained everything.

All this white-man knowing seemed an indescribable grandeur to Sima. They said it was for money, and often they did seem small of spirit. Yet surely not even white men would have ventured forth for all this knowing only for money.

So now he had seen the big water, and he was glad.

His friend, though, suffered from seeing. It made Palea more than homesick—it made him angry. Set him to thinking about how white men had destroyed his people and had ripped him away from his home. It made Palea sullen. And there was no point in that. That only turned things nasty.

Sima saw the canoes start back from the wreckage. They'd spent almost no time there—there must be nothing to save. He studied Palea's long face. "Let's meet them on the beach," he said.

"Bastards," Palea muttered, and started down.

"Stay by my side regardless, lad. Keep your hands off your weapon unless you see me actually fire." Flare repeated for emphasis, "Don't even touch your weapon unless I fire. You might get us all killed."

Sima felt nothing in the world, not the earth under his feet, as keenly as he felt the new rifle in his hands. Flare had taught him to shoot it, and at a reasonable range he could hit. He had fantasies of protecting Flare by felling an enemy. He still couldn't use the word "Indian," even in his mind. The village was Chickeele, he told himself instead.

He was proud not to have been left in camp with Mr. Skye to guard the horses and gear, like Palea.

They walked into the village boldly, every man holding a rifle. The Chickeeles didn't look at them, except for some children who had no discipline yet. The women hurried into the lodges, taking the children, and the men stood at the entrances.

Flare was pleased that it fell into place quickly. An old man appeared carrying his pipe, and followed by three men in their thirties and forties. They invited the whites to smoke and talk in a big cedar hut. Flare assured Sima they'd be safe. They left their rifles outside under a close watch. Flare took only Sima inside with him. The Indians would think that strange, but bugger them.

They smoked. Speaking in the trade language of the region, Chinook, they exchanged expressions of goodwill.

Flare occasionally summed up the talk for Sima—the lad
needed to learn. Out of politeness, Flare waited until the
proper time to bring up the issue. Then he told them mat-
ter-of-factly what the Hudson's Bay Company knew of
the wreck, the loss of cargo and life, and said he knew the
tribe's young men had killed some of the sailors and had
stolen a lot of furs. He met their eyes.

He got polite denials.

The company would not accept these furs in trade,
Flare went on. It demanded they be turned over freely.
Now. For return to their rightful owners, the Russians who
hunted furs from the post at Sitka. Flare's tone said he
would tolerate no disagreement, or even hesitation.

More denials, still polite. Oh, perhaps this band had a
few items plundered from the ship, items they'd gotten in
trade from other Indians. As a gesture of goodwill toward
the whites, they would give Flare these few honestly ac-
quired items, to show their hearts were good.

Flare waited. It was done. Two oilskin slickers, several knives, a sailmaker's awl. Not a single fur.

So Flare smoked once more and made a promise—
that he would find the furs in this village, lodge by lodge,
take them by force if necessary, and return them to the
Russians. He said all this holding the pipe, and told them
he spoke the truth when he touched the pipe. Which was
by God true.

When he repeated all this to Sima, he added, "Keep
your wits about you now, lad. Don't touch your knife. If
we have to shoot, we'll likely be left for the vultures
here."

As they came out of the lodge, Flare ordered the men
to take their rifles and search the entire village, inch by
inch. Tolerate no interference, he said, "and for good
Christ's sake harm no one."

Then men went in pairs. Flare and Sima stayed in
front of the ledge, in front of the village. A half dozen
Chickeeles stood in a triangle around them.

Suddenly Sima understood that he and Flare were hostages. If anything went wrong during the search, if one person resisted and was hurt, these Chickeeles would take Flare and Sima prisoner, or kill them.

Sima felt his heart beat crazily in his chest. He looked helplessly at Flare. The man was simply looking around, his eyes keen, his face calm. Sima had no idea how Flare could do that.

An outcry in French from the far end of the camp. Flare smiled reassuringly at Sima. Sima looked around for a way to run, just in case. There was no cover anywhere, except a boulder as tall as an aspen opposite the council lodge, on the side of camp away from the creek. In case of trouble, Sima decided he would run like hell for the boulder.

One of the French-Canadians came toward them with an armload of otter skins, haranguing at a Chickeele man in French and jerking the furs away from the man's hands.

Flare quietly told Sima to take the furs. The Frenchie went back to the search, still barking at the Chickeele in a language the man couldn't understand.

Flare and Sima stood by the furs in the center of the village. Two more Frenchies brought stacks of otter skins in and laid them down. Flare watched attentively, like when he played cards. Like nothing was at stake except a couple of bets.

Sima's skin was feverish. They weren't going to get out of here alive. Oh, God, he wanted Ribbon again before he died.

Skins kept coming. They were going to have to bring the packhorses even to get the peltries out of the village. Several pistols appeared in the hands of Frenchies.

Separately, two of the Indians around Flare and Sima disappeared surreptitiously. They came back with guns, old fusils.

One of the Frenchies was coming toward them, yelling at a Chickeele woman, and she was yelling back and trying to yank the furs away from him. Flare just watched them calmly.

When the two got close, the Frenchie jerked the furs away from the woman one more time, and she fell down. Then she jumped up, yelling and screeching at the Indians around Flare and Sima, pointing at the Frenchie and the furs, stomping her foot, demanding that they do something.

The Indians stirred uneasily. Flare stared at them, man after man.

Suddenly the woman bit the Frenchie's arm. He dropped the furs on the pile and backhanded her. Hard— she went sprawling.

The first Sima heard of it was a metallic click.

One Indian raised a fusil toward Flare.

Flare looked hard at the Indian and made no move.

The muzzle swung into a line with Flare.

The crash of a shot.

Flare grabbed the old chief leader and put his knife to the man's throat.

Echoes of the shot through the village.

Sima didn't understand.

The Indian with the cocked fusil sprawled on the ground, bloody on the chest.

Every Indian had a knife or tomahawk out. The lone remaining armed man held his fusil on Flare.

"Easy, lad," rasped Flare, his eyes on Indians.

Two Indians kept glancing up nervously.

On top of a boulder stood Mr. Skye. He held one rifle on the group. Another lay at his feet. A Frenchie stood up behind him, rifle at the ready.

Skye roared, "Who else wants to die, you cowards?"

Flare translated the words into Chinook. He brought his knife blade up harder under the old chief's chin. He permitted himself a small, fierce smile.

The old chief said nothing.

The Frenchies came walking and watching, their

guns at full cock. Now they surrounded the Indians around Flare and Sima.

The old chief squeezed a few words out. The Indians grumbled. Stepped back. Lowered their weapons.

Flare nodded at the Frenchies to get the stolen goods.

"Now let's walk out of here, lad," said Flare loudly. "Slow and easy." There was a peculiar joy in his voice.

He started backing up, knife at the old chief's throat. The old chief backed with him. Flare whispered into his ear a sweet song of death.

They made the camp secure against attack. It would take the Indians time to make medicine, Flare said, but a head start wouldn't work. The Chickeeles could kill every man jack of them if they were determined. But the price would be higher than the Indians were willing to pay.

When the leaders came in to make peace, Flare was still hard with them. The old chief was going to Fort Vancouver, he said. He could go as a prisoner. Or the Chickeeles could send several men as guests of the Hudson's Bay Company. The great McLoughlin would be pleased to receive them as guests, he said, and would give them many presents. And then every spring and every fall they would trade their furs to Dale, the trader at Fort Nisqually.

It was a clear deal. The Indians took it.

On the morning of the third day, Flare said to Sima and Palea, "We're clear of trouble." The Chickeeles had truly accepted.

Palea and Sima had trouble accepting the sight of the four chiefs riding in the middle of the brigade. They were half guests, half hostages.

Sima asked what would happen to them at Vancouver. The chiefs would be wined, dined, given presents, feted in every way, and overawed, he said. They would see the fort and the crops and livestock and sawmill and military power, Flare said, and would decide cooperation was the only policy. That was the way of the Honorable Company. It would work. It always did.

Sima said uncertainly, testing it out, "What if we did wrong, Flare? Maybe we did."

"Wrong to save our own lives, lads?" He included Palea. Palea seemed to be going through some bitter passage of his own, and was full of complaints about the world.

"Wrong to go there," said Sima. "Wrong to meddle."

"They stole, lad. They murdered."

"Not from us. Not our people."

"Lads, if we tolerate stealing from any white men, they'll steal from all white men."

"Palea and I aren't white men."

"You are, half. Palea may well be."

They rode in silence for a moment.

"We Shoshones don't set ourselves up to rule everyone else."

"Aye, lads. Believe me, half the time it seems right enough, half the time I think it's a rotten business. The whole time I can't figure out another way to live here."

"Then get out," snapped Palea.

"The world is mine to walk," said Flare equably. "I'll not have it otherwise."

"Your Hudson's Bay Company is stinking up the earth," Palea said.

Maybe the missionaries had the right idea, Sima said. They brought very few guns, they worked by persuasion, not force, and they had a doctor to heal the sick.

Flare eyed the lad and answered, "I cannot speak about the missionaries." He thought he'd best say nothing against them, not yet. The lad was promised to go to the mission for the winter, and learn reading and writing. "As a Hudson's Bay man," he declared, "I've done me best to make things work right."

In the early days of the Northwest Company, he said, the traders gave liquor to the Indians, and the destruction of white and Indian life was terrible. Since Flare got started with the HBC, the company had refused to let Indians have liquor. He himself had applied this policy strictly, and it turned out best. The company also forbade wanton killing of Indians, and severely punished men who drew blood without cause.

"But everything's your way, your white-man way. Even 'right' means your white-man idea of right. You get what you want. And you want to rule."

"Nay," said Flare. "I want to live."

"How are the Indians of this Pacific Coast living since you came here?" Palea said challengingly.

"They're dying," said Flare. "Just like the Sandwich Islanders. Hawaiians," he corrected himself. He looked sympathetically at Palea. "Three quarters of those near Vancouver are already dead from diseases their bodies can't withstand. I don't know why."

"It's what you really want," Palea said hotly. Sima was about to burst in, too.

Flare held up a staying hand. "What I want?" Flare chuckled a little. "Nay, not a bit of it. Think to the future. When the Indians and the wild lands are gone, there'll be a world run by rich swells, tight-assed preachers, and power-mad sheriffs. They'll put fences everywhere, tax our whiskey, and tell us no women without a bloody marriage license. No place to roam for the likes of me and Mr. Skye, come those days."

He grinned at the youths. "In the meantime, we can waggle our tails and live."

He chucked his horse and trotted ahead. He muttered to himself, "If we can stay alive."

Palea broached the subject in a gingerly way, as if afraid of disapproval from even Sima.

It was the middle of the night. The two youths had drawn the midnight watch. They were careful to stay awake and keep their eyes working. Skye had threatened them with bodily harm if they fell asleep on watch, and they feared he meant it. Plus, he had a nasty habit of trying to sneak up on them during the watch and crack their heads with belaying pins.

"Among the Shoshones," Palea began, "are there . . . ?" The word he finally used was incomprehensible to Sima. Palea fidgeted, unable to plunge forward. Finally he said in his soft, melodious English, "Men who love other men."

Sima looked at him big-eyed. "Yes," he said simply.

Among the Shoshone there were *teni-wiaphs,* men-who-would-be-women. Men who lived entirely as women, dressed like women, used the language of women, performed only women's tasks—and married men. They also had some sacred functions, a special place in various ceremonies. They lived as they were told to live in a dream. But Sima had been cautioned by Flare not to talk about men-who-would-be-women. The subject made white people crazy, he said.

"I am one," said Palea.

Sima gawked at his friend. He thought of the two men-who-would-be-women in his own band. They acted like women. The white trappers who visited never even understood that they didn't have women's bodies. If Palea was one, why did he dress like a man, act like a man?

"I am in love with an older man," Palea said sheepishly. "Very fat, very kind, a lot of fun. A generation ago, we would have been together. Now the missionaries forbid it." He laughed ironically. "White people love to forbid many things, but this one . . . " He made a throat-cutting motion. "My father is dead. To avoid humiliation, my uncle sent away me with the Englishmen." The youth was miserable, near tears.

Sima looked at his friend in the eyes. He didn't know what to say. He tried at last, "It must be different among you."

"Why?" Palea was anguished.

"Among the Shoshones," Sima said carefully, "a man-who-would-be-woman follows his medicine. He has no choice. It is strange medicine, but it is his."

"And people are not ashamed of him?" Palea asked painfully.

"It is his medicine," said Sima, emphasizing every word.

Palea nodded. He pondered a moment, biting his lip. "I had to ask. You're the first person I've known well enough to ask who wasn't a white man.

"My father's uncle is also a man-who-would-be-woman. But he has to dress as a man and pretend to be a man. He hates the white men for that. Before the missionaries came, he says, only ten or fifteen years ago, Hawaiians honored their men-who-would-be-women. But the missionaries said it was worse than fornication, worse than stealing, worse than murder. Finally the people got ashamed of it."

He looked at Sima crazily. "So I have no home there, either."

"You must follow your medicine," said Sima emphatically.

"The whites would kill me," the boy said simply. "I like very big men, big or fat. Much older than me. Like Mr. Skye." He shrugged. "Mr. Skye would probably kill me."

He looked at Sima affectionately. "I just wanted you to know," he said. "You are my friend."

Sima was late, and it was dawn. Flare didn't feel much like drinking the coffee in his hand. He could have used a brandy. He didn't dare, but he felt the need of it. When he quit drinking, he told himself he'd have a cup of cheer on every St. Paddy's Day, to honor his ancestors, and that would be all.

The coffee was ready. Where was Sima?

He'd promised the lad a treat, and a real treat it was. He was going to take him to Yves Balmat and buy the boyo an American horse to replace the decrepit Messenger. Old Balmat had some good horses, and Flare had more money, at the moment, than he knew what to do with.

Surely, St. Paddy's Day. If he never drank at all, he'd have to look down on himself as a teetotaler, like Dr. Full. Flare had never met a teetotaler he could bear.

But here it was, dawn, and Flare was on watch. Sima must be preoccupied with that lass, because the lad was looking forward to his surprise. Flare raised his cup and sipped. Cold already.

Dr. McLoughlin had asked Flare to take some watch because Flare would be sober. The HBC didn't trade liquor to its employees except from Christmas to New Year's, but no one could control the whiskey, not really. Especially now, when a ship was in, and the sailors were celebrating a few days in port.

Flare remembered when he'd thought it was fun, all that boozing and brawling and gambling and whoring. To sober eyes, it didn't look like fun. He was sure those who got bashed up, or knifed, thought it less than amusing. Not that Flare would mind a wager or two, for sport.

He'd best make some rounds. Flare got up and started walking. His legs worked stiffly in the cold. He'd walk through all the camps and clumps of huts and see who'd gotten half frozen and get them to a fire.

He'd taken care of his own before going to sleep. Mr. Skye had gone on one of his epic drunks and was now in the second day of an epic sleeping-it-off. The man got drunker than anyone Flare had ever seen—anyone who lived through it—and stayed drunk longer. And when he passed out, he seemed dead, and it took him longer to sleep it off. Then the hangover required longer to get over. Everything about Mr. Skye was double-sized.

Flare saw a figure huddled in blankets, stretched out on the ground. It was old Langlois. Flare stirred him with a foot. The old man slapped at the foot. Well, if he'd survived the night, the sun would bring him around. Good thing the winter here was mild.

Sima was in Flare's lean-to with one of the Frenchie

girls, which was no doubt why he was late. At least it wasn't a whore. Flare had encouraged this liaison as much as he could. He'd even used the gift of red cloth and the lass's parents to encourage it. Nothing to keep a young lad close to camp like a willing lass.

True, Sima had promised to go to the mission. Meant to go right after the new year. Meant most earnestly.

True, Flare had a sort of wager with Dr. Full about who would sway the lad, Dr. Full to the way of heaven, or Flare to the ways of the world.

What was more the way of the world than a lively piece of poontang?

And if Sima never got to the mission, why, perhaps one heaven would be lost but another found. Perhaps.

Flare thought it was a mountain cat crying at first, wailing its strange sound that parodied a baby's cry. But it came from the dock. Then it grew, and grew, and became a series of raucous, hacking sobs. And then a scream. A bellow of wound and rage.

Then it scared Flare to his bones. The voice was Sima's.

They were down by the pilings, in the mud.

Sima was on his hands and knees, like he wanted to touch the figure and couldn't bring himself to do it. He sat back on his haunches and hollered at the sky.

The figure was Palea.

His skull was bashed in. It had bled quarts into the mud.

His face was cut and bruised, as from fists.

His cock was cut off and stuffed in his mouth.

"Aye," said Skye, "bloody sure, one of their bloody sailors." He threw it in McLoughlin's face for no reason. The anger was only half volume for Mr. Skye, subdued by his hangover.

Sima sat and stared out the window, his face glazed.

Flare didn't know what to do for Sima. Right now the only thing Flare could do was insist on an investigation, which McLoughlin was doing as well, so no point in pushing. The question was: What would Captain Plummer do?

Flare was already weary of it all. Weary of McLoughlin's trying to overawe with his size and demeanor. Weary of having two huge men in one small room at the same time. Weary of the pitiful story told by a body found in the mud. Weary of trying to persuade the captain to do something and that hadn't even begun yet. Plummer was taking his time, taking his bloody time, a way of saying, I'm the captain of a great ship, and you are nobody. Just like a stinking Brit.

Skye said he knew damn well what happened. The king's Navy—no, queen's Navy, he kept having to correct himself—was full of Rogers, which was nautical talk for buggerers. Jolly Rogers, indeed, Skye called them. One third of the seamen were queer, another third weren't queer but weren't too particular about what they fucked, and the last third spent their time fighting off the first two. Skye said this last with both his hands on his belaying pins.

And bloody sure the lad Palea had propositioned one of those seaman who fought. Since Palea was a wog, a nigger, an Injun, or some other inferior of an Englishman, as they considered it, the seaman did what was in his heart many a time: He murdered.

Captain Plummer rapped softly and came in without waiting for an answer. He was a ferocious-looking man of an imperious eye, a slash of beard, and a substantial belly. In full uniform, thought Flare, so he intends to overawe us, too.

McLoughlin made the introductions. He included Sima, but Plummer offered the lad just a nod, not a hand.

"What news, Plummer?" demanded McLoughlin. So the emp wasn't kowtowing to the fellow.

The captain's face went huge with pleasure. "Gentlemen, we have the culprit. The midnight watch noticed a scuffle"—the bloody bastard termed it a *scuffle*—"made note of the fighter's name, and made a report. This morning the first mate and I confronted the man, an able seaman, with the facts, and pointed out the marks on his knuckles and the blood on his clothes. We have our methods. He's confessed."

"You'll bring him here," said McLoughlin with a snarl. "I want him."

"Oh, I don't know, Dr. McLoughlin."

Now the lad will see British justice, thought Flare. No sea captain will turn one of his crew over to someone else's justice.

"I'll have him and I'll have him now, Captain Plummer. He's committed murder in the dominion of the Hudson's Bay Company, which I represent."

"Perhaps a word in private, Dr. McLoughlin," suggested Plummer.

"These men will stay," answered McLoughlin. "They were his friends, and want to see him get justice."

"Yes, well," said Plummer with affected breeziness. "Perhaps they want to administer so-called justice themselves. Perhaps they don't know what justice is."

Not being bloody gentlemen like yourselves, thought Flare, and one of us a wog, a nigger, or an Injun.

"He must be punished," said McLoughlin.

"The Royal Navy will punish him," said Plummer.

It was simple, Flare knew. The Hudson's Bay Company would try the man and hang him, quickly. The Royal Navy would give him twenty lashes. Or forty, depending on the whim of the captain.

"He committed the crime on land, under my authority," said McLoughlin.

Sima spoke up. "What is wrong? You know who killed Palea, yes?"

Flare smiled to himself. Good for you, lad. True, you

don't have enough coup to talk in council, but speak up for your friend.

Plummer got apoplectic-looking. Flare hoped for a stroke. Sima kept at him. "Now we must get rid of the murderer."

Plummer burst out, "McLoughlin, this is intolerable."

Dr. McLoughlin held up a flattened palm to Sima. "If I know the lad's customs as I think I do, *Captain* Plummer," began McLoughlin, stressing the title, "he does not mean hanging the seaman. Do you, Sima?"

Flare loved it. McLoughlin was insulting Plummer by inviting the Injun lad to talk.

Sima shook his head hard. "He must be banishèd."

Flare excused the boy for the quaint pronunciation. He did that to words he'd only come across in a poem or a Scripture Miss Jewel read to him.

"I'll be d-damned," said Plummer, sputtering, "if I'll let . . ."

McLoughlin held up both hands to silence everyone. "Yes, Captain Plummer," he acknowledged, "this has gotten irregular. My friends are overeager in their pursuit of justice. Understandable. It is perhaps beneficial, though, to hear what local customs require. Indians generally banish those who shed the blood of their tribesmen. They do not kill them.

"Nevertheless, what I now ask from you, Captain Plummer," McLoughlin went on smoothly, "is the person of this seaman, delivered in chains to me. Would an hour be too short a time?"

Ah, it warms the heart, thought Flare, to see McLoughlin insult the fellow. The Scots have a little of the Irish spirit.

Captain Plummer rose. He had no tolerance for affront, especially deliberate affront.

"Gentlemen," he said, "I advise you to be at the dock in one hour. You will see the culprit punished." He eyed them one by one and gave a smile of pleasure. "It may interest you to know that since the victim was a Wog, the punishment will be reduced by half. Since he was a pervert, half again." And he stalked toward the door.

"Captain," called Flare. Plummer turned his head in his pompous way.

"I have something for you." Flare stepped forward with his hand extended. Plummer looked at the hand, puzzled.

Flare cocked it and slapped Plummer in the face. Hard.

Plummer grabbed for Flare.

A huge pair of hands clamped him by the shoulders. "Don't!" commanded Skye. "I suggest, Captain, that you keep your person on board from this hour forward. It wouldn't be safe to come ashore."

"Nor safe for your men, either," added McLoughlin.

Sima, Flare, Skye, and McLoughlin stood shoulder to shoulder on the dock, watching the great merchant ship. She readied lines and sails. When all seemed in order, an officer gave commands. A seaman was hoisted by a rope tied around his hands. Another officer took a whip and lashed the man's bare back.

The seaman screamed. Blood washed his back. Sima imagined nearby sailors got splattered.

Sima forced back the dry heaves and trotted away. Flare caught up with him. "Barbaric," said Sima.

When they looked back, from far up the hill, she had weighed anchor and was moving.

"What now, lad?" Flare asked quietly. Sima was coming along, but he still acted dazed.

"I want," Sima began. "I want to go to the mission."

Christ.

Bloody Christ.

Flare forced self-control. "And why the bloody hell not? Be hot around here for a bit anyway." Funny, it was

Skye who always worried about getting into trouble with the Royal Navy.

Sima turned full to Flare, his face stiff, full of knowing what it meant. "I want to stay the winter there. At least."

Flare said weakly, "So why don't we the bloody hell get going?"

_____ Part Four _____
LEARNING EXPERIENCES

Chapter
Sixteen

Flare made jokes to himself about delivering his son unto somebody's God, like Abraham or some bloody patriarch he couldn't remember. That's the way he felt about it.

Delivering him on a fine new horse, too. Sima was very pleased about the big American horse Flare bought him from Balmat. A young horse, not yet well broke, but Sima looked forward to training it.

He seemed morose about the death of his friend. He mentioned white-man's disease several times, words he and Palea evidently had for the eradicable prejudices of whites. The lad's learning, Flare thought sadly.

On the way up the Willamette River to Mission Bottom, Flare also played out awful scenes in his mind. The worst was that Dr. Full had married every woman at the mission, installed them all in different bedrooms of his mansion, and Miss Jewel wore her bustle in front. That was a jokey way of saying she was very pregnant.

The route was simply up the Willamette a couple of days to what was infelicitously known as Mission Bottom. Flare was irritated with how the country had changed. Now there were two little settlements of Frenchies along the way at an area called French Prairie, men retired from the HBC. Flare knew almost every man jack of them, and was glad to see them.

He told Sima why. They all had Indian families, and wouldn't abandon them for civilization. The wives and their offspring wouldn't like civilization a bit. Flare didn't mention that the civilized people wouldn't like them.

They went straight to find Miss Jewel, and to hell with Dr. Full.

Though Full was already married, it was almost as bad as Flare dreamed.

"Meet my housemate, Billy Wells," said Miss Jewel, indicating a gangly, embarrassed-looking boy in his mid twenties. Sima shook the fellow's hand, so Flare had to force himself. You acted better when you were showing your son how.

Housemate? Was Miss Jewel married?

Flare watched him shake hands with Sima and make conventional noises. The fellow had the shy-smiling, I-ain't-nothing humility of the Bible-poxed American back-woodsman. He practically scraped and bowed when he met anyone. And he was damned good-looking in a boy-ishly American way. Flare despised him on sight.

"He and I live most scandalously," Miss Jewel said with an impish smile. "Come see."

It was as small a structure as you could call a cabin. It made Flare long for an honest tipi, which would have been bigger, warmer, and more comfortable. A divider of flour sacks stitched loosely together hung down the mid-dle. There was room for a cot on each side, and almost nothing more.

"The family I was with, the Leslies, tried to make me a servant. I told Dr. Full I wouldn't put up with that," Miss Jewel said. "When Billy proposed, Dr. Full thought this would be all right for a while. I think, actually, Dr. Full wanted me under the sway of a man, even a little bit." She gave a merry smile to tell Flare how much good that would do anyhow. "Turns out to be more private than being in with a man, wife, and three children." She winked at Billy. "Billy and I will be married, probably next summer. He's finding it hard to wait that long, but he will.

"Billy is a carpenter," she said proudly, "and he's in training to be a minister of the Gospel."

She took time to explain to Sima what engagement was, how marriage was something sanctioned by God, and the like. She was good about that, and had a way of explaining that treated Sima as an equal. She didn't say why they were waiting six more months to marry.

"We've been expecting you," she told Sima. "Let me show you where you'll live."

They were putting Sima in with Alan Wineson, the blacksmith, and his family. The cabin was a little bigger than Miss Jewel and Billy's, and was split into bedrooms for the couple and for the children, who would now include Sima.

She showed them the schoolroom as well, just one room. Sima would be her fourth student, Miss Jewel said, and they were all teenage boys. Sima was ahead of the other three.

"The prodigal son returns, I see," came the voice. Dr. Full-of-Himself.

Full made them coffee. It was weak, but he gave Sima long sweetening to please the boy. Full made himself ingratiating, with an edge of mockery for Flare's benefit. Flare wondered if Sima saw that.

Oh, the man was high on himself. Surely he'd feared Sima wouldn't come. Now he would be full of bribes. Flare had to tell himself some of them would even be good for the boy. Sima would get all the instruction and attention he wanted. And then some. Fattening the goose for the slaughter.

Well, there wasn't going to be any slaughter.

After a while Full made his excuses, and said goodbye to Flare. "I hope you'll come back for services on Sunday," said Full. "I'm going to invite Sima to tell the story of his miracle."

Miracle, after all, was it? The man was unconvinced until he saw how convenient the idea of miracle was.

"I'll be there," said Flare.

"And where will your wanderings take you next?" said Full, smiling hugely at the thought of getting rid of Flare.

"They will bring me near the influence of the prophets of heresy," said Flare. "I mean to stay the winter at French Prairie, where me friends are. Perhaps I'll be undone by one or two of your heretical sermons."

Full looked downright mean. Flare wondered if Sima saw the look and understood. "Attending our church will give you something more for your next confession, as I understand it," said Full with a phony smile.

Flare supposed killing was forgivable if you did it to save your son.

Miss Jewel covered for Dr. Full by gushing with pleasure at Flare's staying. She and Sima walked him to his horses.

Flare had to ask. "And why is it you and Billy are waiting so long to marry? I'd have ye bedded tomorrow."

She blushed. Flare had never seen her do that before. It was as becoming as everything else she did.

"He has asked another for her hand," Miss Jewel replied. "Before I arrived last fall, he wrote back to the States to ask a Boston woman who wants to come here as a teacher to marry him. He's barely met her." She fussed with a button. Flare wished she'd let him fuss with her buttons.

"Things are changed now, of course," she went on. "But I insist that he set things right. In a couple of weeks we'll send letters down to Vancouver for the winter express. He'll write her, withdrawing his offer. When she responds, we'll be married."

"And living like that," said Flare with a smile. "The flesh is weak, Miss Jewel."

She smiled broadly. "All flesh is, Mr. O'Flaherty. Which gives us an opportunity to rise above temptation."

And she touched his arm and pecked his cheek.

Bloody woman.

"I never promised to rise above it," he whispered close in her ear, and she laughed gaily.

Flare offered Sima a hand.

They smiled and shook and said nothing.

Flare wanted to embrace him. Instead he rode toward French Prairie, away from his son.

"Cleanliness is next to godliness," said Hazel Jick.

Sima had no idea what that meant, but he didn't like the look on her face. She was a fat woman, old enough to be a grandmother, with iron-gray hair tied back in a bun, and a big frown. She looked mean.

She ordered him to get his clothes off. *All* of them, she said with a scowl.

It was the day before Sima was supposed to speak in church. He had to get scrubbed, they said, because the Leslie family was lending him some nice clothes for his talk, and he couldn't get into them "like that." He didn't know what "like that" meant. He guessed it was one of those white-man expressions that meant something like, "You're an Indian and there's no helping it."

Today Mrs. Jick was going to "do something about it." Sima was worried. He stood naked in Mrs. Jick's cabin, shivering.

She poured water from the kettle on the fire into the big tub. She snatched Sima's clothes—everything, shirt, breechcloth, blanket, moccasins—and threw them right into the flames.

Sima dashed for the moccasins. Since he uttered not a sound, she didn't catch him until he had them out. Then she snatched them away, pushed Sima back, and threw them back onto the fire.

Sima grabbed them again, scorching his fingers.

"Lice," Mrs. Jick said harshly, sticking out a demanding hand.

"All right," Siam said meekly. He took his knife, cut his grandmother's beadwork off, and gave the moccasins to Mrs. Jick. She stuck them straight into the coals.

She put one finger into the water in the tub, looked at Sima sternly, and ordered, "In."

He stepped straight in and straight back out, whimpering softly.

"It's hot," Mrs. Jick said, "but no hotter than you need."

In two more minutes, after two more efforts, he was in. Then she poured more hot water in. Sima wondered if he was going to cook into soup.

She dunked his head backward, "to get all your filthy hair in the water," she said. "Cleanliness is next to godliness," she repeated sternly.

Then she began to scrub.

Hazel Jick saved grain sacks for when she had to scrub one—they were coarsely woven, and scraped.

You couldn't scrub these Indians too hard. You needed to take off one layer of skin, was what you needed to do.

Lordamercy.

You needed lye soap, too. Hazel made plenty of it. That was one of her jobs. Was, even before her husband died.

Dr. Full came in. He was a good man. Understood that the Injuns needed a firm hand. He stood in that peculiar way of his, like he was always posing for someone to draw a picture of him. He was a lordawful self-satisfied man.

"The first step in making you acceptable in the sight of God is to get you clean," Dr. Full said to Sima.

Ought to have said to rid him not only of the lordawful dirt but also the vermin. If Hazel needed proof that they lived in darkness, the lice would have been it.

"It hurts, Dr. Full," Sima said faintly. He was ashamed, as well he should have been.

Hazel scrubbed hard. This one was squeamish, like all of them, but it would do him no good.

"Getting the body clean is a sign," Dr. Full said to

the boy. Maybe talking would distract him, Hazel thought, and that was all the better.

"A sign of the willingness to scourge the lower nature," Dr. Full continued. Hazel would scourge his filthy body. She doubted Dr. Full could do as well for his filthy soul.

"Put in one way, the task of the human being who would come unto the Lord is to scourge himself of his lower nature."

Maybe, thought Hazel, but the good doctor didn't add that lower was maybe the only nature Injuns had.

"I'll do my best, sir," said the boy. Dr. Full had taught him to be polite, anyway.

Lordamighty, look at them toes. She held them apart for Dr. Full to see. Webbed together, like the boy was a duck. She looked at the doctor significantly and finally dropped the foot.

What was the point? If that wasn't the mark of the beast, she didn't know what would be. And that was with him being half white.

Hazel wondered about this mission to the savages, but it was only her job to do what her Savior told her to do, not to question His ways.

Anyone could see, though, that some critters was higher and some was lower, and an Injun was not one of your highest animals. Forgive me, Lord Jesus, Hazel thought. I know You called me and Carl on this mission. It's not up to me to question the Lord's marching orders, I just march.

But why did God take Carl away then? And leave me alone in this cussed wilderness?

Lordamighty, there wasn't no answer to some questions the wicked human mind could think up. Hazel told herself she'd best leave the figuring to the Good Book, or at least to the preachers.

Dear Jesus, the kid was about to cry. She told him to get out. He jumped like he'd sat on a cactus.

Well, if they didn't want to be scrubbed hard, why

did they let themselves get so filthy? Vermin living in their hair—disgusting!

She made him lie on the table on his back, spread his hair out, and looked for more lice. She thought she'd killed about all of them. She brushed his hair hard to get the tangles and the little carcasses out. The boy acted like he wanted to holler every stroke.

She gave room to Dr. Full. He always wanted to watch this part closely.

She checked Sima's crotch hair carefully. That was the most revolting, lice in their crotches. She brushed the hair out good. As far as she was concerned, no Injun would ever be clean enough to marry a white woman.

Then she slapped Sima on the bottom and told him to put the new clothes on. They were nice clothes for everyday, once belonging to Mrs. Jick's son and considerably repaired by Mrs. Jick, but the savage wouldn't appreciate that.

Hazel would repeat the entire business next week, and the week after—you had to.

She grinned to herself. The savage wouldn't appreciate that, either.

She hefted the tub of water to take it outside and dump it.

Dr. Full took advantage of Mrs. Jick's leaving to make his point. "Sima, we have scourged your body of its dirt. It was painful. I have an important question for you. Don't answer today—think about it. Are you willing to scourge your soul of its lower nature?"

The boy was big-eyed, clearly distraught. "I don't know, Dr. Full," he said, and hurried out of the cabin.

So, in his mind, Dr. Full addressed the boy's earthly father. Now, Mr. O'Flaherty, the question hangs in the balance. Will your son be of things earthly or heavenly? Will he become like you? Or like me?

The question was serious, of course. A soul hung in the balance. But it also amused Dr. Full.—He knew the answer.

* * *

Sima sat beside the pulpit in a frock coat. Flare could hardly believe it. Coat, white shirt, trousers, neck ornament, boots, the lot. All the lad had kept was his body. On the other hand, his hair was still to his shoulder blades, and free-flowing. He was an impressive figure of a lad—slender, lithe, handsome.

Dr. Full was right. Sima would make one hell of an example. He made the Reverend David Leslie, sitting beside him behind the pulpit, look rotund and ridiculous.

Full introduced him only briefly, saying, "The youth's story will speak for itself."

Sima stood and told of his life. He was born, he said, to a Shoshone woman. She died giving him birth. His father was a British trapper the people called Hairy. This father left before Sima was born. Sima was raised by his grandparents, but he was never accepted by the people. They mocked their young of mixed blood, and made it hard for them to become men, to marry, to become one of the people. So Sima decided to find his father and become a white man.

Flare noticed the lad's English was pretty damn good. Sima had more brains than most of these missionaries. If he had more sense, too, they'd be gone from this place before long.

This decision to find his father, Sima said, was a great point in his life. Like you set out in a great ship on a great ocean, not know where you land. He had to go into a different world. Set out to walk one thousand miles alone, very hard and dangerous. Come among new people. Learn new language. Make self new person.

Took first few steps, came miracle. Fell down. Broke leg but fine now, he said with a grin. Went into little death—no conscious. Woke up in new world. Found by white people. Miles gone, danger gone. New world not in thousand miles, but in pass—through little death.

Now making self new person every day. Glad to be here.

Sima turned to sit down, but Dr. Full put a hand on his shoulder. "Sima," he said, "do you seek your earthly father or your heavenly father?"

Sima hesitated. "Both," he said.

Dr. Full beamed at the congregation.

"Do you understand that seeking your earthly father can be a way of expressing your need for a heavenly father?"

Sima looked uncertain. The lad wanted to please. "Yes," he said.

"Will you accept this mission's offer to help you find your heavenly father?"

Now he seemed to smile directly at Flare and said, "You bet!"

After the service almost all the adults went up to Sima and congratulated him on the great voyage he'd undertaken. And congratulated Dr. Full and Miss Jewel on the wonderful work they'd done with the boy.

Flare thought it was a great voyage, too, and he thought Sima was navigating well.

He was very impressed by the way Dr. Full, by putting the right frame around a picture, made it look like the picture he wanted.

Chapter

Seventeen

When Sima came back from changing clothes, Flare and Miss Jewel were waiting, ready to walk to the Leslies for dinner.

Sima showed them his new white-man outfit—not the borrowed clothes for his talk in church, but the ones Mrs. Jick had given him. Pants. You had to undo some buttons and drop the front to urinate (he used Miss Jewel's proper words) and lower the whole outfit to defecate. He looked at Flare conspiratorially. Yes, they were inconvenient, compared to a breechcloth. Shirt—he liked that pretty well. Boots—he hated those, because they hurt. Miss Jewel said his feet would be better when he had some socks. Flare chuckled and said they'd be better when he got some more moccasins.

He told Flare about the assault on his hair, not mentioning the lower hair, but he could see from his suppressed smiles that Flare knew.

"White people don't have enough brotherly spirit to give residence to tiny creatures," Flare said with a grin.

Sima didn't think it was funny.

Sima got through the dinner well enough. He wasn't used to chairs, and found using a fork awkward, but was able to eat the chicken with his hands. He thought Dr. Full gave him a funny look once, when he was tearing apart a thigh with relish. He'd developed a name for that expression—the Well-he's-an-Indian look. For dessert they had something new to Sima, blueberry pie. He thought the best thing about the white people was the wonderful sweets they made.

The worst was the jokes they made. When he didn't get them, he felt anxious again, left out, looking in from the outside. The jokes of other teenagers were the most painful. Sometimes Sima thought the kids were making fun of him. Miss Jewel had a way of knowing when he was feeling that way, and gave him a warm smile.

She had her own troubles, though. She and Reverend Leslie could barely stand each other. The tension between hung like a choking smoke in the air. She thought he and Mrs. Leslie had tried to make her their servant (like a slave, Sima understood). He was a portly, mannered fellow with a self-conscious way of speaking, so Sima couldn't tell when he was joking and when he was acting important. Reverend Leslie irritated Miss Jewel often, and he didn't care. Sima had an expression for this, too: white people.

But this was Sima's time. He had talked to Flare about it and made up his mind. He would learn. He would put himself forward. He would become one of them. This afternoon he would do that by sharing part of himself.

"May I tell a story?" he said in a pause. Dinner was over, and they were drinking coffee around the fireplace. It was wintertime, so he could tell stories.

Everyone look at him uncertainly. "I thank you for your stories," Sima plunged forward. He looked at them one by one, adults and children alike, taking confidence from the eyes of Flare and Miss Jewel, afraid to look closely at Dr. Full, Reverend Leslie, or their wives. "I am delight to know your ancient and honored stories of Jesus, John the Baptist, King David, Job, and others." He'd been surprised to hear the stories just any time of year, and not in winter only, but he liked the stories. "They are . . . " He didn't know quite what to say about them. To him they showed some connection with Spirit. "They are beautiful stories.

"I would like to give you in return one of the stories of my mother's people, a tale of Pachee Goyo, who lived before the memories of the grandfathers of the oldest men."

He looked at Flare for support and got a smile. "Pachee Goyo is a big man among us. He's called Baldy, because he's losing his hair and what's left is gray.

"One day he and his brother Pia-wi-he, which means Big Knife, went to the lake near Wind River where buffalo live underwater.

"Among my people, my *other* people, this lake is a frightening place. A white buffalo was drowned there once. In the winter you can still hear his roar carried across the ice by the wind. People are afraid to go there. If you want to become a man of medicine, of *poha*, you must sleep there one night in the winter. Many men have failed this test."

Sima was watching his audience. That word "medicine" made him nervous. Whites seemed to speak it mockingly, not knowing it meant power of spirit. Still, he thought he had their attention, especially the kids'. Maybe Dr. Full was looking a little superior, but it was going well.

"When Pachee Goyo and Big Knife went there, the lake was not frozen. After they camped overnight, Big Knife suggested they hunt the buffalo who live underwater there. Big Knife said he would bring a buffalo out of the lake. Pachee Goyo was just to wait on the shore and shoot it with arrows when it came out.

"So Big Knife waded into the water with nothing but his breechcloth and a rawhide thong. Suddenly the lake whipped up in high waves. Pachee Goyo shot angrily at the whitecaps with his arrows, one right after the other, cursing the lake for drowning his brother. When all his arrows were gone, he threw his bow into the lake and hightailed it.

"When the lake calmed, out came Big Knife, leading a buffalo. He wondered what had happened to Pachee Goyo, who was supposed to shoot the creature. Big Knife picked a broken arrow out of the water and killed the buffalo.

"Then he saw their great-uncle Basee Wauts the Snail. But Snail had not seen Pachee Goyo. Big Knife butchered the buffalo and gave Snail some fat and the stomach filled with water and asked him to find Pachee Goyo and give him these things.

"Old man Snail crept over mountains and rivers and finally spotted Baldy in a desert. Pachee Goyo was on his knees, very still, his head under a cactus plant. When Snail touched him with a cane, Pachee Goyo complained that his meditation was spoiled.

"Snail gave him the food and water. Pachee Goyo wolfed it down and hurried back to the lake.

"That evening while the two brothers were broiling buffalo steaks, Snail strolled into camp. They gave him meat to take home, but before leaving, he warned them: 'Cook lots of meat,' he said, 'because Pachee Goyo is a big eater. Don't build a fire at night. And don't sleep on the ground—build a platform in a tree. Take the meat up there so you won't get hungry.'

"They did as they were told. When Big Knife fell asleep in the tree, Pachee Goyo finished all the meat and was still sitting there hungry. He told Big Knife he was going down to build a fire and cook some more meat.

"'Don't you dare!' asserted Big Knife. To keep Pachee Goyo from going down, Big Knife gave him the rest of his own meat.

"When Pachee Goyo finished this meat, he was still hungry. He told Big Knife he was going down the tree to build a fire and cook more. Complaining that Pachee Goyo just wouldn't learn, Big Knife said all right.

"Soon Pachee Goyo was eating by the fire. Suddenly he heard a great whirring. The trees trembled, and the fire nearly went out. A huge horned owl lighted and sat by the fire, watching Pachee Goyo.

"Pachee Goyo offered him a legbone. The owl just looked at Pachee Goyo. Thinking maybe Owl wanted to be fed, Pachee Goyo rubbed the bone against the bird's beak and tried to pry its mouth open. Owl didn't budge. Finally Pachee Goyo got disgusted. He clobbered Owl in the head with the bone and knocked it unconscious. Then he went back to eating."

Some of the kids tittered. Evidently they thought Giant Owl was pretty silly stuff.

"Owl's claws shot out," Sima went on, "and grabbed Pachee Goyo. Baldy screamed for Big Knife's help. He sobbed and cried. But Big Knife lay in the tree quietly. He knew that Owl would gladly get him, too. He thought, Oh, Pachee Goyo, why didn't you listen to me and Snail?

"Owl rose up. It flapped its wings. It lifted off with Pachee Goyo in its great claws. As they soared in the sky, the last thing Big Knife heard was Pachee Goyo screaming, 'Big Kn-i-i-fe!'"

"Very good!" exclaimed Dr. Full, jumping up from his chair. "A wonderful children's tale!"

"But there's more," said Sima.

Flare saw the lad was offended by the interruption.

Dr. Full looked around at the Christian adults. He spread his arms. "It's very entertaining, but I'm not certain of the influence . . . "

"Let him finish," said Flare with a growl. "It's one of his people's sacred stories."

"Well, that's what concerns me. What do you think, Reverend Leslie? The subtle suggestion that this . . . invention is like a Bible story . . . "

"Objectionable," affirmed David Leslie.

"Let him finish," Flare snapped.

Miss Jewel intervened. "Sima, would you like to tell the rest of your story?"

"Yes," the lad said simply, with an emphatic nod.

"Most of your audience is eager to hear it," Miss Jewel said. She glared at Dr. Full until he sat back down. Flare thought, He'll make you pay later, Maggie.

"Giant Horned Owl carried Pachee Goyo over mountains, over plains, over ocean," said Sima.

"At last they landed on a small, rocky island. Owl set Pachee Goyo down on a rocky cliff among thousands of skeletons of human beings. The bird teetered over to the fresh corpse of a person. It tore open the body with its big claws and drank bright, live-giving blood from the trunk."

Dr. Full and Reverend Leslie were showing their disgust in their faces for the benefit of the others. Flare wanted to throttle them. But Sima, lost in his narrative, didn't seem to notice.

"Then Owl teetered over to the swamp and drank fresh water. Then it spread its wings, flapped, and headed out across the sea for more victims.

"With the sound of the whirring of the huge wings still in his ears, Pachee Goyo got up and walked around to check out his circumstances. By the shore, among cattails and grasses, smoke rose from a brush hut. Pachee Goyo walked down and peeked in.

"An old woman, a *hepit-soo,* sat by the fire. Her skin was stretched tight over her old bones. She invited Pachee Goyo in and gave him eggs to eat, boiled eggs of ducks and geese.

" 'Many years ago,' she said, 'when I was young, Giant Owl carried me here. It never bothers me. It only eats the others, the ones it brings back.

" 'I know how you can get away,' she said. 'Is there a fresh body for it to eat?'

" 'Yes,' said Pachee Goyo, 'half of one.' Now he felt ready to listen to the advice of an older person.

" 'When it comes back,' said the old woman, the *hepit-soo,* 'lay down where it put you. Now listen. Every time it eats, the bird drinks from the swamp, always in the same place. Take this bow and these arrows. Hide them now behind the rock where it drinks.'

"Pachee Goyo asked where she got the bow and arrows. The old woman said most of the warriors Owl brought back were carrying quivers and bows.

"'When you've hidden the weapons,' the old woman went on, 'find some obsidian and break it into tiny pieces. Put the pieces into the blood of the corpse. Owl will drink the obsidian in the blood, and the glass will cut up its insides.

"'When Owl is finished drinking, it will head for the swamp. Then you've got to move fast and get behind the rock. Owl will stoop for a long time, drinking. Then let fly with every arrow you've got!'

"When Pachee Goyo finished his preparations, he went back to the old woman. She had no more instructions, and she heard Owl coming. 'Get back where it left you,' she said, 'the exact position it left you. You're lucky there's a fresh corpse or you'd be its meal.'

"Pachee Goyo ran back and played dead in his original position. The huge Owl landed, tore at the fresh corpse, and drank the blood with obsidian in it. Finally the bird wobbled down to the swamp, lowered its head, and began to drink.

"Pachee Goyo ran for his life to the rock, grabbed the bow and arrows, and volleyed arrows into Owl.

"The great bird turned, staggered, and fell dead."

Sima saw he had his audience now.

"Pachee Goyo ran back to the *hepit-soo,* the old woman, and told her he'd killed Giant Horned Owl. She gave him some sinew and loaned him her obsidian ax. 'Here's what you need to do,' she said. 'Chop the wings off with my ax and sew them together with this sinew to make a boat. Put dirt on the bottom. Gather up lots of firewood and pile it on one end. But you must build fires at night—*only* at night.

"'When you're finished with that, gather every goose

and duck egg you can find and bring them to me. I'll boil them for you. On the journey you'll throw one egg into the ocean every day. Now get to it!'

"After a while Pachee Goyo got all his jobs done. Then he said to the old woman, 'What are you going to do?'

"'I want to stay here and live my life," she said. She wished him good sailing and good luck finding his people.

"Pachee Goyo sailed on the wing boat for days and nights and nights and days. He threw an egg into the sea every day and built a fire every night. He looked out over the vast expanse of ocean and wondered where he would land, when he would land, whether he would land.

"Eventually he threw his last egg into the sea. That night he built a fire with the last of his wood. He watched the fire sadly, wondering what would happen to him when it burned out. Finally he put his bow and arrows on the embers to keep the fire going a little longer.

"Suddenly, from the darkness, came glad sounds, laughter, shouts.

"It was his *ata*, uncles Bazook the Otter, Babegee the Weasel, and Baboca the Muskrat! They saw the last glow of the fire, guessed it was their nephew Pachee Goyo, and swam out to help him.

"When they crawled onto the wing boat, they were laughing. But Pachee Goyo pulled a long face. 'What's going to happen to me?' he wailed. 'The fire's almost out.'

"They said in a chorus, 'We'll pull you to shore before it dies.'

"They took turns pulling, Weasel first, then Muskrat. The two of them got the boat halfway to shore but one by one plopped back into the boat, drained. With the embers barely glowing, Otter jumped into the water. He pulled the boat terrifically fast. Just as the last fire died, he pulled them out onto the shore.

"Otter lay on the sand a while, exhausted. Then

Pachee Goyo's uncles advised him to spend the night in a tree, and left."

"In the night came the Joahwayho, the scaly man-eaters."

Sima saw the kids were transfixed. And Flare and Miss Jewel, even Mrs. Full and Mrs. Leslie. The fat Reverend Leslie was staring off into space. Dr. Full was fidgeting. Sima wondered why they didn't give the respect of attention to a story.

"Pachee Goyo," he went on, "was perched on a branch trying to sleep when he heard their low, growly voices. They poked about in the trees, looking for human beings. Pachee Goyo could hear them muttering, 'Nothing here. Ugh. Nothing here.'

"Finally the man-eaters came to the tree Pachee Goyo was perched in, and stuck their long poles upward, searching. One jabbed Pachee Goyo in the stomach.

"'I feel a person,' rumbled one of the Joahwayho, 'right here in this tree.'

"Pachee Goyo quietly climbed higher.

"The sticks jabbed at the air.

"'No one's up there,' said a Joahwayho. 'Let's try another tree.'

"'No,' insisted one of the scaly monsters. 'There's a human being in this tree—let's shake him out.'

"So they shook the tree with all their strength. It was like an earthquake. Pachee Goyo hung on with all his might. He got banged around. His knuckles and shins got barked—his head got banged. His teeth got rattled. When Father Sun began to make the sky light, his fingers were worn out—he was about to give up and lose his grip and come crashing out of the tree.

"Suddenly the tree stopped shaking. Pachee Goyo heard sounds of struggle below, sounds of hitting and thumping and kicking. Otter, Muskrat, and Weasel had heard the monsters stomping around and come to his rescue!

"The uncles wrestled the monsters—they broke their arms and hands. 'We are scared!' wailed the Joahwayho. They ran off as fast as their scaly legs could carry them."

One of the Leslie girls clapped her hands. Dan Full cackled out loud, and got a sharp look from his stepfather.

"When Pachee Goyo climbed down, his uncles told him about the perils on the way home. They gave him some food. They sewed him some moccasins with rawhide soles, and gave him some thick leggings to wear. Pachee Goyo thanked them sincerely and set off, set off again into the unknown, set off toward home.

"He walked for days. Once he came to some ground covered with sharp fragments of obsidian. There he pulled on the heavy-soled moccasins, and they got him through. Thinking more and more of his people and their country, the land of smoking waters, he hurried.

"He walked for many more days, digging roots and killing small game for food. When he came to a desert, he put his thick leggings on and walked straight through, knowing there would be rattlesnakes everywhere. The snakes slithered about, they coiled, they whirred, they struck at his legs, they bit his leggings. On the far side he stopped and looked at his leggings—they were slimy with venom. He took them off carefully and traveled on."

Sima thought his audience might be getting tired now, but he could not end the story improperly. He plunged forward into the last trials.

"Pachee Goyo came to a great gorge. He looked down in, but it was completely dark. Suddenly an owl hooted. While the hoot sounded, it lit up the entire gorge. When it fell silent, the gorge was dark. Again—hoot and light, silence and darkness.

"Pachee Goyo got ready and timed the hoots. When the next one came, he ran and jumped with all his strength. He sailed all the way across the gorge, and sailed into daylight.

"That night Pachee Goyo slept on a hill in moonlight. During the night, cries awakened him, cries of people. He saw they were carrying a dying Indian in a buffalo robe. They put the robe and man on top of Pachee Goyo and circled the two of them, wailing and weeping.

"Pachee Goyo shouted impatiently, 'Who's dead around here? Nobody's dead that I see.'

"The people laughed and tittered and ran off. The dying man laughed, too, and ran after them. Everyone disappeared into the night."

"Walking for days and days, Pachee Goyo came to a clear, sparkling stream. He took a bath in it. Afterward he covered himself with white clay powder.

"A stranger approached, with a sparrowhawk perched on his shoulder. The stranger took the sparrowhawk off his shoulder and threw it at Pachee Goyo. The bird flew straight at Baldy's face and landed on his head. Pachee Goyo stood perfectly rigid in his white clay. He didn't even blink.

"The stranger called out, 'What is this thing? Is it human? Surely it is, it has eyes, it has nostrils. But it's not moving.'

"Pachee Goyo stood absolutely rigid.

"'It must be a human being,' said the stranger. 'It has big ears. Bald, too—nice, shiny bald head. Gray hair, too.'

"In his white clay powder Pachee Goyo stood still as a rock.

"Finally the stranger stepped forward. Right into Pachee Goyo's face. He stuck out one hand, picked up the sparrowhawk from Baldy's head, turned his back, and walked away.

"Pachee Goyo breathed. If he had moved, if he had even blinked, the stranger would have struck him dead.

"He washed the powder off, got dressed, and walked on over a mountain. And there a wondrous sight! A circle of brush huts and tipis.

"He hurried toward the camp. Outside the circle,

alone, stood a man in a white buffalo robe, his head bowed in mourning.

"'Why are you out here alone?' asked Pachee Goyo.

"'I have lost my brother,' said the man. 'Many winters ago we went on a hunting trip and he disappeared. I don't know if he's alive or dead.'

"'The brother Giant Owl flew away with?" asked Baldy. 'Pachee Goyo?'

"'Who are you?' asked Big Knife. He peered at the stranger and at last recognized his long-lost brother. 'Pachee Goyo!' he cried.

"He ran into the circle of the camp. 'My brother is back!' he shouted. 'I'll give a feast in his honor tonight!'

"And there was singing and dancing and feasting for several nights, in honor of the return of Pachee Goyo."

Full and Leslie sent the kids out to play. That meant it was time to correct Sima's thinking. Holy Mother of God, back to learning the bleedin' catechism from bleedin' priests.

Dr. Full drew himself up. He looked sidelong at Sima, who looked scared. Full tapped a finger on empty air.

"Sima, my boy," he began, "that was a story of your people, the Shoshones?"

Sima nodded yes.

"A religious story? Or just a story?"

Sima looked at Flare for help. Sink or swim, boyo.

"I don't understand."

"Let's see," Full went on. "It had gods in it, did it not? The giant owl was a god? The snakes were sent by gods? The stranger with the hawk was a god? Or represented a god?"

Sima looked at Flare. The Irishman shrugged his shoulders in an I-don't-know way.

Sima did the same at Full.

Full put on a benevolent manner like an ill-fitting coat. "I sense that there were beings and doings in your story that were supposed to be divine." He paused. He said softly, firmly, tapping each word out separately, "We cannot have that. *There is but one God, and His name is Jehovah.*

"You do not come to us *tabula rasa*," said Full, enjoying the fancy words. "We understand that. You have a religion."

He wheeled on the boy. "You seek true religion. And I believe your mind is susceptible to it. God is opening you to it. That is a blessing."

Sima felt hot with humiliation. He didn't know what was going on, but he knew he had told a sacred story, a story filled with Spirit and wisdom that comes from Spirit, and that Dr. Full was spitting on it. And on him for telling it.

He glanced at Flare and Miss Jewel. Flare looked mad. Sima didn't know what he was going to do. He couldn't be rude in return, and he couldn't get mad. What the devil?

"This stuff is superstition. Men or gods taking the form of animals, childishness, stuff the human race has outgrown."

Dr. Full paced. Sima could see he wanted to say a lot more, and a lot worse, than he let himself say.

Sima didn't understand. He was willing to learn the wisdom of the whites. Were they unwilling even to listen to the wisdom of the Shoshones? Did they think they knew everything? People who couldn't find water on the plains without a guide? Or find game before they starved? This didn't make sense.

"It's not just that we don't want you to tell these tales to the children. Though their minds don't need to be full of . . . fancies. It's that we want you to scourge *your* mind of it."

He turned to Sima and opened his arms in appeal. "Make room for the one God in your mind. Make room for His son, who gave his life for you. Make room for His spirit, who will guide you. You must empty your mind before we can fill it with truth."

Sima was bewildered now. He would not let Dr. Full make him speak rudely or intemperately. He saw nothing he could do but keep silent.

"Do you understand, Sima?" pressed Dr. Full.

Sima struggled with his feelings. It was mad. He didn't know the truth, but he knew he could never abandon Magic Owl or the *poha* Owl gave him. Never. That would be death.

Finally Sima said respectfully, "I hear your words, Dr. Full."

Sima slipped between Flare and Miss Jewel as they left the Leslies'.

"Don't worry about it, lad," Flare said when they were outside.

"What do you think, Miss Jewel?"

He watched her. She was deliberating carefully. "I think you need not reject one wisdom to gain another, Sima."

He nodded. That did not seem a bad thought.

"Lad, I want to say something," put in Flare. "Miss Jewel won't like it."

They both looked at Miss Jewel. "Everyone is free to express his opinion," she said.

"The Shoshone way seeks to liberate your spirit and give it power," said Flare. "The Christians want to subjugate your spirit."

Flare was in a blue funk.

He'd been at French Prairie a week and fallen into an absolute funk. Nicolette Marais had quickly offered him half a cabin. Old Jacques had died in the fall, and she needed the company anyway, she said. She was a prickly creature of middle age with a face permanently screwed into a scowl and a lively tongue. Though she'd looked unhealthily skinny for at least fifteen years, she had some spirit. (Jacques' other wife, Cora, had moved in with another Frenchie and lived a mile or so away. Flare had known all three of Jacques' wives.)

The first night Flare moved in, Nicolette indicated she wanted to share a bed as well as a cabin. And she just wanted to have a lark, she made it clear. No strings attached. She did mention a couple times, though, that two priests were coming, right here to French Prairie, and all the hell-raisers here could make their peace with heaven. She cackled at that.

Flare had a rule about sex. It was like his rule about food: Take what you can get whenever you can get it, for you never know when the next chance will be. So it deepened his funk that he wasn't interested in Nicolette. He rolled up in his own blankets in another room. Made her tongue turn caustic, too.

He stayed innocent the second night as well, and the third. Couldn't figure out what was wrong with himself. Didn't want to go to Mission Bottom and see Sima. Didn't want to flirt with Miss Jewel. Didn't want to ride about the country. Didn't want to yarn with old friends. Didn't want to get laid. Finally he spent two days doing absolutely nothing but sitting against the front wall of the cabin, moping. He couldn't remember ever doing that before, and he couldn't sleep the night between. He wasn't interested in eating. He was in trouble.

It never did get better until Skye came.

Crack!

Skye got a huge kick out of it, sneaking up on an old mountain man like that.

Flare rubbed his noggin, but Skye had used the belaying pin lightly. "If this child had a been an Injun," he roared with glee, "you'd-a lost your topknot!"

He could see Flare didn't take to it, getting the sneak put on him right against his own cabin. Showed that civilization made a man careless, which would make him dead. Aside from that, Flare looked like he'd lost the plea-

sure in life. Skye wondered what happened. Didn't make
no sense—Skye liked the grand game every minute, even
when he was hung over. Couldn't understand those who
didn't.

They had a drink, Sima and Nicolette whiskey and
Flare coffee. They had a fine supper, with boudins. Later,
since Nicolette hinted that Flare was doing her no good,
Skye did her plenty of good, and made her cry out with
the fun of it.

Next morning Flare looked a little more cheerful.

Skye told Flare he had to be off. The emp hired him
to take an express to Walla Walla. From there someone
would hurry it on to Montreal. And the emp had told Skye
to come up to Mission Bottom first and take whatever
mail of the missionaries along, free on the prairie. The
emp was generous these days, wasn't the old rascal?

Then Skye remembered, "What you make of this, old
hoss?"

He handed Flare a letter.

It was addressed to a woman, or girl, Flare had never
heard of Miss Amanda Perkins, in Boston. The back said
it was from Billy Wells.

Oh, Miss Jewel's fellow—fiancé. Flare knew what it
was. The letter Miss Jewel demanded. To his former fi-
ancée.

"So?" Flare handed it back to Skye.

"So the chap gave it to me, quiet-like, and asked
what it cost to send it to the States. Naught, says I, courtesy of the Honorable Company. Well, says he, I'll give
you two dollars to take it down the road and . . ."

Mr. Skye walked to the fire theatrically and set the
letter on the flames. The edges began to brown and curl.

" . . . throw it on a fire. Be sure it burns, he says,
every bit of it. And tell no one here. Bugger give me the
two dollars, too. What do you make of that?"

"I make it we'd best mind our own business," said
Flare.

Flare knew what else to make of it. Billy Wells was cheating Miss Jewel. But why?

When Skye was gone, Flare went for a walk and thought it over. Decided he'd best have a talk with the lad. Which would be enjoyable. Flare didn't like Billy Wells anyway.

Chapter

Eighteen

Flare gave it a week, a most enjoyable week. He rode the countryside. A most beautiful countryside it was, forested and rolling. He liked it—when he wasn't thinking that it would grow crops like weeds, and so would attract farmers, and so attract those who wanted to sell them things, save them, bank their money, and keep them in line, and the other maggots of civilization.

At night he played seven-up with the Frenchies and lined his pockets with coins. When it came to gambling, Frenchies were as childish as Indians. Besides, he was sober and they were drunk. He contemplated how easy life might be from now on. Go to rendezvous, gamble with drunkards, and fill your possibles sack. After the card games, since he didn't have to listen to Skye and Nicolette making the beast with two backs, he slept wonderfully. Nicolette was considering marrying someone else, she said, and he could have her cabin for twenty-five dollars. Why not?

He thought of Billy Wells's puppylike face a lot.

Nothing like having one up on your enemies to make a man feel better.

So, on the day after their Sabbath, he rode over to Mission Bottom. He didn't want to catch them all together, at church services or at dinner after. He wanted to catch Sima alone after school. And see Miss Jewel a tad. And have a fine and private talk with Billy Wells.

* * *

Billy shook Flare's hand eagerly, a tad obsequiously, as was the fellow's manner. "Billy," Flare said cheerfully for openers, "you're a rotter, a liar, and a cheat." He grinned hugely into Billy's stupefied face. "And I mean to put an end to it."

Billy got the damnedest look and lost his fatuous smile and turned back to marking some boards. This lad's manner was that everything and everybody were wonderful. He was having trouble fitting Flare into that scheme of things. He needed a moment to think things over.

Flare decided to help him out. "What are you making, Billy?"

"A coffin, Mr. O'Flaherty." He spoke wanly and didn't look up. "Seems like the main use of a carpenter here in Oregon is making coffins." He took a quick half glance up at Flare, like he hoped it wouldn't be noticed, and picked up one of his saws. "God's will, I guess." He started to work.

Flare put a hand on the boy's shoulder. Twenty-five years old, maybe, but not grown up, as most American men weren't. He supposed some American women liked it that way.

Billy slipped away from Flare's hand. He made a crosscut. Finally he glanced up. "What is it you want, Mr. O'Flaherty?" He put the board into a miter box.

"I *know*, lad," said Flare. Said it pointedly but gently. Billy pretended to pay no attention.

"You're two-timing Miss Jewel." He let it sit.

"I think you'd best say whatever it is you've got to say," said Billy with his back half turned, "and then go along."

"You promised Miss Jewel you'd write back to Boston and withdraw your proposal of marriage to the lass there. Making you free to marry Miss Jewel. She's waiting to hear from the Boston lass, Miss Amanda Perkins. But that won't be happening."

Flare waited for a response. Billy sawed through a

board in the miter box. Without looking at Flare, he reversed the board and started on the other end.

"You wrote the letter, or a letter. I wonder if you even showed it to Miss Jewel, and shed a theatrical tear. Then you gave it to the express to go with the other mail to the States. And gave the express two dollars to take the letter away from here and burn it.

"Too bad for your rotten scheme the express was my friend Mr. Skye. He did burn it. Right after he showed it to me."

"I think you'd best go on now," said Billy in his way of pretending to be calm. Flare could see the disturbance in one eye, which warmed Flare's heart. "I don't take kindly to your lies."

Billy kept his back to Flare, fussing with the coffin boards. He wasn't even going to look at Flare straight.

Flare restrained himself. "Tell ye what, lad, I'll make you an offer. I'll give ye a week. You tell Miss Jewel what you've done. You tell her and squirm and make it all right somehow, if you can.

"I'll be back next Sunday. If you haven't told her, I'll do the job myself."

Flare turned and walked away.

Billy Wells began to hammer nails into the coffin. Flare could feel the anger in the blows whacking out at him.

It felt lovely.

Ah, but didn't things turn out sweet sometimes?

Sima was drilling on his writing, and then spelling, so Flare watched from the back of the room. The four students did lots of repetition, like a chorus: "Act, a-c-t. Apple, a-p-p-l-e." It was the part of school Flare had hated, doing the same thing over and over, like you'd mistook yourself for a clock, forever repeating tick . . . tock . . . tick . . . tock. His father had put poetry into learning, teaching the great lines of the Bard, and Gaelic songs.

Flare thought it would be even harder to bear rote learning when you weren't a child anymore, but on the

threshold of being a man, like these lads. He felt sorry for
them, and for Miss Jewel, who had the job of drilling
them.

What would it all come to? he wondered. You could
teach an Indian to read, but what would he do with that?

Flare wanted Sima to learn to read and figure, and
draw if he wanted, but he honestly didn't know what his
son would make of that in his life. No engraved invita-
tions would be coming from Buckingham Palace. A
Shoshone wouldn't be offered a job on a newspaper.
Maybe he could be a clerk in a trapping brigade. If there
were any trapping brigades five years hence.

He was proud that Sima was ahead of the other lads
in spelling, though he'd started just a few months ago.
The lad was sharp. But was it not a false pride?

The West was a place of wonders and strangenesses.
Life would do a crazy dance on its stage, surely. And the
craziest would be through the children Flare and his like
had got, white and red at once.

He watched the back of Sima's head in a swirling
eddy of feelings.

"Three plus four is seven. Three plus five is eight.
Three plus six is nine. . . . "

Ah, my son.

Sima was distracted. "It's all right, Flare." He
shrugged and repeated, "I guess."

Was the lad beginning to see through the missionaries? But he would have to see thoroughly and be convinced. He'd have to *want* Vancouver or somewhere else.
And then, lad, I'll have a story to tell you about your old
dad.

"Let me see your notebook," Flare said. Sima handed
it over and sat on a stump—the missionaries had cleared a
lot of trees. "This is the worst part," Sima said, gesturing
at the drawings.

He opened a book of Bible stories and pointed. He
was copying the illustration onto his sheet. "Dr. Full

won't let me draw what I want. I have to 'learn from the masters.'" He rolled his eyes. "It's no fun."

Actually, Sima was not copying the book's illustration. He was re-creating it in his own way. It was some disciples casting a net into the sea, and Jesus showing them how, or drawing a moral from it, or something. Instead of sketching the whole, Sima had started in one corner of the sheet and was filling in that corner with complete detail, and giving it all a kind of fanciful touch.

"That's nice," Flare said.

"I hate it," Sima said hotly. "He won't me let work on my *Thousand and One Nights* drawings. He won't even me let draw from nature. And when he saw I'd done sketches of Coyote some, he got really mad." Sima's English was fast but not always right.

"Dr. Full is not a liberal-minded man," said Miss Jewel, coming up behind them, "but we'll get what we want." She mimicked a dependent, flirting woman with her voice: "Oh, Mr. O'Flaherty, would you help poor little me and Sima?"

Flare chuckled. You couldn't not like the woman.

He watched her coach Sima a little. Not coach, really, but ask, and learn from him. Flare always liked watching her, and hearing her voice.

She liked the kids. Right now she was teaching the boys and girls, separately. When the man teacher got well, she'd be back to girls only. Teaching them to cook, sew, clean. She wanted to teach them to read—she'd been trained to teach Indians to read—but the deacons said no. Studies useful to women only, they said.

She said she had to go to the girls now.

"How long will you keep them, Miss Jewel?" asked Sima.

"Why?" Miss Jewel asked back. She had a tickled look on her face.

Sima said, "Oh, nothing," and pretended to concentrate on his drawing.

My, lad, but aren't you embarrassed? thought Flare.

"The girls will be out in five minutes if they've done their work," Miss Jewel said.

"Hey, Flare, wait, will you?" said Sima. "I want you to meet someone."

"Aye, lad." He'd wait if Miss Jewel didn't come back, too. Flare wasn't going to be comfortable around her today. Billy's rotten scheme was poisoning things. Flare couldn't tell her, not for one bleeding week.

Funny, he didn't think he was going to feel good telling her then. But he would do it.

The lass came running up enthusiastically, then stopped short and looked at the ground and across toward the mill and everywhere but at Sima and Flare. Flare kept his face straight. He thought, And after running toward us, lassie.

"Flare," Sima began eagerly, "this is Lisbeth. My friend."

Ah, well, social graces would come later for the lad, after reading and writing.

Yes, Lisbeth McDougal, daughter of Heather and Alexander. "I knew you when you were younger," he said, "and not yet so very beautiful." He gave her a small bow. "Michael Devin O'Flaherty," he reminded her.

She smiled and nodded with embarrassment, and murmured something, her knees rubbing nervously together.

She was truly beautiful, fairer than Sima, but reddish, like mahogany. A lithe figure, not yet as full as would come. A face to break your heart, long and slender and grave, with huge eyes.

No wonder Sima was attracted. Which the poor lad was, and didn't know what to do about it.

"Lisbeth lives at French Prairie," Sima said. Flare should have known. "But her father and mother gone now are. Trapping."

"Her father is a good man," said Flare. "A Scot. Her mother a good woman, a Sioux. Lisbeth has traveled the country and seen more than you, boyo."

"She's my friend," he said unnecessarily.

And perhaps can teach you about living with a foot in each world, thought Flare.

"I must be heading back to French Prairie," he said. He didn't say "home." Nowhere was home but Ireland, and he'd never be back there.

"We are going to walk down by the river," Sima said awkwardly.

"Good day to ye," said Flare, "and good walking."

"Until Sunday," he called after them.

Mounted, he thought of his own first affair of the heart. He'd been sixteen, she the same. She hawked fish in the street where the family print shop was. Flare would carry tea out to her, and they'd sit on the dirty cobbles and drink it. Kathleen Quinlan, her name was, and she was black Irish, raven-haired, skin fair as cream, and eyes blue as the sky you never saw in the west of Ireland.

They'd met a few times on the sly. Once they'd taken half a day and walked out along the seacoast, on the high, grassy cliffs overlooking the pounding waves. They'd held hands and looked at the great waves, and Flare had wondered if they could stay forever and never move but always touch in this small way that made him feel what he'd never felt before. They didn't move for the longest time, until he had to excuse himself to go behind a rock and pee.

Later they'd sat propped against a boulder and talked and fidgeted and kissed once, exactly once, briefly, tenderly. . . . She broke it off and said she had to get home, right away.

When he'd left Ireland, in the autumn of that same year, he hadn't been able to face her. He'd just sent a note. He wondered what had happened to her. He didn't want to know. Just wanted to think of that one perfect day.

Their romance had been naught but feeling. One kiss, that one but a light caress. All feeling and no more happened.

Unlike his later experiences, which were the opposite, all doing and little feeling.

Unlike Sima, because that damned Skye had put him with a whore.

Flare suddenly thought, But you've lain a-plenty since with lasses of sixteen—Kathleen's age, Lisbeth's age. Have you not, my boyo? A bit of cloth, and few bells handed over, and then a lot of the old rub. Aye. With mere lasses, often as not.

The first wave was guilt, the second shame, and after those only a poignant sadness, and longing.

It was Billy who answered the door.

"Did ye take care of it, lad?"

Flare hadn't been able to wait until after church services. He came early to the cabin Miss Jewel shared with Billy, the rotter, and rapped on the door sharply. He wondered if Billy would still be here—maybe Miss Jewel gave him the heave-ho, as the rat deserved.

Billy gave Flare that damnedest look, again.

"Yes, Mr. O'Flaherty, I spoke with her about it."

"And?"

"You'd best hear it from Miss Jewel herself."

She came to the door, looking uncommonly lovely. The only virtue of church, as far as Flare could see, was that the women made themselves look fine for it.

But she was angry. He gawked at her.

"Mr. O'Flaherty," she began stiffly, holding back. "I must ask you not to come here again, or in any way to approach me or speak to me. As far as I am concerned, you are unwelcome in this community. If you continue to come here, I will tell Sima what you've done."

She whirled away from the door and tried to slam it. But Billy Wells held the door with one hand. He gave Flare a sloe-eyed look of triumph, and closed it gently in Flare's face.

Chapter
Nineteen

Flare stood there for perhaps half a minute, stupefied. Then he banged on the door with the butt of his pistol. It would be bloody hell before he stood still for the likes of this.

He held his tongue and banged. Hard. On the fourth or fifth whack he splintered one of the boards of the door facing.

Billy Wells yanked the door open. He locked eyes with Flare. "She *knows*," he said softly, mockingly. And started to close the door.

"I'll see her or I'll tear the cabin down," Flare said.

Billy gave Flare a long look and a half smile. "Sounds like you," he said softly, but not giving an inch.

"By God—" started Flare.

"Tell Mr. O'Flaherty I'll be right out," came Miss Jewel's voice. "We'll talk to him. Together. In the open."

"The terms of this conversation, Mr. O'Flaherty, are that you hear me out, all the way through, until I'm finished. It would be best then for you to say nothing and leave. I suppose if you must put in one sentence, or two, I'll hear it."

Flare waited.

"Do you agree?" she demanded.

Flare nodded. The three of them stood, stiffly. Miss Jewel held to Billy's arm for support or protection or whatever may be. Protection by the man who was deceiving her. Protection from Michael Devin O'Flaherty, who loved her.

He waited because he had to know what the goddamn bloody hell . . .

"I don't mind saying I'm not only terribly angry, I'm terribly hurt by what you've done. I was fond of you, even attracted to you. Now this betrayal . . . "

She fought tears.

Maggie, my love.

"So. Let us enumerate the facts." She looked Flare full in the face. "You came to my fiancé last Monday, in his shop, and in the guise of friendship reported to him falsehoods. You and I, you claimed, were lovers on the trip across the Oregon Road and at Vancouver."

She warned Flare with a finger not to speak.

"You told him Dr. Full and his family know this—everyone on the journey knows it—and the entire community will soon know it." She looked down at her hands. "You even embellished your lies with something about how . . . lusty . . . I am."

Flare wouldn't kill the bastard, not yet.

She turned fierce. "By God, if I am lusty, you'll never know it!"

She controlled herself with a deep breath.

"You went further. You said your friend Mr. Skye loaned us his tipi for a . . . rendezvous. Billy could check it with him, you claimed." She eyed Flare. "Comtemptible, Mr. O'Flaherty.

"Billy acted with great courage. Few men would have done what he did. Though he was upset, he brought your lies to me. In an understanding way. He was even willing to overlook my supposed . . . wantonness. Because he loves me. But he has insight into people, and with the help of God it didn't take him long to see which of us was lying and which telling the truth."

Now she put both hands up flat. She wanted to finish uninterrupted.

"I must say, Mr. O'Flaherty, that I told you more than

once, and told Sima, what an appealing man you are. I
also observed that you make no attempt through the grace
of God to subdue your lower nature in favor of your
higher. I said that must in the end corrupt you. You have
now proven it." She stretched the syllables out: "Unredeemèd man."

Now came the fire. "I insist that you are not to attempt to speak to me again under any circumstances. Or
to Billy. You have no further business at this mission."

"I want to see Sima," Flare put in.

"If you talk to anyone at all here, I will tell them
about your lies. Anyone, including Sima. I want you away
from him."

"The liar here is Billy."

She stifled a sob. She shook her head decisively.

"I take it back, Mr. O'Flaherty. There's one place in
the mission I'm willing to see you, and hear your voice.
That would be on your knees in the church, begging the
forgiveness of God."

And she stalked away.

Billy was whispering something sweet to her. He
didn't look back.

Flare didn't want to get on Wolf Tone, he didn't
know why. He stood there wanting to stomp the earth to
death with his moccasined feet.

A dozen feet from Wolf Tone's picket pin was a pine
sapling, slender as a man's wrist, and limber.

Flare kicked it. Hard. With one moccasined foot,
then the other. Over and over again.

It hurt. He kept kicking.

In a couple of minutes he reduced the sapling to a
stump of splinters.

Getting on his horse, he looked at the shriven thing.

Wolf Tone, he thought, loud in his mind, perhaps
your Irishman is quite mad.

Late that afternoon Flare recognized his trouble. He
was profoundly afflicted with a desire to roam.

This trouble had first come on him as a lad in County Galway—sure and how the warm western sea fetches in to remind you of the rest of the world. From there it sent him to the New World, the Fortunate Isles of the Uttermost West. Then it came on him again in Montreal, and sent him to Indian country. He had honored it on these two occasions, and on almost every other. It was an old friend, loyal and dependable. He would give it the tribute of obedience now.

"I'm going to clear the hell out!" he told Nicolette.

He gave her this letter to send up to Mission Bottom, carefully sealed, addressed to Sima with no outward sign of the correspondent.

> first quarter, moon of the popping trees
> Dear Sima:
>   Something has come along, I regret I cannot just yet say what, but I must take advantage. I shall be gone for a bit, and then return near the beginning of spring. I plan to go to see Dr. McLoughlin with you then, to get your news.
>   Work hard and learn well. Draw what you want to. Remember that your qualities of spirit are so fine that those missionaries have naught to teach you. Enjoy your time with Lisbeth.
>   Your friend
>   and obdnt. servant,
>   M. Devin O'Flaherty

Flare saw no need to warn Mr. Billy Wells that vengeance would be coming. He bethought himself that vengeance is a meal best eaten cold. And heartily, he added, very heartily.

Then he tied onto his packmule, cinched up his saddle, and took to the trail. Amazing how simple life could be. And how beautiful, when you kept it simple.

Chapter
Twenty

Sima was miserable.

He wanted to complain, and he couldn't. Only one person understood, only one person didn't correct him, explain to him that things he hated were wonderful, or at least were good for him. Flare. But Flare was gone. Gone without warning, gone without good-bye, gone. . . .

That was the most grievous of his complaints, and no one would sympathize with that one. He thought Miss Jewel would, but she told him in her tolerant and kindly and therefore condescending way that Flare was good riddance.

Also, Dr. Full told him to leave the likes of Lisbeth McDougal alone. At first Sima thought Dr. Full was implying that Sima wasn't good enough for Lisbeth. "We're both mixed-bloods," Sima protested. But that wasn't it. Dr. Full had a great future in mind for Sima. He would make a living through his art, and other stuff. Sima didn't want to make a living, he just wanted to live.

Right now, though, he didn't like where he lived. He bedded down in the main room of the Winesons' cabin with the three boys, the oldest fourteen. The Winesons made a point of putting no son on the floor to sleep, but they slept on blankets on hard boards. Sima had to sleep on the packed dirt floor. On the other hand, the dirt didn't seem to him as hard as the boards. He was used to Mother Earth.

Why didn't white people want to sleep on Mother Earth? Why did they think it was pagan—whatever that meant—for him to call her Mother Earth?

Lots of things you didn't try to understand, you just marched forward.

Jane Wineson was a silent, sullen, worn-out woman who seemed not strong enough for life. Miss Jewel had put a stop to the way she made Sima do all the chores. She'd told Mrs. Wineson he was no servant. But Sima still helped her a lot, she was so tired all the time. And she still put him on the floor to sleep.

The one Sima resented was Alan Wineson. He worked during the day in the smithy, and spent all of every evening reading the Scriptures. He was a big man, tall and heavy-limbed, with a loud, rasping voice. Often he would declaim, in a tone of more authority and respect than meaning. Sima could never tell what the words really said when Mr. Wineson read out loud, but he made lots of it sound like harsh corrections from a crazy-mean father, and other parts of it like miraclee that made all tremble before it.

With all this Scripture-reading, Mr. Wineson never did a thing for the family at night. When he quit black-smithing every day, he quit working. Sima and the small boys had to buck up the wood, Sima had to split it all, and the boys stacked it. Plus all the other chores, especially hauling water.

Sima would have complained, but he was afraid of setting Mr. Wineson off. Truth was, Sima thought something was wrong with the man's brain.

What worried Sima the most was the way Mr. Wineson talked about Lazarus all the time. He was crazy on this Lazarus. Flare had a word for the way the missionaries were about religion: "obsessed." Mr. Wineson was obsessed about Lazarus. Sima wished Flare were here to talk to about it.

Wineson kept saying, every night after dinner when they talked about Scriptures: "If Lazarus could rise from the dead, why cain't we? Surely we can show as much faith as a Jew eighteen hundred years ago, cain't we, surely?"

Sima liked the story of Lazarus. It seemed to have some Spirit power in it. And Sima considered that he'd kind of Lazarused himself, falling, breaking his leg, passing through the little death, and being waked up by Flare. Miraclee.

Mr. Wineson came to Sima, in almost a begging way, and asked what he described as a mighty and holy favor. Would Sima draw one of his colored-pencil pictures of Lazarus coming forth from the jaws of death? Would he? That would mean more to Mr. Wineson than anything in the world.

Maybe more important, Mr. Wineson said as though transported, it would give Sima a chance to let God's grace flow through him, through his mind, and eyes, and his heart, and his very arms and hands and fingers into the pencil and onto the paper. He could be an instrument, a vessel. . . .

Mr. Wineson trembled with a holy fervor.

Sima said he would do it. He was glad to draw the picture. He liked the subject, and it would please Miss Jewel and especially Dr. Full. Which he'd decided he'd better do.

Fact was, though, Sima thought Mr. Wineson was addled. Maybe seriously addled.

Sure and there is a god, thought Flare. He was the god of adventure, of men sallying forth for a little risk, a little gain perhaps, and a monkeyload of fun.

Sure and that god appeared to Flare in the form of Mr. Skye.

When Flare got downriver to Vancouver, full of anger and nothing to do, Skye was just back from Walla Walla. He had a plan.

"You and me'll play a wicked tune on the devil's fiddle this time, mate," he exclaimed.

There was an American merchantman in port, and

Skye had arranged for passage to Yerba Buena, at the big bay in Alta, California. (He wouldn't have set foot on a British ship for love nor money.) He'd paid their passage already—had to spend Dr. McLoughlin's money for the express for something, didn't he?

He and Flare would start by having a fine old time in a fine sailor's port. That appealed well enough to Flare. He could have plenty of fun without getting drunk, as long as there weren't any Protestant missionaries around.

Then they'd slip up to Santa Rosa mission, Skye said, and have a look at the wonderful old Spanish buildings and fine vineyards and vast herds of cattle and the thousands of horses there. So many horses the padres didn't know how many, and didn't care, they might as well be wild horses. And then with some volunteer help— there were, by God, mountain men living around Santa Rosa—they would cut out a few hundred of the horses, not stopping for a proper bill of sale, and drive them back to Oregon and trade them.

"Earn ten years' wages in a month or two, we would," said Skye.

"Aye, or steal it," said Flare, and the two men laughed. "What's the difference?" they said.

Neither man had to mention Old Bill Williams and the Utes. They tried the same trick a couple of years back. Tried to drive the horses all the way to mountain country, from Californy clear east of the Salt Lake, and lost most of them along the route. Like life, you got the gelt— gold's gold—but you lost it along the way.

Skye's plan was better. They wouldn't have to drive the horses a thousand miles, less than half that far, it was an easier route, and they could be trading them to Indians right along. Leave California with a powerful lot of horses, arrive in Vancouver with some horses and a powerful lot of furs. Which the emp would gladly buy.

Flare said he'd have his gear aboard well before they weighed anchor.

A little sallying forth will do me good, he thought.

Purge my mind of Billy Wells until it's time enough to deal with him.

Billy Wells started in on it one Saturday night. She just finished washing her hair—she was always a little dishabille washing her hair—and Billy kept angling one way and another about getting married now. He absolutely wrung his hands and twisted his body this way and that and looked like he was in abdominal pain. "Miss Jewel," he said in anguish, "I just have to get married *soon*."

She gave him a reproving eye and covered her shoulders better. She thought he just had a nice, bright, spanking case of animal lust, and that was fine, as far as it went. She could say no to him from here to kingdom come. Moaning and groaning and twisting his body around wouldn't help him a bit. He would grow by overcoming his lust, just as she did by overcoming hers.

Mr. O'Flaherty hadn't touched her and Billy wasn't going to. No man would until she was married.

And she wouldn't get married until Billy got a letter from Miss Amanda Perkins of Boston setting him free. She didn't intend to get married and have that Miss Perkins show up here on the next ship.

Something seemed positively wrong with Billy about it, though. He acted like he was in real agony, not just a little body heat. Well, a lot of good that would do him.

He had a sneaky look about him, too. She knew furtiveness, she'd seen it plenty of times on men. She couldn't figure, though, what Billy thought he could get by being sneaky. It certainly wasn't going to be her body he got.

Huh! Perhaps Billy Wells did have something of an immature character.

But then she thought back on how he handled it when Mr. O'Flaherty came along with those lies, and she admired and loved Billy all the more.

That was his real self. He was just growing into it. She would give him time.

* * *

Alan Wineson didn't pay much attention to Dr. Full's sermon. Just before church, Sima had shown him the picture of Lazarus coming forth from the very grave.

Mr. Wineson was thunderstruck.

Lazarus shone on the page with a holy light.

The Lord's hand showed here. The Lord entered the page and made Lazarus glow. He showed the light still residing in the resurrected from the everlasting light, which he gloried in in heaven for three days.

Lord, what that celestial light must be! Light to make the sun itself as a graying ember.

The Lord had wrought a miracle with a humble vessel. He had used the Injun boy to bring that light into the world.

Manifestly, this small miracle was a promise of the great one to come. How could Alan Wineson longer wonder about the power and the glory of the Lord God Jehovah?

Lo, now the blindness was lifted from the eyes of His servant Alan Wineson.

Lo, faith gushed forth from him as from a bounteous spring.

Now. *Now* was the time.

While Dr. Full *talked* about faith, Alan Wineson would act in faith.

The blacksmith left the letter at the foot of the hearth, under it the miracle drawing, and on both a stone.

He wasn't so good with spelling and such, but God would help his dear wife and his beloved children understand. The letter said,

> Ree joyce! I go unto the Lard! In 3 days wil I bee rezur rected unto my be loved on this urth. I wil come fourth from thee grave in the shining rayment of His glory!

* * *

Alan Wineson felt ecstatic. He fell onto his knees on the hearth, before the fire, and prayed aloud.

"Lord, you have chosen me, a sinner. Thank you. Holy be Thy name. You lift me up to do this great deed for my family, this mission, and Thy glory. Praise be unto You."

Alan Wineson was thrilled that God had chosen not one of all the learned men, all the holier-than-thou, all the blessed, Scripture-quoting women. He had picked a common man, a blacksmith, Alan Wineson. Just as, two thousand years before, he chose mere fishermen to be His disciples.

"Praise Your name. I ask not that this cup passeth from me. I hold high the chalice and drink of it. O Lord, I think not of the pain of this act which the Lord Jesus endured. I know Thou will lend me Thy strength to pass through the valley of pain and even through the gates of death, there to see Thee. In Jesus' name, amen."

He balanced above the fireplace and leaned over his right foot. His bottom bumped the mud-and-stick chimney awkwardly. Though he had chipped places for his feet, until he got the work done, balancing would not be so easy. But God would give him whatever strength he needed.

He would only be able to nail the feet and one of his hands. God wouldn't expect more.

Resolute, the blacksmith put the point of the biggest nail he could find to the arch of his foot and raised the hammer. Wielding a hammer was something God had made him good at. He thought the first swing better be the one that counted.

With thanks on his lips, Alan Wineson gave a mighty blow.

After a while he realized that he had survived the pain.

He smiled beatifically. He murmured, "Thank you."

He swung once more, with the strength of his faith.

With a roar of pain he fell sideways.

His big body swung down like a pendulum.

His head and shoulders smacked into the coals of the fire.

The nail held him upside down, wriggling.

Alan Wineson bellowed. He didn't have the time to doubt. His hair was on fire.

While the others were having fellowship in front of the church, Sima found Alan Wineson nailed to the fireplace.

He nearly gagged on the stench of burned flesh and hair. He started screaming.

For a couple of frantic minutes he couldn't get the nail out of the chimney. When he did, Wineson flopped mostly clear of the fireplace, luckily.

Sima dragged him off the hearth.

He couldn't tell if the man had any life left in him.

No one had come. Sima ran outside the cabin and bellowed.

Sima watched while Dr. Full ministered to Wineson. The man had a strong heart, said the doctor. He cut the curtains of flesh away from the raw places and rubbed grease on them. In an orotund voice he encouraged Alan Wineson and asked the mercy of God.

Alan Wineson lived nearly an hour.

Jane read the letter out loud in an odd, declamatory voice. Then she reached out to hug her children and fell unconscious to the floor. Dr. Full brought her around.

Sima read the letter two or three more times. He felt drawn to it and repelled by it at once. It had some ugly power of spirit. He never touched it.

Sima sat outside with Lisbeth. He held her hand. If Dr. Full saw, he would get even more angry. Sima didn't want to go away from the family right now, away with Lisbeth. Much as he wanted to talk.

He murmured to her. He knew he was incoherent. He said how strange it was that no one in the family mentioned the possibility of resurrection. Neither did Dr. Full. It didn't even seem to occur to them.

Crazy. If they thought their Scriptures had spirit power, why did they act like . . . ?

But they never for a moment considered . . .

Lisbeth didn't like his heresy. She tried to shush him. "The ways of God are mysterious," she said.

He looked at her. And looked. "Yeah," he said, "but this *is* just crazy. So are the Scriptures. That's what I think."

She seemed to shiver and withdraw from him a little.

"These Methodists are heretics," she said. Protestants. Not the true church.

They sat together. Sima felt like her hand kept him from going mad.

Dr. Full asked if he could speak to Sima alone.

"Not now," said Sima, gripping Lisbeth's hand even tighter.

Dr. Full took a deep breath and plunged ahead. "You understand, my son, that the blacksmith was merely crazy? His madness was . . . private. This was not the act of a civilized man, a true Christian."

"Sure," said Sima. He resented the way Dr. Full treated him like a child.

Dr. Full punched him lightly with his fist, gave him a quick nod, and went on his way.

Sima had learned to tell white people what they wanted to hear. They didn't take less.

He held on to Lisbeth.

He missed Flare. He missed Flare bad.

Chapter
Twenty-one

Sima woke up on the floor at the Winesons, two mornings later, with the awareness that he'd been lax. *Mom-pittseh,* Owl, had told him to heal, walk well again, then prepare himself, and finally seek his *poha,* his spirit power.

He'd had the cast off for several months, had walked fine for a couple of months. He had accepted Owl's help, yet was slow in taking on the task Owl had given him, in gaining power, in becoming a man. Yes, he was afraid to touch the bird that brings words of death. Did this mean he would be a white man and not a Shoshone any longer?

He knew it was time.

And it would be a relief to be away from these white people for a few days. The smell of the death of Alan Wineson was rank in his nostrils.

Since they would be intolerant of his mission—even Miss Jewel—he wouldn't tell them. He'd just leave, and listen politely to their corrections when he got back.

At French Prairie he asked old Pierre for help in preparing for his mission. Sima knew a little of the customs of the *takuslitoih kahni,* sweat lodge, and knew he should have an older man of his people to help him prepare, *newe pohakente,* a man of experience, a man of spirit power.

He did not have such a man. Not even among his
people was there such a man for him—he was banished.
And if he was not banished, help would have been granted
reluctantly or not at all—he was a *numah divo*.

So he was on his own. He was deciding this was the
nature of his life, to grow as a solitary plant rather than in
the garden of a people. Left on his own, he would take
help wherever it lay.

Old Pierre was willing to help. But he didn't want the
drawings Sima offered to him. Drawings meant nothing to
Pierre. Since Pierre knew that Sima had nothing, however,
he would accept Sima's old horse, Messenger.

That gave Sima a pang. He was afraid Pierre meant
to make Messenger into stew. But the horse was little
enough to ask, and what you gave should mean something
to you. Done.

Pierre assured Sima that he had lived among Indians
all his life, had many Indian wives, many Indian children,
had sweat many times, knew well how to run a sweat
lodge, how to solicit the help of Spirit.

Sima suspected that Pierre had never been given the
way to conduct the ceremony. Otherwise he probably
would have said so. To observe the ceremony and copy its
gestures were not enough. A man blessed with the power
had to give it to you. But there was no choice. Sima accepted preparing in this half-correct way as simply another sign that he was an orphan in the world.

The two of them built the bonfire, heated rocks from
the size of Sima's fist to the size of his head, shoveled the
rocks into the hole in the center of the low sweat lodge,
crawled inside, and closed the door, creating utter blackness.

Pierre prayed in a language Sima did not recognize—
not French—and poured water on the rocks. The steam
rose, and Sima felt again the familiar, welcome stinging.
He switched himself with white sage. Pierre prayed once
more, then Sima. Then they opened the lodge door and
cooled off, and closed it for another round.

In the first round, the round of four pours of water onto the rocks, Sima asked Owl for guidance in what he was about to do.

In the second, the round of seven pours, he asked for a proper attitude.

In the third, the round of ten pours, he asked for strength to endure.

In the last, the round of uncounted pours, he asked for perseverance and courage. For whatever power Owl might be willing to grant him. And for the presence of Spirit in his heart always.

Pierre showed him where the owls flew along the bottom, helped him trap several mice, helped him build the trap. They had a different kind of owl in these woods, he said, one he'd never seen anywhere else, a spotted owl.

It was a pit big enough for Sima to sit in and move around, covered with sticks. A round of firewood provided a big step for him to get out. Sima would put the bait on top and wait.

Old Pierre fixed Sima with a wry, quizzical eye. "You know better'n fall asleep, don't you?"

Sima flushed. But the old man couldn't know he'd fallen asleep trying to steal Paintbrush, getting himself banished. No one here knew. And that failure had been the beginning of miracle in his life.

The first night it seemed easy. He neither ate nor drank. He never got desperately sleepy. He waited. He sat still. He imagined the drawings he would do on the dirt walls if he dared move. He talked to the spotted owl in his head.

Nothing happened until the sun came up. He went back to Pierre's, ate with the old man, slept, and waited for nightfall.

The second night it was nearly impossible. He was fidgety from the start. Then his body grew heavy, and he felt a great torpor come over him. His mind fought it, but his spirit was languorous and lethargic. He could see sleep alarmingly near. At the same time, at random, he was shuddery.

He grew desperate. He had known a man of his people who fell asleep in an eagle trap. *Pia-kwinaa,* Eagle, had stiffened one of his knees, and he walked with a limp afterward. Sima dreaded being crippled.

Once he pricked the back of his hand with his knife. That brought him alert for a while.

Another time he wanted desperately to go jump in the river to wake himself up bristlingly. But he dared not leave the trap.

Finally he did what he thought he dared not do. Pierre had given him a powder to help him stay awake, with an amused warning about how it smarted. Sima rubbed it in his eyes. For ten or fifteen minutes he wriggled and writhed and wept from the burning. It kept him snappily awake for an hour or so.

The sun came, but no owl.

On the third night, before the Seven Sisters even indicated the middle of the night, something happened. A sound, or a change in the sounds of the night. A shadow, a flicker of blackness. The faintest snapping sounds among the twigs.

Sima nearly panicked. Owl was here, but Sima could not see him.

Tick! Shifting of shadow!

Sima grabbed.

His left hand grasped air, but his right got a stiff, scaly leg.

Owl made a whuffing sound. Slapped its wings violently against the wind. Sticks flew out of the way.

Sima got hold of the other leg.

Stab!

Sima jerked his right hand away.

Ow! He bit off curses at the owl.

He grabbed and grabbed with his right hand until he got the leg back.

Ow! He stepped up on the firewood and jumped out onto the ground.

A flurry of pecks on the left hand. Pecks on the right. The wings driving him crazy.

He would go mad. He had to do it. Now.

Sima began to dance. Holding the owl high, he darted back and forth. He fluttered his elbows like wings. He hopped, he weaved in imitation of the owl, he circled, and he did it all again.

As he danced, Sima raised his voice to the night sky in song:

> Mom-pittseh, Mom-pittseh,
> Mom-pittseh, Mom-pittseh,
> Coming to me through pieces of light and dark.

He sang solemnly. With reverence.

Then he sang the song once more, smilingly. The owl still pecked at him, and hit him with its wings, but he hardly noticed. He sang, he bellowed, and he laughed while he sang. He loved the earth and the sky. And wind. And flowing waters. And the powers. Most especially Owl. Gladness flowed through him like blood.

Finally, reluctantly, he ended the song. He stopped dancing. He brought the owl to eye level. It had stopped fighting. Perhaps it was exhausted, giving up. Perhaps it was surrendering its power to Sima willingly. By the moonlight he could see a dark, oval shape, faint lines of wing and face, and a pair of lustrous eyes. The eyes glowed bright, mysterious, utterly unreadable.

He gripped both legs with his left hand, put his right behind the bird's head, grasped hard, and twisted. Twisted firmly, for a long time. He heard cracking, crunching sounds.

He set the dead owl on the earth. With his knife he opened its chest. He put a finger on the small heart, still quivering. He cut it open.

Now. He held the bird high overhead, as though offering it to Father Sky. The heart's blood flowed down, onto the heels of his hands, down his arms, onto his chest and belly.

He spoke freely. *"Numee Nan-kak Ook."* Hear me, O Spirit. He thanked Spirit. He thanked Owl. He poured forth his heart in a new gladness.

He left the blood on his body—later he would draw himself so he would always know where to put the paint. He took the owl's claws. He took the heart. He took the skin. By moonlight he walked back toward Pierre's cabin, an empowered man.

Chapter
Twenty-two

 After the second night, at dawn, Flare packed Skye out of the eastern side of the bay by Yerba Buena, head down on a mule.

Odd how it seemed fun when Flare was drinking, and dumb when he was sober. He knew what was coming. The boozing would go on for three or four days and the foul-spirited sobering up for three or four more. There was still the whoring and card-playing for Flare, but he'd had enough. He felt too old to enjoy fighting, or watching others make asses of themselves. It hadn't even been a sailors' port, just a dirty little town and a cantina.

He used the rest of Skye's express money and a hundred of his own dollars to get outfitted. He bought a new saddle horse—Wolf Tone was at French Prairie, for there was no honor in taking your best horse on a pony raid. Since it seemed to have a haughty attitude, he called the new horse Doctor. He bought himself a new Californio saddle with his guiding money, complete with silver-embroidered mochila and bridle. He got another saddle horse, and some mules, including an extra-stout one just to pack Skye. He tied the drunken sailor on with a diamond hitch and packed him north. He got to Santa Rosa the second day.

He didn't bother with sight-seeing around the mission. To Flare, Spanish priests were even spookier than Irish. You didn't even get a "Top o' the mornin' to ye" be-

fore you got the eye, searching out your shame. And no
sense in sticking your puss in the fathers' faces, for them
to remember. They liked to have something to hold over a
man.

There was a garrison of Mexican soldiers at the village, which had a jail to put a man in.

Skye was sober enough to ride before they got to
Crawford's place, three or four miles from the little village, and a fine place it was.

Jim Crawford was affable, but something seemed
wrong. They'd ridden together, the three of them, for six
or seven years. Craw was some, as the mountain men
said—trapping man, drinking man, fighting man. Best
hoss throwing a tomahawk Flare knew. Up to beaver in
every way. And he was still their friend—greeted them
with bear hugs, and joy in his eyes. Yet in some way he
was different, Flare couldn't say how. It was elusive, like
a floor that looks flat but is slightly slanted. Or was it
Flare's floor that was slanted?

Craw showed them his place and his life with pride.
Acres and acres of orchards. Two wives, a Crow and a
Blackfoot—got on fine, he said, when their tribes never
did. Fine litter of kids, too many for Flare to keep track of
the names. Three of them were teenagers, and not Craw's
to start with, but a Nor'west man's—mine now, he said
happily. He didn't know if he wanted to run off horses,
said he didn't sport around the country much anymore.
But he knew who would want to, and he might go along
himself, for old times' sake. They'd chew on it after supper.

Billy Wells was making himself a right nuisance
about getting married.

Right nuisance—Miss Jewel thought it was funny
she would put it that way. That was O'Flaherty's language.

She didn't feel quite so harsh toward Mr. O'Flaherty
anymore. They'd never be friends again. But when you

were lost in Satan's darkness, you acted bad. That was that. She should have known, and expected it.

But Billy Wells didn't have that excuse. Billy Wells had the light of Jesus in his life. And Billy Wells wouldn't leave her alone.

"Miss Jewel, I cain't wait. I don' wonna wait. I yearn for you so."

Again: "Miss Jewel, God made us so man would wont woman. God told us to be fruitful and multiply."

Et cetera, et cetera.

She held her pipestone-colored hair with her left hand, the pins between her left fingers, and tucked and pinned the hair, as she did every morning. She turned her head from side to side. This morning she felt like pinning it truly high, making a mound on top of her head. Then she would be tall, tall as Billy Wells or any man around the place. She cocked her head this way and that. She liked it.

She stood up to go to the school. The part of the day she enjoyed the most, now that it was exasperating to be around Billy Wells, was teaching Sima. The boy took to book-learning only moderately, but he loved to draw, and had wonderful skill. She was learning from him.

The thought that Sima's skill seduced Alan Wineson into suicide crossed her mind, but she banished it. Alan Wineson got crazy all on his own.

When she opened the door, Billy Wells was coming back along the path. She stayed on the doorsill. Whatever he had to say, and she didn't want to hear it, she meant to be towering over him while he said it.

He looked up at her. He was hangdog and insolent at once, a particular talent of his. She was getting plenty fed up with Billy Wells.

He angled this and that a couple of times, in his usual way.

Finally she said, "Billy Wells, if you have anything worth saying, spit it out."

He shuffled his feet. Appeared to decide. "Miss

Jewel," he said, slyly as could be, "everybody would want us to go ahead and marry right now. Dr. Full included. Everybody. If we was to tell them *the whole truth* about us."

The look on his face was a schemer who'd won.

Well, that was that.

"Billy Wells," she said, enunciating with great clarity, "I am now breaking our engagement. I forbid you to set foot in this cabin again. When you finish work, your belongings will be piled in front of the door."

He didn't get it. He still whined. "It's gonna snow." He pointed up at the hazy sky, which, as far as Miss Jewel could tell, snowed once in a blue moon. "What will I do?"

Madness got hold of her, real madness for a moment. She said, "Go stick it in a knothole."

She slammed the door.

She leaned her forehead against it.

She sobbed furiously. She pounded the door with her fists. She banged her head against it.

After a minute or so, she made herself stop. No man was going to make her act that way. No man. That's what they wanted. They wanted women to depend on them helplessly. They could all go stick it in knotholes.

But she wanted . . . she wanted . . .

It was insane. Impossible.

She looked through a crack in the door to make sure Billy Wells wasn't still standing there. He seemed to be gone. She opened the door.

She had to get to school. She had to teach . . . dear Jesus, she had to teach four Indian boys to read and figure. While all the Indian girls learned to cook and sew.

She stepped outside. She looked around at the pleasant morning. The men were all at their jobs, making the mission run so it could spread the Word. The women were all in their cabins, washing the men's clothes and patching their long underwear. She cupped a hand to her mouth and hollered out to the fresh morning, "You can all go stick it in knotholes!"

Craw said at breakfast that his boy Garrett and Garrett's friend Innie did want to roust some hosses, so he reckoned he would, too. They'd start today by rounding up some fellow thieves over in Napa Valley.

On the ride over, Craw showed them the country with the pride of a proprietor, He was right. Flare had a sense of a blessing on it. It wasn't just the rolling hills, or the fine tree cover, or the orchards on the slopes, or the pleasant valleys warming up green with new grass, even in February. This country had two seasons, Craw said, spring and summer, both gentle. That sounded grand to Flare. But it was not merely that. It also was the blessing.

He pulled up his horse at the top of a divide and just looked around. Craw was right, it was shining. And Flare got a kick out of sitting at the top of the ridge. In Indian country, you didn't silhouette yourself.

Then Craw told the damnedest story. Said a painter fella came out from Philadelphy on a ship, landed at San Francisco, come out to Santa Rosa with a pack horse of easel and big, stiff sheets of fancy paper, wanted to hire Craw to show him around. Fella didn't need any showing around, country safe as the back forty, but the dollars would pay for more fruit trees, and he wasn't such a bad fella anyhow, even if he was an *artiste*. So Craw sent Garrett here along with him during the day, and fed and lodged the hoss at night.

Well, this *artiste* couldn't hold his tongue from going on about the light. Said it had a way about it here. Reminded him of the sunlight in the North of Italy, which was a similar climate, and the most romantic place in the world, whatever that meant to say. In the paintings, fella said, the light wouldn't look like it came from the sun, would seem to kind of glow forth from the countryside itself. Said he'd get it down in watercolors here and then big oil paintings out of them in his studio. Sell the oils to people in Philadelphy who had too much money, which sounded right enough.

Craw didn't know about any sunlight coming from any ground, and he never saw any watercolors he'd rather look at than the actual, real-to-God hills and rivers. But on lots of winter afternoons, late afternoon especial, he did think there was something about the light in Californy.

"God's finest country," he summed it up.

Flare wished Sima could see it and paint it in those watercolors. Holy Mother of God, Flare chuckled—him and Sima, Catholic and heathen, sun worshipers both. Well, at least the sun was real.

My heart aches when I think of Sima, Flare thought. Then he snapped at himself, Next ye'll be wearing bleedin' skirts and ridin' sidesaddle.

Skye said it might be God's finest country, but the people here befouled it—crowded it up. People always made things worse, he said. He looked sidelong at both Craw and Flare, and Garrett and Innie riding beyond them. "Worse especial for breed kids," he added.

"That's why we moved to Californy," said Craw. "It was here or Taos, and you can't grow orchards in Taos. Seems like it's gonna be diffrunt here. Spanyard and Injun, now a few Americans. Even some Russians over to Bodega Bay. Half the people mixed-bloods anyway, no call to look down at anybody else."

Innie snorted. He and Garrett were a funny pair, not related by blood, but looking alike—good-looking lads of middling size, strongly built, with the reddish-black hair breeds sometimes had. Flare thought Innie had enough anger for a war party—bitterness, too. He didn't say much beyond what was sociable. Funny, his anger and bitterness, living with the Crawford family. Garrett was genial and easy, like his dad. Craw always liked the world, however it was.

They got to Old Yount's in time for supper, and in time for Yount to get out the word for the mountain *cam-*

pañeros to come share a cup—Flare and Skye had blown
in.

They straggled in one by one and two by two, told
Flare and Skye they were glad to see those beavers still
had their hair, accepted a cup, squatted against a wall. A
half dozen Flare knew from the mountains and a half
dozen others.

Flare was surprised so many mountain men had left
the beaver country for the settlements. Aye, and beaver
was down, but life in a town? Life at half mast, as Skye
sometimes called it?

Over the cups their stories came out. Most were busy
making crops by day and children by night. Most were
bored. They asked questions about beaver and the price of
baccy and what was doing to Laramie. They marveled at
the just desserts them Blackfeet got, near wiped out by the
pox. They acted disgusted, those that didn't know, that
missionaries had come across, and held their tongues
when told that Flare himself had guided some. To a man,
they sounded homesick.

Save for Craw. Craw sounded content with what he
was doing, rewarded in some way that eluded Flare's
eyes. But then Craw was maybe fifty, had come to the
mountains with Henry in 1810, had had his full time in
the mountains.

Flare angled in and asked quietly why they'd left the
mountains at all. Maybe a beaver couldn't make money,
but he could roam, explore, live.

It was time, was the consensus, no more than that.
Most of them sounded like they wished it wasn't.

Well, hell, Flare thought, a man doesn't have to let
thirty-nine birthdays spoil his fun.

Toward midnight Flare and Mr. Skye sounded out the
thought to them.

Why, old sons, we could run off some horses, drive
'em north, and trade 'em.

Old Bill Williams done that, warn't worth it.

There be settlements in Oregon, use for horses. It's not so far.

There's planting to be done.

Plowing's for those as like it.

One old hand, Dick James, said the padres might not take kindly to their horses gettin' stole.

E. L. Bulow said he didn't give a damn whether they took kindly to it or not.

Murphy Fox said they cared nothing about those horses, had no claim on them anyway. Bunch up in Alexander Valley the *vaqueros* hadn't even seen, let alone put a brand on. Good horseflesh—yellow duns, steeldusts, copperbottoms, and bluecorns—no spotted ponies in California.

"Like to see that Oregon country," said Bulow.

Wide grins and sly looks everywhere.

"It's agin what they call the law here," some observed.

"That's as may be," said Mr. Skye.

More grins.

"Mebbe troubles," someone else said.

"Praise be," said Flare.

Grins everywhere.

"Shining times," drawled young Garrett.

It was on Wednesday that Billy Wells went to Dr. Full. He had a heavy heart, he said, and Dr. Full heard many sighs from him.

"I need to unburden myself," he said. "Not a confession—I'm no papist, I know you can't absolve me."

He fidgeted and looked up shyly and in general didn't seem to know what to say. "I have something weighing terrible on my mind," he ventured. "I need to get right with God. And with my fellow man. Truly, with my fellow man. I need to speak what's in my heart. Tonight, really."

Dr. Full told Billy, "Why, yes, go right ahead." Out

of compassion, Dr. Full said, "Sooner would be better, surely. Tonight would be fine."

Billy Wells looked gratefully at Dr. Full. He asked if he could testify first at prayer meeting tonight. Before he lost his courage.

"Of course, my son," said Dr. Full.

Billy left Dr. Full's office looking shamefaced and heartened. And grateful for the help.

Dr. Full felt mystified. He knew all that went on in his little community. One of his special skills was putting it all together in subtle ways to make things work somehow. He put his hands into the morass that was the human heart, the iniquity, and made it all come together for the glory of God.

For once, though, Dr. Full was stumped. What had Billy Wells done? And what did he want? Dr. Full saw clearly that Billy wanted something, but Dr. Full didn't have any idea what it was.

As for the sin, he could imagine as much from Billy Wells. But surely not Miss Jewel.

"Brethern and sistern," Billy Wells began, "I would like to tell you tonight, as I've often heard from many of you, how the Lord Jesus has lifted up my heart. But I can't, that's the truth, I can't. Because I have dipped my heart in pitch."

He hung his head. He couldn't look at anyone. He had noticed that Miss Jewel was not here tonight. He had hoped she would keep to her pattern, and he gave thanks for it.

"I hurt. Lord, how I hurt.

"I'm a coward. Truly I am. I have a dark secret, and I wouldn't be trying to find the courage to tell you tonight, except that the hurt is so awful.

"So I pray that laying myself prostrate before you will ease the hurt. That's my coward's hope. I dare not even think yet that if I ask sincerely of the Lord Jesus, He will forgive me."

He thought of his deeds that needed lifting from his
heart. In imagination, he once more touched Miss Jewel's
bare, voluptuous breast. He kissed her and pressed her
back on the bed. He rose over her.

The memory of these deeds made him shiver as truly
as if they had actually happened.

"Though Scripture says forgiveness is His promise, I
am so lost in iniquity that I cannot even hear His sweet
words now, calling me to His bosom."

He shed a tear or two, and let himself look around
through the tears. They were with him. He saw it in their
faces, and he felt it—they were with him. Oh, sweet
Jesus.

"I have betrayed your trust. And Dr. Full's trust. And
the trust the Lord put in me. Even while seeking to become ordained, to become an instrument of God's will, I
betrayed His trust.

"You put me in a cabin with Miss Jewel, knowing
our faith was firm enough to resist the temptations of the
flesh, that we are people whose spirits are stronger than
their bodies.

"I have sinned. I stand before your judgment, and the
judgment of the Lord God almighty and terrible, and I
confess that I have sinned."

For a while he could not go on. Tears were running
down his face and onto his shirt. He did not trust his
voice.

Louder, with less quaver, he said, "I confess that I
have sinned with Miss Jewel. Grievously."

Again he felt the sickly sweet deliciousness of his
fall into sensuality. He shuddered.

The congregation was fearfully quiet.

"All men are sinners," he said.

"Amen," a man's voice called.

"I am a sinner," Billy declared firmly.

"Bless you," said a female voice.

"I stand before my God a sinner," Billy declaimed
loudly.

Oh, sweet Jesus, it was true. Already he could feel it. He could feel the cleansing hand of the Lord God in his breast. Oh, thank you, Jesus.

He got down on his knees where he stood. He threw back his head toward heaven. He opened wide his arms.

"Lord God almighty, I repent. Christ Jesus, I beg for your mercy.

"My heart is black. I pray you, Jesus, make it white once more."

Other men testified that night, shyly, crudely, in a homey way, that they had sinned carnally as well. Until they confessed, they lived in a terrible darkness. Once they opened their hearts to God and asked forgiveness, heavenly light came into their eyes.

And witnessing that light, their loving wives forgave them. Having foolishly risked all, they were so grateful for forgiveness.

No woman offered similar testimony. Thought Dr. Full, it is ever thus.

Dr. Full offered a prayer that acknowledged the courage of Billy Wells and praised his Christian upright-ness. He had fallen, true enough, as all men fall, but tonight he had raised himself back up, and stood in grace in the sight of God and man.

They closed the meeting with a wonderful old hymn:

> *Just as I am without one plea,*
> *But that thy blood was shed for me,*
> *And that thou bidd'st me come to thee,*
> *O Lamb of God, I come! I come!*
>
> *Just as I am, and waiting not*
> *To rid my soul of one dark blot,*
> *To thee whose blood can cleanse each spot,*
> *O Lamb of God, I come! I come!*

This was Billy's story, the cleansing of one dark blot, which was why Dr. Full picked it.

> *Just as I am—poor, wretched, blind;*
> *Sight, riches, healing of the mind,*
> *Yea, all I need, in thee to find,*
> *O Lamb of God, I come! I come!*

When the meeting was over, Dr. Full himself led the way to Billy, embraced him tenderly, and told him how close he felt to Billy now, and promised to pray for Billy tonight and every night.

Almost every woman in the congregation gave a similar reassurance to Billy privately, and several men. Dr. Full watched carefully, and it went as he expected.

Well, he thought. Even Miss Jewel was fallible.

He pondered.

She knew his door was open. He would wait.

Chapter
Twenty-three

A rap on the door.

Billy Wells, come back slithering on his belly?

He'd gotten his belongings from the stoop while she was gone, and Miss Jewel was sweeping up the cabin. He would come back, she was sure. She would show him no mercy. She was embarrassed that she'd let herself be charmed by such a man.

"Who's there?"

"Maggie, it's Annie Lee Full."

Miss Jewel felt a thrill of gratitude, and then told herself no. She was lonely, but the truth was, Dr. Full's wife had been a woman to keep her distance.

It wasn't just Annie Lee but Elvira Upping and Susan Johnson as well, the women she'd come across the Oregon road with. They came in, looking at Miss Jewel with eyes full of emotion.

So they knew.

Tears flushed Miss Jewel's eyes.

The tears flowed. Miss Jewel let them run down her cheeks.

Annie Lee Full opened her arms, and her eyes spoke her womanly feeling to Margaret Jewel.

They understood.

Miss Jewel hesitated, took one queasy step forward, and let herself fall into Annie Lee's arms.

Maggie let go and bawled.

                         * * *

Annie Lee held Miss Jewel. Susan Johnson hovered close and made cooing sounds. Elvira Upping ran to the Full house and got tea to brew, as a particular treat for Miss Jewel.

Margaret Jewel wept for perhaps five minutes, the biggest cry of her adult life. It felt awful. When the sobbing eased, she felt better about one part: She had not permitted herself sisterly intimacies with other women—it seemed so much like the weakness men always smiled indulgently about. Now she knew what she'd been missing. It seemed especially nice that Elvira had come—Miss Jewel thought she'd sensed enmity from Elvira.

She recovered swiftly enough, and felt peaceful. Actually peaceful, for the first time since Billy began snaking his way up to her.

"Oh, Annie Lee, it's so terrible," she said, and burst into tears again.

"Yes, dear," said Annie Lee Full sympathetically.

Miss Jewel laid her head on Annie Lee's shoulder again. Women were marvelous. A woman felt for another woman.

"You don't know," Miss Jewel said. "He . . . "

Elvira offered the hot tea, and Miss Jewel took her cup gratefully. She held it with both hands, loving the warmth.

"He wouldn't leave you alone," Annie Lee said with a nod.

"He nagged you night and day," said Elvira Upping.

"He begged," said Susan Johnson.

"He prostrated himself," said Annie Lee. "He rubbed up against the furniture like a hungry cat, and said he was going to go mad if he couldn't have you."

"Yes, yes!" Miss Jewel exclaimed, laughing and crying at once. The three woman comforters looked at each other with sisterly smiles. "How did you know?" Miss Jewel asked.

"Oh, women *know,*" Annie Lee said. Three pairs of eyes were tickled.

Miss Jewel burst into tears again. "It was awful." Suddenly she was sobbing, remembering.

After a bit she raised her face bravely into their eyes. She studied the souls in those eyes and saw nothing but affection and understanding. She let herself bask in it. It felt wonderful.

Tea sloshed onto her hands a little. Elvira handed her a handkerchief.

She looked from face to face of her friends.

They didn't know the worst, Miss Jewel thought. They don't know that Billy Wells actually threatened to administer poison to the entire community.

Miss Jewel decided instantly that she would not tell them. It was too despicable, and it didn't matter now. Her friends understood how men crept around begging, true enough. They didn't know how really snaky . . .

Miss Jewel felt besmirched by what Billy had threatened to do. She wanted it out of existence. She was sure that, on reflection, even Billy would repent of it.

Miss Jewel would accept the sisterly affection of her friends for her broken engagement. She would not tell them all of her afflictions.

She studied Annie Lee's face. Once she had thought it a tired, subjugated face. Now she saw it was a face of cares, troubles, faith, and gallantry in the midst of the vicissitudes of life. Why she had not seen, until now, what this woman had to offer another human being?

"Maggie," Annie Lee said warmly, "we do understand. We are touched to see what our understanding means to you. But our understanding . . . our love . . . are not enough. There are two further steps you must take."

Miss Jewel was puzzled. "I don't understand."

"It is one thing to open your heart to your friends," Annie Lee said. "But it isn't enough. You must come to all the sistern and brethern and speak. They are waiting to welcome you into their hearts. Most important of all, you must openly ask the forgiveness of God."

Miss Jewel felt her heart shrivel. "I don't know what you're talking about," she said coldly.

"Oh, Maggie," said Elvira, "if only you'd seen Billy. He was beautiful. He felt so awful about his sin, and it was awful, but when he confessed, the Lord transformed him. Transformed him." Her face was rapturous with the memory.

"We all loved him in that moment," said Annie Lee.

"Tell me," said Miss Jewel, "exactly what he said."

Annie Lee Full knew that Satan hardened hearts, and you could never tell where or when he would succeed, at least for a moment. With a look she asked Elvira and Susan for even more understanding for Maggie, their sister in sin.

Then Annie Lee reported to Maggie fully what happened last night at prayer meeting. She let the beauty of it shine through her words. She let the love she and the entire congregation felt for Billy glow from her tale. She let Maggie hear how the merciful love of God had ennobled Billy and all his listeners.

At last she reached out and grasped both of Maggie's hands. "Maggie," she said, "all this is waiting for you. But only you can take the step of opening your heart to this community. Only you can ask forgiveness from the Lord Jesus."

Maggie stood up. She withdrew her hands. She looked at the three of them most peculiarly. Annie Lee could not have described it, but hateful was not exactly right.

"Get out!" hissed Maggie.

They went not in anger but in sorrow.

Sometimes Satan wins, Annie Lee told the others outside the cabin. Remember, his victories are but temporary.

*   *   *

It took nearly a week to get the herd really going. In the Alexander Valley they split up. Two men volunteered to go kick horses out of the canyons on the west side of the valley. Flare took another pair; the youngsters, Craw's son Garrett and his friend Innie, not yet out of their teens, rode canyons on the other side, scouring the rest out.

That left Skye, Bulow, and Fox to round up the horses grazing everywhere on the valley floor and ease the main herd north. Flare thought they made the damnedest trio. All of them were over six feet and the better part of three hundred pounds and dwarfed little mustangs as they rode. If big trouble was going to come, it would be on their shoulders, which would permit them some entertainment.

Flare had some fun bringing in the horses. Innie had worked with *vaqueros* on the big ranches and had some skill with his *reata*. It was a handsome piece of work, sixty-five feet long, braided of rawhide, cured with liver and brains, supple and alive in your hands. Innie could swing it once around his head and lay it over the head of a horse neatly as a collar, or could forefoot the critter—rope him by his front two feet, dally the *reata* on the saddle horn, and jerk him down.

Flare and Garrett had a good time trying. Flare hung the loop on his powder horn once and his spur once, which gave Innie a fine laugh. That was well enough. Sometimes you taught people by letting them teach you.

Their first night out they camped without a fire. Both lads were the sons of mountain men, Garrett sired by Craw and Innie by a coon Flare had never known, now gone under, and Innie lived with Craw's family. Garrett was a good-tempered fellow if ever there was one, a pleasure to be around.

Garrett told Innie stories borrowed from his old dad.

"Last time this child was up this canyon come on a she-griz. Old Ephraim wasn't glad to see me. Run me uphill. Had her whipped till my horse fell. Went cartwheeling. First saw I'd lost my rifle, laying twenty feet away. Then saw I'd lost my horse, flying up the canyon.

"Old Ephraim considered. Though she might prefer horseflesh, there was something to be said for me being handy."

Innie smiled a little and looked sidelong at Flare to see if they were being strung along. He got no help.

"She come up snuffling and snorting the way they do, slow-like, though you know they're quick as cats.

"I laid still. Dad told me they'll pass you by lots of times if you're still."

Innie snickered a little, to show cynicism. Flare saw it didn't shine to be thought gullible. Even for a youngster that couldn't know nothing yet.

"I moved just my eye, to check my priming. Hadn't lost it.

"Ephraim come right close, snuffling and snorting—like to tore up my nerves but this child was still. Finally she just reaches out and slaps at my leg, playful-like.

"Damn, but they're strong. Like to took my leg off. Warn't a cool evening I'd show you the scar on my thigh.

"Wall, that done it. Up I leaps and fires that pistol point-blank at her heart.

"Ephraim cocks her head funny, like considering what to think of that."

Innie looked enthralled now.

"I couldn't wait to find out if she were hit mortal or merely amused, and I had one bad leg. So I jumps on her and drives my knife into her chest, right up to the Green River." He touched the hilt of his knife, a slow smile on his face. "Then she grabs me big. Boys, that's what they mean by a bear hug. I could smell death, thar in her arms, her breathing on me." He just looked at Innie a bit.

"What happened?" busted out Innie.

Garrett gave Innie a straight look. "She killed me and et me."

Flare told stories, too, but he didn't feel like telling yarns. He told real stories, just as they happened. What

he'd done with old Craw, what he'd done with old Skye.
Though they were both madmen, always looking to fight
or fuck, Flare didn't let that show. He told them about the
real life of a beaver man, times starvin' and times shinin',
deep drafts of both hard and grand. He truly remembered,
not just the deeds but also the feelings.

Then he realized he felt like he was saying last words
at a funeral.

"So boys," he finished, "you best ship out for the
South Seas, or the like. Beaver's done."

Neither of them said so, but he could see they didn't
give a tinker's dam if it was done. They were going.

Since it was safe country, Garrett finished the
evening playing an instrument Flare had seen only once
before, the harmonica. Handy thing—you could put it in
your pocket. Old Batiste Charbonneau, a fellow Flare had
never liked, used to play one, probably still did. Garrett
seemed an appealing fellow, Flare's notion of a pied piper.
In Flare's honor he played "The Girl I Left behind Me":

> *The dames of France are fond and free,*
> *And Flemish lips are willing,*
> *And soft the maids of Italy,*
> *And Spanish eyes are thrilling;*
> *Still, though I bask beneath their smile,*
> *Their charms fail to bind me,*
> *And my heart falls back to Erin's Isle,*
> *To the girl I left behind me.*

Ah, Kathleen!

> *For she's as fair as Shannon's side,*
> *And purer than its water,*
> *But she refus'd to be my bride*
> *Though many a year I sought her;*
> *Yet, since to France I sail'd away,*
> *Her letters oft remind me,*
> *That I promised never to gainsay*
> *The girl I left behind me.*

Ah, Maggie!

> *She says, "My own dear love, come home,*
> *My friends are rich and many,*
> *Or else, abroad with you I'll roam,*
> *A Soldier stout as any;*
> *If you'll not come, nor let me go,*
> *I'll think you have resign'd me,"*
> *My heart nigh broke when I answer'd, "No,"*
> *To the girl I left behind me.*

Ah, the curse of being Irish!

> *For never shall my true love brave*
> *A life of war and toiling,*
> *And never as a skulking slave*
> *I'll tread my native soil on;*
> *But were it free or to be freed,*
> *The battle's close would find me,*
> *To Ireland bound, nor message need*
> *From the girl I left behind me.*

It nigh made Flare sentimental.

He rolled up in his blankets. He thought about his son. And then about Miss Jewel, until he got irked by that business with her and Billy Wells. And then about Sima again. He would get back to the mission and get his son out of there, and have a new partner to ride with. That fantasy fulfilled him. He didn't really suppose Sima would spit in his face. Would the lad?

Flare didn't sleep that night. Everything he thought about tasted sour.

The next morning he got Garrett and Innie to do the job at hand, drive the ponies out into the big valley. That's when it started raining. The sort of rain that goes on for a week in that northern Pacific Coast country.

They saw neither hide nor hair of padre or angry *vaquero*.

* * *

"Dr. Full," Miss Jewel said over the rim of her coffee cup, her eyes bright and defiant, "I am not guilty."

Easily, Dr. Full said, "We are all of us sinners, Miss Jewel, all guilty."

"Of this particular charge, Dr. Full, I stand before my God innocent."

She does not appeal to me for any verdict at all, thought Samuel Full.

She'd had her say. Dr. Full got up to pace, as was his habit. He looked at her, turned away. What could he possibly say to her?

Yet Dr. Full welcomed this opportunity. Crisis always brought change, and his mission among his flock here was to make that change for better, to shape the people on the anvil of God's will.

He'd heard her out. He saw the passion in her denial of sin. Last night he'd seen the abject sincerity of Billy Wells's confession. The issue was urgent within his flock. It could divide them badly, or weld them together. He needed time to consider.

Even if he didn't, as a matter of policy he would have given the answer he now gave: "Miss Jewel, I need to take this to the Lord in prayer. Please come back after supper."

She nodded once and marched toward the door. He touched her reassuringly on the upper arm, but she withdrew from his touch.

"All will work together for the good," he told her.

Miss Jewel looked at him skeptically. Then she went out into the rain. It had rained for days already. It looked as dreary as she felt.

Dr. Full put himself onto his knees and asked God for clarity of mind in resolving this painful issue. Then he rose, paced, and let his mind hover around the facts of the situation, as he often did in crises.

Extraordinary . . . an extraordinary woman. He admired her, he always had. He admired her independence, prideful as it was. He admired her courage in coming this evening to confront him. He thought she had character, and, of course, intelligence.

Which did not change the facts. She was a woman. Had she been a man, she would have made a worthy opponent. But she was a woman. She had brandished her refusal to stay in her own sphere, to play a woman's part in life. Inevitably the opportunity to teach her a woman's place had to come. This was it. Dr. Full thought that was to the good.

It was not necessarily in a personal way that he liked it, he told himself. As leader of this community, he relished it. It was an opportunity.

He had heard her story of the interchanges—intercourse, he punned in his mind—between her and Billy Wells. In its own terms her account was plausible, perhaps persuasive. Dr. Full was not blind to the deceit, and self-deceit, all human beings were capable of, including Billy Wells.

Yet he liked Billy's story. Dr. Full enjoyed the forbidden thoughts it brought to his mind, as other people did. He was pleased by the iniquity it bespoke, the eternal condition of mankind.

Billy was a less admirable person than Miss Jewel, less mature, less formed. But Full did not mind his faults. He liked flawed vessels for doing God's work. They were humble, malleable.

Miss Jewel until now had proved unmalleable. A nuisance in a man, intolerable in a woman. And against God's will, Dr. Full reminded himself. To make woman man's helpmate had been God's decision, not Dr. Full's. The wisdom of that decision had always been manifest to him. A True Woman was pure, pious, domestic, and submissive.

Dr. Full returned to his knees and thanked God for His help. His knees hurt in that position after a short time, a fact he would not bring up to his congregation.

He got the coffeepot off the stove, filled his cup. He looked toward the cabin where she now lived alone and wondered what had happened there. He thought he could make a shrewd guess, but did not allow his mind to stray in that direction.

He watched her face again in his mind's eye. She had told him her truth in perfect composure, then awaited his decision equally. Admirable. For practical reasons she hoped he would see things her way. In more enduring terms, it didn't matter to her. Her refuge was her truth. Thoroughly admirable.

Strange, though—her virtue was a poor tactic with Dr. Full. It kept her beyond his reach, ungovernable. Billy's vice (if such it was) was infinitely more useful.

Besides, there was fundamentally no question here. Dr. Full was no fool. He had heard Billy's confession with his own ears. He had seen his congregation's dramatic response. He had felt the fever raging through the community the past twenty-four hours. Even people who previously disapproved of Billy Wells today went to his workshop to embrace him and whisper words of support.

Like all leaders, Dr. Full knew a groundswell when he saw it. He could not have reversed the tide lifting the body politic into one great swell of feeling had he wanted to. Which he didn't.

He reminded himself carefully that he was committing no injustice. He did not *know* who was telling the truth and who was lying.

_____ Chapter _____

Twenty-four

_____

Rain and all, they moved those horses easily over to the valley of the Sacramento and straight on north. The valley was high, wide, and handsome, making things easy. They moved the horses right along. Flare figured the danger was from the Mex soldiers. The Indians around here weren't even horse Indians. So they made distance day and night, dozing in their saddles. It was a satisfaction to travel with mountain men, who didn't complain when the life or the country got hard. Or winter turned out to be the rainy season, not the cold season.

Innie seemed to think herding animals, using your skills of horse and rope, was a fine life. It struck Flare as irksome as herding missionaries. The critters didn't quarrel, it was true. But if you worked for a mission or a big *rancho,* you'd see the same ridges and creeks every day of your life, and chase stupid beasts. While your horse slipped around in the mud, far as Flare could tell.

Folks in Texas and California raised a lot of cows and a few horses, he'd heard. They could have 'em.

Up the Sacramento River into country dominated by one solitary peak that looked like a volcano. Flare and Craw and Garrett and Murph rode in and palavered with the Indians who lived near the foot of the volcano, gave them tobacco and cloth.

No troubles. Flare and Skye and the others had to

talk sharp to the young fellows, especially Innie, to make them keep their eyes out for the troubles that never came. Straight on to the north and then a little west, into the Siskiyou Mountains now, rough going.

Up canyon, across divide, down canyon, through the rain, slipping and sliding, until they came to the Klamath River.

This was what had been nettling Flare's sleep. It was running out of its banks, high and hard, the rush like the rumble of hoofs, the waves snapping up like horses' tails, white and angry.

For two days they scouted the river's banks, up-stream and down, looking for a better place to cross. The ford Skye found, a few miles downstream where the river was wider, was the best they could do. A little slower there. Not a man of them liked it at all.

When you got horses into a river, they acted crazy. Kicked each other, jumped on each other's backs, turned around and tried to swim into the herd, every damn thing. If you lost a hundred horses, there'd be little profit in the venture. Worse, you'd look a fool to yourself.

Best thing to do was tie the critters nose to tail, send a savvy rider into the river leading them, drag them till it got deep, and pull until they had to start swimming. It would take time. Days. It was the only way.

Only Innie saw it otherwise. Even when he wasn't angry, Flare noticed, he was a moody lad, and right now his mood was to drive the lot into the river and see what happened. He switched between saying "It'll turn out fine" and "It don't matter." When he saw every man was ignoring him and just getting ready to do the job, he shut up.

When there was work to be done, sometimes Innie pitched in and labored like the very devil. Sometimes he'd do nothing at all, like he wasn't part of the outfit, sharing all. At other times he seemed to make a point of doing double the work of any other hand. You could never pre-

dict which would be which, or whether the youngster
might growl at you. Human beings were a study, Flare
thought.

Flare thought the finest discovery around would be
why Garrett did nothing but enjoy his life, turn it into
laughter and music, and Innie hated his. It was the same
life.

Skye took the first bunch, and all hands watched nervously.

Into the current, gently, slowly, letting the pony feel
the cold first, and then the pull of the water. He stopped,
fretful, eyes down at the freezing brown rush. Aye, matey,
it might be full fathom five for us both, true enough. Then
a touch with the spurs to make him move.

He did move. Gutty little pony, proved it before oft
enough. Skye turned and looked at the string. The first
horse had its feet in the river now, not liking it a bit,
pulling back on the rope.

Rope dallied on the horn of Skye's Spanish saddle.
Pony upstream of the others. When the current took them,
the rope wouldn't sweep Skye off the saddle—they'd go
away from him. Could let the string go if you had to.
Must not, because of money. Each horse a half dozen
plews, the ten worth a month's trapping, or even two.
Must not because of pride.

The water roiled around the pony's belly now, and it
fought for footing. Didn't want to swim, no, not a bit of
that. Touch of the spur. Beast's confidence in man. Pony
pulled forward.

Water in Skye's moccasins and leggings now, bloody
cold.

The pony lost its feet, flailed. Swung downstream
fast. About to go over. Skye pulled the head upstream, and
the pony righted and began to swim. Still swept downstream, then swimming took hold. Pulled. Right enough
now.

Strong pull on the rope. First damn horse stopped
hard, forefeet planted.

Cracking sounds—Flare and old Craw using their quirts on the horses at the back. They bolted forward and knocked the front ones into water.

The planted horse came tumbling; they all came, they all began to swim. Skye got his pony balanced and gave it the spur and the critter pulled hard for the far shore. That's a matey.

Oh, bloody Christ. The river swooshed up to Skye's waist and his chest, colder than the hand of death. He spurred and made his quirt whistle. A wave smacked him in the face.

He fought for breath. He didn't know where he was in the river, going in what direction. He kicked the pony hard.

The pony found bottom, clambered forward, sank into current again.

The whole river roared over Mr. Skye.

The pony found bottom, Skye kicked it. Feet on the bank. Clattering out. Backward pull on the rope. Rope ripping Skye out of the saddle. He turned his pony toward the horses coming out. They pranced onto the shore, nervous-footed, mad-eyed.

Skye dismounted and shook himself like a wet bear.

It doesn't get any bloody easier, thought Flare.

It was his third trip across, and he was still leery. Bloody river. He'd have nightmares about being down with the fishes and the turtles tonight. He always did, when he had to ford high water. If he'd been a sailor, like Skye, on those big seas he'd have died of his dreams.

He looked back at Craw and shook his head. Craw grinned. Craw used to say fear was a boon, it kept a man's bowels cleaned out. His backwoods talk.

Skye and Flare and Craw and Murph had made all the trips today. The lads were back up the canyon, holding the other horses. They itched to make the hard ride, but

Flare said they'd wait for tomorrow. Maybe water would be down tomorrow.

He looked at the water, brown with mud, dirty with floatsam, choppy, and in every way nasty. Flare figured he was made for a dry country. He dreaded his dream tonight.

He wondered if the new and unproven horse, Doctor, would be the death of him on one of these trips. He touched Doctor with his heels, and Craw put the quirt to the wild ones. Flare plunged in.

He would never get used to this cold.

The next morning the water was down, a tad, at least.

It was first light. Hosses making fires and some breakfast—which was needed when you rode through a freezing river like an idjit.

Flare squatted by the water. Truly, he thought, a little down.

Time for the young lads to act like men. Time indeed.

Skye and Fox holding most of the crossed herd up-canyon on the far side. Bulow and Dick James holding some on this side. Flare and Craw and Garrett and Innie to do the leading across—that was the scheme of things.

It was hard. For Flare, it was living.

A fellow came to difficulty. All sorts of difficulty, naturally, from learning accounts to outwitting a competitor to walking twenty miles in a day. The sorts of difficulty that held Flare's mind in sway were the mortal ones. You stood up to a man who was twice your size and of murderous mind. Maybe he backed down, maybe you survived the fight, maybe the awful urge in you actually made him go down, didn't matter. Or you walked into an Indian village with nothing but your wits for weapons and your life in the balance. Or you rode right among the buffalo, the great beasts rampaging, a stumble meaning certain death, and tried to keep your mind clear enough to get a clean shot. Or, Flare supposed, if you were a bloody

British lord, you took your jumper fast over big logs trying to catch the fox.

One way or another, you risked your precious hide. Your precious life.

And suddenly in the middle of it all, you felt a way you'd never felt before—blood roaring through your veins, eyes seeing colors twice as bright, sounds keener. Air grand in your nostrils, and your lungs. Skin prickling. Balls clanging.

Alive, alive-ho!

Flare had taken his fair share of big risks, and then some. He'd chosen a life of them.

He'd seen a lot of other men take their first, and discover the feeling. He liked seeing that, truly liked it. Now, funny, he had some years on him, and maybe the big ones had lost a little of their zest. But he liked showing young men the way, seeing them brave forth, and start living because they dared.

Like Garrett and Innie today.

After breakfast the four of them drove twenty horses down. Flare cursed himself for yesterday. He'd let the entire herd come to the bottom of the canyon, which had been dumb. If something spooked them, the whole herd would have been in the river, and no telling how many you might lose. Innie had told a *vaquero*'s story about cattle stampeding into the Sacramento and starting to circle, right there in the river, headlong flight round and round in flank-deep water. Stumbled, fell, got knocked down, trampled. Most of them drowned.

So they'd bring the horses down a few at a time today. Lasso 'em—that was the word Innie used. Innie and a couple of other coons were good at it, and Craw was coming right along. Catch those hosses by the neck. Improvise halters and get 'em tied together. Without the California hands, Flare and Skye would never have been able to get this job done.

Now time to let the new lads earn their keep, and find out how to love your life.

Craw took the first bunch, to show the way. A fine swim, no trouble. On the far side he waved his hat as though to say it was Simon-simple, and pretend it wasn't particular cold.

Flare just gave Garrett a nod and a small smile.

Garrett could feel the eyes on him. Except for his dad and O'Flaherty, he'd stay right here. Seemed dumb, really dumb. His stomach felt like a jumble of river ice.

He looked back.

In he went, watching the rope. It came taut and the horses began to move, Flare rousting them sharp from behind. All in good order, himself upstream, them nicely spread out below and moving.

Jumping Jehosaphat, it was cold.

Well, he was crazy, but he wasn't a coward.

He whipped his horse hard and they were swimming and the whole bunch was swimming. Jesus, it was cold.

Flare watched Innie get lined up. The lad was either too damn eager or too damn scared, Flare couldn't tell which. But it was like losing your virginity. You were as you were, as there was naught for it but to go ahead.

"Move on in!" Flare shouted at him.

The lad did, with a close eye on the line and the horses. Good lad, on out. In good control.

Flare sat his horse at the ready just upstream, and Craw and Garrett watched closely from the far bank. Though Flare couldn't think what good any of them could do if aught went wrong.

A rumble.

Flare looked around. What the hell was it?

The horse herd, galloping downcanyon.

"Go!" he yelled at Innie.

Flare whipped the line of horses hard as he could.

Too goddamn late.

The lead horses were on him.

Whump! A horse shouldered Doctor fiercely on the rump.

Doctor almost went over.

Flare lost his seat in the saddle. He fought for one foot in the stirrup. He grabbed the saddle horn savagely.

One foot was on the ground, and he could see nothing but flying feet and bobbing heads and rumps.

Whump!

Doctor took the bit in its mouth and scrambled out of the way.

Flare dragged along behind.

He swung up in the saddle and saw instantly.

Innie was trying to lead the string fast, but he had no chance. The lead horses in the herd crashed into the rear horses of the string, jumped on them, knocked them over.

Innie couldn't ride across because his rear horses were pulling back on the rope.

"Let go the line!" Flare screamed at Innie.

He had no chance of being heard over the din.

He kicked Doctor into the water. Maybe he could get to the line and cut it. "Let go the line!" he screamed again.

Held fast to the end of the rope, Innie was being swept straight downstream.

Doctor wouldn't go into the melee, threw its head, stayed upstream of the herd, began to swim hard.

Flare saw Innie throw the rope away with a big arm fling.

The entire herd was between him and Innie. He let Doctor have its head to swim across.

He stood in the stirrups and watched Innie.

The lad was buffeted by the wild horses, but he kept his seat. Good lad!

They were still in water only flank deep, and the horses were leaping on each other's backs. One crashed into Innie's mount from the side. Horse and rider went sideways and under.

A moment later both came up, Innie in the water but clinging to the saddle horn.

A horse screamed and jumped on top of Innie, front feet flying.

Then Flare could see nothing but heads and rumps leaping into the air.

In his mind's eye he saw the rocky bottom, hundreds of hoofs, skull and bones between.

The sky was filled with the screams of horses.

Flare and Doctor clambered up the far bank and wheeled to gallop downstream. He had to do something for Innie, dead or alive, and something for the horses, dead or alive.

Craw was ahead of him. And swinging that damned *reata*.

What the hell for?

Craw's throw shot out fifty feet and fell useless into the tossing waves.

Then Flare saw. Garrett was swimming horseback on the edge of the herd. The damn fool was trying to get to Innie.

Craw jerked the *reata* back, swung, and flipped again.

Perfect neck throw.

"Craw!" Flare shouted. "No!"

Craw had already seen and let the rope go slack.

Garrett grabbed the loop and fought it off his neck.

When he got it more than head high on his hand, Craw coolly jerked him out of the saddle.

Garrett swam for the saddle horn, but his mount went plunging ahead. The lad looked back toward Craw, bobbing in the waves, and shook his fist high in the air.

Craw just flipped the loop back to Garrett. It rode up and down in the waves. Garrett grabbed it with both hands. Craw dallied, and the lad came like a pendulum to shallow water.

While Garrett came up the bank yelling at his father, Flare kicked Doctor downstream. Let 'em bellow, he thought. The lad wanted a gesture noble but futile, and perhaps fatal. The father wanted his son alive, breathing, walking the earth.

Downstream, Flare might see something of Innie.

Then he saw Dick James riding along the far bank and waving. Flare stopped and watched. Dick took off his hat and gave the sign for enemies nearby.

So. Damn. The herd didn't just stampede, it was spooked.

Flare sat his horse and looked across at Dick. He gave a big nod and motioned downstream.

First there was Innie to find. Garrett's saddled horse to find. And the herd to round up.

And while you're doing it, he thought, your hair to hang on to.

Chapter
Twenty-five

A light tap at the door. Annie Lee Full saw it was Miss Jewel. Her husband nodded at her. It was inconvenient that he had no study where he could consult privately with those who needed him. Another hope for the coming of civilization. Annie Lee held the door open for Miss Jewel, then slipped out into the darkness of the early winter evening.

She walked toward the Wineson cabin. By custom she now walked a little with Jane after supper every night. Poor dear, married to a man anyone could see was mad. Now widowed and left to raise three children alone. Annie Lee gave her no advice on these evening walks, merely human companionship, the solace of fellowship in the midst of pain.

She'd offered solace to Miss Jewel yesterday and been rebuffed. It did not disturb Annie Lee to be rebuffed. Pride was momentary. Life buffeted people, and everyone needed solace sooner or later, and she was glad to give it. Annie Lee had a good heart. She did wonder, sometimes, why she generally felt more pleased to see people hurt and grieving than happy and optimistic. What she never liked to see, though, was people prideful. Like Miss Jewel.

Annie Lee tapped on the Wineson cabin door and turned back down the path toward the mill. Jane would come along quickly.

* * *

Dr. Full was going to tell her once more, she knew, that it was all going to be all right. Miss Jewel supposed it was his attempt to make her feel better, which was crazy even for him. Her mind was bedlam, and feeling better was a sea change away. She could barely hear and couldn't think.

"Miss Jewel," Dr. Full concluded, "only God is omniscient. I do not know all here. I can only go on what I see before my eyes. What I see, when all is said and done, is a man and a woman. Each makes certain claims. One humbles himself before God, the other stands prideful. One admits sin, the other insists on innocence."

The look he was giving her was intended to portray a loving but aggrieved friend, she was sure of that.

What on God's green earth did he think she could do now?

She clicked it over in her mind again. Billy confessed sin, falsely. In so doing he accused her of sin, falsely. Everyone believed the lying man, no one believed the innocent woman. Her only way out was to confess.

She would go insane.

She stood up. Her legs felt mechanical, her body numb. She wondered if she would fall. Somehow she kept standing. She opened her mouth to speak.

Screams came out. Horrible, soul-scoring screams like Miss Jewel heard in her dreams.

Her mouth was open and the room was full of screams.

No, the screams were in her head.

Then Dr. Full bolted for the door.

Screams outside by the river.

Miss Jewel ran, stumbled, then ran hard right behind him.

Annie Lee and Jane sat down on the riverbank, just above the mill. They both liked the mill. Annie Lee couldn't tell why Jane liked it. She was so peculiar these days you couldn't tell much about her at all. Anyone

would be peculiar if her husband was so crazy he cruci-
fied himself. All you could do was be with her a little. She
would accept that much.

Annie Lee rubbed the sleeves of her wool sweater
fondly. She usually wore this heavy white sweater on
these walks because it looked nice in the moonlight.

Annie Lee liked the mill because of the sounds it
made. All the little creaks and groans suggested labor to
her, effort, painful toil, the stuff of human life. But the
sound of the water flowing through the mill, pushing the
blades, dripping back into the river, that meant work done,
accomplishment. The river shooshed down the millrace
and up against the banks and over and over itself and onto
the great mill wheel and turned the mighty paddle to do
the work. To saw the boards that made the houses that
made Oregon fit to live in.

Dr. Full had used the mill one Sunday in a sermon,
and the sound reminded her of what he said, which was
very different. The mill showed the inexorability of life,
he said, the way things flowed on and flowed on and
never stopped or changed but just kept coming. Annie Lee
felt that about life. To her it was inexorably sad. The grief,
the grief rose here and fell there, but like the mill wheel it
churned ever on.

In the dark above their heads the great wheel turned.
They saw only a shadow against the sky, but they heard
its ceaseless, sibilant shoosh.

Annie Lee listened to Jane jabber. She didn't say
much in these evening talks, really, a bit about the kids,
sometimes something about her mother, often something
about her childhood. Lots of times what she did say didn't
make much sense. When she talked about being a kid,
sometimes she swung her legs over the bank and waggled
her feet in the dark above the water and giggled. Those
were her best times.

Tonight the river was up. Annie Lee could see the
moon dimpled on the water of the millrace just below
their toes, and she could hear the extra power of its push

against the paddle blades. That was good. A mill put the good Lord's nature to work for man. When it rained, as it had rained on and on for the last week, nature worked its muscles even harder.

She would have to tell Samuel that, and he could put it into a sermon. Though he didn't use many of her ideas. It wasn't her sphere. She knew her sphere, and was pleased with it.

"Look here," Annie Lee said, "you didn't see in the dark." She stood up and flattened her skirt against her spraddled legs. Jane crooked her neck queerly to look, like she was looking around a post that wasn't there. "It's a new skirt I made out of that calico that came."

It was full and had oversize pockets. Annie supposed Jane couldn't see the dark skirt as well as the white sweater, but she made sounds of approval.

"I made one for you, too," she said, "the blue instead of red." ◀

She pulled the folded skirt out of one of the big pockets. Jane took it in a subdued way. Annie Lee had been afraid Jane would act funny and say no. All she wanted was to make the poor woman smile.

Annie Lee twirled and made the skirt balloon, full of the night air.

At that moment a little more of the underside of the bank gently let go and eased into the water. The bank had been doing that since the millrace was dug, and had been doing it rapidly during the past week of rain. This time it was only a small amount, a handful or two or dirt. A moment later Annie Lee put a dancing foot near the edge, and that was enough.

The bank caved in.

The earth cracked and toppled. Annie Lee Full, still twirling, pitched outward. She turned in the air and fell back. Because the water was deep now, her head did not hit the rock hard enough to knock her out.

But it made her woozy. She didn't think about Jane.

She didn't think about getting her feet on the bottom and getting out. The wooziness even protected her against the freezing temperature of the water a little. It was cold, but after a moment it didn't matter so much. She tried to move her arms, but they were too heavy in the soaked wool sweater. There was something acceptable, inexorable about it all.

The current sucked her down the millrace steadily at first, and as she approached the great wheel, she felt its hand take hold powerfully, like the will of God.

When the earth gave way, Jane Wineson started to scream. The water froze the scream in her throat.

She found the bottom, scrambled to her feet, lost the bottom, and went onto her hands and knees under the goddamn freezing water. She clawed for the surface.

She was in a fury. She got to her feet. She was angry at God. She hated the world. She lashed out at it with both hands. She stepped into a hole and lost her footing and went down again. As the current took her, her clawing hands hit roots. She grabbed on savagely.

Exposed roots of a big tree, she saw. She grabbed and pulled herself into the root ball. Farther into shallow water, only knee deep now.

She looked up. She was under the body of the tree, tangled in the roots, caught. She couldn't go upward, she couldn't go sideways, and she wouldn't go back into the deeper water.

She looked around, petrified.

She calmed a little. I'm all right, she thought, the tree has me.

That was when she saw the white blob moving steadily away downstream. And in her mind identified the blob as the sweater, and Annie Lee.

Floating into the mill wheel.

Jane screamed for help. She climbed hard into the roots, but only came against the bottom of the tree. She

looked at the dark, icy water, the only way out. She would
never be able to go into the water.

She screamed. She found all the agony of her life in
her guts and screamed it out.

Miss Jewel sat by the body of Annie Lee Full. It was
half in the water. So was Miss Jewel. She was also muddy
and cold and terribly, terribly tired.

The life went out of her a little when she jumped into
the millpond, she had felt it. Dr. Full had gotten to Jane
first, but somehow Miss Jewel knew what had happened
and ran downstream of the mill wheel.

She spotted Annie Lee's white sweater in the still
pond below the wheel, floating gently, circling, at peace.

Miss Jewel plunged in, grabbed Annie Lee under the
arms, and started to pull her to shore. She looked at Annie
Lee's face, and it was peaceful. Something about the face
made Miss Jewel reach out and touch Annie Lee at the
hairline.

The skull gave like the white of a hard-boiled egg.

Miss Jewel put her arms around Annie Lee and held
her and put her head to her breast.

All at once the cold from the clothing, the cold of the
water, and the cold of death sucked the life out of Miss
Jewel.

It was all she could do to stagger toward shore, drag-
ging the husk of Annie Lee Full.

Then she sat. Just sat by the body. A couple of men
ran up and asked what was happening. She told them. Astonished, they touched the body, felt for signs of life.
Then they ran off to take care of Jane.

Poor Jane. Miss Jewel had seen her, trapped there in
the roots. But there was nothing for Miss Jewel to do
there. From the shouts she knew one of the men was
going to Jane with a rope. But Jane wouldn't take it. The
fellow had to hoist and carry her out.

After a few minutes Dr. Full came and squatted and
held his wife's dead hand.

Someone else, Elvira Upping, held a burning rag stuck in a cup of congealed bacon grease over Annie Lee's face. Funny, in that light the face didn't look beaten up. Beneath, the skull was crushed, but the face looked reposeful.

Miss Jewel looked at Dr. Full's face. It was fixed. Distant. Utterly unreadable.

She got up and walked toward her cabin.

She sat in the open doorway and looked out at the wilderness. At midnight she couldn't see much, but she knew what was there and what wasn't. Beyond the buildings and clearings of the settlement, there was nothing but trees, and mountains, and desert, and mountains, and rivers, and plains stretching beyond sight, beyond imagination, beyond hope. Two thousand miles of it.

This was a place of death.

There was no way out.

Involuntarily, Miss Jewel jumped.

The cold of Annie Lee's body had run through her like an electric shock. She waved her arms and waggled her knees to make sure they worked.

Would her voice work? Rasping with fright, she tried. "I am lost."

Again, louder. "I am lost."

Thought: Right now she would give the world to see Michael Devin O'Flaherty.

A voice came back from the shadows. "Miss Jewel?"

"Who's there?" she cried. "Sima?"

He came into the moonlight. Sima. Lisbeth behind him.

Maggie ran to him, hugged him, babbled at him foolishly, wept. Lisbeth put her arms around both of them, weeping. They were a six-legged animal, rocking and hugging itself.

These were her children, the only children she would ever have, they were precious. She had been angry with him. He'd disappeared from school for nearly a week without warning and wouldn't say where he'd been. She would never be angry with him again.

They went inside. Sima made hot tea while Lisbeth helped Miss Jewel change her clothes.

They talked. And talked. The two teenagers stayed up all night with her. They talked about everything. Sadly about the Winesons. Mockingly about Dr. Full. Regretfully about Annie Lee. Happily about Flare. She told them about Billy's lies, and somehow it got funny, and they all laughed raucously and foolishly.

It was crazy, but when the sun came up, they felt like they'd survived something. They were exhausted and happy.

Chapter
Twenty-six

Flare found Innie floating in an eddy about half a mile downriver. Floating face up, which Flare had never seen before. His eyes had a strange look, like he was halted in the midst of doing something, about to raise a hand, maybe, or just say, "Hey!"

The face and head were trampled, bruised, cut, what you will. One hand was boneless as cabbage leaves. When Flare dragged the body out, it felt limp as a rag doll. He didn't open the clothes to look.

He looked a last time at those eyes, ready to speak or holler or frown or . . . whatever. Innie's traffic with life was interruptus, unfinished, fruitless, pointless.

Nothing was as peculiar as life.

He left the body. The others would want to have a burial, maybe. After they found all the horses. Flare had to get along and teach some Indians a lesson, and get some horses back.

The tracks didn't tell much. Neither Flare nor Skye knew the Indians of this country much. American fur men never spent any time here. Dick James, who knew them a little, said the moccasin prints of the Klamaths, the Rogue Rivers, and the Umpquas looked the same to him. He also said they were ornery, unpredictable Injuns.

Like all Indians, thought Flare, until you knew their minds.

Skye and most of the men took on the job of getting the horses together and moving them north. Flare, Dick, Craw, and Garrett tracked the Indians. The bastards had fifteen or twenty head, no more. They were headed over the divide to the Shasta River, from the look of it. Why had they spooked the herd down the canyon, across the river, instead of running it up the canyon? Stupid, maybe, or murderous.

Time to lift some hair.

He looked at the little camp through the Doland. Right handy a Doland was, and he would keep a telescope if he could stay sober and not gamble it away, or get it lifted by Indians like these.

It had been plain easy. The tracks ran over the divide, down into the Shasta River Valley, and upstream. High, wide, and handsome. Not that there was any way to hide the tracks of that many horses. They were making time, but Flare and his outfit were making better. He had come up on them at dusk, as he planned. They might not like to fight in the dark.

But this was pathetic, a sign of what the Indians had come to.

Flare knew how it would go among most Indians who still were Indians. A warrior would have a dream, or other medicine insight: He should lead a raid, and on that raid such-and-such would happen, and the raiders would cover themselves with honors. He would go to the men of his choice, tell what his medicine said, and ask them to join him on the raid. Then, if they didn't have medicine leading them to do something else, and if they had confidence in his medicine, they would join the party. In a few days a bunch of warriors would be agreed on, likely including a teenage boy or two to hold the horses while the warriors did the work. They would make medicine to assure success, and go.

This was a bunch of teenage boys. Klamaths. None of them could have any medicine to amount to anything.

They were just out looking for trouble, out of control. The older men would reprimand them when they got back. If Flare let them get back. In the old days—even ten years ago, Flare thought, before the diseases played havoc with them—the customs of the tribe would have kept these lads in check.

He watched them through the Doland. There were four in sight. They'd built a squaw fire. The horses were in a rope corral back in the trees. Probably one more there, on watch. Maybe another, no telling where.

Flare slid back from the crest of the hill and told his companions what he saw. He said nothing about his sadness, but Craw and Dick would know.

"Let's take 'em," said Garrett. Garrett was angry. Garrett had lost a friend. And he was scared. He'd seen death up close, maybe for the first time.

"What are we waiting for?" he said.

So Flare laid it out.

Why Flare didn't kill him he didn't know. The sentry had his back propped against a fir, whittling with a white man's pocket knife, alert as a stump.

Flare moved up on him stealthily, in utter silence, step after slow step. He carried his pistol cocked. If the sentry heard him and reacted, Flare would shoot him. At the sound of gunfire, Dick and Craw and Garrett would open fire on the camp.

Maybe inalertness wasn't dumb. Maybe it would save the life of the sentries and his mates. By accident.

Flare took a step no more than every half minute. The soft fir needles made no sound, or less sound than the scrape of pocket knife on wood. Flare eased up until he was behind the fir the sentry leaned against, so close he feared the bastard would hear his breathing.

Then he clunked him solidly with the hammer of his tomahawk.

The kid rolled his head a little and dropped.

* * *

It was crazy. It was dumb. Flare did it anyway.

He tied the kids' hands and hoisted him on a shoulder and walked within conversation distance of the fire. The others must have thought it was the sentry coming back. They didn't notice the extra heaviness of the step. Their ways would get them killed one day.

He held the kid in front of him with his left arm. Titillating, to stand there in the shadows and watch them and listen to them. Stand within their ken, unseen.

In the Chinook trade language he said loudly, "Don't move or I'll kill your brother."

He held a cocked pistol against the sentry's head and grinned fiercely.

"Don't move or I'll blow your head off," came from the darkness. Dick's voice in Chinook.

"This child'll make sausage of ye." Craw, in English.

Even Garrett got into the spirit of things. "I'll cut your balls off."

Flare heard the three of them coming through the darkness. Someone was shuffling his feet and beating them double against the ground, to sound like two enemies. Probably Craw; he had that trick.

When they got into the firelight, Dick told the Klamaths to get down on their faces in the dirt. Warriors would have spit and told the whites to do their worst, which the whites probably would have done. These were kids, so they lay down in the dirt.

"What you wanna do, Flare?" Craw asked.

Flare asked Craw to tie the kids' ponies nose to tail, to be taken along. Garrett took all their weapons and possibles. Dick tied them hands and feet.

Why are ye soft, old man? Flare asked himself. Why leave them alive? They killed your friend. He didn't know why. But maybe the tribal fathers would be less angry this way. Or maybe Flare didn't have a taste for killing anymore.

Flare worried about Garrett. He looked like he was

about to bust with animal rage, or fear, or something. Flare told him to go help his dad.

When they were ready to go, Garrett raised an opposition. Didn't want to give them such a good chance, he said.

Not a good chance, Flare answered, afoot and without weapons. Might not ever get home.

And might get out of these ties in ten minutes, said Garrett, and come after us. He wanted to knock them cold.

Craw agreed with him.

Flare nodded at Garrett. One by one he clunked them.

When the lad was done using his tomahawk, Craw spoke up.

"Ye've killed that un. Tell by the sound on the skull." It was the sentry. "Since he's dead, scalp him."

Even in the firelight Flare saw the lad pale.

Then he took the knife off his belt and stepped over the body.

Craw instructed him. "Take the crown part of the hair." Garrett grabbed too much. "A hand span's worth mebbe," said Craw.

"Now pull it taut. With your left hand." Garrett switched. "Where it wants to raise the scalp, cut a circle right around. Good."

Flare noticed that one of the captives could see what was happening. His eyes were full of rage.

"Now sit down and put both feet against the head. Not right on the part you're gonna pull. Good. Now give it a good, clean snap with both hands."

Garrett took three or four jerks. Finally the scalp came with a THOCK.

Garrett threw himself to the side and vomited.

"Good," said Craw. "Now mebbe you'll grow up be better'n your pa and not do it."

But Craw made him take it along. To remember, he said.

Chapter
Twenty-seven

 Early that morning Miss Jewel wrote a poem in her journal:

> *Face thine enemies—accusers;*
> *Scorn the prison, rack, or rod!*
> *And, if thou hast truth to utter,*
> *Speak and leave the rest to God.*

Dr. Full was waiting for her outside the Indian boys' schoolroom. He greeted Sima pleasantly, and asked to speak to Miss Jewel alone. Sima went on in.

Miss Jewel was amazed at how even-keeled Dr. Full seemed. The minister had lost his wife. His children—stepchildren, actually—were without a mother, his bed empty. Yet he carried on his duties seamlessly. She wondered what his inner strength was. Then she caught herself and felt embarrassed. His inner strength was the Lord God Jehovah, of course.

"At noon will you please give the students some assignment and meet with the deacons, Miss Jewel?"

"It won't help, Dr. Full."

"Nevertheless."

She shrugged.

"At my house, then, at noon."

He smiled, perhaps making a point of being agree-

able. He walked the path toward the church, to go forward
a little with God's endless work, she supposed.

She had come to an odd conclusion about that unal-
terable smile. It was his way of treating people equally
when they behaved well and when they behaved badly.
He often said men were sinners in their natures, raised at
moments by the grace of God. By treating everyone
equally at all times, he was directing himself to that sin-
ful nature. It never changed. The way he treated them
never changed. His sympathy for them as sinners never
changed. His offer to help them toward grace never
changed. Probably he was right.

Miss Jewel went into the schoolroom. Right now she
didn't give a damn about Dr. Full's theories or his deeds.
The only people she gave a damn about in this entire community were her Indian students. She looked at Sima and
Lisbeth. They were sitting together, until teacher separated the girls and boys for domestic learning and book
learning.

Miss Jewel loved to look at them. She thought what
they felt for each other—excitement, concern, generosity,
desire; in a word, love—that was truly the gift of God.

They lived in a world of love. She lived in a world of
loneliness and despair.

"Miss Jewel," Dr. Full began, "we come here this afternoon in the hope that you have something new to say to
us."

There was Dr. Full and Parky and Reverend Leslie,
who disliked her, and four others she didn't know well.
She looked around at them. Three men of God, indoor
men, and four with the weathered faces of men who
worked outdoors. Big, calloused, worn hands. Some
knobby knees, big ears, big bellies. They were of all ages,
occupations, temperaments. She supposed they had devo-
tion to God in common. And a commitment to a way of
doing things, which included establishing man's sphere
and women's sphere and so holding on to man's rule over

woman. Dr. Full was addicted to ruling women. Leslie had tried to turn her into a domestic servant. Even Parky expected deference.

She hated being here. She shouldn't have come.

"What can I tell you?" she said helplessly. "A man has made accusations against me. He can't back them up. They aren't true. Everyone in this community listens to him instead of me. Everyone assumes I'm guilty without any way to know. My character is worth nothing. No fair trial, but I'm condemned."

"Your character is considered," said Dr. Full. "Your fallible, human character. And it is loved."

She just looked at him. "I did right."

"Isn't this just a lovers' quarrel?" asked Leslie.

She stared him down, then looked at each of them, man for man, in the eye. "There's nothing more to say." She tried to hold their gazes. They looked at their knees. "Truly, do you want me to lie? What would be accomplished by that?"

There were no answers but nervous hands, shifting feet, downcast eyes.

"What do you want me to do?"

"Perhaps we'd best ask it the other way," Dr. Full put in gently. "What do you want us to do?"

"Let Billy Wells and I tell our stories in a formal way to the community—say, like a debate. I will tell exactly what happened."

"I think this community already knows what happened," said Dr. Full.

Miss Jewel felt the rage rise in her throat, hot and vile. She swallowed it and went on. "Billy Wells won't stand up in public and tell those lies to my face," she said. "I don't think he has the courage." She also thought that when the women heard her story, heard just the way he sidled up to her week after week, how he'd angled, how he'd begged, they'd *know*. Women *knew*.

"Billy is gone to the Dalles," said Dr. Full. "We've sent him to start a new mission there."

Miss Jewel stared at him. "Unbelievable," she said at last.

"Billy is a child of God, as you are, Miss Jewel. Like every human being, he is within the reach of God's redemption."

She understood. The rage lashed out. "*Damn* convenient for you."

The men looked at each other. That word. Well, they were understanding men, but this was the woman they'd chosen to teach children!

Miss Jewel stood up to leave. "I don't understand," she said. "I'm sure you want me under your thumb. But not this much. What is it you really want?"

Wringing hands and shuffling feet.

She started out.

"Miss Jewel," Dr. Full put in quickly, "the deacons are obliged to tell about a decision they've come to."

She stopped and looked at him. She enjoyed towering over him and looking down.

"As of this date, you will no longer be teaching the Indian children."

She felt dizzy and faint. "I don't believe it."

"The deacons feel that you are a questionable moral influence on them."

She looked her anger at them, one by one.

"Not only have you cohabited with a man all winter—"

"You approved that! You suggested it!"

"—you also shared your cabin last night with one of the Indian boys. One who is sexually mature."

Oh, Lord. She couldn't mention Lisbeth being there. That would get the child in trouble. She rose. She tried, "Sima is a son to me."

"Miss Jewel, I assure you, we take this action reluctantly. I invite you to return this evening to pray with me, and with the Lord's help—"

She slammed the door on his voice.

She stood outside, trembling.

She wanted to fight. By God, she wanted to fight. But who, how, was she supposed to fight?

When Miss Jewel left the schoolroom, she said she wouldn't be back today. They would have another teacher this afternoon.

Sima and Lisbeth looked at each other, their hearts in their throats. This was a better chance than they'd hoped for.

They looked around at the other kids. A boy was reading, two girls were knitting and chattering, the rest were staring at the walls. Lisbeth got the cloth sack out from under her sewing materials, the sack full of corn bread and side meat. They looked at each other and stood up, and looked at each other, and daringly walked toward the door. When they got outside, they ran for the trees in a burst of delight.

As though sworn to silence, they didn't talk, didn't laugh, just set off fast for the cave.

It wasn't really a cave, more of a big overhang, a recess in the bluff. It had a seep. Sima had brought firewood here, bit by bit. It had pieces of rope for snares. It had blankets. Though less than an hour's walk from the mission, it was well hidden.

This was Sima's special place. He came here when he got worn out with the mission people. Except for Lisbeth and Miss Jewel, that was all the time these days. He fantasized about living alone here, snaring and shooting game, drawing, spending his days in beauty without the encroachment of another human being.

For some reason, they whispered, like they were on a secret mission. Sima built a small fire—the March day was cool but not cold. Lisbeth stuck the strips of side meat on forked sticks and broiled them in the small flames. The fire made the recess cozy.

They ate. They sipped at the cooling run of water on the rock wall. Sima spread the blankets, and they lay on

their backs. Sima nervously began to tell her about his
fantasy.

He wanted to make a huge painting on this slanted
ceiling. A painting done with strong, vibrant colors made
from red and ocher and white clay, and the black of ashes
and other more modulated colors made from bitterbrush
lichens, raspberries, and blueberries. When you faced the
rock wall, he pointed out, you were facing east. Where
earth met gray rock, he would paint the beginning of
every day's sunrise, a molten, red, bubbling. . . . He made
gestures to show how the red would flow and undulate.

Next to the sun, near the ground, the figure of Magic
Owl, flying. Hesitantly he opened his shirt, holding her
eyes with his, and showed her one of the two owl claws
tied against his inner arms. She would understand.

Above Owl, like the sun itself, a wheel of the four directions. Black for the west, where the thunder beings
live. White for the north, the home of the white buffalo
and the cleansing winds. Red for the east, whence begin-
nings come. Yellow for the south, where we are always
looking.

When you slept here, ate here, sat here, and looked
out on the forested hills of the Oregon country, you would
be sitting in a place made sacred by the painting.

He saw this painting in his mind as clearly as a
dream. He used that word consciously, knowing she
would understand that he meant waking dream, vision
through power. He was not yet sure this was the cave
Power meant him to paint. When he saw more clearly, he
would begin.

He looked at her. She seemed to be paying more attention to him than his imaginary painting.

He pointed to both ends of the recess, where the rock
walls curved in. These he would populate with smaller
figures, another Owl there at the south, War Eagle at the
west, Magpie at the north, Meadowlark in the east. Then
still smaller figures, Coyote and Spider, and maybe. . . .

She leaned over him, smiling impishly. She touched his lips with a finger. She kissed his lips, ever so gently.

His body tingled. He moved his lips against hers, exploring. Sensations rose in him like waves, lifting him, swirling him.

He held her face with his hands and looked at her. He kissed her eyes and eased her back onto the blanket.

He kissed her—hard, soft, with passion, with tenderness, more ways than he could imagine.

After a while he put his hand on the top button of her cotton blouse. He undid that button and kissed her collarbone. He undid the next button, and the next, and kept kissing, farther down, between where her breasts would be.

At last he folded one flap of her blouse to the side. He looked at her breast, a warm brown with a rose-colored nipple, small, exquisitely shaped. He kissed delicately around the outside of it, then around the nipple, then the nipple itself, gently, sweetly.

He had never felt anything like he felt here, now, touching Lisbeth. He was tremulous with . . . fear? Excitement?

He lay her blouse completely open. He nuzzled her breasts.

He stripped off his shirt, pulled her against him, felt her breasts warm and sensual against his chest. He kissed her lips.

After a while, perhaps a very long while, he took off the rest of her clothes. And his own. And came over her.

She wrote it blindly, in haste and rage. Otherwise she knew she wouldn't have written it.

St. Patrick's Day 1838

Dear Dr. McLoughlin:

I write to ask you formally for a position teaching Indian children at Fort Vancouver. I am trained for this work at the Wilbraham Academy in Massachusetts, and have for some years regarded it as my life's work. My commitment to bringing these children the light of civilization is complete.

You will wonder why I do not wish to continue in my similar position here. The fact is that I am falsely accused of indiscretions. That has made my situation intolerable, as I'm sure you will understand. I believe it would be more acceptable were I not innocent.

As I wish to leave this community immediately, I look forward to hearing from you as soon as possible.

Yr obdnt servant,
Margaret Jewel

Miss Jewel took the letter to French Prairie and found a Frenchie who would take it to Vancouver for twenty dollars.

Lord, twenty dollars. That was more than half the money she had in the world.

What would she do if Dr. McLoughlin said no? Walk to St. Louis? Alone?

Sima and Lisbeth went to the school at noon. They'd stayed at the cave all afternoon, all night, all morning enjoying what they'd discovered, exploring its textures and dimensions.

Sima was happy. And amazed. He felt like a wall had crashed to the ground and a new world shone behind it.

Through the window they saw that Miss Jewel wasn't doing the teaching. Miss Upping was in there.

Sima didn't know what to think of that.

They were probably in trouble. The families they stayed with had surely reported them missing. The trouble seemed trivial, like some people scurrying about, seen from high on a mountain.

It would be just as well, though, to see Miss Jewel first. They went to her cabin.

She told them she'd been dismissed as the teacher for the Indian children. In the blankness of her face Sima saw her pain.

"Why aren't you in school?" she asked.

Sima told her they'd been out all night together, at a place he liked to camp.

They put their arms around each other's waists, and looked into each other's eyes, and let Miss Jewel see.

It wasn't necessary to say more.

Miss Jewel felt a pang of joy. Strange—feeling joy, through the awfulness.

She took them both into her arms. She smiled at herself. If she hugged them, they couldn't ravish each other in front of her. Which they were aching to do.

"I love you both," she said.

More briskly, "Now. You're in trouble." She thought. "Don't let anyone see you, and get out of here. I'll say you went to French Prairie yesterday. You told me you were going. Lisbeth is staying at—what's the name of your neighbors there?"

"Langlois," Lisbeth said.

"Lisbeth is staying at Langlois'. Sima is staying at Nicolette's."

"Why did you go?" She considered. "I'll just say you were upset. Everybody's upset."

"Now get. Be sure no one sees you."

Sima guided Lisbeth to the door, turned back to say thanks to Miss Jewel.

"Nicolette's is empty, you know," she told him. The old gal had married Pierre, who was ancient.

"You'd best come back tomorrow," she added.

The thrill in their faces was embarrassing. Sima nodded at her with restraint and was gone.

Aiding fornicators. Was she terribly wicked?

Helping love blossom, she corrected herself.

Sometimes this damn religion seemed to nurture hatred and root out love.

* * *

20 March 1838
Fort Vancouver

My dear Miss Jewel:

Your request touches my old heart. The
world is unjust, and it is unjust that so fine a
person as you should feel herself in a difficult
situation.

You are most welcome here, of course, and
I personally would be glad of your company.

I cannot offer you quite the position you ask.
Our pupils here are all Catholic, like their fathers
before them. You can see the unsuitability.

I do, however, open the door of hospitality
wide. You would be a welcome guest, of course
with no charge, for as long as you like. At a time
of your choosing I could arrange transportation
to the States for you on one of our ships.

I personally look forward to your arrival at
your earliest convenience. The bearer of this letter is authorized to escort you to this fort if you
choose.

Yr. obdnt servant,
John McLoughlin

She thanked McLoughlin's messenger, told him she
would need no escort, and dismissed him. She thought she
should give the man a few dollars as a thank you. But her
financial situation was desperate already.

In this vast wilderness, she had nowhere to turn.

"Sima, I want to talk to you about your future."

Dr. Full was groping. He didn't know how to approach the boy. Didn't know where the boy's mind was.

So much had happened. Mr. O'Flaherty had run off.
Miss Jewel disgraced. Alan Wineson dead. Unthinkably,
Annie Lee dead. The boy infatuated with Lisbeth McDou-
gal. Dr. Full knew such puppy love had inordinate sway

over the minds of the young. Carnal sin had even a greater sway, and the boy might be trapped in that swamp. Dr. Full was worried about his Alchemized Savage.

Sima sat nervously on the edge of one of the Fulls' kitchen chairs. The boy refused tea and coffee, refused all amenities, just sat and waited. From appearances, unwillingly.

Dr. Full never knew what the boy was thinking. Sima would say what white people wanted to hear, Dr. Full knew that. It annoyed him, the arrogance in it.

"Sima, I see God working powerfully in your life. Do you feel Him?"

Sima didn't look up at Dr. Full. He didn't know what to do, how to answer. How odd for Dr. Full to bring this up. How could he not know that, because of the way he treated Miss Jewel, Sima despised him? How could he pretend that wasn't between them?

Sima couldn't just answer the question simply anyway. Of course, he felt Spirit in his life. He had been born in Spirit, raised to honor Spirit. Spirit was in him and in everything.

Dr. Full meant something else, though. Something like a code that . . . Sima wasn't sure. But he knew he didn't want what Dr. Full was talking about. He wanted to keep being Sima.

He shrugged. "I don't know," he said.

"You learn fast—read, write, figure. You draw wonderfully. Where come these gifts but from God?"

"I don't know," Sima said. Being around white people was pretending all the time. Except for Flare and Miss Jewel.

"When you think back on your life, notice how it has changed. Last summer, when you left your tribe, you were a savage. You have been alchemized into something shining. Only God can do that."

Sima wanted to be out of here.

"Perhaps it's too soon. This summer, perhaps, you could look back on the year since we found you with

God's help. When you look back, you will see a transformation. A miracle."

Sima stared at his knees.

"Perhaps then you will make a profession of faith in the Lord Jesus Christ. He shines through you even now, radiant and holy."

Sima let it go.

"Perhaps I can give you now a glimpse of your future. It is glorious beyond imagination."

Sima thought, he means beyond the imagination of a savage.

"We would like you to go to the United States on a ship, perhaps next fall. The Methodist Episcopal Church will pay your passage. Our members there will house you, feed you, clothe you, take care of everything.

"You will do something for us—speak to our congregations, and let them see what redemption can do for one of your race." He wants to show off his trophy, thought Sima, his Alchemized Savage, thought Sima. "And we will do something for you—help you apprentice yourself to an artist, a master of drawing and painting."

Sima felt flushed. He didn't know about that. Someone to show him how to do things, maybe, skills of the pencil, the brush, the palette. But maybe someone to order him what to paint and how to paint.

It didn't matter anyway.

"What are your thoughts about this?"

Sima thought about whether he should answer. After a while, he looked Dr. Full in the eye, and with a deliberately soft eye and soft voice said, "You know. Next month I will be going to Montreal with the Hudson's Bay men to look for my father."

Miss Jewel went everywhere with Sima or Lisbeth, which made it better and worse at the same time. Better because she didn't have to bear it alone. Worse because everyone spoke to Sima and Lisbeth and acted as if Miss Jewel didn't exist.

When she went to the river to fetch water, for a walk, to the privy, she didn't exist.

The congregation of Mission Bottom was shunning Maggie Jewel.

Though she knew Sima and Lisbeth wanted to spend every spare moment alone, they mostly stayed with Miss Jewel. They were gone only at night. She wondered when they slept. And where.

When just Miss Jewel and Sima were together, and someone did speak to him, Sima answered, "Bottom of the morning to ye, you ass."

Miss Jewel corrected him, of course, but Sima paid her no mind. He seemed angrier about the shunning than Maggie was. Noon or night, he growled, "Bottom of the morning to ye, you ass."

She knew it was conscious and deliberate. They were making a point of cutting her off from succor. They were unanimous about it. The only person who said anything to her, once, was Parky. He spoke to Sima, got the usual vulgar rebuff, looked off across the river, and murmured, "I'm sorry, Maggie." After that Miss Jewel would head back the way she came to avoid Parky. She felt it would kill her if even he snubbed her.

Miss Jewel decided the shunning was fair. They were within their rights. But they couldn't know how it hurt her. She was on the outside once more, looking in on human society, as she had been in the temporary homes she'd been in, foster homes. There she languished, suspended in an awful pain. She saw what other people had and hardly noticed. Family, community, belonging—she had none. It made her take two resolutions: She would always be independent, able to take care of herself, able to support herself, because you never knew. And she would find a place where she belonged. That was what her church meant to her.

Now Miss Jewel had lost everything. How could she be independent two thousand miles from civilization?

How could she even earn a living? How could she belong
to people who despised her?

She swung from utter despair to deep despondence.
Mostly it was despondence. She sent Sima off to school,
though the new teacher, Elvira Upping, wasn't equipped
by training or temperament to deal with Indian students,
especially Indians at completely different levels of learning. Then Miss Jewel lay around all day, doing nothing.
She wrote a lot in her journal at first, all the lurid details
of the lies and the maneuvers, but soon she didn't care.
She didn't leave the cabin except to go to the privy, because she didn't want to be snubbed. She just lay about.

She wondered what would happen when they ran out
of the stores of flour and beans they had in the cabin.
Sima said he would hunt and make sure they ate. Would
the congregation try to starve them out? Surely not, but . . .

From Miss Jewel's journal:

> My mind is still cast down. I pray—I ago-
> nize—but still something rests upon it which I
> cannot describe. My spirit groaneth within me
> as I go about my work; my mind is restless and I
> do not find peace. It really appears to me that
> God is preparing some event for me which now
> I do not understand. I have met so many disap-
> pointments as to cause me to be weaned from
> earth. . . . Perhaps I am wrong and take erro-
> neous views, but I have prayed that if I am de-
> ceived the Lord will undeceive me. I want very
> much to know the will of God concerning me,
> and I think I can never rest contented till I do.
> My case is, I think, singular. I know of no Chris-
> tian that ever felt as I do. I am sensible that
> some unseen hand is leading and directing the
> events of my life, and shall I not be grateful that
> I am so much regarded as to be led on, even
> through affliction, for some wise purpose? I will

be thankful and bless God that he afflicts me
and deigns even to notice me.

In the evenings Sima read stories from *The Thousand
and One Nights* and Miss Jane Porter's *Scottish Chiefs* to
Miss Jewel and Lisbeth. The two were her last contacts
with the world of human beings. She made tea for the Indian students one night when Sima brought them, but they
were uncomfortable, and she asked him not to bring them
again. She fantasized sometimes about telling Flare that
she knew now who was a liar and who wasn't. But mostly
she withdrew from human contact.

She didn't care. She was dead to the world.

She wrote a poem in her journal:

> *Though waves and storm go o'er my head—*
> *Though strength and health and friends be gone,*
> *Though joys be withered all, and dead—*
> *Though every comfort be withdrawn,*
> *On this my steadfast soul relies:*
> *Father! Thy mercy never dies!*

Chapter
Twenty-eight

 Flare patted Doctor. He liked to keep the critter nearby on watch. Flare could hear in the dark, but Doctor could smell. Smell Injun.

Unfortunately, Flare was hearing too many noises that told nothing. The horses snuffling, clomping, occasionally nickering. Once in a while a shout, or voices raised in song. Skye's loud, half-drunken bellow, mostly. The men were celebrating, and tippling.

He guessed they did have something to celebrate. Flare and the lads caught those Klamaths and took care of them. Brought the ponies back. Mainly they'd gotten the herd over the roughest country and were down on the Willamette, at Mackenzie Fork. Safe country, sort of. Not far to go to French Prairie, where they'd trade lots of the horses. An easy go on to Vancouver, where they'd trade the rest of them. And head home with some dollars in their possible sacks.

But Flare felt wearied by it all tonight.

He shook himself. Got to get out of this feeling of deadness.

He thought of his plan. Meant to save six of the best horses for Sima. Give the boy something to take back to his tribe, making things all right at home. Man couldn't live on the outs with his blood relations. But he could take care of his obligations and move on.

276

"Flare."

A soft voice.

"Flare."

Craw's voice.

"Come."

Craw walked close, sat. He got out the white clay pipe he still carried in a *gage d'amour* around his neck. Loaded up, handed Flare the tobacco. Flare loaded up his own pipe.

"Murph relieved me. Want to jaw a little."

Flare waited. He supposed it was such tame country he could talk on watch. Too bad, in a way. They used a lucifer to fire up.

"Garrett wants to go to trapping."

"Nothing there, Craw. Beaver's a dollar a pound."

"I told him that."

"Here Before Christ will hire him." It was the American trappers' bitter name for the Hudson's Bay Company, which always insisted its rights were prior to anybody's.

"Doing what?"

"Sailor on the timber boats. Back and forth to the Sandwich Islands. Winsome lasses there, they say, Craw."

"I'll tell him. All of it. Believe he'd rather go mining."

Flare puffed and sat and looked at the stars.

"What were we after, Craw?"

"Making the blood sing."

"Why doesn't it sing anymore?"

"Does for me, Flare. Slower maybe. Different tune, for sure."

"We killed a lad, Craw." Meaning Innie. "Two lads, truly." The Klamath sentry, too.

"Life looks cheap when you're young. 'Pears a long stretch, too."

"Was it worth it?" Flare asked.

"Half a year's wage, coupla months' work."

Flare tapped the ashes out of his pipe. "Why do things seem so sour to me? Getting old?"

"Might be. 'Nother word for getting old is growing up."

Flare gave him a silly grin in the dark. "Never tried that."

To Dr. Full's gratification, Billy Wells and the others rode in early on Sunday afternoon. The community welcomed them warmly, and some of the women got together a second dinner, side meat, sop, and other things the travelers hadn't eaten for weeks. That night the men reported their progress to the congregation, and it sounded splendid.

As he listened, what Dr. Full really thought was how splendid was Billy Wells. Put in charge of a difficult project, Billy had come through. He looked good—three weeks of clearing trees had shaped him up. He had a new air of authority, the sort that comes to a man growing into what he should do, what God asks him to do. He had a clear eye. His manner was not so insinuating as before—he was a little more direct.

Dr. Full was very satisfied. That's why, when Billy came to him with that special request after church that evening, Dr. Full said they must discuss it with the deacons tomorrow morning. Billy would be reporting to them anyway, decisions would be made about funding for the mission, and how many colonists to send there, and who would go. They could bring it up after all that business.

Privately, Full thought it was a good idea. A very good idea.

Billy Wells had a flair for the dramatic.

He, the deacons, and Dr. Full spent all morning working out the plan for the Dalles mission, practical men working out practical affairs. The deacons did not always know God's will, as Dr. Full seemed to, but they knew something about how to build a wilderness outpost and make it work. After two hours, things were in good shape.

That's when Billy made his surprising request. "Gentlemen, I want to take a new wife to the Dalles."

The deacons looked at each other uncertainly. Parky said, "Billy, appears to me she's spoke to that," and everyone chuckled. The community hadn't been able to do much chuckling about Miss Jewel lately.

Billy grinned and gave an elaborate shrug. "Let's let her speak for herself."

He opened the church door and jerked his head.

Elvira Upping stepped into the doorway.

Billy and Elvira held hands sometimes, and looked at each other fondly, and told the deacons how they had discovered each other. Billy said Elvira had come to him as a great comfort after his fall, and helped him set his feet on the right path again.

"I saw the light of the Lord shining forth in him," she explained. "He was washed in the blood of the Lamb. At first I just wanted to show him my personal support as a Christian. But soon God led me to see how he and I—"

"We've each spent the last three weeks praying about it, far apart, and we feel led to it," Billy said. "There's not much more to say than that. We feel led to it."

While the couple sat outside, awaiting their decision, the deacons debated only briefly. Parky was dubious. He asked sharply, "Samuel, do you know what on earth you're doing?"

Dr. Full choked back his anger. He'd never been able to get Parky to show respect consistently, or even to be uniform in addressing him properly. In a carefully curbed voice, he said they all should submit to where God was leading them.

Parky let it go.

The deacons were practical men, men with some years of experience with marriage. They liked the way the young folks mooned at each other. They thought God meant man and woman to get paired up. They weren't so sure it made that much difference which one you paired

up with. And they damn well thought a fellow starting a
new mission in the wilderness was best supported by a
helpmate.

Billy and Elvira were told they might have the ceremony Saturday, kneel with the community on Sunday to
ask God's blessing on their enterprise, and head back to
the Dalles Monday morning and get to work.

The mountain men, plus Garrett, drove the horses
into French Prairie just before sunset on a perfect spring
day, the wind gentle, the sky robin's-egg blue. Flare felt
like the setting sun was shattering an exquisite afternoon.

The Frenchies said how glad they were to see all that
fine horseflesh. Tomorrow they'd trade, and tomorrow
night hold a feast and a dance to celebrate skinning the
Americans.

Skye led the boys off to get drunk. The only two who
didn't want to drink, Flare and Craw, stayed with the
horses.

This time it was Flare who brought out clay pipe and
tobacco. He'd been wondering about it since the other
night. "How come you upped and left the mountains all of
a sudden, Craw? Didn't even wait for rendezvous, as I recall."

Craw snorted a laugh. "Don't exactly know. Felt different. Everything. Real different."

He looked around a little, lit his pipe, pondered. Flare
waited.

"You recollect the spring of '34? We was on the
Madison? High up?"

Flare nodded.

"Handy died, remember?"

Flare remembered. Craw and Handy paired up and
trapped up toward some of the boiling springs. Handy,
who was called that for a reason Flare never knew, went
exploring and broke through the crust of the earth and put
both legs into some of that hot water. Craw brought him

into camp on a travois. After about a week his legs got all inflamed and he got a high fever and died.

"It was then I started thinking of going somewhere else, doing something else, didn't know what. Just dissatisfied.

"I hadn't known Handy much afore I paired with him that time, but he had a Bannock wife and a little boy. They were with her folks over to Henry's Lake at the time. He hated to be away from that boy. Kept talking about staying with that bunch of Bannocks all the time and . . . doing whatever. I wondered then. Whatever didn't seem like enough for a white man to do, but Handy wanted to do it.

"When we buried him, I got to thinking on what he'd done, and what he wanted to do, and the want he got left with. What he'd done was grow up to be man-sized and then fight and fuck all over Injun country, blood runnin' high. Then look around to see what was next, and . . . " Craw made a scissors motion with his fingers.

"I had my woman, just Helen then, hadn't got together with Pine yet, plus Garrett and Isabelle. Susie's out of Pine. I began to think about that." His fingers scissored again. "Wanted to do something else. Something more. Didn't know what." He shook his head, chuckled at himself. "Californy," he said, and grinned at Flare.

"What have you done?"

Craw looked away. Kept his head turned. Looked back. "Reared my children up to be human beings," he said.

Flare sat, fidgeted. "Mine grew up without me. Whoever they are, wherever they are."

Craw nodded, puffed. "They do that," he said. "Mine grew up most of the way while this child was trying to outwit beaver. You know what, though? When you teach someone to be a grown-up, you learn yourself how to be one." He gave an embarrassed grin. "Might even act like it sometimes."

"If you try it, do you like it?"

Craw grinned foolishly and shrugged. "It's like there's stages. You're a kid and you play kids' games, and that feels good. Then you're a young buck and you play grown-up boys' games, and that feels grand. I don't hold with those as never goes adventurin'."

"Fight and fuck all over Injun country," said Flare uncertainly.

"That shines. Then one day you ain't a young buck, and young bucks' games don't feel like enough. You want . . . Helen and Pine and Garrett and Isabelle and Susie."

He gave a wry look. Flare let it sit.

"Craw," said Flare, "I'm gonna dub you Sir Nut."

"Naw," protested Craw. "Na-a-a-w."

"Truly I am. Get on your knees."

They invented it drunk, around a campfire, years before. That summer a scientist fellow named Nutting rode with them, studying plants. He had a habit of getting philosophical with big subjects around the campfire at night. So the game was, if a man spoke big foolishness, or pomposity, or a bunch of big words, he got dubbed Sir Nut. He couldn't refuse the honor.

Grumbling good-humoredly, Craw knelt in front of Flare. "By the power invested in me as Grand Poobah," intoned Flare, "I hereby dub thee Sir Nut."

He tapped the ashes of his pipe onto Craw's balding head.

Craw jumped up laughing and slapping at his head.

Flare jumped back, well back. Must have been a hot spot or two in those ashes.

"Whoo!" hollered Craw, laughing. "Whoo! That's what I get! Whoo!"

When Miss Jewel heard about the wedding coming on Saturday, she turned to her Bible and read. After a while she copied some verses from *Jeremiah* into her journal:

> Be not afraid of their faces, for I am with
> thee to deliver thee, saith the Lord.

Thou, therefore, gird up thy loins, and arise and speak unto them all that I command thee; be not dismayed at their faces, lest I confound thee before them. And they shall fight against thee; but they shall not prevail against thee; for I am with thee, saith the Lord, to deliver thee.

But what should she say? Who should she fight?

Part Five

A BRAVE NEW WORLD

Chapter
Twenty-nine

The wedding day was more than Miss Jewel could take. In a way she would have liked to stand right there and watch her Billy Wells get hitched to none other than Elvira Upping. Just went to show, she thought.

Went to show what?

She didn't know. She chuckled sardonically. But now that the church had given her the boot, she had some richly vulgar thoughts.

The spectacle might be fun, but she wouldn't be able to bear the shunning. They would celebrate the joining together of man and woman, and then have a big dinner on the grass in front of the church, and everyone would maintain this elaborate charade that said Maggie Jewel didn't exist. They would go around with stiff backs turned to her. Not one person would speak, or nod at her, or offer her tea.

Oh, her moods were black these days.

Funny how your feelings played tricks on you.

She didn't want Billy Wells. She saw him for what he was, a weasel, a chameleon. But her fantasy wasn't as smart as her wide-awake brain. Her fantasy made lots of fairy-tale pictures of her and Billy together. Making love. Teaching the innocent. Making love. Raising children. Waking up together. Making love.

No, fantasy wasn't smart. It raised up Michael Devin

O'Flaherty last summer, half man, half devil. This winter it raised up Billy Wells, all worm.

If she stayed here today, fantasy would make her cry.

It would be disgraceful to cry over a worm.

She went into the yard, where Sima was splitting wood. She smiled to herself, thinking how glad he would be.

"Let's go to French Prairie today," she said. Lisbeth's parents had come back two days ago, and she was there, so Miss Jewel didn't have to give a reason.

"Nothing to do with Lisbeth," she said.

He dropped the maul and grinned.

First sign of life from Miss Jewel in days, Sima thought. Didn't ask questions, just got his rifle and saddled his fine American horse and got her mounted and they set off.

He liked French Prairie. Even when Lisbeth wasn't there. People lived in shacks and tipis and even lean-tos. They wore skins. They ate meat they hunted and berries they gathered. Most of them were Indians by blood, and even the Frenchies and few Scots were Indians by learning.

Sima felt like life at Mission Bottom was all about pretending you weren't one of the beasts. You wore spun cloth, not the hides of animals. You were embarrassed about needing to go to the bathroom. You never talked about sex. You ate what you cultivated in nice rows. You were too good to be earthly.

God, if only word would come from Dr. McLoughlin. But not quite yet. He didn't want to leave Miss Jewel in trouble. He wanted to see Flare before he headed out. He wondered if he could take Lisbeth with him.

They came to the edge of the clearing of the cluster of cabins called Jarvis's and saw some fellow pissing in the grass in front of old Baptiste's cabin. It made Sima

smile big. Miss Jewel started to smile, he saw, but killed
it.

It wasn't until they rode closer, and heard him holler,
that they realized it was Flare.

Flare knew damn well it was them. Knew it damn
well. What other white woman rode astride? He shoved
his prick back behind his breechcloth before he started
hallooing. Mind your manners, lad, she's a lady.

He went running up to them.

"Top o' the morning to ye," with a fine, wide smile.

They said something friendly back.

Ah, it's right awkward, isn't it? You want to hug both
of them, but look at the spot you've put yourself in. Sima
doesn't know you're his father, and Miss Jewel thinks
you're the griz of all liars. A fine job of living you've
done.

He stood a few steps off, looking at them sheepishly.

Sima offered a hand, and Flare gave him an *abrazo*,
saying it was a custom he'd learned among the Spaniards
down in California. Actually, he'd learned it years before,
in Taos. Felt good to grip his son. And he touched his hat
to Miss Jewel, up there high on that horse.

"I'm glad to see you, Mr. O'Flaherty," she said
warmly. Her face looked flushed. "I want to tell you immediately how sorry I am that I accused you of falsehood.
Billy Wells was the one who was lying, I know that now."

Flare was taken aback. He held his hands up and she
took them and dismounted, almost into his arms. He
looked into her eyes. He wished the woman didn't always
make him feel weak-kneed.

"Now that we have a bit of an understanding," he
said to her, aware of sounding more Irish than usual, "do
you think you could call me Flare? That 'mister' makes
me feel like me father."

"Thank you, my friend," she said. "And I'm Maggie."

"That ass Billy is getting married right now," Sima said ironically. "To Miss Upping."

Flare saw pain in her eyes. He stepped away from her or else he'd embrace her. Miss Upping, he thought, fitting enough, that tight-ass. Turds of a feather flock together.

"Let's not talk about this now," said Maggie. "Sima will fill you in. I want to have a good time."

"You've come on the right day, lass," said Flare. "We just rode in last night and we mean to feast today."

"And lift a cup," Miss Jewel said with a smile.

"Surely some will do that," said Flare.

"And dance to Monsieur Jacquet's fiddle?"

"A jig or two, lass."

"Sounds grand," said Maggie. "I want to dance with every man in the place."

"A right bastard, yes?" asked Sima with a smile, checking the term. They were walking toward Flare's surprise for the lad.

"A right bastard," said Flare grimly. "And Dr. Full is, too."

Sima had given Flare the whole story, a nasty bit of work by Billy Wells, backed up by the good doctor. It didn't make sense to Sima. Flare claimed it was because the missionaries despised the strong and fawned on the weak. He couldn't tell if Sima thought so, too.

Flare studied Sima's face. Surely the lad wouldn't be tempted to model himself on the missionaries now. Surely. But he was a lad to keep his own counsel.

The shunning was rotter stuff. There are no cruel like the righteous, Flare thought.

He'd damned well better get Maggie Jewel out of this miserable situation. Damned well.

They came to the little corral with the horses. "Here's the surprise, lad," Flare said with a gesture. Sima's face looked . . . afraid to hope. "We did well on the pony raid. A dozen horses—six for me, six for you. You may choose your six—they're all fine."

Sima looked at Flare, looked at the horses, back at Flare. He offered his hand gravely. "Thank you." He was a good lad.

"The six are yours to do as you please with. But here's an idea. Good ones like that would soften a lot of hearts back with your people. Clear your back trail." And get you away from these missionaries.

Sima nodded thoughtfully. "Thank you," he said softly.

Flare looked at her across the big fire pits. The Frenchies were roasting a couple of elk whole on spits. Would be fine doings, though not quite so fine as buffler.

She was chattering gaily with two breed women. He chuckled. Maybe they were talking about how to make a lazy stitch, why English selvidge was the best cloth, or what new baubles might be down to Vancouver. Or gossiping about how Madame Sacré Bleu was in a family way again, how young Merde hadn't learned to keep his prick in his pants, and whatever. It tickled him to think of that highfalutin Miss Jewel making woman talk.

She looked like she was having a grand time. She needed it, according to Sima.

Sima had disappeared with Lisbeth. Flare sent silent blessings with them into the bushes.

He walked around to a bunch of men smoking and talking and shook with Alex McDougal. A square-jawed, blunt-talking fellow, graying and balding, never without a pipe in his mouth, not a bad fellow for a Scot. Didn't see his wife, Heather, a Bob Ruly from the Red River settlements—Bob Ruly was one of the Sioux tribes. Though named Heather, and a half-breed, she was uncommonly dark, and had the tongue of a shrew. Flare sat with the bunch, lit his pipe, and looked over at Maggie sneakily.

She's too tall for you, Michael Devin O'Flaherty, too serious, and far too religious. Bad as hooking up with a Brit.

What's wrong with ye, lad? What are these thoughts

of domestic life you're entertaining? Ye'd not be content minding a store. What would be happening when your heart got to itching to see the other side of the mountain?

Besides, she won't have ye. Which shows she's right smart.

He looked at her. He'd never had feelings like these before, and he didn't like them.

But then he'd never had a son before.

Nor thought of wanting a wife, and more sons, and daughters.

It gave him the willies.

'Tis a brave new world, Flare said to himself mockingly, that has such creatures in't.

Sima and Lisbeth were spooned up together, naked as God made them, wrapped tightly in a blanket. Though it was a lovely April day, evening was coming, and she asked for the blanket after they made love. She was getting chill.

She wiggled her bottom against him to encourage him. He murmured and kissed her neck and ears and caressed her breasts and belly. She liked what she heard, but she wasn't sure. He was talking about taking her to Montreal.

Montreal—it sounded grand. Her father told her all about it. Fancy carriages and French gowns and silver plates to eat from. She'd like seeing that. But they'd never let her have any such luxury. Her father didn't even dare take her mother there, for fear of the insults on the street. Like her mother, she was just a mixed-blood girl. Which was all right only in the whorehouses.

She loved loving Sima, but she didn't see how women sold themselves to men they didn't know, men who used them quickly and roughly and threw them away.

She didn't think she liked white men much. Except her father. She didn't know many white men. The Frenchies were all mixed-bloods, like her.

Sima was trying to get her to answer whether she

wanted to go to Montreal. If they went, she'd get to stop
at the Red River settlements. She had friends there, good
friends. Of course, Sima might not like some of the attention the male friends would pay her. She was hardly notic-
ing Sima's words, just his hands. Soon she decided she'd
better shut him up. She knew exactly how to do that.

Maggie danced until she was ready to drop.

There were gigues and reels, fast songs and slow,
vigorous and languid, athletic and romantic. She really
did dance with every man there, she thought, including
several who smelled questionable, and a couple with roving hands. Mr. Skye picked her up clean off the ground
and twirled her in the air, which was thrilling.

The music was wonderful. Voyageurs' songs, they
called them, mostly new to her. There were two fiddles
and Jew's harps of all sizes. The harps made a chorus, a
drone, the way she imagined bagpipes must sound. The
fiddles sang melodies above, now sprightly, now wicked,
now sentimental, now dreamy, often melancholy.

A melancholy one was "À la Claire Fontaine":

> À la claire fontaine,
> M'en allant promener,
> J'ai trouvé l'eau si belle
> Que je m'y suis baigne.
>
> (chorus)
> Lui y a longtemps que je t'aime
> Jamais je ne t'oublierai.

In several verses it told the story of a young man,
walking one night by a clear fountain, who tells the
nightingale to sing while he weeps. He has lost his lover.
When she asked for a bouquet of roses, he refused. Now
she is gone. He will never forget her.

You would never have thought these rough Frenchmen, who looked half like animals and who acted and

smelled half like animals, were really men of sentiment. But they loved their old songs. They roared out the words to the lively tunes and wept in their rum through the maudlin ones. They sang what they could never say.

The drunkenness, however, was going to be considerable, with Mr. Skye leading the way. She was glad that Flare didn't partake, and would be able to see her home safely.

Only one more dance, she told Skye, who insisted. It was "Passant par Paris," a lively drinking song, and she wore herself out jigging it.

> *Passant par Paris, pour y vider bouteille,*
> *Passant par Paris, pour y vider bouteille,*
> *Un de mes amis il me dit à L'oreille:*
>
> (chorus)
> *Gai, Bon, Bon*
> *Le bon vin m'endort et l'amour m'y reveille.*
> *Le bon vin m'endort et l'amour m'y reveille.*

Skye whispered the translation of the chorus in her ear with mock suggestiveness: Wine puts me to sleep, and love wakes me up.

When she collapsed onto a log, Flare spoke quietly to one of the fiddlers. Then he turned to the crowd and said, "One Irishman shall give you bunch of drunks a taste of the finer things of life. This is 'The Young May Moon,' by the Irishman Thomas Moore, the greatest living poet."

> *The young May moon is beaming, love,*
> *The glowworm's lamp is gleaming, love,*
> *How sweet to rove*
> *Through Morna's grove,*
> *When the drowsy world is dreaming, love!*
> *Then awake!—the heavens look bright, my dear,*
> *'Tis never too late for delight, my dear,*
> *And the best of all ways*

To lengthen our days,
Is to steal a few hours from the night, my dear!

Now all the world is sleeping, love,
But the Sage, his star-watch keeping, love,
And I, whose star,
More glorious far,
Is the eye from that casement peeping, love.
Then awake!—till rise of sun, my dear,
The Sage's glass we'll shun, my dear,
Or, in watching the flight
Of bodies of light,
He might happen to take thee for one, my dear.

It was gorgeous. The one fiddle double-stopped sweet harmonies. Flare closed his eyes and sang long, lovely lines fragrant with feeling. It was beautiful and touching. She supposed it was the Irish soul in him.

When he finished, Flare said, "Now, what the song means is that if it was May, we'd all get loved tonight." He put a nice little twist on "loved." Rough laughter around the fire.

Peculiar man, Maggie thought. He puts forth feeling, then pulls it back. Like all men.

Crack!

Shouts. She couldn't make out the voices. Or the words.

Crack! Crack!

A screech of pain. Sima.

Miss Jewel jumped up, and she saw Flare in front of her.

Sima came hopping, skipping, trying to run. Mr. and Mrs. McDougal trotted behind him, Lisbeth behind her parents, bawling. Miss Jewel could barely see by the light of the bonfire.

Crack!

Screech of pain from Sima.

Mr. McDougal was . . . whipping Sima with an ox whip.

Miss Jewel started for him and bumped into Flare.

Oh, she saw, Sima was trying to run while he pulled his pants up.

Lisbeth wasn't wearing anything but a blanket.

Alex McDougal blistered Sima with a torrent of curses. Maggie had never heard such profanity. Heather McDougal pitched in, too. In her French the English words "goddamn Shoshone" were repeated over and over.

"Stop him," she snapped at Flare.

Flare shook his head. "Boyo's got to learn to handle this kind of trouble on his own."

Sima hopped off into the bushes. Mr. and Mrs. McDougal turned and started giving Lisbeth a tongue-lashing. The girl cowered. Heather McDougal kept saying "goddamn Shoshone."

"Why does she talk about him being Shoshone?" asked Maggie. Meaning, she's a half-breed, too.

"Lass, Indians have their prejudices as well. The Sioux and Shoshones are old, old enemies. But the bad part is that, to the Sioux, the Shoshones are ignorant trash Indians."

She looked at him, unbelieving. Then she sat down on the ground and laughed helplessly, and held her head, and laughed and laughed, and cried.

Flare put his hands on her shaking shoulders and laughed with her.

Chapter
Thirty

She wanted to pull away from these people for a little now. They were good folks, in their way. She couldn't help liking them. She had to remind herself that every man jack of them had killed and scalped and consorted with low women. Even the horses they were celebrating were stolen. Unredeemèd Man.

At any rate, they were not her folks. She moved back and sat on the porch of a cabin, alone. She'd spent the day not thinking a bit about her dilemma, just having a good time. That had helped. Time enough, soon, to *think,* productively, about her predicament. Instead of moping, girl. Time tomorrow to think, and act.

For sure she'd learned a lesson. She couldn't survive by herself. Simple as that. Certainly cut a girl down to size.

Long ago Maggie Jewel had decided she'd never depend on a man, or for that matter on another person, for what she truly had to have. She'd been in foster homes where you had no right to anything, and she'd hated it. Then, later, she'd decided that by the same token she wouldn't be left out. She'd make a place for herself.

And now it's all boiled away, isn't it, honey? And what's left?

She smiled at herself, remembering. Her mother came from Vermont. She used to say the stresses of life to some people were like the fire under the bucket of liquid from the maple tree. When you made the stuff boil, you were supposed to get syrup. Some you boiled and got an empty bucket.

Life's boiling you, girl.

You do in life exactly what you don't mean to do. She was now dependent as could be, at the mercy of the mission folk. And completely excluded. Not to mention, she'd lost the thing she started out to do, teach Indian children.

To top it all off, she didn't have a clue what to do about it.

So you'd best get to figuring, girl.

Alex McDougal came to the fire, and Flare eased in next to him. Lisbeth was with her mother. Flare wondered where Sima was.

McDougal's eyes were still full of fire.

"You and I did the same," Flare said softly.

"Doon be telling me my affairs," muttered McDougal. He sucked on his pipe for a while. "Said they were in love," he spat. "What I saw was in rut."

"Aye," said Flare. "Just children themselves."

"I'm not ready to start in raising tiny ones again," said McDougal.

"Ye may have trouble keeping 'em apart," Flare said lightly.

"Ooh, I donna think so. Heather and I talked it over this last trip. We'll be going back to Red River."

"Red River," said Flare. Sad for Sima.

"Aye. She wants to be with her people. Wants Lisbeth to marry into her people. Besides, the bloody missionaries are spoiling this country."

He grinned lewdly at Flare. "As long as two thousand miles is longer than six inches," he said, "we'll be safe enough."

Safe. But no more kind or wise, thought Flare.

*   *   *

"Sima's mourning," Flare said. "May I see you home?"

She nodded gratefully. "Is he all right?"

"His bottom is well enough, but his feelings smart considerable. I told him Lisbeth and her family are heading for the Red River settlements. To stay. He's railing against the fates. My friend Murphy Fox is telling him the course of love never did run true. Before long Murph will give him a dram or two to drown his sorrow, which won't hurt the lad. All 'round he'll get through the night."

They turned the horses down the trail in the dark, and rode slowly in silence. It was a gibbous moon, a couple of days before the full moon. The gibbous moon always struck Maggie as odd, incomplete, unsatisfying. A life not whole, like hers. Or Flare's.

The moonlight splashed and dappled the trees, the new leaves, the earth, the spring grass.

"I loved your song," said Maggie. "You have the soul of a poet."

"The Irish are strong in the art department," said Flare, "because the British have all the craft."

"I think you're an American now," Maggie said.

"Aye, the Brits have dispersed the Irish, too. That's one of their ploys."

"Always jokes," she said affectionately. "I want to tell you something, Michael Devin O'Flaherty. Despite your clowning, you're a fine man."

He didn't speak for a moment. When he did, the sass and the lilt were gone.

"I want to tell you something, Maggie Jewel. What that Thomas Moore song brought to my mind tonight. You may not think I'm so fine when you hear it."

He looked across at her in the dark. They stopped their horses. He didn't speak.

She reached across and touched his arm. "I am your friend, Flare."

* * *

"Sima should hear this first," he began. "As he will as soon as he wakes up in the morning."

He took a deep breath, let it out. "He's seeking his father. That father is me."

She drew her hand away. Then she thought, and put it back.

He told her about the webbed feet. He told her about Pinyon and his winter among the Shoshones. He spoke of bright, young love, beaming down. He spoke of his innocence then. He spoke of the feeling he had for Pinyon. He spoke with regret of not having sense enough to treasure it. Too young and ignorant, he said.

"But heavens, Flare, why haven't you told him?"

"I'm a coward, Maggie. He told us all how he hates his father. Nothing new, I suppose, right down from that bloody patricide Oedipus."

"No coward," she said.

He was silent for a moment. "I'd just found him. I was stupidly surprised to discover that I had strong feelings about him. I can't bear to lose him, not yet."

She nodded, then nodded again. "Does anyone else know?"

"McLoughlin. He knew from the moment Sima asked the name of his father. The trader who spent the winter of '18 among the Shoshone was I. McLoughlin keeps records of such things. He said if I don't tell Sima, he will."

Flare watched her a moment. "And that bastard Full knows. He spotted the webbed toes on both of us. He made sure I knew how much Sima hates his father, how Sima will spit on me." Flare thought a moment. "The bastard threatened to tell Sima to get rid of me."

"Dr. Full is a wicked man," said Maggie. "And Sima doesn't hate his father. He loves you. He will be deeply moved when you tell him."

Flare let it sit. "I'll tell him at first light. He's got all he can handle tonight. Good Christ, but I want the lad to come ride the world with me."

* * *

"What will you do? In your new life?"

Flare shrugged. Since he thought beaver was done, she wondered what directions he would take. He'd mentioned switching to the trade in buffalo hides. He'd told her William Clark, the superintendent of Indian Affairs, had suggested he'd make a good Indian agent for the Platte River country.

He answered simply, "Live."

They rode on in silence. It was a good silence. Maggie felt splendid. Something good was going to happen for this man and boy she cared for.

They reined up in front of her cabin. Flare dismounted and helped Maggie down. He stayed back this time, but held on to her hands. He looked at her for a long moment. "Maggie," he began, sounding clumsy, "I have other words unspoken."

She waited.

"I love you. Will you be my wife?"

She burst into tears.

He held tightly to her hands.

"Maggie Jewel," he said, "I beg you to hear me out. I heard you out once without a word."

She nodded, but her head was half turned away, and the tears flowed.

"I love you. I cherish you. I believe you care for me.

"Truth to tell, Maggie, I've grown up some recently, and I want to make a different sort of life. With you. And Sima.

"What sort of life? That offer to be an Indian agent probably stands. You could teach the Indian children, which is what you want. That Platte River country is good, close to civilization but in the wilds."

She almost sank to her knees.

"Listen to me, Maggie." She half lifted her head. "Taos is a good country. American and Indian and Spaniard get on fine. Plenty of need for a teacher.

"And Californy's a good country. Grand. Mild all year, anything will grow. Americans and Indians and Spaniards all together again, a new kind of world.

"I want to start a new life, Maggie. With you and Sima.

"That's what I have to say."

He waited.

It took her a moment to change tears for words.

"Oh, Flare," she wailed, "just go away." She pulled her hands back. "Please, go away."

She ran for the cabin, sobbing.

Chapter

Thirty-one

Before breakfast Miss Jewel dressed and went to see Dr. Full.

It was clear to her. Since she could remember, she'd wanted to come to the West and teach Indian children. Dr. Full and his wickedness were beside the point. She wanted to serve the children. She wanted to do what God called her to do. Right now the dream tasted bitter in her mouth. It wouldn't always.

So she would damned well do what she must do.

She smiled at herself. That language was Flare's sort of talk, and she would have to leave it behind, even in thought. No place for it in her world.

She would make her confession. She would say she had sinned with Billy Wells. She had lusted, and fallen to temptation. It was true—she had lusted, had sinned in her mind. If she hadn't done everything they would understand by her words, that was their problem. She'd sinned, that was a fact. She would say so. A little deceptively.

She would survive.

She went past Mrs. Jick, who made a point of turning her back and not speaking, and past the children, who maintained an embarrassed silence, and found Dr. Full in the kitchen.

"I must speak to you about the condition of my soul," she said, almost stammering.

"Of course," he said gently.

Dr. Full stepped outside onto the grass with her. The children weren't right since Annie Lee died, he said, though Mrs. Jick helped out. Everything upset them, including his pastoral talks with members of his flock.

Everything in his manner suggested Dr. Full was simply her minister, solicitous as ever about her spiritual well-being.

Nevertheless, she told herself.

She thought back to when she had first met him, she thirteen years old, he sixteen. He had always had this air of concern. It was expectation—demand—in the guise of concern. Impossible expectation. Meant to be impossible. He was her brother—even if he never admitted it—but the one thing she was sure of was that she would never be able to please him. She wondered for the millionth time what he wanted from her.

Nevertheless.

"Dr. Full, it is my decision that I must set myself back on the right road with my brothers and sisters here, and with God. I have come to state my willingness to do whatever is necessary." She nearly choked on the words.

Nevertheless, she told herself. In five years today wouldn't matter.

He considered, nodded his head a couple of times, finally asked mildly, "What do you suggest?"

"I want to confess publicly and ask God's forgiveness." She wished she could put more contrition into her tone, be more placating. But it was enough that she was willing to do it. And she was. Whatever was necessary. It was that or give up everything.

He looked at her for a long moment, studying her. At last his face softened. He stepped forward and put his hand on her shoulder.

"I'm sorry you've suffered so. The decision to shun you was painful, and not one of the deacons liked it. With great personal pleasure I will meet with them this noon and tell them of your change of heart."

He stepped back. Looked at her fondly, or his version of fondly. "Miss Jewel, I hope for your sake that your change of heart, which I thank God for, will be enough."

Good Christ, what else? No, he was just talking.
And . . . *nevertheless.*

"Please be here at noon. When I've prepared them,
they may want to hear your repentance in your own
words."

She inclined her head submissively.

Flare woke late in the lean-to, after first light, and
Sima's borrowed blankets were empty. His gun and horse
were gone. Back to Maggie's, probably.

Flare rolled out, sat, looked around. Fog lay gentle
on the wide grasses of French Prairie.

He felt a great void in his chest. No wife, no son.

He wanted Sima, and he wanted him now. Or, goddamnit, he wanted to be rejected like the ass he was and
be done with it. As Maggie had rejected him.

Goddamnit!

But Sima was surely at Maggie's, and Flare didn't
want to see her again. Not yet, anyway. Too much
heartache.

He would go to the river and bathe. He liked to dunk
himself in freezing rivers for as long as he could stand it
and then give a banshee cry to relieve the tension and stay
a bit longer and then go charging out and run around on
the bank naked and roar like a grizzly. Satisfying, that
was.

There would be time enough to talk to Sima a little
later. Maggie wouldn't tell him.

Sima was packed and headed out. He had no packmule, but few belongings. He could ride downstream with
Flare and the horse herders, but he thought he'd go alone.

He was damn mad. Furious. That stupid woman hat-
ing Shoshones, more prejudiced than a white person. Old
man McDougal, so near dead he didn't remember what
love felt like.

If he left right now, he'd beat the McDougals to Vancouver, and see Lisbeth there.

He'd see Flare later, at Vancouver. And then his great adventure—Montreal, and his father.

Surely on the way to Montreal they'd stop at the Red River settlements.

He wasn't taking any food away from the mission. He'd stop at French Prairie and ask Nicolette for a little. One of the other Indian boys ran off home a month ago, and the mission folk called taking a little food along for sustenance stealing.

White people had a way. Or mission people had a way.

He had his foot in the stirrup when he thought. He had to say good-bye to Dr. Full. Surely he'd learned that much good manners from his grandmother. Regardless of how Sima felt now, the man had brought Sima to his village as a guest.

Dr. Full paced, furious.

"It doesn't make any sense!" he shouted at Sima. "Hang out with Frenchies, who are bad as . . . ? Roam the wilderness? What for?"

Sima had told Dr. Full he was going to Vancouver to join a brigade, no more.

He was sitting on a stump in front of Dr. Full's cabin. He did not want to debate religion with Dr. Full. Sima's mind wasn't closed to white-man medicine. But he was beginning to think that while white men knew a lot *about* God—theology, they called it—they didn't know God, directly, personally, intimately. They didn't even have spirit helpers, like Owl.

Dr. Full half squatted, put his hands on Sima's shoulders, looked into the boy's eyes, and said, "Don't you see you can't give up the progress you've made?"

The boy just looked down at his knees. Dr. Full didn't talk, he railed at you.

Dr. Full turned away and went onto one knee. O Lord, he prayed silently, I've made mistakes. But I value this Indian boy. I value his soul. He's heading away from redemption and into everlasting hell. Lord, he is only an Indian. Give him Your strength and light so that he sees *now*.

Dr. Full got up, paced, didn't look at Sima. He had to think. That damned McLoughlin. Unlike the other Christians, Dr. Full had thought him generous. Now Dr. Full knew better. McLoughlin secretly promised Sima a job in the spring. The offer dangling, all winter, tempting the boy. The man was an enemy of God and deserved unrelenting opposition, may God damn him to hell.

Suddenly Samuel Full brought himself up short. He was skilled at listening to hidden meanings. Weren't there some here?

He turned gently to Sima. "Why else are you going? Aside from the job?"

Sima hesitated. So there was more.

"The brigade is going to the Red River settlements. From there I can go to Montreal."

"And why do you want to go to Montreal?"

"I want to see the big world of white men," said Sima.

Dr. Full heard more hidden meanings. "Why else?"

Sima shrugged.

Dr. Full stared at him, demanding.

"To find out who my father is," said Sima. "The HBC has records there, Dr. McLoughlin says. They will tell."

Dr. Full considered.

"Sima, have you enjoyed your time with us?"

Sima considered and decided to say yes. Anything else would be rude. "Yes."

"Will you come back to live with us?"

"I don't think so."

"What do you think of our understanding of God?"

"Your great stories from the Bible are very beautiful," Sima said.

"Do you believe in God?"

"I see Spirit everywhere in the world, in everything."

Dr. Full heard well, and knew what the boy was not saying. "What do you *not* like about us?"

Sima hesitated. Hesitated some more. "You make each other unhappy," he said. "Much"—he banged his fists together like the word wasn't enough—"fight."

"My friend, that comes not from our religion but from a lack of grace," said Dr. Full.

Sima gave a maybe-so shrug.

"Sima, don't you see it's your *heavenly* father you need to find?"

Maybe-so shrug.

Dr. Full changed his tack. "My young friend, I can make you a better offer. As I said, we'll send you East. Free. Place to live, free. Food, free. We'll have someone check the Hudson's Bay archives for you. Please."

Sima stared downward. He shook his head slightly. No.

Damn it! Dr. Full considered most seriously. His last ammunition. All right, here goes.

"Sima, I know who your father is."

Sima felt his chest rise.

Dr. Full eyed him strangely, but Sima had not time for Dr. Full's strangeness.

"I have known all along." Emphasizing the words now. *"He made me promise not to tell."*

Was this bastard telling the truth?

"He didn't want you to know."

Suddenly Sima knew. Over a high, whining scream out of the land of dream, he knew who his father was.

Why, Flare? Why? Why?

Sima waited, trembling.

"The records will show that the Hudson's Bay man who lived with your people in the winter of 1818 was Mr. O'Flaherty."

It was true. It was true. Why? Why?

"If you feel unsure, ask Mr. O'Flaherty to show you his toes." Dr. Full pointed at Sima's moccasins and smiled.

Toes . . . goddamn web feet . . . from his father. Sima wanted to vomit.

He backed away. He started running.

"Ask yourself what kind of man wouldn't want his son to know," called Dr. Full.

Sima heard nothing but the scream inside his head.

Miss Jewel had never been so anxious. Sitting on one of Dr. Full's stumps, anxious, she'd wrung a handkerchief wet, and on a cool April day, soaked the armpits of her dress.

It was Parky who finally came out of the meeting of deacons. He stumbled toward her like a man who's lost a friend. "They want you," he said curtly. He led her in with a tender hand on her elbow.

It was Sheppers Smith, not Dr. Full, who asked the questions, like a lawyer at a hearing. He got to his feet and looked at the deacons like a jury. "The people have watched you close your heart to God, and to them. Why do you want to come back now?"

She had her discipline in place. "I've had a change of heart," she said with feeling.

"How are we to see your change of heart?"

"I want to open myself to the congregation. I want to confess before all that I sinned with Billy Wells." To sin in your heart is the same as sinning outwardly, she reminded herself. In her heart she had sinned with Billy Wells. "I want to ask God's forgiveness, and then live an open life before man and God."

Sheppers looked at the other deacons. They leaned forward, exchanging knowing glances, pleased. Miss Jewel was ashamed of herself.

"Miss Jewel," he went forward, "we have considered this most carefully. I'm personally touched by your repentance. The deacons are gladdened by it. We're sure the congregation will be as accepting as we are, and we welcome you back in Christian love."

"Thank you, Mr. Smith. I am afraid. I pray for God's help."

God help me. The words are all true. Their meanings are lies.

"But your acceptance as a member of a Christian community is not the only issue before us today."

What now? She felt herself going numb.

"You came here as teacher of the lost children we are sent to save. The deacons of this church have suspended you from that position, and we have composed a letter to the mission board which certified you explaining our action."

He turned and looked down at her with an unreadable expression. "The truth is, we are not satisfied that you are the person for that responsibility. For reasons that have nothing to do with weakness of the flesh. I wonder whether we can also take care of this matter now."

She waited. There was nothing else to do.

Had she lost all?

Sheppers looked at Dr. Full with suppressed . . . what? This is what it means, she thought, that phrase "dancing on my grave."

"Our concern is that you are a poor example for the children you teach. Teachers imbue an understanding of life less by precept than by example."

He turned. He drew himself up. She saw he would hand down his verdict now. "It is the decision of this board of deacons that to reattain your position you must show a change of heart more substantial, and more difficult for you, than a confession of momentary straying." He hesitated, apparently searching for words. "I'm sorry to say it, but you are willful, headstrong. You suffer from pride of intellect and will. Every Christian must cultivate submissiveness to God's will. He must lose himself, that he may be found."

He came to her and looked down pointedly. "This is particularly true of a woman. God made woman to submit to man. We find you . . . lacking in submissiveness. Some of us would put it more strongly."

He whirled away from her, preaching now to the deacons. "Ordinarily, this would be a matter only for you, your husband"—here he paused and fixed her with an eye—"and the Lord God. Not a concern for this board.

"However, we think you will unconsciously, and all too effectively, communicate your attitude of insubordination to the children. And that is unacceptable.

"Do you have anything to say on your own behalf?" He kept his back turned to her.

She asked softly, "What can I do to show you that it isn't true?"

Sheppers looked up and down the line of seated deacons, and lingeringly at Dr. Full. He turned back to Miss Jewel, and she was amazed at the look on his face. A man springing the trap. "Dr. Full is your pastor. You should counsel with him about that, and then pray about it."

As a body, the deacons stood up to leave.

Sima ran up to his pony in a blind fury. He didn't know whether to moan, sob, wail, shriek, or bellow. His pride in self-control—his *Indian* pride—kept his face a little straight. He had the reins and was into the saddle in one jump.

Someone grabbed the reins.

Flare.

My goddamn father.

Sima jerked at the reins. He wanted to be *out* of here. Anywhere. Away from my bastard of a father who denies me.

Flare held the reins hard, and looked hard at Sima. His eyes brimmed with tears.

"Sima," said Flare, "I'm past due telling you something. I want to do it right now."

Sima kicked his horse. The pony lunged. Flare threw himself to the side, dragged the pony's head along, held the horse.

Flare stood, shook himself, and looked gravely at Sima.

Sima jumped off the horse and ran.

Flare took off after him, and to the devil with the horse.

Over a log. Around a tree with a double trunk.

Going hard—Flare began to wonder if a father could keep up with a grown son twenty years younger.

Breath coming hard now.

Sima jumped down the bank into the creek, splashed downstream fast.

Flare ran along the top of the bank and gained a little. He would never gain enough.

He had to try something. "Ow-w-w!" he hollered.

Sima turned to look.

Flare took another step and without breaking stride launched his body toward Sima.

Crash of bodies. They fell down in a tangle. Came up sputtering and shaking water off.

Flare threw one foot across Sima's lap, hard.

"Wait!" he said into Sima's face. "Be quiet."

He reached with a hand and slipped the moccasin off his foot. Lying back into the water, he lifted the foot high. Spread the toes with his fingers.

The toes were webbed.

"I should have told you long ago," said Flare.

Suddenly hot tears choked him. "I-I-I am your father."

He held his arms open.

Sima leaned into his father's arms.

They sat in the creek and hugged and wept.

Her dear brother. She would have to persuade her brother, who had never acknowledged she was his sister, that her heart was obedient, malleable.

She was now delivered up to the mercies of a man who had sought dominion over her for her entire life. And never gotten it. Until now.

She shook her head slightly in wonder. Then she said softly to her Lord God that she would accept whatever he required of her, and looked up at Dr. Full.

His face was full of . . . what? Tenderness, maybe. Tenderness, she hoped.

She started to call him Samuel, but caught herself. "Dr. Full," she said, "what are we going to do? The one thing in the world I want is to teach those children."

He nodded. He sat next to her, touched her gently on the wrist.

"I think you know what the issue is," he said. "Let us pray for God's help in resolving it." They knelt together.

"I was scared to tell you," said Flare. "I'm so ashamed. I was just plain scared."

They held each other at arm's length and simply looked. After a while, Sima said, "Why?"

"You said you hated your father."

Flare laughed out loud. "You said your father's name

was Hairy, H-a-i-r-y. All of us thought you were saying
Harry, H-a-r-r-y."

He moved away and sat on a log. He laughed more,
it was so dumb. "When I saw your toes and knew it was
me, I was scared."

He looked up at Sima, standing over him. "You have
reason to hate me."

Sima shook his head, fighting tears again.

"I was ashamed. Ashamed I hadn't been there every
day for you. Ashamed I'd put you through all that pain."

Sima sat next to him. Flare said, "Most of all, I
thought you'd curse me and kick me out of your life."

Sima put an arm around Flare's shoulders.

"I didn't think I could stand that. I'd just found you."

Now Dr. Full seemed expansive, easy, generous.

"The deacons are only half convinced you need more
discipline," he said. "Some of them think you only needed
a husband, and some children to keep you busy." He
smiled sweetly at her. "I'm so grateful that you have accepted God's gift of light to show you the way."

He smiled broadly. "The deacons don't know you.
I'll never forget how bullheaded you were from the start.
When I read Scripture aloud, you wouldn't listen; you
would read some book of your own."

She shrugged. She'd just wanted not to be controlled
every moment.

He was enjoying reminiscing. "You wouldn't accept
leadership at all. That's the reason I told Mama you were
a Jewel, not a Full." He turned to her suddenly. "You were
my favorite, you know. Because you had spirit."

He turned serious. "Spirit in the service of the Lord,
put to the uses God made for it, is the most precious of
human virtues. Willful spirit is the most troublesome of
vices. And now you see that."

"I feel I do," she said. She was determined to see it
through.

"For those who have consecrated their beings to

God," Dr. Full began, "it is a question of understanding what His cause requires and entering into a compact to do it, whatever it is. Of surrendering self into the larger bliss of the whole. It is in that spirit I make this suggestion."

Flare and Sima walked along the river. They talked.

Flare told about the competition he and Dr. Full staged, a contest to show Sima who was the better man, which was the better way of life. They both chuckled about that.

Flare told Sima about his grandparents, shopkeepers in County Galway, simple people, fiercely Irish, fiercely Catholic, fiercely anti-British. His father had been in love with poetry. Gone now, both of them. Maybe Sima would like to see Ireland one day. "A God-cursed country," Flare said sadly.

He told Sima about his freezing journey across the North Atlantic to a brand-new continent, full of opportunities and dangers, and about how scared he was the first time he saw Indians.

After a while Sima said he wanted to sketch while they talked, and went to his packs for his sketchpad.

Flare sat and looked at the flowing river.

He loved rivers. He loved the way the water tumbled and played. He loved places like the falls downriver, where you could see water do its playing right on the surface. He also liked to think of all the little creeks that came into a river continuing to spin and undulate along, part of the river yet distinctly themselves, playing like otters in the greater mass of flowing liquid, separate melodies intertwining with each other, the inner music of rivers.

Aye, he thought, you truly can never put your foot into the same river twice.

"The criticism you've felt in the last few weeks," Dr. Full said to Miss Jewel, "has been offered in Christian love. I have been aware of Christian love for you during every moment of it. And in this last year I've become aware of how much I admire you. You have strength, and intelligence, and a warm heart. You were a pillar of strength on the journey, and a pillar of strength when Annie Lee died.

"Wonderful gifts God has given you."

He seemed to reflect a moment, and then he slid onto one knee. He seemed uncomfortable in that posture, but he plunged forward. "Now I come as supplicant," he said.

He took one of her hands in his. "I've spent hours and hours on my knees to God about this," he told her. He shifted self-consciously. He looked into her face. Since he could not read it, he dived in.

"Margaret Jewel, I ask your hand in marriage."

Chapter
Thirty-three

She hardly heard whatever else Dr. Full said. Something about his children, something about the integrity of the family, something about the isolation of the unmarried state, something about God's will that man and woman should be one flesh, something about the two of them as a two flames become one bright fire for Jesus Christ. He even made some sort of joke about her finally getting to be a Full.

She didn't laugh or respond in any way. She wasn't attracted or repelled or anything else. She was a jumble.

Finally she withdrew her hand and stood up. "Dr. Full," she said, "I thank you for this offer." She had difficulty getting her breath. "It's so sudden—I don't know what to say. If I may, I'll bring you back an answer. Soon. Tomorrow at the latest."

She walked out without looking back.

In front of his cabin she began to tremble. She could barely control herself well enough to walk. She broke into the shakes and had to sit down in the grass.

Finally she did walk. Down to the mill. She had not been to the mill since the awful night Annie Lee died.

She could not tell what her thoughts were. She felt heaved up and down randomly by crazy feelings, and she could hardly tell what her emotions were. Tears trickled now and then, but they brought her no relief. She walked aimlessly, flotsam in a heavy sea.

She sat on the grassy bank where she could hear the mill. She sat and listened to its river music. For her the mill was a thousand musical sounds—shoosh, gurgle, tinkle, whisper, rumble, murmur, creak, she was fascinated with them all. Sometimes they made a kind of harmony. Today they were a senseless clatter.

She did not think of being a child again, she simply felt like a child. She felt lonely, terribly lonely, as in the days when her ma was first gone. She remembered talking to the mothers and fathers who took her in and having no idea what was going on. She remembered how rejected she felt, these nice people meaning well but not understanding . . . at all. She remembered . . . lots of things, some of them good, some of them bad, all of them pungent as strong smells, old, ripe, sometimes rich, sometimes sour.

She began to sing. She wasn't aware of when she started, but then she got going strong. She would sing and imagine that the mill was accompanying her. She sang old hymns, "Nearer, My God to Thee," "The Old Rugged Cross," "What a Friend We Have in Jesus."

Then she sang "Wayfaring Stranger." It was one of her favorites, and she floated it out, plaintive, above the sounds of the mill and over the wide, slow river.

> *I'm just a poor, wayfaring stranger,*
> *While traveling through this world of woe.*
> *Yet there's no sickness, toil, nor danger,*
> *In that bright land to which I go.*
>
> *(chorus)*
> *I'm going there to see my father.*
> *I'm going there no more to roam.*
> *I'm just a-going over Jordan.*
> *I'm just a-going over home.*
>
> *I know dark clouds will gather 'round me,*
> *I know my way is rough and steep;*

Yet beauteous fields lie just before me,
Where God's redeemed their vigils keep.

(chorus)
I'm going there to see my mother,
She said she'd meet me when I come.

I'm just a-going over Jordan.
I'm just a-going over home.

Then she sang the one she'd heard the boatmen sing one night, floating down the Ohio River. She'd heard it before, but never in such a such setting, the rough, strong voices echoing eerily across the water. They were the voices of backwoodsmen, primitive men, men who couldn't read or write but knew how it felt to be in a strange land far from home.

Oh, Shenandoah, I long to hear you.
Away, you rolling river!
Oh, Shenandoah, I long to hear you.
Away, we're bound away
Across the wide Missouri.

Oh, Shenandoah, I love your daughter.
Away, you rolling river!
I'll take her 'cross the rolling water.
Away, we're bound away
Across the wide Missouri.

Farewell, my love,
I'm bound to leave you.
Away, you rolling river!
Oh, Shenandoah, I'll not deceive you,
Away, we're bound away
Across the wide Missouri.

Somehow the singing made it all right. She could go back.

After she walked a little, she saw Flare and Sima by the river.

Right then, like a miracle, like a revelation, she knew what she wanted to do. Knew utterly, and found a kind of peace.

They bounded happily toward her. They told her how grand they felt. They hugged each other. They laughed about how Dr. Full had tried to separate them by telling Sima the secret. Sima showed her his latest sketch of Flare, a head that caught his dash and style.

She had trouble keeping track of all their tales of joy. She tried to respond appropriately. At last she asked Sima if she could speak to Flare alone for a moment. She took his arm.

"Flare," she said, "I want something important from you."

"Anything," he said.

"I must go speak to Dr. Full now. Will you take me to French Prairie afterward? For the night?"

"Sure." He loved her, he'd do anything.

"Will you let me stay with you?" He was using Nicolette's old cabin.

"Sure." He searched her eyes. "What is it you want, Maggie?"

She looked at him. She supposed her eyes must look mad. She took her hand off his arm and tried to say it merrily: "I want you to take me to bed and jolly me good."

"Tomorrow?" Dr. Full repeated.

She nodded. "At noon." She kept her composure. "Would you ask Parky to marry us? I'd like that."

"Of course."

"Please excuse me now, Dr. Full. I have lots to do before noon tomorrow. The most difficult is to say good-bye to Sima and Mr. O'Flaherty." She had told him how happy they seemed in their discovery of each other.

Dr. Samuel Full cocked his head at that. Then he

considered his new opportunity in life, smiled admiringly at his woman, and said, "Things have worked out for the best, my dear."

"You're sure this is what you want," said Flare at the front door of the cabin.

She nodded several times. She grinned a pretty good grin. "Carnal abandon," she said.

She didn't say that she had only a glimmer of what she wanted beyond tonight.

Maggie Jewel was flying, and she thought she damn well might crash.

At first light she got up. Ouch! She was sore. No one had told her losing your virginity made you sore. Losing it, the devil. She'd flung it to the four winds.

She woke Flare. She slipped back into bed with him one more time. He gentled her, whispered to her, caressed her. Then he found ways to make it not sore.

Afterward she made him shut up and listen. She told him exactly what she wanted. It took some explaining.

"At noon," he said, making sure. "The wedding's at noon sharp."

"You bet," she said. She gave him a cockeyed grin and headed for her horse and her cabin. She meant to get married looking her best.

Watching her go, Flare thought, Maggie Jewel is considerable woman.

Chapter
Thirty-four

Susan Johnson and Mrs. Jick arrived five minutes after Miss Jewel got to the cabin, sent by Dr. Full to help her get dressed. She wondered if they'd stopped by earlier and found her missing, and wondered where the bride-to-be was before breakfast. The idea tickled her.

She loved the way her body felt this morning—tired and used, so that she moved slowly and deliberately, but alive and sensual and sassy, all mixed up together.

Time to get started. She had known from the time her ma died that no one would ever give her a proper wedding, so when the time came, she would have to stand up in whatever she had. She had collected some things bit by bit over the years. She got out the silk dress she had kept for nearly seven years and never worn. It was empire style, saffron, with a gay canary and tangerine sash, a sensible woman's one gesture of flamboyance. Mrs. Jick set to ironing it.

Then Miss Jewel and Susan oohed and aahed over the dainty pair of silk shoes she'd saved for the occasion, and the elegant little hat. It was all a little colorful for a Methodist minister's bride, but you didn't get married twice.

"You're going to look scrumptious," said Susan several times. She acted delighted by the fancy display they were going to make of the bride. Thank heaven she wasn't

Old Sobersides. Miss Jewel wondered if Susan could smell carnality on her, a grand, fecund pungency.

Miss Jewel thought the congregation would be truly surprised by how fine she could look when she wanted to. And taken aback by her lack of sobriety. Which was just how she wanted it.

She had no cosmetics, she was no painted woman. She saw a certain grandeur in plainness.

Miss Jewel was glad for tradition. Dr. Full wouldn't see her until she appeared at the altar. So he would just have to let her make as big a show as she wanted to.

At about a quarter to twelve the mountainmen began to collect outside the church.

Parky wasn't surprised. They'd come from French Prairie before for a funeral or two. And Mr. O'Flaherty was a friend of Miss Jewel and Dr. Full, and would naturally come to their wedding and bring his friends. Well, maybe Parky was surprised so many mountain men came.

They made a fine sight in their brightly colored blanket coats, which they wore on this cool spring day, with calico shirts, knives in their belts, hair slicked back. And they brandished their smiles like flashing blades. Something about a mountain man was always a strut.

Parky was talking with the members of his congregation, who were far from mountain men. They dressed somberly and comported themselves soberly. They shone forth their sense of high purpose—they were not in the wilderness for adventure, or frivolity, or self-gratification, like the Frenchies. Parky thought they could use a little more frivolity. Nowhere was it written that life should not be enjoyable.

On his way into the church he stopped to howdy Yves, and Jacques, and Baptiste. He wanted to make them feel welcome, mostly Catholics, as they were, in what they saw as a house of heresy. Not that they were really Catholics. What they had was more superstition than religion, and it was pagan as much as Christian.

He spoke in passing to Old Young and Black Mac. He didn't even know if they were Protestant or Catholic.

He howdied Mr. O'Flaherty, Mr. Skye, and the Indian boy Sima, standing together silently and watching everyone, and passed inside. He looked around the sanctuary. That was Parky's favorite word for it, sanctuary. He always found it a place of quiet, peace, and communion.

Back home there would be plans to be made, ceremonies to be observed. Out here you just rough-and-ready married them. And they just rough-and-ready started keeping house together and went back to work the next morning, getting on with the business of pushing the wilderness back and raising high the light of the Gospel.

Parky thought that was fine. But he missed the small graces that made a real society. One day there would be a real society here, and it would be gracious because he and his kind prepared the way.

The pianist struck up the music, and Parky began to feel good. To him the piano was more than an indulgence. The human heart raised itself to God, he thought, through music. It had come all the way from the East Coast in the hold of a ship, and to Parky the expense was worth it.

The mountain men were standing around the sides of the church. Restless fellows, they always were, roving eyes and shifting feet, never content to sit, especially not in a chair, and perhaps nervous here in this Christian building.

Miss Jewel came from the back of the church, down the little aisle toward the altar. She looked splendid, under the circumstances. Mr. O'Flaherty was escorting her, and would evidently give her away. That was irregular, but the wilderness made everything irregular.

Parky felt dubious about this uniting of Miss Jewel and Dr. Full in marriage, but she had asked him personally to administer the vows, so he consented.

Dr. Full stepped to the altar from the side of the church, a fine figure of a man with his black frock coat, erect carriage, leonine head, and air of authority. Parky did not always think Dr. Full wise in the way of the human heart, but God had given the man great gifts, and he would grow as a man of the cloth. This morning he simply radiated that overawing energy of his.

When everyone was in place and the music paused, Parky began. "Brothers and sisters, we are gathered together in His sight today to see these two joined together as man and wife."

Dr. Full interrupted in a stage whisper. "Miss Jewel has something to say first."

Of course. Parky knew and nearly forgot. Again irregular, but the bride and groom insisted.

"To bring herself before man and God as she chooses, Miss Jewel has a few words to say."

She turned and faced the congregation.

She began, "I come before you to make a confession."

She drew herself to her full height, conscious of the hair piled high so it would make her taller, and looked into the eyes of the congregation.

"I have sinned," she told them, her voice low, intimate, as though she were opening her heart to each one.

"Yes, we all have sinned, but I have sinned particularly, and grievously. Now I want to start fresh with each of you, and with God, by unburdening my heart."

Dr. Full felt as vigorous as he'd ever felt in his life. He stood beside Miss Jewel and looked on his congregation in raging pride. They all saw. They all understood. They all felt his triumph.

"The sin I committed was fornication."

Though everyone knew, when she said the word, murmurs flickered through the congregation. Dr. Full smiled broadly.

"The word of God," Miss Jewel went on, "tells us that sexual communication is reserved for a man and woman who love each other, and who are man and wife. I sought gratification outside those boundaries. Gratification of the body.

"It's true I've denied this sin to this congregation for weeks. I've refused to confess, I've proclaimed my innocence.

"But I stand here this morning to confess my guilt, to ask your forgiveness, and to ask the forgiveness of God."

Dr. Full started to turn back to Parky. It was time now for the saying of the vows. He was mildly surprised when Miss Jewel went on.

"I must make my confession more particular." She could not have described the flood tide of emotion rising in her, overflowing into the next words.

"I committed this sin repeatedly, but with only one man, and only on one night.

"Last night.

"With the man who stands next to me."

Pause. "Michael Devin O'Flaherty."

She turned full to Flare.

"It is you I love, and you I will now marry."

They permitted themselves a moment to look into each other's eyes in joy.

Over the gasps and mutterings of outrage Flare heard Dr. Full emit a loud, animal groan, as from a gut-shot animal.

A lot of people started to rise out of their seats. Dr. Full grabbed for Miss Jewel. Everyone stopped, frozen, when Mr. Skye grabbed Dr. Full from behind and bellowed, "Belay that, mates!"

His hand had Dr. Full's hair, and his pistol was jamming the minister's head far enough back to sprain his neck.

The mountain men had spread down the side aisles. Pistols and blanket guns were out from underneath their blanket coats, held muzzles to the ceiling, at the ready. Flare looked ready for a fight, and fiercely happy.

In the icy silence Maggie spoke to Parky. "Reverend Smith," she said with an immense grin, "will you please administer the vows to me and Mr. O'Flaherty? I think maybe quickly?"

Flare thought Parky actually chuckled before he intoned the first words.

And over the vows, solemn and joyful, came the exuberant voice of Sima. He sang his father and his new mother a song of blessing, a song calling all the powers of the four winds to bring a benediction to this union:

> *Hiyo koma wey, Hiyo koma wey*
> *Hiyo koma wey sheni yo*
> *Hiyotsoavitch, Hiyo tsaovitch*
> *Hiyo tosavitch sheni yo.*

Chapter
Thirty-Five

Flare's watchword was, "Keep an eye on your back trail."

The newlyweds, Sima, Mr. Skye, and several Frenchies went a couple of hours down the Willamette toward Vancouver. Then, while the mountain men went on downstream, left a conspicuous trail, and made camp, Flare, Maggie, and Sima slipped over a divide to the east, driving their dozen California horses. That bunch of preachers couldn't read a trail, wouldn't know which tracks were mounted men and which a loose herd. If Dr. Full came skulking around looking for a lucky shot, the mountain men would take care of him.

Just the same, Flare, Maggie, and Sima would skip Vancouver, go down to the Columbia an unusual way, and head straight for Walla Walla. And just the same again, they would keep a move on. The wedding night Flare gave Maggie was dozing in her saddle and stretching out exhausted for an hour or two while he and Sima took turns on watch.

By the second night they'd covered a lot of ground, too much for a bunch of preachers, and their back trail was clear. They made a proper camp, and Flare put up his canvas lean-to for the newlyweds and made a bed out of blankets and buffalo robes. He told Sima to stand watch out of earshot, which gave the boy a kick.

At first Flare thought Maggie was about to cry. She'd joined herself to a pagan and a madman, and he'd gotten her into trouble and run her half to death the first two days. What a marriage.

He fed her pemmican out of a parfleche. She made a brave attempt to eat it.

He put her head in his lap and rubbed the scalp under her long, pipestone-colored hair. It was beautiful hair. She was a beautiful woman. He loved her until it ached.

Now that he'd done it, would he be able to take care of her? Now that she'd cast her lot with him, could he make her dreams come true?

Yes, boyo, a grand romantic gesture. A long chance she's taking, truly. Are you thinking yet that it's a long chance for you as well? You're both mad, perhaps.

Nay. I say love is enough. I say love is all there is.

Long chance this way, no chance other ways.

He rubbed for a long time without a word, and she uttered nothing but an occasional sigh. He saw a tear trickle down her cheek.

She thought she was crazy. She didn't understand herself. Without understanding, she had the damnedest conviction that for once in her life she'd done right, absolutely right.

She felt wild, mad, exhilarated with freedom.

Scared as hell, too.

What of everything she'd lived for?

She would always love God. She'd changed her mind about which human beings walked His way.

She'd always want to teach Indian children.

She'd always want to live with a certain snap and sass.

Maybe she was ready to go adventuring and see where it took her.

Maybe? She'd put herself into the hands rubbing her scalp and neck and shoulders. Utterly. She was out of choices now.

"Well, lass," he said at last, "what will it be? Shall
we go to Missouri and be Indian agents? Go to Californy?"

She cut him off. "Let's go talk to Sima."

Flare's suggestions were Missouri, California, and
Taos. He described Californy as grand, a wonderful country where it's always spring or summer. Taos as a place of
peculiar beauty where a breed boy would get along. Missouri as a most sensible choice.

"We'll want to visit Sima's people first, wherever we
go," he said. "And I expect you're strong for stopping in
at the Red River settlements." Sima braved a smile at this
idea. "Lots of travelin' ahead."

They looked at Sima.

He spoke hesitantly, but with a new confidence. "I
want to go to my people for a while," he said. "And take
the horses."

Flare nodded approvingly.

"I have a task to undertake. Four days. June would be
the right month."

Flare understood. His son wanted to go on a quest for
vision, for medicine. First he wanted one of his own people to prepare him properly.

"I don't know where I'll go after that," Sima said.

Indeed he didn't, Flare thought. You never knew
where the force of life would take you.

Sima grinned. "Maybe wherever you go."

They went back to the lean-to. He asked her where
she wanted to go. "The world is wide to us, lass," he said.

There's a lame sort of joke, Michael Devin O'Flaherty, she thought. She said, "Shut up and rub me."

He rubbed. She wiggled sometimes, and moaned
softly. She was half out with fatigue.

Finally she sat up. She pushed him down on his
belly. She rubbed his neck and shoulders. Her hands felt
strong, and she kneaded firmly.

Finally she turned him over onto his back. She kissed him lightly on the lips. She looked at him, and touched his nose with a forefinger.

"I don't know where we'll head, Michael Devin O'Flaherty." She looked into his eyes to see what world was there. "Where we'll go, really, is adventuring." Scared again. Tremulous.

"I want you to fill my belly full of babies, and we'll spend our days raising them up."

She looked into herself for a moment. She saw high seas and no landfall.

Then she slipped on top of him. Wiggled all over.

"I'd like to get started on that part right now."

Afterword

This book is perhaps as much historical fantasy as historical novel.

The physical settings are real—the Intermountain West, the Pacific Northwest, and California of the 1830s, Fort Vancouver, the Methodist Episcopal mission on the Willamette, and other places. So are some of the characters portrayed in this book—for instance, John McLoughlin, chief factor at the Hudson's Bay Company establishment. The cultures, both Anglo and Indian, are drawn with what I hope is scrupulous fidelity. (The story of Pachee Goyo is borrowed form Rupert Weeks's *Pochee Goyo*.)

My missionaries are not historical portraits (since history doesn't tell lots that's crucial)—they're impressions of the sorts of Christians who participated in that well-intended and misguided effort. (One of them actually did try to crucify himself in the horrifying manner described here.) The most important of the evangelicals, my Margaret Jewel, is closely modeled on the mission teacher Margaret Jewett Smith. Her liberated style, her conflicts with the men in charge of the mission, her betrayal by her fiancé—all these are historical. The journal entries and poems attributed to her in this book are the ones she actually wrote and published. (The reader can pursue the people of Mission Bottom further in *The Eden Seekers*, by Malcom Clark, Jr.)

The other characters—Flare, Sima, and the crew—are the children of my imagination and my love. I hope readers have as much fun living with them as I did.

One scalawag, Mr. Barnaby Skye, is borrowed from the books of my friend and colleague Richard S. Wheeler. Thanks for the loan, Dick.

Some readers may get the impression from these pages that of all Americans I'm most fond of the Irish and the Indians.

Sure, them and the Welsh, and all others who see the magic in the world.

—WIN BLEVINS
Jackson Hole, Wyoming
December 1, 1991

ABOUT THE AUTHOR

WIN BLEVINS was born in Arkansas, attended Hannibal-LaGrange College, and graduated from the University of Missouri, where he spent most of his time playing music and writing bad poetry. He went on to receive graduate degrees from Columbia University and the University of Southern California, and taught at several colleges and universities while devoting his "free time" to more music and (better?) poetry.

The Rockefeller Foundation saved Blevins from life as an academic by making him a fellow in its Project for the Training of Music Critics. Thus trained, he reviewed concerts and plays for *The Los Angeles Times,* and became principal music and drama critic of *The Los Angeles Herald-Examiner,* and later entertainment editor and principal movie critic of that paper.

In 1973 he published his first book, *Give Your Heart to the Hawks,* an anecdotal tribute to the mountain men, which has been in print ever since. Blevins is also the author of innumerable newspaper and magazine articles, four screenplays which producers have been wise enough to buy but not yet to produce, and two novels about the mountain men, *Charbenneau: Man of Two Dreams,* and *The Misadventures of Silk and Shakespeare,* two previous novels in the Rivers West series, *The Yellowstone* and *The Powder River,* and an ambitious dictionary of Western words, *The Dude's Dictionary.* He is general editor of the series "Classics of the Fur Trade."

As a young man Blevins fell in love with the West, and has spent as much time as possible climbing its mountains, rafting its rivers, hiking its deserts, and exploring its history. He lives with his wife and the youngest of his three children in Jackson Hole, Wyoming.

If you enjoyed Win Blevins's epic tale, THE SNAKE RIVER, be sure to look for the next installment of the RIVERS WEST saga at your local bookstore. Each new volume takes you on a voyage of exploration along one of the great rivers of North America with the courageous pioneers who challenged the unknown.

Turn the page for an exciting preview of the next book in Bantam's unique historical series

RIVERS WEST: Book 9

THE TWO MEDICINE RIVER
by Richard S. Wheeler

On sale in Spring 1993 wherever Bantam Domain books are sold.

Chapter One

She felt his gaze again, and turned her back to him. A nun's back, she supposed, severe black broadcloth and a black knit shawl, though she wasn't a nun. Her long blue-tinted jet hair told him that.

Beneath her she felt the sinister throb of the *St. Ange,* the steam demons slowly churning the great paddlewheel at the rear, pushing the shuddering packet into the swift chocolate water of the Missouri. She clutched the rail and watched St. Louis diminish in morning fog, dark low buildings on long bluffs under a castiron sky, and with it, a part of her life.

She had grown used to the stares of men, even at age fifteen and even as a convent girl. It had started two or three years earlier among the brothers of her classmates, and their fathers, and sometimes their beaux. The sisters had noticed too, and had alternately delighted at the attentions men paid to Marie Therese, and scolded and warned. But mostly, she thought, they had delighted in it. How the Sisters of the Sacred Heart loved to encourage good Catholic marriages!

But it puzzled her even so. Just as the unwavering gaze she felt upon her back puzzled her now, when she wished to be alone with the image of St. Louis growing dim on the gray horizon. It must be that he noticed her height, she thought. She towered above the other girls; above many men. It didn't embarrass her as it might some girls. Her father's blood hadn't made her tall, but her mother's Piegan blood, the blood of Meadowlark, had fashioned her. The thought of her mother awakened some sort of unfathomable emotion she couldn't identify. She hadn't seen Meadowlark for eight years.

An amulet of yellow agate, shaped into a tiny buffalo, dangled between her breasts, suspended by a cord of rawhide. It was Meadowlark's gift to the seven-year-old girl about to go down the great river to be schooled. Marie Therese had swiftly hidden it back then, when she learned such things were idols and forbidden. But now she wore it. Now she was beyond the clutch of the sisters. Meadowlark's gift was a powerful totem of the Piegan people with good medicine in it; but above, resting on the loose bodice of her black broadcloth dress, dangled a fine silver crucifix suspended from a necklace of turquoise-colored beads.

She watched the wooded black shores roll by, and heard the slap and gurgle of water hammering on the low hull. Dark smoke from the twin chimneys of the *St. Ange* sometimes whirled down on her, leaving grit and ash in her nostrils. And still the boy behind her gawked.

Perhaps, she thought, she should turn and face him; let him see her blood. Let him see her yellow-brown flesh and her heavy cheekbones. She had never understood why Indians had been called redskins. Hers was golden brown, and so was the flesh of all of her mother's people, the Pikuni the whites called Piegan, the Kainah they called Bloods, and the Siksika they called Blackfeet. Let him see her flesh and that would stop the staring. It often did. No matter how welcome mountain children had been in St. Louis, she had found that barrier everywhere, unspoken. Sometimes even among the jolly sisters.

She had to turn and face him anyway. She felt trapped at the varnished rail, with no place to go but overboard into the cold murky river. Her few things had been stowed by a porter back in the women's cabin aft, over the thundering paddlewheel, beneath one of the six bunks in that common room. She'd go there, where men were forbidden, now that the city had been ripped from her vision and the monotonous wooded shores offered nothing.

She turned to face the boy, some proud reserve in her face, and met his gaze coldly. He surprised her a little. His face looked as dark as her own, a little redder perhaps, and the features of two races melded in him as it did in her. Skinny, she thought. Hair oddly red on an Indian face. Dressed in a gray wool suit jacket and baggy britches.

"I didn't know you had gray eyes," he said.

"Please stop staring at me," she replied. Her solemn gray eyes had been one of the gifts from her father, Charles Pierre Jacques Eduard de Paris. They didn't fit in her Pijuni face; they didn't belong, and they always startled people.

From him she had those eyes and a thin nose and sharp chin-line and small bones and a knowledge of French and English and maybe even some of his peculiar arrogance. Yes, she thought, she especially had that. He'd always seemed somehow above the American fur Company's other engages and even looked different from them, slim and patrician, while they were burly and rough and hearty.

"I think I know you," the boy said.

She'd been pushing past him, but paused.

"I think you're Marie Therese de Paris. I remember when you went away."

He surprised her. She stared back, dredging memories from her childhood. She wasn't sure at first. Could he be that boy?

"You are Peter Kipp."

He grinned triumphantly. "I've been to school here, same as you," he said. "Only we aren't Catholic."

She stared uncertainly. He'd been such a quiet boy. Now he seemed different, bold, almost insolent, with a wide grin that mocked her. "You kept looking at me," she said, to put him off balance.

"I couldn't help it. You're beautiful, Marie Therese. Now that I'm grown up I see things—"

"Neither of us are grown up."

"I'm seventeen."

People had joked that Peter Kipp's father was the American Fur Company. In 1840, when he was about five, a Salish women had come to Fort McKenzie and handed the red-haired half-breed boy to the factor there, Alec Culbertson. The child is yours, she had said. His name is Peter. And she'd left without revealing anything more. Peter.

They'd all studied the boy's face and red hair and guessed at the father, drawing blanks always. Young James Kipp, even then a veteran American Fur Company trader, took the boy in and raised him, or rather, his lovely Mandan wife Ipasha, or Good Eagle Tail, had. No one ever supposed Kipp had sired the child.

"I must go to my cabin now," Marie Therese said.

"Why do that? We have a whole steamboat to see. Don't you want to see it? We can go anywhere, I guess."

"I don't like the boat."

"Why?" he asked, intensely curious.

"The underwater spirits are bad."

"Bad medicine!" He laughed. "Bad medicine! Do you still believe that stuff?"

She refused to reply. Meadowlark had told her long ago that the things under the water were dark spirits, like the things under the earth. The *St. Ange* crawled with them. She felt the packet shudder with dark spirits, felt the steam from dark fires make the boat go upstream against the current.

"I see you do," he said a little scornfully. "This isn't magic. It's the modern machinery of white men, harnessing the powers of nature. The fires made steam and the steam pushes two big pistons connected to pitman rods which are connected to the paddlewheel. It is all perfectly sensible to rational minds. It is all science. Didn't they teach you that Indian religion is all superstition?"

"Yes," she said reluctantly. The sisters had told her that all the spirits the Pikuni respected were idols and evil. Marie Therese had tried to believe them; tried to believe that the only God was the invisible one above and the visible one on the cross. It troubled her.

"Then you should forget all those silly myths. Just because our mothers had them doesn't mean they're right."

She was suddenly aware of the small polished amulet under the black bodice of her dress. It troubled her, too. Everything that divided her mother's beliefs from her father's beliefs troubled her.

"Let's go looking around," he said. "Since the fur

company chartered the *St. Ange,* it's like we own it, almost."

She didn't reply, but didn't resist. She hadn't intended to explore the great evil fireboat because of the bad spirits she felt everywhere. She meant to cloister herself in the cabin. But Peter's enthusiasm tugged at her.

She followed the boy past cords of firewood destined to make steam, past deck passengers making camp as comfortably as they could. Peter headed for the companionway that would take them up to the boiler deck, where the cabins and staterooms were, as well as the segregated men's and women's lounges fore and aft. But he didn't pause there. He tackled the next companionway, while she tagged behind, her heart racing with the sudden exertion. This one took them to the top deck, the texas deck, a dizzy height above the river. The pilot house perched here and just behind it the texas, or officer's quarters.

"See!" he cried. "Feel the power of it! Don't you see?"

She felt the power, the throb of the engines. Just above her the twin chimneys belched black smoke and ash. Whitemen had harnessed the power of fire and water to make the *St. Ange* run against the Big River. That was the Pikuni name for the Missouri—the Big River. In the pilothouse she saw a steersman and another in trim blue uniform, Joseph LaBarge, the ship's master, pilot, and owner. No man, they said, knew the wild river better. Before her, rising from the main deck, were wooden booms and spars, and beyond them, the shimmering dark flood that would take her home . . . home to a place she'd never seen and a father she barely remembered.

Dizzily she peered down at the dark river far below, feeling the power of the whitemen in the shuddering boat. Near the prow she saw two priests. She knew the name of one of them. Any Blackfoot would. She cried out, feeling the water demons convulse the packet, and ran for the companionway.

"Where are you going, Marie Therese?" Peter cried.

"I'm afraid," she said, descending the stair as fast as her skirts would let her. She reached the boiler deck and raced down the corridor dividing the staterooms, reaching the women's lounge, a tiny cubicle actually, and then the women's cabin behind it. Just beyond it the wooden paddlewheel splashed and rumbled and sprayed her fear back upon her.

They stood at the bow of the boat on a sultry afternoon watching sweating deckhands hoist long lengths of ash and oak aboard to feed the hungry firebox. Eighteen cords a day, and whenever wood wasn't available from the woodyards along the banks, Captain LaBarge sent his crew and passengers to the forested flats along the steaming river to cut fuel.

She wore her cream dimity dress with the frills about the neck, but in the oppressive heat of the glistening river snaking by, it seemed as heavy as her black woolen broadcloth. From the time she'd arrived in St. Louis and the lower river, she'd hated summers and hungered for the dry cool air of her homeland far, far away. Her underthings stuck to her and her body felt greased and dirty, as if the moist air would not let her flesh breathe.

Peter didn't seem to mind. The ebullient boy didn't mind anything, including her cold stares and reluctant companionship, and in truth, she thought, she'd become fond of him. He made her laugh. His shining hazel eyes were seeing the universe in ways her own eyes hadn't, and slowly she'd come to enjoy that, and him.

"Marie Therese," he said solemnly. "Would you listen carefully, and even if you oppose what I ask, would you take me seriously?"

He peered earnestly at her, his face glistening with sweat, his eyes searching her own and then travelling longingly to her breast, whose contours were visible under this shadowy dimity unlike the concealing wool of her broadcloth.

"Yes, Peter," she replied, sensing his earnestness.

"Would you marry me? I love you."

"Peter!"

But she saw such longing in his face she didn't laugh,

though the question was ridiculous. Behind him she watched sweat-blackened hands carry the rough logs up a gangplank and pile them neatly near the firebox.

"Marie Therese. I know you're young. Fifteen's young to marry. I know I'm just starting. I'm going to rise in the fur company. I'm going to the top. I'm going to become a chief trader at one of the posts. Maybe even a partner of old Chouteau, like Alec Culbertson. I'm going to do it, Marie Therese . . ."

She smiled at Peter, knowing what her answer would have to be. But still she enjoyed this. No one had ever proposed to her before. The sisters had talked about it all the time. Say Yes to a good Catholic man, they had said, but don't let him touch her until after the nuptials. Now here was a boy, not a man, and a protestant too. But that didn't matter.

"Marie Therese, we're mixed bloods, you and me. You know how it is. What they think of half-breeds. Some of them call us bastards, or mountain children, because there are no priests and ministers up the river. You know how it is. But if we marry, if we stay together . . . Don't you see? The fur company's a safe place for us, don't you see? What does it matter, what they think down here? We'll be up there, where it's cool and good. I can make us a good living with the company, don't you see? I know all the things of the whites. We can take these to our mothers' people—the Pikuni, the Salish, and give them—"

"Peter," she said. "I don't like the world of the whites. What they do. What they think. How they treat me. How they treat my mother's people . . ."

"You haven't answered me."

"I can't. Not now. Maybe not ever, Peter."

"I'll ask you tomorrow," he replied. "And the next day and the next. I will ask you every day to Fort Benton and then I'll ask you every day when we get there. I love you, Marie Therese."

She smiled. "You are a protestant." She meant to say, You are a Christian, but didn't. She could not say what she was; only that other spirits tugged her soul.

He fell silent and together they watched from the varnished rail as the *St. Ange* built up steam again until it throbbed from the escapement pipe and oily clouds of smoke belched toward ivory skies. She'd scarcely seen here a deep blue sky of the sort she had grown up with, on the high Missouri.

The sun dazzled off the water so viciously she wished she'd worn her one hat with its broad brim that shaded the eyes. She felt the prick of oily sweat collect around the shining buffalo amulet between her breasts. She could not marry Peter. Something else tugged at her. Something dim and strange had been forming in her soul—she liked that whiteman's word, soul—that would lead her along strange paths. Beautiful paths.

"I am Pikuni," she murmured to him, but he didn't notice. He paid rapt attention to everything on board, and now he watched the deck hands in their dirty cottons drag the gangplank aboard.

She felt the steam demons again, the dark hissing power of the *St. Ange* as it shuddered free of the muddy levee and out upon the copper river. Far above, on the white-enameled texas deck she saw Mrs. LaBarge, Pelagie, who had come along with the captain this trip. And their children. They had two staterooms just behind the men's lounge far forward.

She saw the priests, still in their long black cassocks with red piping, and wondered how they endured the steamy heat in their black clothing. One of them, the Jesuit Pierre-Jean DeSmet, had become a legend on the upper river and among her people. The other was new to her. Christopher Hoecken, she'd learned on the second day of the voyage. She'd learned the names of other passengers, too, such as Doctor John Evans, a geologist. A man who examined the bones of mother earth. Somehow, he disturbed her. His irreverence for the earth mother disturbed her. Would he not let the spirits rest?

Around her on the sweated burning deck a motley crowd of American Fur Company people, French Canadians, Scots, Missourians, Assiniboin, Sioux, Crow, and breeds like herself, all rank with oozing sweat, found shade against the murderous sun, and waited for lavender twilight and river mist. She thought of her narrow bunk and the shade of the women's cabin. But its fetid air and closed society deterred her. The few white women on board, bound for St. Joseph or Leavenworth mostly, had studied her dark skin with cold disapproval, unable to prevent such contact as they had, but not yielding an inch to her. Later, above Leavenworth or Council Bluffs, virtually everyone remaining on board would be connected some way with the company. But until then she had no place to call her own.

An easterly tailwind pushed the packet, carrying on its hot breath the foul smell of the waterclosets perched aft on the main deck and projecting out from the coaming so that wastes dropped into the brown river, unless they streaked first along the stained hull just ahead of the wheelhouse. Couldn't these white people ever be clean? Why didn't they take sweats and wash each day in the river no matter how cold, as her mother's people did?

She found shade on the north side of the boat, and relief from the heavy nauseating odors around the stern. Peter followed her, as he always did, almost a shadow, wanting to squander every second on board this bad medicine ship with her. She didn't mind. His blood was something like her own, Salish and perhaps Scottish Canadian, but at least mixed. And that made him precious to her. And he had become her protector, too, fending off stinking lice-ridden men in buckskins and greasy calicos, whose stringy hair hadn't seen soap in months, if ever. Men with lidded eyes and something hungry in their frank sweeping gaze that always paused at her breasts and thighs.

Beside her a man with a wild mop of brown hair sketched deftly on a pad, catching a dozing mountain man slumped against cordwood. She peered at the sketch and marveled.

"You like it, yes? I am Rudolph Friedrich Kurz of Berne, Switzerland," he said in heavily accented English. "You are a daughter of the mountains, yes?"

She nodded warily. That could mean anything.

"I will sketch you next. What tribe do I see in your face, mademoiselle?"

"Pikuni—ah, Piegan. Ah, Blackfeet."

"Ah! You are from far above! That's where I am going, far west and north where the air is cool and this—this steam doesn't . . ." His voice faded off. "You have free will. I see it in you, free will. I will catch your inner spirit, your freedom!" Something in that excited her. Could this artist catch the true thing inside of her, the Pikuni spirit, the medicine power that separated her from white men, that separated her even from her father?

"I would like that!"

"Sketch me too," said Peter. "My mother is Salish."

Forward, near the booms, amidst a welter of crates mounded on the grubby deck, a crowd gathered around a writhing young man of the mountains, who lay groaning and gasping air through his honey-colored beard.

The growing crowd caught her eye and chilled her. Kurz, still sketching, scarcely noticed. Peter glanced forward uneasily and then turned away. But she watched.

Slowly the man's writhing subsided, and then he lay quiet except for great irregular gulps. His flesh looked blue beneath the brown stain of outdoorsman's flesh. She stared at this bad medicine, seeing the Under-Earth Spirits dance about him, just how long she didn't know, mesmerized by something evil that she had known would come, she had felt in this *St. Ange* ever since she stepped aboard and felt its chill.

And then the hot deck echoed with a terrible wail that rent the boiling June afternoon, a word she had heard too often that year of 1851 and the previous years as well.

"Cholera, cholera. . . ."

Chapter Two

Death . . . a plague packet.

It seemed to Peter that cholera perched atop the pilot house far above, pointing now here, now there, striking men by whim, with no respect for virtue or sin. The *St. Ange* plowed grimly up the white-boiled river while news of its cargo raced ahead by fast horse, faster by far than its slow passage up the twisting flood.

They docked at deserted woodlots whose proprietors had fled, and loaded the long lengths of cordwood, carefully measured by the mate, under a broiling lemon sun. At each site Captain LaBarge left a receipt in a bottle, payable upon the ship's return or negotiable at St. Louis.

On board, people shrank from one another, ceased talking, stared bitterly into space, sweated in the heavy air, ignored the sullen ash that cascaded from the chimneys onto them. Cabin passengers took to their bunks, dreading the burning deck.

A few died swiftly, as the first man had. Most died slowly, over two days or three, dehydrated by the convulsions of their bowels, unable to keep down any liquid. It struck some so swiftly they had no time to race to the cabinets aft. They could only drop their britches and spew the waste of their spasming bellies over the side, where it smeared its way down the white hull and into the murky river. Some couldn't wait at all, and the filth soaked their dungarees and oozed noisomely out upon the worn gray planks of the deck. Others, in the oppressive heat of their cabins, filled foul chamberpots so fast the cabin boys couldn't empty them. Cabin and stateroom passengers had only the enameled sheet-metal pots whose lids failed to contain the stench within.

Marie Therese had angrily retreated to her women's quarters, and Peter hadn't seen her in days, and wondered if she'd been stricken. Bad medicine! she'd cried. White men's evil! Until the white men came up the river, bearing their evils, her mother's people had scarcely known disease. But in 1837 the pox had come wrapped in a foul blanket aboard the *St. Peter*—why did they name their evil ships after saints?—and slew a third of the Pikuni, almost all the Mandans, and the Arikara and Assiniboin. . . . Did whitemen slay everyone? she asked, and then turned away, in tears. Peter hadn't seen her for three days.

Peter trudged the ship as if it were a hot frying pan, afraid to touch anything, peering at varnished handrails with black suspicion, detouring around the few other passengers who walked, refusing to eat the poisoned food, terrified to put his lips to murky river water.

Death was everywhere, lurking, waiting to pounce. Just that hot morning he had watched a man who seemed to be in good health standing beside the rail amidships.

"Oh, no," the man had said quietly, walking stiffly rearward toward the closets. He'd emerged from them flushed and fevered. Wobbling forward to the foredeck, he settled down, his back to cordwood, and clutched his convulsing torso . . . doomed. The thin, dark Father Hoecken had spotted him, and had taken the man's sweated cold hand into his own.

"Our good Lord awaits you on the other side, in Paradise," the priest had whispered.

"I don't want. . . ." the man muttered.

"No one wants to die. But we go when we are called. What may I do for you? Are you baptised? Have you anything to confess?"

"Not Catholic."

The priest had nodded quietly. "Are there messages? Have you loved ones? Do you want to make a will?"

The man vomited, the treacly stuff sliding green across the hot deck.

"Yes," he'd whispered. "Tell my wife . . ."

Peter had watched, transfixed, as the bearded man in butternut homespun coughed out names and messages, while the Jesuit quietly pencilled words on foolscap.

The man didn't die. He lay gasping and blue-fleshed as the pearly sun fried him through the afternoon. No one dared drag him to shade. But Father Hoecken brought him a tumbler of water with a little whiskey in it. The man gulped the liquid, and then vomited it out, wheezing. Peter stared frequently, morbidly curious about the moment when breath left the man; curious about what would happen. What would that man feel when it happened? Peter wondered whether he would see God and angels just beforehand . . . or demons . . . or nothing at all. What would it be like? He could scarcely imagine it.

Not me! he thought. Not me! I'm too young!

But he knew he wasn't too young. Terror drove him forward to the prow. That put death behind him, not ahead. Death back there, not up here! He closed his eyes, concentrating on his stomach. Was that quiver a first sign? He wiped his heated brow. Had he fevered? His forehead burned!

He felt a new throb in the hammering steam engines, felt them slow. He peered back above, high up to the pilot house, and made out the captain gesturing to the wheelsman, shouting down the speaking tube to the engineers here on the main deck. The silent ship settled slightly in the coiling green current and then slid northward toward a gentle wooded shore with a meadowed hill rising above it. Not a woodlot in sight, and it puzzled him. Slowly the silent packet eased toward the bank until the paddles ceased splashing and the boat glided almost to land.

Then he understood. Six crewmen with spades stood ready. And at their feet lay two bodies wrapped in ship's canvas. And above them stood the Jesuit Pierre-Jean DeSmet, florid and beefy-faced, a missal in hand, an ivory stole threaded with gold over his neck. Captain LaBarge had stopped for a burying.

Something in Peter cried out to walk down the plank they were sliding out, to flee the packet while he could. It didn't quite reach land, disappearing into muddy water three feet from shore. He could run! Run! Deckhands splashed to the grassy bank and made the boat fast, fore and aft, to saplings.

"Who are they? Who died?" Peter asked a gaunt weathered man beside him, the geologist John Evans.

"Fur company men . . . Cadotte and Rambeau. Deck passengers—it seems to affect the deck passengers worse."

Peter knew Eduard Rambeau—he'd labored for years at Fort McKenzie. "I don't want to die!" he exclaimed.

Together they watched crewmen trudge up the verdant hill and begin digging under a chalky sky, sweating in the glare of the river. Far above, Captain LaBarge watched silently from the texas deck.

"Who are you, lad?" asked the geologist.

"Peter Kipp."

"James Kipp's son?"

"Sort of," Peter said shortly. "I live with them. I've been at school for seven years."

Something abrupt in his tone evoked a gentle caution in the older man. "There's a way to fight the cholera, Peter. I've seen it work. Use a little spirits in everything; soak your food in spirits. Dip bread in it. Never drink plain water, but mix some spirits in."

"How do you know that works?"

"I've seen it work. I'm out a lot—out beyond the cities, out where the claws of cholera stretch to rake us, on the California Trail, and the Santa Fe. And I've been on the boats. Peter, lad, do as I ask, eh?"

"I don't drink spirits. I'm too young."

"Spirits are dangerous and you're wise, Peter. But use a little now. A little in everything you eat. Or at least wine with every meal. I've been telling that to a lot of people on board. Some follow it; most don't."

"Is it scientific?" Peter asked. Science impressed him more than anything he'd learned in St. Paul's School for boys, run by the Anglicans.

"I'm afraid not. We know no cause and effect. But if science observes and records results, then I'd say yes, it's scientific. So use spirits. Table wine. Or a little whiskey."

Peter had scarcely eaten since the packet had been

stricken with disease. Meals were served on folding tables set up in the men's and women's lounges, mostly meats and vegetables cooked in a galley aft on the main deck and brought up to the boiler deck.

"I'm not hungry," Peter mumbled.

"You look starved. Eat, lad. But only as I say."

"Have you told the women? There's a friend of mine—Marie Therese de Paris. Would you tell her?"

"I have. The young lady refuses. She seems quite angry."

The deck hands were lowering the long limp cylinders of canvas into the red clay on the hill above, and Peter watched silently, a safe distance from death. A breeze caught the robes of the two priests and flapped them as they read something. Peter caught a Latin word or phrase on the moist air, but could scarcely hear. Far upstream in a cooler and dryer land, two mountain widows would learn of this. Except for the distant murmur of priests, a suffocating quietness gripped the *St. Ange.*

They watched the burial party return down the long emerald slope and board silently.

"It's scarcely begun. And we haven't made Independence yet," Evans muttered.

BANTAM DOUBLEDAY DELL
PRESENTS THE
WINNERS CLASSIC SWEEPSTAKES

Dear Bantam Doubleday Dell Reader,

We'd like to say "Thanks" for choosing our books. So we're giving you a chance to enter our Winners Classic Sweepstakes, where you can win a Grand Prize of $25,000.00, or one of over 1,000 other sensational prizes! All prizes are guaranteed to be awarded. Return the Official Entry Form at once! And when you're ready for another great reading experience, we hope you'll keep Bantam Doubleday Dell books at the top of your reading list!

OFFICIAL ENTRY FORM

Yes! Enter me in the Winners Classic Sweepstakes and guarantee my eligibility to be awarded any prize, including the $25,000.00 Grand Prize. Notify me at once if I am declared a winner.

NAME

ADDRESS   APT. #

CITY

STATE   ZIP

REGISTRATION NUMBER   01995A

Please mail to: LL-SBA

BANTAM DOUBLEDAY DELL DIRECT, INC.
WINNERS CLASSIC SWEEPSTAKES
PO Box 985, Hicksville, NY 11802-0985

OFFICIAL PRIZE LIST

GRAND PRIZE: *$25,000.00 CASH!*

FIRST PRIZE: FISHER HOME ENTERTAINMENT CENTER

Including complete integrated audio/video system with 130-watt amplifier, AM/FM stereo tuner, dual cassette deck, CD player, Surround Sound speakers and universal remote control unit.

SECOND PRIZE: TOSHIBA VCR *5 winners!*

Featuring full-function, high-quality 4-Head performance, with 8-event/365-day timer, wireless remote control, and more.

THIRD PRIZE: CONCORD 35MM CAMERA OUTFIT *35 winners!*

Featuring focus-free precision lens, built-in automatic film loading, advance and rewind.

FOURTH PRIZE: BOOK LIGHT *1,000 winners!*

A model of convenience, with a flexible neck that bends in any direction, and a steady clip that holds sure on any surface.

OFFICIAL RULES AND REGULATIONS

No purchase necessary. To enter the sweepstakes follow instructions found elsewhere in this offer. You can also enter the sweepstakes by hand printing your name, address, city, state and zip code on a 3" x 5" piece of paper and mailing it to: Winners Classic Sweepstakes, P.O. Box 785, Gibbstown, NJ 08027. Mail each entry separately. Sweepstakes begins 12/1/91. Entries must be received by 6/1/93. Some presentations of this sweepstakes may feature a deadline for the Early Bird prize. If the offer you receive does, then to be eligible for the Early Bird prize your entry must be received according to the Early Bird date specified. Not responsible for lost, damaged, misdirected, illegible or postage due mail. Mechanically reproduced entries are not eligible. All entries become property of the sponsor and will not be returned.

Prize Selection/Validations: Winners will be selected in random drawings on or about 7/30/93, by Ventura Associates, Inc., an independent judging organization whose decisions are final. Odds of winning are determined by total number of entries received. Circulation of this sweepstakes is estimated not to exceed 200 million. Entrants need not be present to win. All prizes are guaranteed to be awarded and delivered to winners. Winners will be notified by mail and may be required to complete an affidavit of eligibility and release of liability which must be returned within 14 days of date on notification or alternate winners will be selected. Any guest of a trip winner will also be required to execute a release of liability. Any prize notification letter or any prize returned to a participating sponsor, Bantam Doubleday Dell Publishing Group, Inc. its participating divisions or subsidiaries or VENTURA ASSOCIATES, INC. as undeliverable will be awarded to an alternate winner. Prizes are not transferable. No multiple prize winners except for Early Bird Prize, which may be awarded in addition to another prize. No substitution for prizes except as may be necessary due to unavailability in which case a prize of equal or greater value will be awarded. Prizes will be awarded approximately 90 days after the drawing. All taxes, automobile license and registration fees, if applicable, are the sole responsibility of the winners. Entry constitutes permission (except where prohibited) to use winners names and likenesses for publicity purposes without further or other compensation.

Participation: This sweepstakes is open to residents of the United States and Canada, except for the province of Quebec. This sweepstakes is sponsored by Bantam Doubleday Dell Publishing Group, Inc. (BDD), 666 Fifth Avenue, New York, NY 10103. Versions of this sweepstakes with different graphics will be offered in conjunction with various solicitations or promotions by different subsidiaries and divisions of BDD. Employees and their families of BDD, its division, subsidiaries, advertising agencies, and VENTURA ASSOCIATES, INC. are not eligible.

Canadian residents, in order to win, must first correctly answer a time limited arithmetical skill testing question. Void in Quebec and wherever prohibited or restricted by law. Subject to all federal, state, local and provincial laws and regulations.

Prizes: The following values for prizes are determined by the manufacturers' suggested retail prices or by what these items are currently known to be selling for at the time this offer was published. Approximate retail values include handling and delivery of prizes. Estimated maximum retail value of prizes: 1 Grand Prize ($27,500 if merchandise or $25,000 Cash); 1 First Prize ($3,000); 5 Second Prizes ($400 ea); 35 Third Prizes ($100 ea); 1,000 Fourth Prizes ($9.00 ea); 1 Early Bird Prize ($5,000); Total approximate maximum retail value is $50,000. Winners will have the option of selecting any prize offered at level won. Automobile winner must have a valid driver's license at the time the car is awarded. Trips are subject to space and departure availability. Certain black-out dates may apply. Travel must be completed within one year from the time the prize is awarded. Minors must be accompanied by an adult. Prizes won by minors will be awarded in the name of parent or legal guardian.

For a list of Major Prize Winners (available after 7/30/93): send a self-addressed, stamped envelope entirely separate from your entry to Winners Classic Sweepstakes Winners, P.O. Box 825, Gibbstown, NJ 08027. Requests must be received by 6/1/93. DO NOT SEND ANY OTHER CORRESPONDENCE TO THIS P.O. BOX.